TO BE A DUKE

TO BE A DUKE

OTTELIEN LISANNE DYKSTRA

Published by Called To Life Publishing
Grand Rapids, Michigan

ISBN Paperback: 979-8-9918185-0-6
ISBN Electronic: 979-8-9918185-1-3

Scripture quotations taken from the King James Version, under the public domain.

Cover artwork by Miss Marbles
@marymarblepoppins

Printed by Ingram Spark
First Printing, 2024
Ingram Content Group
1 Ingram Blvd.
La Vergne, TN 37086

To the late Eloise Anderson, of Aurora Pond.
May I share with you your namesake in eternity.
And to my Lord Jesus, the Most High,
without whom this wouldn't be possible.

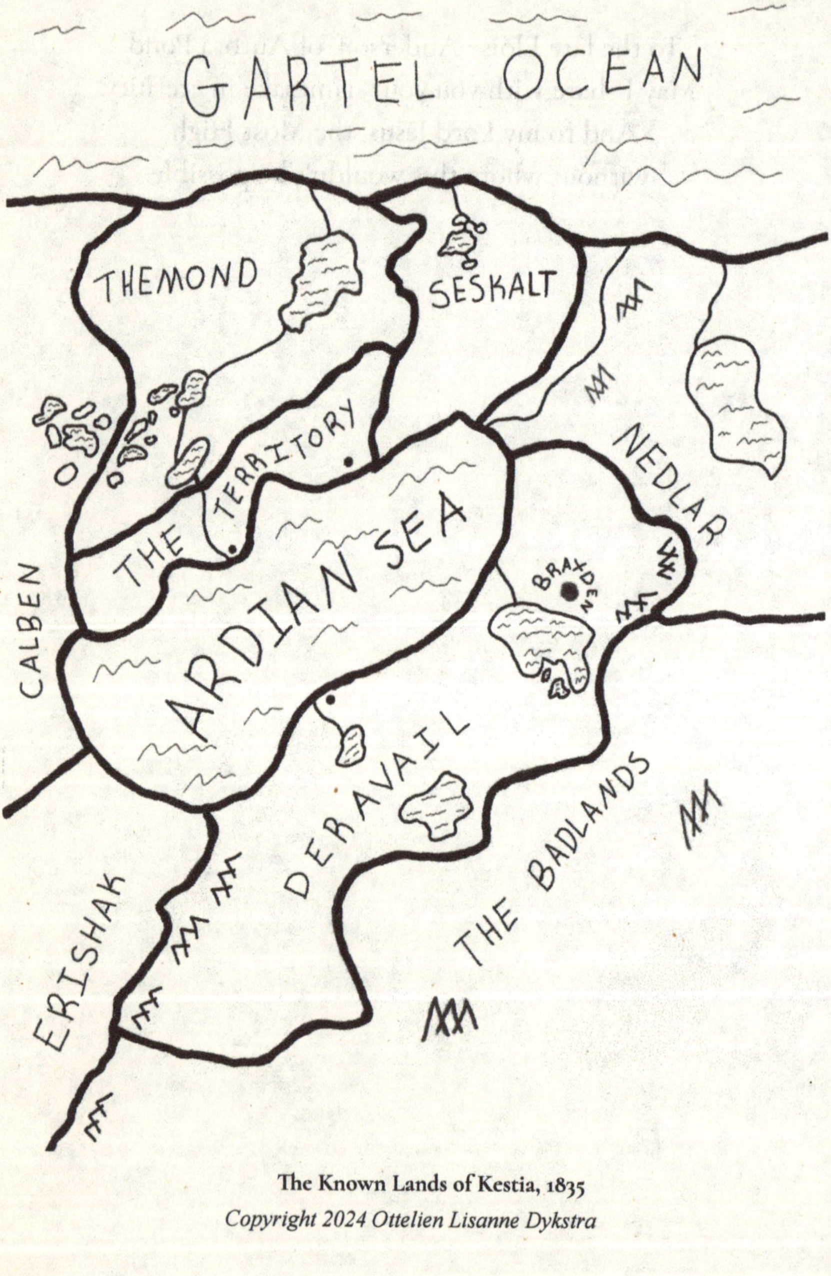

The Known Lands of Kestia, 1835

Cast of Characters

Bryant Wooldridge, Duke of Whittaker
Lady Eloise Wooldridge, Bryant's Mum

Corbin Entwistle, Earl of Waldron
Shepherd Whitley, Marquis of Pwyll
Brigham Roberts, Baron of Grimes

Lyz, Bryant's valet
Eyri Bowen, a servant at Angarth

Lady Olivia Mosstyn
Alden Kegg, Earl of Arioch
Marjorie Morris, Brigham's sister

Prologue

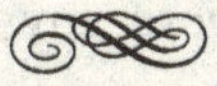

April 15th, 1826, Kestia Anno Mortis
Battenhold Academy
Braxden, Deravail

Bryant Fintan Wooldridge, the duke of sheep, bound into the school's courtyard. Well, he wasn't actually the duke of the sheep. In truth, he was the Duke of Whittaker. Among his friends however, he was Bryant, the duke of the sheep, and he never despised it more than he did now.

Earl Corbin Entwistle currently held Bryant's hat in his hand, swinging it around in the air as he called Bryant by his unofficial title. The two eleven-year-olds were nearly brothers which, of course, came with a bit of harmless teasing.

"Give it back, Corbin!"

"Sorry, Your Grace. I quite fancy this hat! Mind if I keep it?" Corbin leered. Their chase paused as two boys hurried down the school's steps. Running out of the schoolhouse to join them in the courtyard were Shepherd Whitley, son of the Duke of Stuart, and Brigham Roberts, the heir of a baron. The lads quickly joined in the game, tossing the cap between themselves. Bryant's frustration grew as the others kept the hat away from him. Before long, the young duke could barely keep his emotions in check.

"Give it back!" He yelled, throwing a punch at Shepherd. Shepherd, in turn, screamed at the top of his lungs. Their game was quickly put to rest as the headmaster, having heard the scream, strutted up to the boys.

If the look on his face were any indication, all four of them would be cleaning the dormitories for weeks. "What is the meaning of this?" The headmaster tapped his foot impatiently as Corbin nervously gave Bryant his hat.

Shepherd was the first to speak, pointing a shaky finger at Bryant. "Headmaster Abberton, Bryant punched me!" Bryant's eyes grew wide as he realized the trouble he could be in. Getting detention twice in one term was not going to please his mother. His first lashing all year was sure to disappoint her. As any normal boy would, he desperately wanted to hide his face in shame, but the words of his father echoed in his ears.

You are the son of a duke, Bryant. Keep your head high. It shows to the world that you know the authority you carry.

He was the duke now. It was his responsibility to accept the punishments for his actions, to accept the consequences of letting his emotions rule over his reason.

"Have you anything to say in defense, Your Grace?"

Bryant swallowed before speaking. "No, Headmaster Abberton. Shepherd speaks the truth. I punched him." His eyes wandered to Corbin, feeling the boy's stare. A small nod from him caused Bryant to raise his eyebrow ever so slightly, confused.

"Headmaster Abberton, may I add something?" Corbin spoke up. Bryant tugged at the hem of his shirt nervously. The others watched in curiosity.

The headmaster's head spun to face the young boy who stood squarely, taking a note from Bryant to stand confidently. "You may, Lord Waldron."

"Bryant only punched Shepherd because I stole his hat. The three of us were tossing it between ourselves, see, and Bryant got mad at us. It's my fault that Shepherd got hurt. I ask that you punish me instead of them, because I'm the one who started it."

Abberton watched the young boy as joy, a rare emotion for the man, sparkled in his eyes. "I appreciate your honesty, Lord Waldron. Integrity is a becoming trait of any respectable gentleman." A small smile—if one could call it such—spread across his face. "For the collective honesty of your group, the punishments will be decreased to an afternoon of extra chores in the stable. I expect all of the horses residing there to be properly groomed."

"Of course, Headmaster Abberton," Bryant replied, letting his fidgety hands fall to his side. The others murmured their agreement before respectfully bowing to Abberton and making their way to the stable.

Ten minutes later, all four held brushes and buckets of water. The array of horses before them had each choosing favorites that would be groomed first. The afternoon passed quickly, aided by the laughter of a few small water fights and the occasional mudslide. Just as they were finishing up, however, a boy from the nearby village appeared with a telegram.

"Who is it for?" Bryant inquired.

"Brigham Roberts, sir," the boy responded. "I was told he would be here."

Brigham raised his hand. "That's me." He took the paper from the village boy and read it, concern in his face growing with each line he read. "It's my father."

"What about him?" Shepherd questioned, worry lining his face.

"The king's advisor requested he be sent to a sanatorium for paranoia, and the king agreed." Tears welled up in his eyes as he read the telegram again. Despite his desire that the message would change, it didn't. He nearly let one of the others read it aloud to confirm that he wasn't misreading it. However, the news of his father wasn't the only message contained in the telegram and the second was just as personal. One the other boys wouldn't regard as very important, for none of them had sisters and couldn't possibly understand how fiercely Brigham, even at eleven years old, was protective of his own.

His older sister's fiancé severed their engagement on account of the baron's supposed insanity.

Brigham stormed away from the stable, clutching the telegram firmly in his hand. His friends attempted to follow him but he glared at them until they left him alone. In his mind, none of them would understand the bitterness aimed at the cad who showered Brigham's sister with promises of a future together.

Hours later, Brigham lay on his bed, staring up at the ceiling. On the bed next to his, Bryant appeared to sleep peacefully. Brigham knew better, though; he knew that his friend was too worried to sleep. Bryant was like that. Always concerned about how other people were doing.

"Bryant," Brigham voiced as he continued to stare at the ceiling. "Can I tell you something?"

"Of course you can, Brigham."

"If you ever break a girl's heart, I'm going to punch you harder than you've ever punched Shepherd," he stated flatly.

Under other circumstances, Bryant would have laughed at the statement, but he knew how serious Brigham was. "I'll remember that."

And he did.

Chapter One: Front Page News

November 4th, 1835
Neoma Mansion

Bryant Wooldridge, Duke of Whittaker, stared at himself in the mirror, amazed at how *old* he appeared. His title weighed heavily on his shoulders, no lighter than it had in his youth. His life, as life often does, turned out far different than he once expected.

Just before his eighth birthday, his father perished from consumption, hoisting the title onto him. His studies quickly turned from simple arithmetic and literature to learning what his duties would be when the time came.

He had spent his eighteenth birthday overseas, taking care of a territory given to his title following the Themondian War. A man named Damtri had reached out, appealing for protection from the nearby Themondian raiders. Entire villages had been destroyed and he needed to take back control of his property. Property that, until receiving the letter, he hadn't known was his.

His nineteenth was celebrated alone in a newly built home, a mere two days before he booked passage back to Whittaker County. Loneliness had nearly overtaken him as he realized that his friends were entering society without him. Homesickness almost did the same with the understanding that his mother must have been just as lonely as himself.

And now, at twenty years old, he desired nothing more than a year at home to catch up on the things he had missed—the House of Lords' decisions and the affairs of his mainland estates. Instead of assisting with the harvest and doing paperwork, however, he was attending his first season in an attempt to find a wife and continue the duchy, as was his duty.

At twenty years old, he was attending his debut ball.

"Are you ready, Your Grace?"

"I believe so, Lyz." He chuckled to himself, hoping to calm his nerves. "It isn't as though anything can change if I'm *not* ready. They're expecting me." With a quick farewell to his valet, he walked out into the hallway and closed the door to his borrowed room. His stomach churned with unease as he plodded down the wide pathway towards the stairs.

It was a feeling he remembered well. He'd entered a great many situations like the one he now faced, relying on the approval of those before him for the night to end pleasantly. For a moment, it felt like he was walking into the governor's building for the first time. He could almost smell the salt of the breeze amidst the candles and potpourri.

The ceiling rose as he approached the steps. Likewise, the walls opened up to reveal a grand room with gold paneled walls, marvelous chandeliers, intricate candle-stands, and a flurry of guests. Halfway down the dark staircase was a balcony that overlooked the room of dancers and musicians: the perfect vantage point for surveying his peers.

He sucked in a deep breath, hoping once more to calm the unease that stormed in his gut. Would the *ton* judge him for going to the territory instead of the House of Lords? He could have sent someone to sort things out in his stead, but he felt as though *his* presence was needed there. Sending a manager to oversee the project while he dined in luxury wouldn't have sat right with him.

He shook his head, ridding himself of the negative ponderings. If his peers didn't approve of his decision, nothing he could do would change their minds. He found no sense in dwelling on things out of his control. He plastered on a smile and continued on, not stopping at the alcove to get his bearings before stepping onto the dance floor.

...

Society held its breath as Bryant scanned the crowd. The papers somehow found it noteworthy that his debut was happening later than it "should" have. Multiple columns had already been written regarding which events he was attending and who they suspected he'd take notice of.

It was all for naught, of course. Despite the attendance showing some of the most eligible young women from the most prominent Deravailian families, he hardly noticed the eligibles. Instead, his gaze was on one soul that meant more to him than the world itself: his mother.

All around him, he heard gasps of surprise as he walked to her side. He ignored them. Mother was the most important person in his life and he wanted to display that family must come before titles and conniving engagements.

He stopped a foot away and bowed low to the ground. "Mother, will you do me the honor of a dance?" When he met her gaze, he noticed tears lining her eyes.

"The honor is mine, Your Grace," she whispered hoarsely. The two stepped onto the dance floor and Bryant led her through the steps. She took a deep, happy breath as she recognized the tune and asked, "Bryant, did I ever tell you that my first dance as a debutant was a mazurka?"

His eyes twinkled as he continued leading the dance. "You may have mentioned it a time or two." She had, in fact, mentioned it more than just a time or two. For that very reason, Bryant had arranged for the band to play a mazurka as the first dance of the evening.

As the dance drew to a close, he spotted Shepherd and Corbin on the alcove overlooking the crowd. He returned his mother to her friends before climbing the stairs to meet his own.

"What all is new, gentlemen?" Bryant inquired, noting the teasing smirk on Corbin's face as well as Shep's glazed-over look.

Heads of blond and black hair, respectively, turned his way. Corbin flashed a grin. "Not much, Your Grace. Someone has a sweetheart, is all," he informed, a wicked sparkle twinkling in his eye. The statement earned him a sharp look and a jab from Shepherd's elbow.

Bryant's eyebrow lifted in quandary. "Who is she?"

"Lady Ruth Watton."

"Ruth Watton?" He tapped his chin. "Her name sounds familiar."

"She's the daughter of the Marquis of Gili, Wyatt Watton." Shepherd answered without thought, evidently trying to keep a blush from his cheeks.

Bryant glanced at Shepherd's distant look and grinned before asking Corbin, "Is she sweet on him too?" When Corbin nodded, he nudged Shepherd forward. "You should ask her to dance."

Shep reeled back vehemently, unease in every wrinkle on his long forehead. "Are you certain?"

"I couldn't be more sure. Why do you doubt yourself, Shep? You're a marquis, the heir of a duke. I doubt a single woman in this room wouldn't be willing to at least *dance* with you. Go ask her." He emphasized every word.

"Your Grace, everyone knows that my title is just a courtesy. Until the Most High sees fit to call my father home—which is unlikely to be any time soon—I have no true title. It could very well be that the duchess-to-be leaves this world before my father does."

Corbin sighed and shook his head. "Shepherd, if she isn't interested, you can move on. You've just turned twenty, after all. There's plenty of time for you to find someone who is happy with your courtesy title if it doesn't work out with Lady Ruth."

He nudged Shepherd towards the girl and gave him a look that said he would start pushing if Shep didn't move voluntarily. With a quiet groan as his only resistance, Shepherd strolled across the room towards Lady Ruth. Uttering words Bryant couldn't make out, Shep offered his hand to his intended. She took it, a bright smile spreading across her face.

As the couple made their way to the dance floor, Bryant's gaze flickered around the room at the wallflowers who watched the dancers with envy. One in particular stood out to him. Bryant recognized her, even from this distance, as Brigham's sister. The siblings, born a decade apart, nearly looked like twins.

The woman was nearly thirty and had long ago married, but it was not the love match she had been hoping for. Those dreams had been dashed to pieces the moment their king sent her father to the sanatorium, condemning the family as lunatics and scaring away any potential suitors—and friends—before they had the chance to learn the truth.

Only one man refused to withdraw his attention: an old, wealthy merchant. Though she wanted otherwise, Marjorie accepted his proposal, tying herself forever to the fringes of society. A tragedy he often wished he could change.

"We should try some of that ourselves, you know," Corbin interjected, dispelling Bryant's mullings of the past and unchangeable circumstances.

He raised his eyebrow. "Whatever do you mean, Lord Waldron?"

"Dancing, Your Grace. Shepherd isn't the only one whose eyes have been on a certain young lady." He gestured to Marjorie. "You should ask her to dance with you. She seems lonely; she has ever since she got married."

He wanted to offer, but the press would riot if he danced with two ineligible women in a row. They'd perhaps even stir up a rumor about her that could have been avoided entirely. That wasn't the sort of change he wanted to bring about. "Brigham said he was going to dance with her tonight," Bryant responded shortly. His mother had said as much, anyway.

Corbin nodded. "And Brigham needs to dance with other women just as the rest of us do. He is never going to find a bride if he only dances with his sister. I'm sure she'd appreciate dancing with you."

With a moment to think about it, he replied, "I'll ask her for a set later, after I've had a chance to get used to the crowd."

A comfortable silence fell between them before Corbin added, "You know, Your Grace, I've noticed that she isn't the only one you've been watching."

Bryant hummed. "Oh? Whom have I been watching?"

"Nearly every eligible woman in the room. Even as you were dancing with your mother, your focus was on those around the room. Which of them will you dance with next? They're all pining for the chance to woo the only eligible duke of the season, you know." Corbin's eyes sparked mischievously, as though he was about to run to the papers with a complete list of Bryant's dance partners. "You'd better find her quickly, for the next set is starting soon."

A sigh escaped Bryant as he turned from Corbin's stare and towards the railing overlooking the ballroom. He *had* been scanning the fringes of the room as his mind spurred with ideas. His peers would take note of the girls that he danced with tonight. Was there any way he could make that not a curse?

He approached one lady in a cream colored frock and bowed respectfully before her. "May I have the honor of dancing this next set with you, my lady?" The woman stared at him, not attempting to veil her shock. She blinked slowly before regaining her composure and nodding. Bryant took her hand in his and led her to the dance floor.

They made it halfway through the set in painful silence. "Have you been to the theater yet this season?"

She responded quickly. "I haven't had the chance yet, Your Grace. Through the grapevine, though, I hear the current play is extravagantly done."

He found it difficult to keep the pity out of his smile. He *had* seen the play and it was rather simple. Even the press neglected to exaggerate the set and costumes. Either this lady had unkind friends to give her such inaccurate information or she hadn't thought to ask anyone and panicked when the subject came up.

"It is quite beautiful. Even simple things can be made extravagant when done correctly." He could only hope that he had been the first to bring up the topic.

The music dimmed quicker than he had expected, leaving an awkward pause before he offered, "Shall I escort you to the refreshments table?"

"No," she said harshly, wincing as though her tone was more rough than she expected. "No. I believe I shall chat with some friends after you return me to my mother."

He complied, gently offering his arm and accompanying the young lady to her mother's side. The gentlemen nearby glanced over at the exchange between the three, not missing a beat after Bryant stepped away. Within seconds, Lady Cordelia Edmondton was on the arm of an esteemed viscount.

A soft smile graced His Grace's face as he scanned the room for his next partner. One Lady Olivia Mosstyn stood out against a swarm of lovely ladies, her olive green dress starkly different from the creams, pale pinks, and whites of the younger women. The dress, though evidence of her multiple seasons, complimented her and caused her dark hair to shine—something he was sure the woman intended.

Their mothers had been friends, once upon an age, and Lady Olivia was one of the few present that Bryant could say he actually knew. As a child, she was bossy and unkind. He had every reason to believe that translated into how she presented herself; meticulous, perfection, inerrant. Granted, as he hadn't seen her in several years, she might have grown in grace, instead.

He strode towards her, not minding the stares of the nearby women as he bowed before her. "Lady Olivia, might I have this next set?"

The woman seemed humored. "You want to dance with me?" She looked him over before replying, "I would be honored to dance the next set with you, Your Grace." Her tone indicated that she was not. All the same, she took the hand offered to her and stepped out with him.

The instruments struck up a slow waltz and Bryant led her through it with grace. He marveled at how quickly she found the rhythm. Her movements were elegant and fluid, as though the dance had been practiced and repeated too often to truly be enjoyed. "Have you enjoyed yourself this evening, my lady?"

"Indeed I have, Your Grace," she responded, not missing a step. "Have you?"

That almost annoyed him. The fact that she could answer questions with perfect social grace and still not falter in her strides made him question how many times she actually rehearsed this dance. Did it mean anything to her to be able to dance in such a grand place, or had the years spent on the sidelines destroyed the magic for her? Did she hold the art as highly as he did?

Her smile held firm on her face, clearly fake. Obviously, she did not.

"Certainly," he answered. "The music is quite exquisite, wouldn't you say?"

She responded only with a nod, her mouth pressed in that eternal fake smile. It would be nice to dance with a woman that actually enjoyed the moment, even platonically.

Bryant sighed internally and led her through the rest of the dance, returning her to the fringes the instant the music swelled to a stop. The women nearby swooned beside him, all attempting to make themselves more noticeable. Bryant glared at all of them and walked to the refreshment table, hoping—praying—to find a girl that cared for more than his title.

Do not grow weary of doing good. His father's words, taken from the scriptures, echoed in his mind. If Lady Cordelia danced with other high titled gentlemen after dancing with him, the same could be true for the other wallflowers and gentlemen's daughters. If the world only saw his title, perhaps he would bend it into a good thing. He could help people with his power, using society's own expectation and reaction to do so. Or, so he hoped. His plan that depended entirely on other people couldn't be guaranteed to work. At the very least, he wanted to try, starting with a certain Marjorie Morris.

The woman smiled at him, one corner of her lips tilting up higher than the other. "Hello, Your Grace. Are you looking for my brother? I believe he's caught up in a novel or some such thing in the library. Despite Mother's attempts at getting him to socialize with his peers, he's completely opposed to the idea of appearing in the ballroom." She added a polite laugh at the end, but her discomfort was visible.

"Actually, my lady, I came to ask if you would do me the honor of sharing a dance with me. You seemed in need of company and I thought I could provide some, if only for a few minutes." He extended his hand in offering.

Marjorie stared at it, unsure of how to respond. "Your Grace, I'm flattered, truly. But—"

Her mother interrupted her. "Come now, darling. You haven't danced at a ball since you were a girl. Enjoy yourself tonight. There's nothing in the rule book about married women being forbidden from dancing with old friends." Her mother nudged the girl forward.

"I suppose it couldn't hurt anything," she hesitantly relented. "I'd be delighted to dance with you, Your Grace." Marjorie took his arm and stepped away from the wall. All eyes turned towards them as whispers filled the room. Heat rose in her cheeks as she stared at them all, turning her gaze slowly toward Bryant. Her worried brown eyes met his.

"Relax, my lady. There's no reason to be nervous over a dance." He sent her a reassuring smile. "They're only staring because they're jealous. No one is going to judge you for this." He paused, a thought occurring to him. "If your husband asks, tell him to talk to me. I'll explain everything." That seemed to settle the girl's nerves. Strange. Perhaps she really was just worried about causing a scandal. Or, perhaps, there was more to the situation than what stood at surface level. He attempted light conversation that he hoped would shed some light on her thoughts. "How long have you been married, my lady?"

"You don't have to keep calling me that, Your Grace. Marjorie is fine."

"Nonsense. I shall call you *my lady* for you are one." He spun her around as the routine called for. Life's joyful glow steadily returned to her cheeks.

"I married just after Brigham finished at Battenhold; a summer wedding, so he could be in attendance." She smiled at the memory of the day, bringing some light back into her weary features. For being only nine and twenty, she seemed far older. Dark circles hung under her eyes that didn't suit her unnaturally pale skin.

When the music ended, Bryant escorted her to the refreshments table and reached for a glass. "Would you like some punch?"

"Punch would be lovely," she answered, taking a cup from the tray. He couldn't help but notice just how thin and shaky her hands were. Had they always been so?

Taking care to not spill, Bryant poured punch for her and then himself. "Did you enjoy yourself, my lady?"

"I did, Your Grace. I'd forgotten just how much fun dancing could be." She took a sip of the punch. "This is good. I wonder what they used to make it. I could bring the recipe home and give it to Chef."

"Chef?"

"Our cook. I'd love to have this at evening book studies. Perhaps even at a party of my own." She smiled wistfully, face drawn in longing. "I'd love to host a party."

"Why don't you?"

"My husband is rather tight with his purse when it comes to such things. No new wardrobe for the season, no parties of my own beyond small gatherings. Book clubs and things of the sort, you know." She winced at expressing the implied criticism. "No one would show up, even if I did host."

Bryant didn't know how to respond beyond apologizing. If he knew the man better, he would have spoken with him about allowing Marjorie to have a party. The poor woman needed some friends.

She noticed his hesitation and shrugged lightly. "All is well, Your Grace. After seven years of marriage, I'm quite used to it." At least she'd answered his question before she took a sip of punch and sauntered off to her mother.

All wasn't well, and he thought she knew that. The man married her because of her father's money; he knew no one else would want her. After the news from the king, not a soul would give her so much as a passing glance. As she walked back to her mother, however, he noticed several people taking notice of the girl. A few matrons even stepped up to engage in conversation. A brilliant smile lit up her face.

Perhaps his plan would work after all.

...

Duchess Eloise Wooldridge surveyed the room, scanning faces for acquaintances long since introduced. Several of her friends from finishing school dotted the area with their grown daughters. A few of the sons she recognized as Bryant's friends from Battenhold, but most were a few years too old for their paths to have crossed.

A loud voice approaching her brought a smile to her face. "Eloise! How pleasant it is to see you at last!" The matronly Carmen Rhees, wife of the Earl of Kilsship, plodded steadily towards her. "However have you been, dear? Your son is here this year, is he not?"

"That's right, Lady Carmen. He offered his first dance to me," she stated, trying to avoid another tear slipping down her face.

"Oh, isn't that just the most darling thing? I wish my boys had thought to do that. They don't quite understand the wishes of us older ladies to dance as though it were still our first season. Which dance did he—"

"The mazurka," she interrupted. "My favorite; the one I danced with his father when we first met, may the Most High rest his soul."

"That is precious." Carmen laid a hand on her heart. "How are you doing, dear? Seeing your son out as a grown adult without your husband here?"

She spoke hesitantly, gathering the words to express the cries of her heart. "It's difficult, for sure and certain, but I'm managing. I'm so proud of who Bryant has grown to be and I know his father would be too, if he were only here to see it. I remind my son of that every day. His father loved him dearly."

The older woman nodded sympathetically. "If you ever need anything—some company, someone to talk to over tea, perhaps—feel free to extend an invitation. I'm rather lonely now that my youngest is married and moved on. It would be lovely catching up with you."

"Indeed, Lady Carmen. Thank you for the offer. Are you free next Tuesday?"

Her lips pursed as she dug around her handbag for her calendar. "Give me just a moment to check, dear." Her eyes flitted across the page. "I don't believe I have any appointments on that day. Afternoon tea, then? Lovely." She reached into her bag to grab a pencil and jotted it down. "Until then, my dear."

"Until then, Lady Carmen." Tea on Tuesday with Carmen. She'd need to inform Mabyn as soon as she was able to. Given that she'd already scheduled tea with both Lady Seylor and Lady Parliger, she'd need a second mind to keep track of her commitments. Never had a season seemed so busy. One of the many joys of motherhood, she supposed.

A pale, brooding face caught her attention. "Alden Kegg?" She mumbled to herself as she crept closer, trying to get a good look at the lad. "My stars, it is." She walked up to the man, a bright smile on her face. "Viscount, what a pleasure it is to see you. I don't believe our paths have crossed since Battenhold."

He turned to face her, matching her grin. "Duchess Whittaker, what a surprise. I'm delighted to officially make your acquaintance. It's been too long." He kissed her hand as was customary. "However, it is *Earl*, now. My father passed away some time ago."

"Oh, I'm terribly sorry. It has been so long that I had forgotten." She remembered vividly now; the headlines claimed that the late Earl had been brutally murdered. The case hadn't been solved. "Lord Arioch, then, is it?"

"Indeed, Your Grace." His gaunt face held little emotion beyond the fake smiles that all of society wore. "Is His Grace well? Bryant, that is."

"He is well, yes. Dancing with one of the young ladies, I presume."

"I was hoping to catch him sometime before I leave tonight. We've a good deal of catching up to do, but I suppose it must wait until another time."

"Or," Eloise began, "you could join us for afternoon tea tomorrow. That would provide you an opportunity to have proper conversation away from these stuffy ballrooms. We should be home in time for it." She smiled as the earl nodded his head in agreement. "I look forward to it."

Chapter Two: Passing Glance

November 5th

The sun awoke slowly, savoring the November day and banishing the midnight hours from the world, covering the city in a blanket of fog. The *ton* dawned leisurely, for with the new day came traveling from Neoma Estate to every man's own home. Lyz packed up the Wooldridge family belongings and, along with a footman, loaded them onto the family's carriage while Bryant said his goodbyes.

"We'll see you at another party sometime soon, won't we?" Shepherd inquired. "I'm not going to be able to take on my first courtship alone. I hardly know what I'm doing."

Corbin laughed and bumped Shep's shoulder. "And you think we do? You're the first one of us to begin any kind of serious relationship." His tone fell a notch. "Aren't you rather glad we convinced you to talk to Lady Ruth?"

That earned him an annoyed glare. "Yes. I am. You all were right. For *once in my life*, I was wrong." He rolled his eyes as his peers chuckled. "With the way you three have acted since the ball, I'd think you were still schoolboys."

"You can't exactly expect us to change from boyish and gleeful children to stoic and serious men just because Bry's first season has come about, can you?" A grin lit Corbin's face as he spoke. "It isn't as though this single year marks the moment we all grow up—even if it *is* the first one that we're all together for the season. That sort of transformation only happens in Brigham's books." He sent a teasing glance to the man in question.

Brigham, in response, looked up from his book. "Hardly so." He huffed and returned to the book, scanning the page for the spot he left off.

Corbin kept his face straight for only a moment before bursting out in laughter. Upon realizing that the only laughter was his own, he coughed and *ahem*'d. A short, pudgy man approached him. "Ah. Excuse me, gentlemen. My chariot awaits." The grin didn't leave his face as he left.

Bryant let out a sigh. "That troublemaker. One of these days, he'll grow up like the rest of us—"

"And when he does, you can be sure that the end of the world is upon us." Shepherd interrupted, a grin not unlike Corbin's tugging at the corners of his lips. He felt a *whack* on his arm as he chuckled. "I have only been wrong once in my life, Your Grace. I'll not be proved wrong again."

The joke was almost out of character. "I'm not so positive that's right, Shep, especially coming from you. After all, you have always been the most mature of the group. First to read, first to receive favor in the House of Lords, first to fall in love—"

He was quick to correct him. "It is not love yet, Bryant. I've only danced with Lady Ruth the one time. We hardly know each other." He shook his head. "It is merely affection and adoration at this stage. I'll call it love once I know that I want to marry her, and I shan't propose until I know that she is as willing to work towards a healthy, happy marriage as I am."

"A wise sentiment, Shepherd," Mother stated, joining the group. "If more of our fellows thought the same, more couples would attempt to remember their commitments to each other." She let out a disheartened sigh, meeting Bryant's eyes when he wrapped an arm around her comfortingly. The simple gesture added a soft glow to her expression. "I'm quite proud of you all. You've done well to show me that our nation will be in good hands when the time comes."

"Rest assured, Your Grace, that this responsibility is one we gents take seriously. It is, after all, our duty to the nation to hold fast to tradition and the teachings of the Most High."

Mother nodded her head and smiled. "Well spoken, Shepherd." She turned to Bryant. "The carriage is ready and the footmen have packed our things. We'd best be off." With every bit of elegance as she did everything, she gave Shepherd and Brigham her goodbyes and well-wishes and strutted off, Bryant's assurances to join her trailing behind.

"I'd best not keep her waiting for too long, Shep, but I have a question for you before I leave." He paused, awaiting Shepherd's approval before continuing. "What do you suppose love feels like?"

Shep's brow furrowed, his eyes glazing over with thoughtfulness. "I don't suppose you have an easier question somewhere for me, do you?" Bryant shook his head, a hint of a smirk on his lips. "We're meeting up for billiards tomorrow like we planned, correct? Ask me then. Perhaps in the time between then and now, I'll be able to develop an answer for you." A deep, gentle voice called the marquis away, and soon all four were happily with their families.

...

The carriage plodded along towards Angarth, the town residence of the Wooldridge family. Bryant kept his gaze fixed on the few acres of land outside. The tenants under his care labored in the cold sun, preparing the land for seed before the harsh winter snow set in.

A soft voice touched his ears. "Bryant, do you recall Earl Kegg from your days in Academy?" His mother's timing suggested more than a desire to reminisce. Promptings by the Most High, she'd always said, when she was on mission to make something happen.

"Naturally," he replied. "Why do you ask?"

"I invited him for tea this afternoon. See, he'd been invited to the party last night as well and, knowing how few people he knows and not wanting him to take on the season with such dauntingly few connections, I thought it would be kind to extend an invitation for tea. At any rate, an earl is only as good as his wealth and his connections nowadays." Bryant nodded absentmindedly. He didn't remember much about the man, if he were being honest. They were friends, once. "You don't mind, do you?"

"Not at all, Mother. You may invite whomever you wish. Angarth is *your* estate, after all."

"I know, dear, I simply..." she paused, gathering her words. "It's different than inviting one of my cousins or one of the ladies from my sewing club. We haven't had a gentleman guest at either estate ever since your father passed all those years ago." She cleared the emotion from her throat, but couldn't shake it from her eyes. "I feel it's only right to ensure you approve of my inviting a man into our home after all this time."

"You have my complete permission, Mother. Besides," he stated as the carriage drew to a stop, "he's far from the first gentleman to grace our manor in the last decade. You've neglected Corbin and Shep and—"

"They hardly count as guests, Bryant," Mother countered on a laugh as the footman offered his hand to assist her. "You've known those boys since before you could read."

Bryant followed her out of the carriage. "All the same, there's no reason why you shouldn't be allowed to invite someone into your own home." He paused to greet their housekeeper. "Mrs. Kendrick, I trust that everything has been well since our departure?"

"Indeed, Your Grace. Harold stopped by asking for a few parsnips in exchange for work in the stables, as he often does. Beyond that, we've had only one visitor. The parlor is ready for afternoon tea as soon as Your Graces have freshened up from the trip."

A grin lit Bryant's face. "A lovely way to tell me that I smell, Mrs. Kendrick."

The woman sighed, shaking her head. "You'd best get on with it, Your Grace. Her Grace's guest is waiting."

He gave Mother a confused glance. "He's arrived already? We only left the party an hour ago. How did he get here so quickly?"

Mother rested a hand on his shoulder reassuringly. "I invited him at the ball, Bryant," she explained. "He mentioned that he was leaving that very night."

"I wonder why..." He shook his head and bid his mother farewell before retreating into his chambers. His broad-shouldered batman helped him out of his traveling coat into a charcoal afternoon jacket. "Lyz, did you happen to catch a glimpse of Mother's guest?"

The valet shook his head. "I was ushered to the stables upon our arrival, Your Grace."

"Harold?"

"Harold. The boy can't seem to understand that some horses require an expert rider. Why he respects me and not the stable hands, I'll never understand." He let out a sigh as he handed a new set of boots to Bryant in exchange for his muddy ones. "Out of curiosity, why do you ask?"

"I find it odd that he would arrive early, knowing Mother and I stayed the night. It's hardly two in the afternoon and yet he's sitting in our parlor, having arrived some time ago."

"Perhaps he is eager to see your mother," Lyz hastened to soothe any worries. "For what it is worth, Your Grace, I've asked Eryi to keep an eye on our guest in your absence. The Kendricks are fine people but, if you don't mind my saying so, they are a tad too trusting."

"I don't know what would provoke an earl to misbehave, Lyz, but I am grateful for your initiative." He glanced at the clock on the mantle: just past the hour. "I suppose I ought to go greet my mother's guest. Wish me luck." He plastered a light smile on his face before making his way to the drawing room.

The bounce in his step, to an observer, was boyish and giddy, even as Bryant's insides churned with nerves. He rarely entertained guests in his youth, ladened with responsibilities that he was. Any sort of guest in the territory was there at his bidding, to work through a hazard or a threat, unless said guest came without invitation and as a risk to his person. Guards were employed at all hours to ensure his safety and the safety of those in his care.

This young man harbored much distrust for guests as a result, even if his mother invited them personally to partake in her home.

He rounded the final corner, and entrance to the drawing room, before halting in his tracks. Alden Kegg stood in the middle of the drawing room, looking as primmed as he possibly could. As the man, his own age, turned towards him, he couldn't help but notice the many wrinkles and lines in his face. "Kegg," he began, struggling to find his words. They looked so different, for being so similar. "Welcome to Angarth. It's a pleasure to see you again."

"Your Grace," Kegg greeted. "It is good to see you. I'm rather surprised our meeting has taken this long. Surely, though, your business in the territory was extravagantly more important than your place here."

He opened his mouth, trying to grasp a response. "It was," he stuttered. "People were dying and I was able to provide protection. Is that an issue?"

"Not at all, Your Grace." His eye twitched as he continued, gesturing to the doorway. "Ah, so the lady of the house arrives. Thank you ever so much for inviting me to tea." He offered his arm to Mother, guiding her to a seat. "It was quite a surprise bumping into you last night."

"Indeed," Mother said with a smile. "A pleasure, of course. It's always lovely whenever I encounter one of Bryant's old friends. What have you been up to in the days since Battenhold?"

"Caring for my estate, mostly," he answered, irritation tingeing his tone. "Father left the place in near ruin. Mother's brooding didn't help things. By the time I received the land, a great deal of work was in order to repair what they had neglected."

Bryant watched the man's eyes as he spoke, finding his annoyed tone odd. "My condolences, Alden. I had no idea that you'd lost so much."

"Surely you understand it yourself, Your Grace. Losing a parent is never easy." He eyed the duchess. "And my condolences for the loss of your husband, Your Grace. I know it would have been better to say when we were introduced years ago, but I didn't have the sense then to realize what Bryant's title meant." He shook his head solemnly.

"Your delayed condolences are accepted. Thank you." Spotting a new shadow lining the floor, she motioned to the servant standing in the doorway. "Don't linger, Cristyn. We'll take the tea in here." She assisted the young woman in setting the tea tray down on the low table. "How do you take it, Lord Arioch?"

"Weak, please. With cream and sugar. An odd combination, I know, but I've always had peculiar taste."

Mother fixed his tea and offered it to him before pouring stronger tea for her and Bryant. "Plain as usual, son, or are you feeling adventurous today?"

"Plain, Mother. Thank you." He took his tea, finding Kegg's mannerisms on the whole entirely strange. No 'thank you' to follow his tea, arriving before the host; his taste certainly wasn't the only thing peculiar about him.

He was the first to speak, as well. "If you've time, Your Grace," speaking to Mother, "I'd love to tour the grounds. A promenade, perhaps."

"That sounds rather pleasant," she offered. "Perhaps I can convince Aneira, our cook, to pack a picnic for the three of us. The grounds here are quite extensive, despite being in town, and to view everything would take some time. There's a lovely spot for a picnic dinner near the pond."

A bright grin lit his face almost unnaturally. Bryant couldn't look at it long without feeling unnerved. "It's settled, then. We'll go out just after tea."

"Perfect." Mother relaxed into her chair, comfortable with the arrangement. Much more so than Bryant was. "I am so glad that you accepted my invitation for tea, Lord Arioch. Many years have passed since your time at Battenhold and I'm eager to hear what you've done since then. And, of course, what events you plan to attend this season. If you don't mind my saying so, I have a vast knowledge of the young ladies who are out this season, should you be interested in finding which one will be the match for you."

Bryant sighed audibly, exaggerating it only to show his distaste. He had lost count how often this same information had been orated to his own ears."Mother, I hardly think that Alden will want to know who exactly is going to be at every event he is attending and which silks they prefer over others."

She sent him a glare that said *I'm only being polite* as Kegg spoke up. "I appreciate the offer, Your Grace. Truly, I do. However, I already know which young lady I plan to win over, if she'll have me."

"Is that so? Who might the young lady be?"

"I'm sure you know her. Lady Olivia Mosstyn."

If Bryant hadn't been paying attention before, he certainly was now. Olivia was hardly a match he'd consider if he were going for a marriage built on love and kindness. "Lady Olivia, you say?"

"Yes. An odd choice, as well I know. But, as I stated before, I—"

"You have peculiar taste," Bryant finished. "I do hope you know what you're signing up for, Lord Arioch. I might be new to society, but even I am aware that Lady Olivia is known for her loud, distasteful opinions. I fear that you'll end up a bachelor for life because she didn't approve of your handkerchiefs."

"Bryant, don't say such things!" Mother scolded. "It isn't polite to speak of Lady Olivia in such an unpleasant, exaggerated way."

"Forgive me, Mother. I only thought to take a page out of the lady's proverbial book and speak my honest opinion." If looks could kill. Guilt stabbed at his gut for his harsh words. Corbin's arrogance must be rubbing off on him. He schooled his expression and turned to Kegg. "Why, then, Lady Olivia?"

"Because Lady Olivia is a determined young woman with a delightful spirit," he responded concisely. "She'll make a fine wife; I'm sure of it." There was enough confidence in his voice to assure Bryant that he was entirely serious.

"To each his own, then."

...

The stars hung overhead before Alden finally departed. Really, they ought to have offered him a room for the night, but Bryant was so put out with him that he didn't dare extend a hint of an invitation. He couldn't stand the man, regardless of their supposed similarities.

Mother took him aside. "We're attending another ball the day after tomorrow, hosted for Caitlyn Pryce. I have it on good word that both Lady Olivia and Lord Arioch will be in attendance. Please, please, Bryant, if you love me, do not interrupt this. Lord Arioch has been through enough in his life as it is. He doesn't need your disapproval added to that list."

"What are you asking of me, Mother?" A simple enough question, though he feared its answer. If she expected him to be nice, he couldn't promise anything. The mere thought made his blood boil.

"Simple: don't interfere between him and Lady Olivia. Let them be happy together if she'll have him. Whatever your misgivings about the young woman, she can be quite pleasant when she intends to be. *In fact*, I'm scheduled to have tea with her mother in a fortnight's time. If only I could drag you along, perhaps you'd see for yourself what a fine young lady she is."

He shook his head. "I am no more interested in getting to know Lady Olivia than I am Alden Kegg. The man has changed greatly since I knew him last. There's something about him that sets me on edge. I don't like it, Mother. I don't trust him."

Her expression fell further. "Please try not to be so hard on him. He's experienced your grief twice-over. I'm sure that can explain any unpleasantness in his demeanor."

Her words stung him as heat swirled into his cheeks. "I'll take that into consideration," he mumbled, making his way up to his quarters.

There waiting, as ever, stood Lyz. "Is everything alright, Your Grace? You look troubled." His voice dropped to a whisper. "Lord Arioch didn't steal the silver, did he?"

A breath of a grin crossed his face as he answered. "Not at all, Lyz. It's only that your attitude about him is entirely correct. I don't trust him either. Mother, on the other hand, is enamored with the idea of setting him up with Lady Olivia Mosstyn at Lady Caitlyn's debut ball."

"What sets you on edge about him, if I might ask?"

"I'm not entirely sure, and what I have noticed could be entirely nothing. He mentioned his parents' deaths, and what they left for him, without any sort of sorrow; rather, he was put out by it. That shouldn't cross me the way it does—everyone grieves differently, after all. It's only that his manners are atrocious. He didn't even thank Mother after she poured his tea."

Lyz frowned. "Rather odd for a gentleman of his standing, wouldn't you say?"

"Exactly my thinking. Atrocious manners aren't exactly a reason to distrust someone though, is it? Surely I should have more evidence before I write him off as a bad character." He sighed in exasperation. "Perhaps I am simply apprehensive at his being a guest. Hosting visitors didn't exactly bring joy in the territory."

They sat in relative silence, both pondering the question until Lyz spoke up. "Cristyn served tea, did she not?"

"She did," he responded with a furrowed brow. "What of it?"

"She is an excellent judge of character, Your Grace. If anyone would know his true intentions, it is that dear girl." Something in Lyz's tone suggested darkness and pity. "How did she react to Lord Arioch?"

He took a moment to recall the scene, trying to analyze Cristyn's actions. "I don't quite remember; only that she lingered in the doorway and fumbled with the tray while she set it down. Mother helped her stabilize it before she spilled anything." She was rather new at her current position, having just moved up from scullery maid. Any missteps could easily be explained by nerves or inexperience. Then again, she didn't wobble or trip before, and she certainly never stood in the doorway while he talked with his mother. A guest could change that.

Lyz seemed to be on the same path of thought. "I'll ask after her when I am able. She may be of a similar mind as you and me. And if she is, I wouldn't trust Kegg with *any* of those young women."

"You do realize how serious that accusation is, Lyz." The cold gravity in Lyz's usually warm eyes gave him chills.

"I wouldn't say it if I didn't mean it, Your Grace."

He knew that. He only hoped that Lyz made an exception for once. Such accusations weren't dealt with easily, and especially not when all they had to go on was a duke and a few servants who 'had a bad feeling.' They'd need evidence against the man. Unfortunately, evidence of this nature could only come at a cost they didn't dare afford. "Very well then. By all means, interview Cristyn about him. I'd rather risk hurting Mother's feelings than risk Lady Olivia herself."

"I will find her posthaste. In the meantime, Your Grace, I suggest you speak with Eryi. He may be able to shed light on this as well."

"How so? Lyz, what do I not know about my staff members?"

He responded with a solemn grin and, "You'll simply have to find out, Your Grace," before slipping out the door and down the hall.

Chapter Three: Long Winded

November 6th

When the weather was fine enough to support the trip, Gentlemen of all sorts flocked from their homes to the city's many clubs. One such club, The Vagabond Lion, so named for the second sons which frequented it, stood just across from Outrey Park, making it a popular spot for post-race drinking. Today, however, it housed two of the finest men in Deravail, seeming quite at odds with their chaotic surroundings. Odd though they were, the corner billiards table served as the meeting spot for Bryant and Shepherd from their youth.

Bryant set up the rack as Shep lined up his cue. "Do you wish to discuss it now or shall we wait a moment to settle in?"

"Now is fine," Shepherd responded as the cue ball sent the others flying. "I believe that it would help us first to define our terms. What do you mean by love?"

His brow furrowed as he scanned the table. "To be honest, I am not entirely sure. True love, I suppose. The kind of love that lasts."

"I see. I don't know what that sort of love feels like, Bryant. I haven't experienced it. The closest example I could give you is that of my faith; that is, my love and loyalty to the Most High. I know His love is one of sacrifice, one of compassion, and one of faithfulness. But that love is different from a love of romance, however similar they might seem." Shep moved around the table, knocking a ball in. "I wish I could give you a better answer."

"Don't worry about it, Shep. That does help me. After all, we are instructed to love our wives similarly, which encompasses all of those things." He hesitated, taking his turn before continuing, a newfound nervousness evident in his jerky movements. "If I may, Shep, I have another question."

"You are always free to speak your mind, Bry."

He set his cue down. "I may have stumbled across a dilemma. Two, actually, and I don't know what to do about either."

...

Bryant wandered around the expansive ballroom in search of Corbin. Rumors spread throughout the room that Shepherd had danced with Lady Ruth twice already this one night and he needed to have them confirmed. He spotted the mop of pale blond hair leaning against the far wall, surrounded by a ring of suits and bright smiles. Just as the earl raised his glass to call out another joke, he interrupted.

"Lord Waldron, may I have a word?"

A mixture of worry and mischief crossed between his eyes as he propped himself back up and bid farewell to his gents, following Bryant to a more private area of the room. "What is it, Your Grace?"

"I've just heard something tweeting on the breeze, that's all. Have you seen Shep around?"

A pure grin burst out on his face. "You mean Lord Lovebird? He's over there, on the outskirts of the dance. His *third* dance with Lady Ruth and the night is still young. If he's not careful, he's going to find himself in the gossip pages tomorrow at the center of a scandal." He cheered his glass in the couple's direction before taking a sip. "Care for a drink, Your Grace? Lady Caitlyn's mother has arranged for the best champagne I believe I've ever had."

"None for me, thanks." He paused to look over the swarm, scanning for one head in particular. "Have you seen Brigham?"

Corbin sighed. "The duties of a duke, I suppose. Always worried about the problems of everyone else. Next you'll be asking after Marjorie or Shep's parents or my aunt and uncle—"

"Actually, I was inquiring about Brig to ask about Marjorie. Not that it hasn't been pleasant to waltz with the wallflowers, but I was hoping to ask how she has been since my debut."

"I haven't seen him. In all honesty, I'm not surprised. He's never been as social as you, Shep, and me. His mother is standing over there, though, so I suppose he must be here somewhere." Bryant followed his gesture in the woman's general direction, noting that Marjorie sat beside her looking worse for wear.

"Where do you think—" he cut himself off. Brigham had his specific hideaways. "I'll be in the library if you need me, Cor." He hurried down the corridors, asked a passing servant for directions, and made his way to the library. As expected, his target sat in a corner of the room, his nose fully enveloped in a book. He whistled to make his presence known.

Brigham met his gaze as he stood, setting his book aside. "Hello, Bryant. Am I needed?"

"Only by me," he replied, making his way to the nook. "How are things going? With Marjorie, I mean. We danced at my debut and she seemed nervous."

His eyes lost their light as he shook his head. "She's happier than ever, having all those ladies chatting with her at events, but her husband isn't kind. I wish I could help her, Bry, but I don't know how. She will not divorce him no matter how bad it gets;

she's told me that already. I fear for my sister's wellbeing, but there's nothing I can do to help her."

"Why not tell the police? Surely they will be able to step in if there's trouble." The constable could investigate, take one look at the woman who surely has bruises on her soul, and decide that her husband has committed a felony against her.

"She would hate me if I stepped in. She's all but convinced herself that this is fine, that his behavior is normal among husbands. You and I both know she is wrong. Mother knows she is wrong. All the same, she would hate me if I forced her to cross that line."

Bryant spoke his line with reverence to the words. "As Shep would say, sometimes the best thing we can do for someone is the thing they don't want."

Brig met his eyes with a wearied gaze. "Give me time to think about it. I need to know, without a shadow of a doubt, what I should do before I act."

He nodded, respectful for the moment, trying to deflect the worry eating him up. "Should I refrain from dancing with her until you sort all of this out? I wouldn't want to make this worse for her."

"I don't think that is necessary. John knows that we're good friends, I should think, and you are only being nice. Not to mention that you, as a duke, could report him for suspicious behavior and have him arrested easily."

The hesitation made him question Brigham's decision to wait. Clearly, the man was terrified for his sister. "Brig, are you sure you don't think we should step in yet?"

"It's not the right time." With a sharp breath, he picked up his book. "Was that all? I'm at the most riveting part, you know," he stated joylessly.

"I was going to ask if we'd ever see you out there, but I suppose I just got my answer." A sad, sympathetic smile stretched across his face as he tipped his hat. "Farewell, Brigham. Have fun with your books." He closed the door softly behind him and made his way back to Corbin.

His friend gave him an amused smile. "Back so soon?" At Bryant's half-hearted grin, he continued, "I take it you found him."

"Indeed. Our conversation was... enlightening, to say the least." He spoke hesitantly, unsure how he should phrase what Brigham wanted left alone. The weight of it hung heavy on his shoulders, his desire to help crushing him the longer it existed. Marjorie deserved better.

"And Marjorie?"

"I've made her popular, it seems. The spinsters and matrons who used to ignore her now enjoy sharing the latest gossip." He sighed. "If only it were enough."

"Bry, you've done all you can. Let Brigham handle this one. You don't need to save the whole world, just your part of it." He gave him a nudge towards the ballroom. "Might as well dance while the night is young or tour the gardens while there's still light. I'll be off in the side room playing cards with Lord Tristan if you need me. Unless you'd like to join us?"

"Cards have never been my strength. Not your sort of cards, anyway. I'll find someone to dance with, I suppose." He bid Corbin farewell before scouting the room. A group of young women stood on the outskirts, whispering in conversation. "Might as well start there," he mumbled as he made his way over.

One Anwyn Davis stood out. She was two years his senior, according to his memory. She turned down two previous proposals because she hoped to find a love match, or so her story went. "Lady Anwyn, might I have this dance?" With such lofty dreams, he had to try to help her cause.

"I'd be honored, Your Grace." She smiled with dimples—a charming trait—and took his offered arm. "Do try to not get jealous, Lady Olivia," she spouted over her shoulder. Olivia retorted that she did not care. Anwyn turned back to Bryant, her eyes challenging Lady Olivia's words.

Was Lady Olivia setting her cap for him? Kegg wouldn't like that. Neither did he. If only Lady Ruth had a twin sister, for she *was* his sort of lady. Soft, gentle, with a demeanor of grace and kindness. Not one that spewed arrows in the direction of those who dared to disagree with her. "I have it on good word that Earl Alden Kegg fancies her."

Anwyn's eyes widened mischievously. "Is that so?" A grin spread over her face. "That's hilarious. She thinks him a right scoundrel and a reprobate. I'd feel sorry for the man if I didn't desire to be there when Olivia rejects him. Poor Lord Arioch, but Olivia isn't interested in the slightest."

He tried; that was enough for Mother's approval. "Poor fellow." He did his best to keep the sarcasm off his tongue.

Apparently, there was no hiding from Lady Anwyn. "You don't fancy Lady Olivia, then. A pity. You would have made a beautiful couple." She sighed as they took their place in a row with other couples as the music started. "Oh, I do love this one. It's a pleasure to dance it with you, Your Grace." She smiled brightly, dimples gleaming. "The other songs have lost their spark after having to dance them so often, but not this one. *Never* this one."

"It's the favorite of Lord Grimes as well, or so he claims. A shame that he's not here to hear it."

Her smile fell. "Baron Roberts? The two of you are friends?"

It was odd to hear a lady react to Brigham's name with distaste. Growing up, their peers would joke and sneer when he was around, for sure and certain, but the ladies tended to keep outward disapproval towards him away from the public. "Yes. We went to school together. He, Lord Waldron, Lord Pwyll, and I have been friends since we were boys."

"Are the rumors true?" She dropped her voice to a whisper. "Was his father really thrown into the sanatorium? Is their family crazy?"

Anger burned across his face as he answered bitterly. "His father's sentence was made for disagreeing with the king's decision to enact a genocide during the war. Their family is not crazy. I'll not have you or anyone else spreading such rumors about them."

Her face flushed. "I'm not spreading rumors, Your Grace. I simply heard from Lady Cordelia that he was a great recluse and that his sister is hardly ever seen in public. Everyone loves their mum, but they wonder if she hides her children from the world."

"I can assure you that they keep away from society of their own volition. Marjorie keeps to herself because she's married and Brigham..."

Socializing hadn't been Brigham's taste ever since the kids at school started teasing him about his father, jeering that he'd go insane too. Over the course of a few weeks, some of the older boys convinced him he was going mad by jumping out at him, howling outside of his dormitory, and lying about noises they made around him. It drove poor Brig to the edge. One night, he hadn't been able to sleep. He opened the window and stared outside until Bryant joined him. They looked at everything below them until Brigham whispered, "I'm not crazy; right, Bry?" He turned to face Bryant with teary eyes. "What if they're right?"

Bryant shook his head, clearing the memory from his view. "Brigham doesn't deserve what the *ton* has made him out to be. He's only reclusive because of the rumors. You would be as well if everyone in Braxden twittered about how crazy *you* are because of your father."

"I suppose I hadn't thought about it like that," she answered quietly. The music came to a close. Bryant bowed as she curtseyed before he went off into the gardens to clear his head. He'd only passed the threshold when his reply came back to him.

"You're not, Brig. I promise you, you're not. They're just mean." He squeezed Brig's shoulder comfortingly. "Even if you were, it wouldn't matter. We'd still be friends. I promise. I'm not going to leave you." He pulled Brig into a hug. "Neither will the others, Shep and Corbin. We're friends, the four of us. That means forever, no matter what."

"No matter what," Brig whispered. "Are you sure?"

"Yep."

"What if we die? You can't reverse death," he argued.

Bryant grabbed his copy of the scriptures and flipped to a page. "'Even in death, yet we shall live, for we are a kind that belongs to the Most High. In that day, He shall collect His own to be with Him forever. None can take from His hand; who shall let it?' See, Brig? Even after death, we won't be separated. The Most High will gather us all together to live with Him in the Perfect Day."

"What if I stray? It's hard to believe, Bryant. So many bad things have happened this year with my father and Marjorie and at school. I don't know that I believe in Him. Why would He let these things happen if He loved us?"

He flipped to a different page. "One of the Followers wrote about that for one of the early churches. Here, it says 'but this happened that we might not rely on ourselves, but on the Most High, who raises the dead.' If the Most High can raise the dead, He can give you the strength to keep going. It'll happen someday, Brig.

Your father will be released. Your sister will be happy again. The bullies will stop once they get bored."

"I don't know that I can believe all that, Bry." He spoke in barely even a whisper, just a breath with a broken rhythm.

"You can ask Him to help you. I did, when my father died. We don't understand why bad things happen, but we can use them and purpose them to grow in our faith instead of our fear. My mum taught me that. Believe with me, Bry. We can all get through this together."

Brigham hadn't moved for a long minute, simply soaking in the words as Bryant prayed for him. A tear filled his eye as the memory faded. He thought about that moment almost every day. Every single time he heard a whisper from a passerby; every time he noticed someone sending a glare in Brig's direction. He didn't deserve the hate his family name gave him. None of them did.

He took a seat on the side of the fountain and looked out at the stars. The Most High had promised a vast many things. He promised them peace, love, and His presence. Boldness when they should speak out, wisdom when they should keep quiet, and the diligence to know the difference. Shepherd had been blessed with that several times over. He never lost his tongue, never dared raise his voice when it wasn't necessary. Corbin stood on the opposite end of that, speaking out almost always but being quiet when he knew he should. But Brigham? He didn't speak up even if it *was* necessary, out of fear of being labeled a coward and a lunatic.

That left him, then, to take the last quarter: speaking up when it wasn't necessary, not knowing when to keep quiet. He thought back to his conversation with Brig about Marjorie and his replies to Kegg's desires for Lady Olivia.

Too often did he speak out of turn, making a joke when he shouldn't, offering something that opposed society's rules. If it hadn't been for Brigham's insistence that he keep quiet, he would have spoken with the constable tomorrow. He'd been tempted even after Brig declined the offer. Mother would tell him, "you've done a kind thing, but you need to put it to rest" as she ought to. He couldn't force his own plans on the Roberts family, no matter how much he thought they needed it.

Footsteps approached, matching a familiar face. Shepherd took a seat next to him. "Corbin said that I'd find you out here. How is Brigham?"

"He insists that he must take care of this himself. I've been told to leave it alone, at least for now," he said briefly. "How has dancing with Lady Ruth been?"

His mouth pulled up into a grin as a blush lit his cheeks. "You heard about that, did you? Corbin has eyes everywhere, I suppose." He cleared his throat and continued. "She's an amazing woman; kind, compassionate, gentle. Everything I've ever wanted in a wife and more."

Bryant noticed the 'wife' and raised an eyebrow. "Wife, hm? Are you considering marrying her already?"

Shep's grin faded into a softer smile. "It's only been a week, Bry. Give it more time before asking me questions like that, will you? I've barely had time to stop stammering over my every word. We've managed a mere handful of proper conversations because I can't get my sentences in order."

The thought made him laugh. Shep never crossed his words. Ever. Imagining that a woman had the ability to do that in one week was like watching one of Corbin's pranks back at Battenhold. "I'd like to see it, Shep. Hard to believe that a single person can render you speechless."

"I've gotten past that state, thank you very much. I don't stammer now that we have been around each other enough. I hate to burst your bubble, but you'll have to wait for some other time to see me in such a way."

"What sort of other time, Shep? When you propose? Your wedding?"

He pressed his lips into a firm line. "We'll see." He sighed. "What do you suppose love feels like, Bry? I know we discussed it the other day, but it's hard for me to put these feelings in words. I just suppose that a chap in a courtship ought to know what it feels like when you're in love."

He shook his head, replying with, "I don't know if I have the answer to that. The actions of love for sure and certain, we talked about that yesterday; but the feelings?"

"I know, it's an impossible question for two bachelors who have never been in love." He sighed, resting a hand in the cool water of the fountain.

They sat in silence, both pondering the answer. For himself, love had always been shown through action. His father spending time with him up until his death, his mother teaching him what he needed to know to fill in for the late duke. She took care of his father when he was ill and cheered him up when he was disheartened. Every step of the way, she poured herself out in love. "I suppose that you know you're in love when it seems that living a single day without that person feels like it could kill you."

"How do you figure?"

"When my father died, my mother cried for days. She told me that it felt like half her soul was gone with him. They certainly loved each other."

"Surely there's more to it than feeling torn when they leave," he suggested. "Otherwise, how would we know until we've almost lost them?"

Bryant nodded and fixed his gaze on one of the many statues dotting the area. "I can only assume that love feels like affection, like you want to give her the world and everything in it. I can't help but think that love is more than a feeling, though."

"How do you suppose?"

"Paul describes love as many things. A feeling isn't among them. It is patient, kind, content, it keeps no record of wrongs. My answer then is this: we know we love when we persevere through the temptation of giving up on showing that love. As I said yesterday, we love by mirroring the Most High's love for us, with all of its sacrifices."

He smiled. "Are you sure you've never considered joining the church, Bry? You'd make a fine preacher."

"I'm sure, Shep," he said with an eye roll. "All the same, do you suppose that's it? The Most High demonstrated His love for us by sacrificing that we might be forgiven, by forgiving us to the highest degree, and continuing to pursue us when we turn away. Isn't that what love is? Commitment through the worst of it all?"

Shep met his gaze before nodding. "Yes, I think that's it. The decision to demonstrate love even when it gets difficult. I like that. Thanks for helping me sort out my thoughts, Bry. I feel a bit more capable now to tackle my first courtship." He spotted Lady Ruth standing by the threshold. "Speaking of, I've a promenade to offer to a certain young lady. If you'll excuse me." He stood and made his way to the lady before they sauntered off together.

"See you around, Shep."

Chapter Four: Calling Cards

November 12th

The most wonderful and terrifying woman in the entire world set her cup of tea down on the low table and opened her mouth to speak. "Bryant, dear, you should call on a lady or two that you danced with last night. It's proper etiquette, as you well know."

Bryant groaned. This is what he dreaded. Out of every subject tutored to him, social etiquette had been his least favorite. In a world where he was the caretaker of thousands, he needed to pay visits to keep face. What face? The only duke that the *ton* knew was the strange duke who was two years late to his first ball. That was all they cared to know. Why would he try to make them see anything different?

"Dear, take that look off of your face. It's not as impossible as you might think. And it *is* a good idea to try and meet some of these young ladies. One of them is going to be your future bride. It's best to get a head start now."

He didn't fancy throwing himself to the lions just yet. If only he could manage more time to prepare. Alas, any time he might have managed had passed long ago. All he could do now was use what he'd been taught to get through all of the courtesy calls and small talk. Unless, that is, "What if she all but falls into my arms like Shep's lady friend?"

An unlikely turn of events, though he'd far prefer it to paying *call*. Anything to keep from being out on his own and scrutinized. What if he accidentally breached the wrong subject or gave her flowers she didn't like? What if the style of his cravat failed to reach her expectations?

Mother clicked her tongue. "You're stalling, love, and there's no reason for it. Women aren't as impossible as you're making them out to be. It isn't the same as showing up to talk with Shepherd or Brigham, but it isn't difficult either."

He gave her a look that hopefully reminded her of him on his first day of school—terrified to be alone and desperate to stay. All that earned him, however, was a (not so) endearing laugh. "You're too hard on yourself. The sooner you put yourself out there and actually visit a lady, the sooner you'll realize that it isn't as bad as you fear."

She was right. He knew she was right and he resented it. But what could he say beyond telling her that he didn't have interest in any of the women he had danced with the night before? Lady Anwyn was far too willing to believe conspiracy theories and lies for him to ever take her seriously. Lady Caitlyn hardly looked at him for the duration of the song, only finding time to bat her eyelashes at a man across the room.

He'd danced with Marjorie again, though. Surely he could call on her. A married woman would forgive any sin in regards to his mannerisms and she was Brigham's sister. It would be like calling on his cousin or another relative. He found nothing intimidating about that.

"Very well. Have it your way, Mother. I shall call upon one Lady Marjorie Morris after we finish our tea." He gave her a half-grin, noting the mischief warring with seriousness in her eyes.

With an exaggerated sigh, she relented. "I suppose that will do for today. *However*, I highly suggest you pick a lady who isn't married later on this week."

He would; by then, surely, he wouldn't be intimidated by taking flowers to a woman he hardly knew and talking nonsense for upwards of an hour.

"She mentioned last night that she is visiting her brother today. You will want to check Brigham's estate first before going to her home. It would not do to show up uninvited to the house of a married woman when she is not home." Before he could respond, she added, "Marjorie's favorite flowers are daisies. I believe there are enough of them in the flowerbeds for a bouquet."

"Of course, Mother. Thank you." He rose from his chair, donned his cap, and headed for the door. Just outside, he stopped in his tracks. A carriage had already been prepared, complete with a bouquet of daisies in the hand of a footman. He allowed himself a sheepish eye roll as he climbed into the cabin. Apparently, he was more predictable than he thought.

The coachman called to him from the bench. "To where shall we be off, Your Grace?"

"Cargan Estate, Pedr. I've a mind to visit the Baron Grimes while I may." He turned his gaze from the coachman to the scene outside of the carriage. Thoughts swam around his head like fish in too small of a pond.

He really held no interest in his dance partners last night. None of them seemed to care about him either, for that matter. It had been his impression that a duke—an eligible, young, wealthy one, at that—would have his pick of a bride from the marriage minded debutants. Not a single one showed the least bit of interest. The most attention he had received was, of course, from Marjorie, and he couldn't very well marry her.

Was the rest of his season doomed to be much of the same? Would a woman always dance with him for appearances rather than to seek true love? Did any of them have butterflies the way Ruth had for Shep, and vice versa?

His own stomach sat void of fluttering, to his dismay. Though, given that his dance partners all had their eyes on other men, perhaps that was a blessing. He sorted through the faces of every nobleman's daughter he knew—even the gentlemens' daughters—searching for any that seemed to set off those bells in his head.

They didn't.

He knew well that he wasn't immune to such feelings. Back at Battenhold, he quite fancied a girl whom he saw near daily—the sister of one of his peers. They exchanged notes on occasion before they'd been too old to do so appropriately. Perhaps if he found her again, they could renew what they had previously.

Alas, he remembered hearing that her family had moved to the new territory across the Ardian Sea. That would have been nearly six years ago, given that it coincided with the end of the war against Themond. He would not find a bride in her.

Relief for his thoughts came at last as Cargan edged into view. He'd put away with this nonsense and focus his brain on something other than finding a wife: bringing a bit of cheer into his friend's sister's lonely life. He grabbed the flowers from the other seat and climbed out of the cabin. "I should be no more than an hour, Pedr. Best come at half-past to be on the safe side." He doffed his hat to the coachman and bounded up to the door, knocking thrice.

Brown, curly hair met his stare. "Bryant? What brings you by?"

"Brigham? Why are you at the door and not your footman?"

The boy shrugged. "It's Benneit's day off. Figured I might as well take over while Marjorie is visiting, since she's spending more time with Mother than with me."

"Ah, that brings me to why I'm here. Is your sister with your mother right now?"

"No, not currently. Mother was feeling a bit poorly so she decided to rest. Marjorie, I believe, is in the conservatory believing that she can make flowers grow faster by staring at them." He added a hint of a grin. His eyes flickered to the flowers in Bryant's hand. "Are you here to call on her, then?"

"Indeed. Mother all but forced me out of the house, insisting I call on someone that I danced with last night. I thought to myself 'I danced with Marjorie last night' and that was that." He hesitated before adding, "Single women terrify me, Brig."

He let out a sigh that was filled with far more understanding than humor. "I can relate to that. How Shep manages to speak to Lady Ruth without stammering like a fool, I'll never understand."

"I'm pretty sure it was Corbin's relentless teasing that did the trick. I'd run off with a woman too if I was the sole aim of Corbin's teasing for an entire night."

That pulled the laugh from Brig that he'd been aiming for. It took some of the nerve off of visiting for the first time on his own. "Come in, Bry. No sense in my taking up your visit on the threshold before you've had the chance to see my sister."

"Thank you, Brig." He followed his old friend in through the foyer and down a hallway to the drawing room. Patterned couches sat perpendicular to each other, one facing a door and the other a window with lace curtains. A lavish rug sat between them, supporting a teakwood table with lace doilies.

The boys took their seats, relaxing into the worn fabric. "You know," Bryant began, "I've always loved this room. It's far cozier than the drawing room at Angarth, despite my mother's attempts to keep it welcoming. Perhaps she keeps up with the latest fashions instead of making the room her own and keeping with it. Did your mother embroider these pillows herself?"

"She did; back when she was our age. Her mother took care to preserve them, giving them to her as a present when Marjorie was born. "You'll want these for your own drawing room someday, dear," she had said." He mimicked the elder woman's voice with a grin. "At least, that's what Mother claims she said." His smile softened as he gently rubbed his thumb across the surface of the thread.

"I wish my mother had kept some of hers. I'd have liked to set them up in a nursery when the time comes." He could picture it now: a yellow-walled room dotted with flowers and animals. A rocking chair in the corner with the pillows neatly set against the back. One or two of the pillows in the crib or on a rug where his wife sat coddling their newborn. A lovely idea, if it ever came to pass.

"That would be nice, wouldn't it? I'm sure whomever you marry would think so as well. Combining the past with the present, introducing the old to the newer generations." His eyes glazed over. "I do truly hope you get to have that moment, Bry."

That tone. He knew that tone and he despised it.

"Don't say that as though it will never happen to you. You'll meet her someday, Brig. I know it. No matter what the papers think of you or what whispers still linger." He gestured to the window. "Out there is a woman who will look past misconceptions and meet the real Brigham Roberts and she will be happy to take your last name as her own." His voice almost tinted with rage, livid that his own people turned against him for something so incredibly stupid. Brigham's father wasn't even insane.

His rant was met with a small smile that ended at its creases. "I suppose I'd best go fetch my sister, then. I'll only be a minute." He stood, the chair creaking below him, and left.

A deep sigh escaped him. Brig might never believe that he will find love just as Shep had, just as Corbin and himself could. He set the matter aside for now, for a figure with a lovely freckled face and curly hair stood in the doorway. "Good afternoon, my lady."

"Good afternoon, Your Grace." She smiled and sat across from him.

He held the bouquet out. "These are for you. Mother said daisies were your favorite."

"Her Grace was certainly correct. Thank you, Your Grace." She accepted the bouquet, smelling the blooms before setting them on the table.

"Please, call me Bryant. We're friends enough, aren't we?" He could have sworn he'd said the same thing a time or two before, but no matter. Perhaps she didn't think of him as family. There was no older sibling in Bryant's family for her to befriend, after all. He had a cousin, but she was younger even than he was.

"I suppose so." Her tone held a wariness that he wanted to avoid. The last thing she should feel was discomfort in her own—albeit former—home. Steer the conversation away from the pleasantries, then. Take it somewhere personal.

"Brig mentioned that you love the conservatory. Do you often spend time there?"

"I do. I've always been fascinated by plants and their various cycles of life." He didn't expect her to be interested in botany. She always seemed more like Brigham, preferring to pick up a book rather than trying to experience the real world. "We've kept our conservatory in its best shape since my father was taken. Mother insisted, given that it was my father's favorite part of the house. I suppose I inherited my fascination from him." Despite the gloominess of the memories, a small smile lit the corners of her lips and lingered in her eyes.

That bit of cheer gave him hope that he was on the right path. "I know that daisies are your favorite *flower*. Has a plant stolen your attention moreso?"

The smile filled itself out, spreading across her face in full bloom. "Lavender; though, lavender is technically still a flower. Its scent never ceases to calm me on a stormy day. The beautiful range of blues and purples has always cheered my soul."

He'd have to arrange for a bouquet of lavender to come by later. "What else do you enjoy about the fauna?"

"A better question would be what I don't. There are endless reasons to give my love to our conservatory. Each plant tells a story. Each has its own unique journey in finding its bloom. Those that don't bloom grow in other ways, adding to the scene with vibrant greens, blues, and yellows."

What an interesting outlook on life that could be. He reasoned it was how she managed to come to terms with everything that happened in her own journey. If she wasn't meant to be a flower, she could be an ivy or a fern, meant to add to the beauty of another's blooms.

If that was beautiful, why did it inspire only sadness?

"That's lovely, my lady." He didn't quite know what else to say in response to the pangs that hit his heart.

Luckily, she changed the subject. "Are you going to Lady Goddard's masquerade ball on Saturday? Brigham tells me that he plans to dress as a prophet; I don't quite remember which one. Elijah or Dhiarmuid, perhaps. All the same, he intends to use feathers to recreate a sort of beard on his mask."

"As a matter of fact, I am. Mabyn—you've met Mabyn before, haven't you? My mother's lady's maid?—offered to create a mask for me. I'm going as a detective."

"What does that entail?" The intrigue in her eyes alone was enough to make his day. He could consider his mission successful.

"A custom hat (one cannot play the detective with a gentleman's top hat) and a capelet. A beautiful grey plaid capelet to match the hat. I've also got a magnifying glass, of course, and a wooden pipe. Do keep in mind that I don't intend to use said pipe during the ball." He grinned. "Mother was aghast when I mentioned that Lyz—my valet—managed to secure an ancient one for me. It took a full ten minutes to convince her that I only planned to use it for my costume."

She matched his grin. "I would expect nothing less from a gentleman. If I may say so, Your Grace, everything that Brigham has told me about you is plain as day truth. Your grace, your generosity, the kindness you bestow even when no one has asked it of you. I'm eternally grateful that the Most High saw fit to give my younger brother such a godly man for a friend." Her smile held true, adding a twinkle to her eye and a crease to her brow that highlighted a mark he didn't notice before.

It looked almost purple, though she clearly tried to conceal it with powder. A bruise, perhaps? What sort of fumble could cause her to bruise the middle of her forehead? It looked new, given the color. Why did she feel the need to hide bruises from her family and their closest friends?

He opened his mouth to ask about it when another voice called her name, belonging to the lady of the house. Marjorie stood, clutching the daisies. “I'd best be off, Your Grace. Thank you again for the flowers, and for taking the time to call on me.”

“Of course,” he stammered, somewhat taken off guard that their time had ended so suddenly. “Have a good day, my lady.” But she was gone before he could finish, disappearing down the hall as Brigham took her place. “Brig, I have a query. Keep in mind that it isn't a pretty one and it isn't likely to have a pretty answer.”

His friend eyed him warily. “What is it?”

“Was that a bruise on her forehead?”

Brig shot him a glare that all but screamed '*don't question it*'. “I don't know what you're referring to.” His shoulders went rigid and he avoided Bryant's eyes. “It's nothing, Bry. That's what she told me, so that's what I'll tell you.”

He sighed. “Does she know it's not nothing?”

“Mother has talked to her about it. You didn't hear me say that, though. She wouldn't like me talking about it, even to you.” The pain in his eyes could soften the hardest of hearts. “There's nothing I can do, Bry, so there's no point in pretending you can do anything either.”

“We could involve the constable. This doesn't need to go the way you think.”

“Yes. It does. She's an adult, Bry, and she's married. I'm a child in comparison. There's nothing I can do.” He sent a glare that gave him chills. “Please, just drop the subject and let me handle it.”

“Why? So you can handle it by *not* handling it?”

Brigham growled and shouted, “If I step in, he might do something worse!” Silence fell between them thicker than ice, and just as cold. His voice dropped to a whisper. “If I step in, he might do something worse.” Emotion clogged his words. “I don't want to lose my sister, Bry.” He grabbed the door, pulling it open. “You should go. We have a house party to attend, do we not? Surely you need to prepare for it."

He lifted his gaze to meet Brig's cold brown eyes. "If you're so scared of losing her, why don't you separate him from her? Call the constable on him and make sure he can't hurt her anymore."

In a voice barely loud enough to hear, he replied, "I'll see you at the masquerade."

Chapter Five: History

November 16th

"What are you supposed to be, Corbin?"

"A raven, of course. Didn't you notice the unusually long point of my beak? Or the black feathers along my cape? What else would I be?" He huffed and turned away from Brigham, staring out the window. "I've never been to a masquerade ball, despite the fact that I've wanted to attend one for all of my three seasons."

"I don't believe any of us have been to one. It didn't seem fun unless we could all go together," Shepherd responded.

"And what great fun it will be when Brig, Bryant, and I are huddled together after you abandon us for a certain Lady Ruth," he jeered sarcastically. All that earned him was a huff and an eyeroll. "Couldn't you spend time with us for a night? Just *one* night, Shep. Like the good old days, back in the two seasons you didn't have a sweetheart. Do you remember those days?"

He shook his head. "I've a duty to my dearest. Can't have a scandal reaching the papers because I neglected to dance with her tonight." A hint of a smile wrote its way into the wrinkles of his eyes. "I wouldn't want our peers to get any ideas."

Brig met his gaze. "That's a little forward, don't you think? You've only been courting her for a fortnight or so."

"Perhaps, but I don't intend to drop a courtship after only a few weeks. She could very well be the one. I've never quite met a woman like her—"

His voice drowned out as Bryant stared out the window at the passing lands. Their very first masquerade ball. Excitement bounced about in his stomach and jittered his thoughts. All the same, the glitter of the evening couldn't keep away his worries. His mind switched between two images; one of Marjorie, the other of Olivia.

Marjorie, because their conversation last week still lingered in his head. She hadn't seemed well and he had definitely noticed a bruise or two dotting her face.

A shudder stole through him as he remembered the fear in her eyes. It was only a dance that should have meant nothing. A dance he *had* intended to repeat tonight. After seeing her ghastly appearance, however, he was having second thoughts. *Let Brigham handle it*, Corbin's voice mumbled. Despite the rolling of his conscience, he was inclined to listen. All the same, he intended to ask Shepherd for his opinion. The man never steered him wrong.

He thought of Olivia because of the clear interest Alden Kegg had in her. If both Lyz and Cristyn had premonitions about him, Bryant feared for her safety. Kegg wasn't willing to lose easily. His affections wouldn't be without a cost. Certainly not, if Lyz didn't trust the earl around *any* young woman. He'd need to keep an eye on the man, and on both young women besides.

What was precious had to be protected.

A jab from Corbin brought his attention back to the group. "Bryant, you need to settle this. Does Shep's costume more resemble a fish or a lizard?"

His brows furrowed as he stared at Shep's costume. "A lizard. A great terrible lizard that any fish should fear." A grin broke out on Shep's face as he inquired, "What is it supposed to be?"

"One of those prehistoric lizards that my younger cousins keep going on about. They're just at the age where they're learning about history and sciences and putting away their faerie tales. The great lizards are a new addition to the textbooks now that paleontologists have classified them. Terrifying, as you might expect."

Brigham spoke up, then, finally brought out of his trance and pulled from the window. "Those aren't *just* faerie tales, Shep. Those creatures are as real as you and me."

Humor sparked across Corbin's face. "Surely you jest, Brig."

"I'm entirely serious," he said with a glare. "I've studied them. There is an entire field guide about them written by a chap named Idris Hopewell. He spent years tracking and studying them during the war and published his findings afterwards. The Daoine Sidhe are just as real as those lizards."

An uncomfortable silence fell between them as Bryant watched Cor's reaction. His cheeks flushed as he spoke, "Then it appears that I was wrong."

"Clearly," he spat. Odd, that was. Brig's temperament made him calm and quiet even in the face of adversity; even when their peers teased and joked about him going mad, he didn't fight back. For him to lash out against *Corbin* of all people didn't make sense, even if Cor did tend to take jokes too far. They'd been friends for a decade. Something was eating at Brigham, and he suspected it was their conversation yesterday.

He would need to find out later, however, for the beautiful Goddard estate edged in his vision. Their carriage halted a moment later. The door swung open and a footman escorted them out of the cabin. What a sight it must be: four boys tumbling over each other in full costume as they bantered and chittered with each other. His mother wasn't far behind, taking the lowly position of the last person to leave the carriage before it was swept off to another part of the estate.

"A lovely building, this," Corbin commented as they made their way inside.

"Indeed. It lends itself to the magic of masquerade balls with the architecture. 16th century, I believe. The height of Deravailian society, back in a time of peace. Braxden *is* one of its oldest cities, after all. I wouldn't be surprised if this manor were one of the last remaining from that time period," Shep commented. Still Brigham said nothing, pivoting himself away from the group.

The other two chatted about this or that thing they noticed on their way to the ballroom which made for an entertaining jaunt. Corbin was still convinced that Shep's costume looked like a fish while Shepherd was far too entranced with the architecture to care.

Just outside the doors to the ballroom, they slipped their masks on, determined to hide their identities from the world until the evening's end. Bryant tied his own, marveling at Mabyn's handiwork. She'd done an excellent job, pulling the perfect fabric to match his detective aesthetic.

A sea of well dressed people met them inside. Musicians dressed in a variety of penguin costumes grouped near the piano. Women dressed in all sorts of bright colors—quite a difference from the usual pale pinks, whites, and yellows that made up their wardrobes. The men almost all dressed lighter, keeping to their original uniform with only an added accessory or two to change up the look.

Quite a waste of an opportunity.

Music swelled as pairs matched up. The refreshment table looked far less intimidating in comparison. Deciding that it would be best to ease into the night, he headed that way for a glass of punch instead of finding a young lady's dancing card.

Just as he took a first sip, something caught his attention. Brigham was dancing. Not only dancing, but laughing. He stepped away from the refreshments, edging his way around the wall to get a better look. Sure enough, that was Brig, dancing and smiling and chatting with the lady he danced with.

It had to be at a masquerade. A right shame that he had no idea who the recipient of Brigham's rare laughter was. The only clue given to him was her dark, ominous coiffeur. Perhaps on the morrow he'd have a better chance at determining her identity. For the moment, he'd be glad to let her make his old friend laugh again.

There'd been so little of that lately. They had their moments, of course. Times where Corbin said something actually funny or one of them tripped over a stone or Shep's wit got the better of them. Nothing like what he saw now. Never where someone Brigham hardly knew managed to make him show more than a scowl or a dark expression. Shep had found his lady, for sure and certain. Could Brigham now join the line?

Alas, as the song ended, they parted ways with him not so much as accompanying her back to whichever matron belonged to her. Though, Bryant mused, she could be here alone. Uncommon, certainly, but not out of the question. Many society girls decided to venture out without their mothers or sisters for one reason or another.

Could the girl be here without supervision *to* see Brigham, afraid of what her parents might think of the match? It was true that in the years since Brig's father's scandal, very few welcomed the Roberts family into conversation. It was conceivable that she managed to avoid an evening chaperone to dance with Brigham.

What better way to find out than to ask the man himself?

He strolled away from the wall, finding Brigham just before he entered the card room. "Who was that, Brig?"

His eyebrow raised in question. "Who was who?"

"Your dance partner, of course. The one who made you laugh like you haven't in years. Who was she?"

A confused grin lit his face. "I don't know. That is quite the point of these events, isn't it? To not know the identity of your dance partner until afterwards?"

"You're telling me that a complete stranger made you laugh more than Corbin's jokes or Shepherd's wit has in five years?" Unbelievable. Outright unbelievable.

"She was funny. Can a woman not have a good sense of humor?" His defensiveness wasn't a good sign. He didn't want the matter touched.

Bryant could respect that. A lot of things in his family weren't to be addressed unless they must. "I don't mean to cross you, old friend. I simply wish I knew who it was that gave you such happiness." He didn't mean his tone to make it sound as though their future had been set in stone.

"If it makes you feel any better, I don't plan on pursuing it. She responded to a question in a manner that I found humorous. There's nothing more to it, Bry. I promise." He paused, hesitant to say what was on his heart. "I've been thinking about our argument and I wanted to apologize. What I said was out of line. I'm just..." he sighed, his breath hissing out slowly. "I don't want to make things worse. This whole situation is unfamiliar to me and I'm lost as to what I should do. If I intervened and it was nothing, the rumors might get worse. My own sister might even start to think that I'm turning mad. But if I do nothing and there *is* something wrong, I'd be the sole reason my sister got hurt." His eyes found the ground, darkening as the storm behind them grew. "What am I supposed to do?"

Shep should be here. He was more adept at giving advice. Although, he had no knowledge of what was going on. At least, not as much as Bryant did.

He took a deep breath, trying to think through what Shep would say. The words came slowly, piecing themselves together as he spoke. "Pray for her safety, for wisdom, for guidance to know what to do when the time comes.

"Be vigilant and look for other signs of her distress. Notice things she tries to hide. Not just bruises, but the shadows in her eyes, the stammer in her voice. When you've found them and you're certain they're there, involve the authorities and make sure she's safe. She can stay at Angarth if it's needed. My staff will be happy to welcome her."

He nodded slowly. "That all makes sense. I'll look out for that. Once I'm sure, though, how do I make certain she is safe until the constable can deal with it? Surely, if the constable showed up at her home, her husband would find a way to lie his way out of it and retaliate later."

"Invite her home. You could have her over for afternoon tea, or for a book club. That will keep her a distance away without her husband being suspicious of her whereabouts." He desperately hoped that what he was saying would help, that it was right. If he misplaced these words and havoc struck as a result, the weight of it would be on his shoulders alone, regardless of anything Brig might say.

"Do you think she'll suspect anything?"

"It's difficult to say just now. Is she the observant type?" If she was, no doubt her worry would be through the roof as Brig watched her.

"In all honesty, I don't believe so. These past few years have muted her senses, I think."

Too often, he realized, Brigham's voice carried sadness. A deep kind that wasn't healed with a simple encouraging word. He'd been scarred just as his sister was. That kind of hurt cut everyone involved. It made his own heart ache in agony. "Keep watch, then. As discreetly as you can, of course, but stay vigilant *for* her as much as *of* her."

"Right. Thank you, Bry." He sighed as though some burden fell off of his shoulders and breathed as if the air had only just become clear.

"Shall we be off for a game of cards in—"

A voice interrupted. One rather dark and brooding that he, frankly, didn't want to hear today. "Your Grace!" Alden Kegg greeted. "What good fortune that I've found you. Your mother mentioned that you were here, but I only just determined that it was really you. The mask does well to hide your identity."

"Thank you, Lord Arioch. How do you fair this evening?" He forced his tone to be steady, not trusting the man no matter what Mother said in his defense. Lyz didn't like him. Lyz's judgment was never wrong, and when coupled with Cristyn's hesitation to even serve him tea, the man must be trouble. He wasn't safe, whatever that would mean later on.

"Quite well, Your Grace; thank you. And good evening to you, Lord Grimes." His tone set him on edge. From the growl of the 'gr' to the slight way he held his 's', his very voice betrayed him. He didn't sound like an earl ought to. In fact, he sounded like a merchant. Brigham doffed his hat before resuming his impression of a stone column. "I've heard through the grapevine that you told someone of my intentions to court Lady Olivia."

Accusation probably wasn't the right word to describe his statement, however he had strung the words. Balanced was the closest thing he could put to it, but even that didn't suffice; it didn't represent the layers to his voice that contained so much more than his words.

Averment, he decided. "I did. My conversation happened upon the subject. I didn't think anything of it." He added an ounce of apology to his tone, just in case Kegg meant it to be an accusation.

"No need to apologize, Your Grace. I had no intention of keeping it a secret. It's quite hard to keep such things hidden, as I'm sure you well know." He gestured to the corner where Shep spoke with Lady Ruth. "All the same, I've a query for you."

He raised an eyebrow.

Kegg continued somewhat hesitantly, as if he was expecting Bryant to answer with more than he had. "Would you put in a good word for me?"

If he had been sipping on a drink, he would have spit it out. Even *if* Bryant liked the chap enough to do as he requested, he hardly *knew* Alden. They barely spent a year as friends at Battenhold and Kegg had clearly changed in the time between then and now. At a loss to say anything else, he responded with, "I'll see what I can do."

What more could he say? To be rude here would give both of them a worse reputation than they needed this early on in the season. To agree would go against his very conscience; everything told him not to trust Kegg.

The corners of his mouth pulled up in a grin. Not the wicked sort that he expected, but one of genuine thanks and cheer. "Thank you ever so much, Your Grace. You know, this marriage could be what saves me."

His brows knit together at that. "What do you mean?"

Alden rolled his eyes with jape, mischief weaving its way into his grin. "Let's be entirely honest, Your Grace. My family's reputation isn't the best. My father died of unknown causes, my mother of 'heartbreak' just a few months later. Circumstances like that don't paint one's family in the best light. If the Duke of Whittaker himself put in a good word on my behalf, any disdain for my family name might disappear. Proceeding that, if Lady Olivia decides she likes me enough to marry me, my reputation would skyrocket. Her family is of the best sort, as well you know. This marriage could save my family name."

He hadn't considered that Kegg might have been an outcast because of the suspicious circumstances surrounding the deaths of his parents. Wanting to leave him with a good word, Bryant responded, "I wish the best of luck to you, then." It would take far more than luck to get Lady Olivia to fall for Alden Kegg since the lady *wasn't*—according to Lady Anwyn—interested in the earl.

He had to wonder, then, if she had set her cap for someone else.

"Thank you again, Your Grace. This means more than you know." His eyes danced around, wondering if he should stay and continue chatting or if he should move on.

Bryant prayed he chose to move on, to go somewhere else so that he and Brigham could spend some proper time as brothers, challenging each other in a game of wits.

"His Grace and I were just about to play a game of moral quarrel, if you'd like to join us." Brigham spoke up, to his surprise. They weren't, by any means, about to play moral quarrel. Shep might have joined them if they were, given that three players were necessary and Shep enjoyed thinking through moral situations.

"I do fancy a game, though I'll admit that I've never been good at discerning which opponent to pick for moral quarrel. Perhaps another game, instead? Klaverjas, perhaps?"

A fun game, if a bit dull. "That will be just fine. Thank you for suggesting it," Bryant responded. It was better than standing around talking, at the very least. In a game, he could keep his mind occupied with thoughts other than of how Alden's tone insinuated the very character Cristyn thought he had.

"Klaverjas it is, then. In the drawing room, just off to the side here? I believe they've the cards for it." Dancing would need to wait a little longer. It was a good thing that the invitation was for a few days.

Chapter Six: Playing Hand

Bryant stared at the cards in his hand, wishing that his teammate would actually decide to make a smart decision. For the game to work, they'd needed to borrow an extra man to make the teams equal. From there, it was a matter of mastering the cards and taking the tricks. If only his teammate had found it such a simple task. The man hardly made a good move all game, choosing to start low instead of high in the hopes of drawing out his opponent's higher cards when the game was young.

Such a strategy could have worked in their favor if Bryant had high cards in his hand to take the tricks afterwards. The only problem *there* was that he didn't. The highest card in his hand was a nel; nine in a standard deck. The third lowest card of the game.

He might have suspected that his teammate had low cards as well, but Alden hadn't played many high cards either—most being a number instead of a crown. By process of elimination, his other must have some higher-up cards that he simply wasn't playing.

"Your turn, Your Grace."

Drat; it was, and he didn't have anything near good enough to take the trick. A right shame, for he'd never best Kegg with the way the game was going. Not that he exactly wanted to, for it meant beating Brig as well. He did so despise losing, though.

"I play a nel, the trick goes to Lord Arioch." Being the highest ranked man among them, they'd declared it his job to remember who took what trick. A brilliant suggestion, given that he could hardly think straight with Lord I-Could-Be-A-Murderer sitting just beside him. Not fair, by any means.

A whisper behind him caught his attention. Men, just out of the corner of his eye, pointed to a ledger and whispered amongst themselves, barely loud enough for him to hear. The Earl of Gregsay and the Marquis of Jenherd, if he wasn't mistaken. Gambling on horses, he'd be given to assume, but their words didn't match that. They whispered of men and debts and wagers and *others*.

Others, being lords their own age. He felt an uneasiness grow within him as he played his next card; his attention stayed on the game but his focus was on the men behind him. Their eyes lit with a disguised panic, as if they were betting on something unfamiliar to them, something as new to the *ton* as the idea of having a duke seeking a bride among wallflowers.

He shivered as Kegg took the hand, eyes hardening with ice as his own name was whispered. "No, that isn't likely," Lord Jenherd replied as he wrote something else into the ledger. "It's only been two weeks, you know."

"I know," Gregsay responded. "All the same, it seems likely to me. His friend followed suit, if the reports are true. It isn't out of the question, if that's what you're worried about. And, if it is, the benefactor will cover it as he has in the past. Who'd have thought that with a single sentence, one man could have the whole House of Lords at his feet?"

Jenherd shook his head. "*I'm* not at his feet, Gregsay; hardly so. I'm not as *stupid* as some of the others. I do not bet what I do not have."

A debtor, then. An interesting thought, he mused, but one that didn't spark danger like the man sitting next to him. Debtors were a normal part of society, even among the *ton*. Then again, they were hardly mentioned among his peers. To admit that one had lost their family's wealth was a fate worse than death.

Fortunately for himself, his mother had kept their estates and accounts within their means in his father's absence, as well as guiding him through the process when he became of age. These men didn't sound so lucky—or else had used up their wealth at the tables or by life of luxury.

"Neither do I, Lord Jenherd, but some things cannot be helped. When this benefactor has promised to cover any bet with no deadline to pay him back, why not bet a little more than I usually would? Who is going to find out? Who is going to care?"

He imagined that their wives and children would should their bets go awry. Little ones never used to hunger pains and cold suddenly thrust into small flats with poor heating. Mothers suddenly donning cottons and wools instead of silks and satins. Not a rough life, but a different one. One that spoke of 'what if' for perhaps the first time.

"Lord Gregsay, I do believe there's a game of whist calling us over in the corner." The marquis spared a glance in his direction before gesturing to the more private corner table.

So much for his eavesdropping going unnoticed. Not that it had been a matter of national security. Nothing was properly at stake. Someone's pride and honor, perhaps, but no one would die because of a benefactor supplying betting money at the tables for his peers.

"Your Grace, are you alright?" Kegg looked at him with concern.

"Pardon?"

"You seem distracted, is all. Something on your mind? Lady Anwyn, perhaps?" The dastardly grin he *did* expect finally showed itself. "This is a house party, as you are well aware. There are plenty of rooms available if you need a moment to refresh yourself. We can finish our game later."

His shudder had to have been visible. It had to be, for it took his very breath from him. "No need; we can finish the game now. I've more important things on my mind than childish endeavors, Kegg." Childish endeavors that left his stomach reeling at the thought and his skin feeling as though he'd just walked into a spider's web. The very idea that he'd act inappropriately at a house party set his skin on fire. "Perhaps I *should* go if that's the kind of man you expect me to be, Lord Arioch."

The grin on his face didn't waver. "There's no need to be like that, Your Grace. It was a simple jest; just a joke as any of these fellows might make."

"Then perhaps I should go home now instead of in a few days' time. I'd sooner be hanged than deal so in the house of another." He rose from his seat. "Good day, Lord Arioch. Lord Humker." He stumbled his way out of the room, storming towards the outdoors.

In doing so, he almost toppled Cordelia Edmondton, who even now had her arm on the viscount from the other day. "Your Grace, what a pleasant surprise. How do you fair?"

He really wasn't of mind to talk to anyone—certainly not a lady just yet. The gardens were but twenty paces away and he needed to reach them before his skin combusted. "How do you do." He nodded in her viscount's direction, taking strides to angle himself away, and hoped they understood he wasn't in a mood to chat.

Fortunately, Brigham popped up and called to him. "Forgive me, Lord Harvers, Lady Cordelia. Lord Grimes is calling for me." He rushed to Brig's side and they hurried into the cool night. "Thanks, Brig."

"Lord Arioch is a right fool for saying what he did. Don't let my silence fool you into thinking I agreed with him. He's an idiot and a coward for laughing that off as a joke instead of owning up to his sins." Brig's voice boiled with the anger that Bryant felt; rage bubbled to the forefront as Lyz's words echoed in his head. *I wouldn't trust him with any young woman.*

"Lyz was right," was all he could manage to say as the stress came to the forefront. He took steady, slow breaths in a vain attempt at calming down. "Cristyn was right. Kegg is not to be trusted with Lady Olivia or any of these young women. He's a danger, a hazard. I need to watch her, to dance with her to ensure her safety. If Kegg lays a single hand on her, I fear he won't stop at a dance." His stomach churned as his supper rose from its place.

Brig laid a hand on his shoulder. "Take a few minutes for yourself before you rush out there. Lady Olivia is no naive child, mind you. She'll see through any odd request the earl makes. She can handle herself until you've managed to regain your composure. I daresay she won't take kindly to a duke hurling his dinner on her shoes."

He almost laughed at that, but the bile that rose up convinced his lungs to silence. Instead, he focused on the cool air that made its way through him. Little by little, the storm between his eyes cleared. His thoughts rid themselves of the fog of anger. Even the churning in his stomach started to calm. Now, he prayed with intensity that what Brig said about Olivia was true. She needed the obstinance now more than ever. "I think I'm ready now."

"Count to sixty for me."

His brow furrowed. "What?"

"Count to sixty. It's a simple enough task to do while tensions are still high, and it should help you calm down enough to dance without tossing away your dinner." He started counting before

Bryant could, as if saying the numbers aloud would encourage him to join.

He did, to his own chagrin. It couldn't have looked normal for a duke and a baron to be counting out loud. "Sixty. Now am I ready?"

"Absolutely. Your tone gives nothing away." He gave a half-smile in assurance. "Bry, don't worry about Kegg. I'll deal with him if he becomes too much of a threat to Lady Olivia." They both knew that his dealing with it meant he'd get Shepherd involved, who would speak to the proper authorities to see what could be done. The public might not listen to Baron Brigham Roberts, but they'd listen to Marquis Shepherd Whitley to a fault.

"Thank you, Brig. I appreciate it." He returned the half-smile before walking inside. His eyes scanned the room, searching heads for Olivia's dark hair and usually green dress. He nearly jumped out of his skin when he felt someone tap his shoulder.

"Good evening, Sir Detective. Care to dance the next set with me?" He didn't recognize the voice. The mask did well to hide her features, at that. Beautiful grey-green eyes stared up at him through the cream-colored mask.

He hesitated in answering, knowing that he was specifically looking for Lady Olivia. Denying her, though, would change the game he'd set. His scheme of dancing with girls who weren't noticeable was his entire plan for surviving his delayed first season. If he didn't dance with this woman whom he didn't know, what was the point of his dancing with anyone?

"I would be delighted, my lady." He offered an arm and led her to the middle of the room just as the musicians started up again. "You know my costume, but what is yours?"

The question pulled more of a grin than he expected it to. "A sparrow."

An interesting thing to dress as, that bird. A canary or a cardinal, he could understand for their bright colors, but a sparrow? Then again, Corbin *was* running around the place in all black with the most pointed beak of a mask he'd ever seen. A sparrow, then, couldn't be entirely out of the question.

"Notice the patches of brown and black lace mixed in with the ivory. Quite clever, I should *think*." Her voice was laced with pride as she took his hand.

It was, he mused, using mixed fabrics to create a spotted effect. "Clever indeed, Miss Sparrow." He twirled her, watching the way the colors of her dress blurred together as they swished.

"Thank you. Did you come with anyone tonight, Sir Detective?"

Was she trying to discern his marital status or his identity? He mused that the question would only be answered if they had time to ask more questions. "I arrived with some peers. No lady on my arm, if that's what you're wondering."

She wasn't wondering, apparently, for she followed it up with, "Which ones?"

He didn't quite fancy giving up his identity yet. It seemed an insult to the idea of the party to outright tell her who he was. "A raven, a fish, and a prophet." Elijah, Brigham had decided once they'd met up at Angarth.

"A prophet? Why, that could be anyone a few decades your senior." Despite the mask covering the majority of her upper face, he could make out a few wrinkles that suggested she'd furrowed her brows in thought, tallying who all she'd seen that night that could be dressed as a prophet.

"Just be glad none of them were dressed as penguins," he joked. Their game tugged a flutter from his heart: one that he hadn't felt since he stopped writing letters to Rhedyn Evanson over six years ago. Warmth spread over his cheeks as he realized it. This sparrow before him had stirred his heart.

Alas, to keep up their questionnaire, he couldn't dwell on it. "Keep an open mind. This is a costume ball, after all, and the imagination can interpret any one thing a hundred different ways." He paused to focus on the next step of the dance, raising a hand to twirl the woman. "You're a lovely dancer."

"Thank you, Sir Detective. I've practiced this dance a fair few too many times." There, in her tone, was a bit of indifference.

Her statement brought with him that tinge of forced humility that had been dealt to him at his debut. He'd been dancing with Lady Olivia, whose steps were far too calculated and perfect to have not been practiced a thousand times; such was that the magic of the art had all but vanished.

His eyes caught sight of the rich color of her dark hair as the pieces fell into place. Miss Sparrow, dancing just an arm's length away, *was* Lady Olivia.

The lady who irked him.

"It shows. In your gracefulness, I mean." He amended the statement, hoping she wouldn't take offense to his almost saying she didn't care. His words tumbled out before he could think about what he was saying. What *was* he saying? This was Olivia, the woman he didn't care about. Why would he attempt to spare her feelings? The notion of being polite hadn't stopped him before.

If she did think his statement offensive, she didn't note it. "Thank you again, Sir Detective. The grace, I'm told, comes naturally." There that indifference was again. The arrogance that wove her tone with every syllable.

If he wasn't sure that she was Lady Olivia before, he was certain of it now. "What inspired your costume, if I might ask?"

"A sparrow. I had thought that was rather obvious." The arrogance more than laced her voice. It stabbed.

Heat bloomed in his cheeks as he clarified his question. "What I mean is, what inspired you to base your costume off of the bird?"

Her expression changed—however slightly—into a softer, more understanding one. "Ah, of course. A sparrow happened to be the first thing I spotted after getting the invitation. Naturally, I chose it as the inspiration for my costume."

"Naturally." The music came to a close. He bowed and offered his arm to her again. "Shall I escort you to the refreshments table, Miss Sparrow?"

She nodded, placing her hand gently into the crook of his elbow. "That was quite fun, Sir Detective. I don't suppose you'd be available for another dance in—say—five minutes?" He would, if it was needed. Anything to keep Kegg from getting his claws on her. Anything to keep her safe.

A soft grin lit his face to mask his fear as he repeated, "Naturally."

Light danced in her eyes, sparking across the beautiful grey-green irises like cloud-lightning. "Wonderful. So then, Sir Detective, what might your fish friend look like?"

Back to the questions, then. "Some say he looks more like a lizard, which he claims to be. The costume does, however, much more resemble a fish." Not the conclusion he'd drawn in the carriage, but a necessary statement to keep her guessing a few minutes longer.

"A lizard, hm?" He searched for the recognition that, yes, she had figured out who he traveled with. "An interesting choice of costume."

"With all due respect, Miss Sparrow, your choice of costume was, well, a sparrow."

Through her mask, she glowered. "Don't interrupt me," she spat as she turned to face the room. "A lizard that looks like a fish."

He spoke again before he could stop himself. "I do believe, Miss Sparrow, that you're overlooking perhaps the most invaluable piece of evidence." He didn't want her to know his identity. She'd only shown disdain for Duke Bryant Wooldridge. Sir Detective, however, had found her good graces. He wanted to keep in her favor.

He couldn't fathom why. Perhaps the butterflies were addicting. Could seem to be so, given that many of his peers chased after one woman and moved to the next in quick succession. Perhaps they found themselves victim to the fluttering that had caught his attention.

"Sir Detective?" Her voice made them stir, fluttering higher than before as if disturbed by the sudden voice. "Sir Detective." The arrogance was back in full force. Her glare stated that he'd gotten lost in his thoughts and that she'd said his name several times. "Hello? Are you there?"

"I beg your pardon, Miss Sparrow. I was caught up solving a mystery. I can assure you, though, that you have my fullest attention." Unless the butterflies got there first, which seemed likely.

He could not be falling for Lady Olivia. She was irate and stubborn. Dancing had meant nothing to her. It had been everything to him once upon a time. The butterflies lied to him. She couldn't be the one that he'd been waiting for his entire life. Lady Olivia could not be the woman he asked to be his wife.

In a moment of stubbornness, he decided they weren't butterflies at all. Instead, it was simply his stomach churning from fear for her. Fear that Kegg might grab hold of her if he didn't stay close enough. Concern that she'd fall victim to his jokes and charms.

Even Miss Sparrow, the most outspoken, obnoxious woman he knew, deserved far better than that.

That suited him just fine.

"The raven is the one you're referring to, is it not? A costume of all black, unless you mean that he is flighty or mischievous."

That had, in fact, been the reason Corbin chose his costume. *Ravens are mischievous*, he'd claimed. Ravens, though, weren't earls. They didn't have a gentleman's nature or a top hat.

"That man over there," she pointed out. "He's the raven."

Bryant followed the invisible line drawn from her fingertip. Sure enough, Corbin's curly blond hair stuck out from the sea of black that enveloped him. "Indeed so, Miss Sparrow. Now, if only you could find the identity of the man, you'd have me figured out."

She turned to face him, a determined grin on her face. "I suppose I'll have to ask him for a dance." With a laugh, she patted his shoulder. "Our dance will have to wait, Sir Detective. I've a more important matter to attend to." She whisked away to Corbin's arms.

He almost wished Cor denied her the dance, but that wouldn't exactly be fair to either of them. It wasn't jealousy that gripped him. Couldn't be, for there were certainly not butterflies flittering in his stomach. It was fear. Perhaps Kegg stole Corbin's costume and donned a blond wig to look like him.

But, no. Kegg was a fair bit shorter than Corbin. That was definitely his idiot raven friend dancing with his sparrow.

He wasn't jealous.

Chapter Seven: Scars

November 17th

Corbin slid into the seat next to Bryant at the breakfast table, shoving a forkful of eggs into his mouth before speaking. "Your Grace, you'll never believe who I danced with last night." His tone held nothing but mischief—the same mischief that stuck a grin to his face.

"Oh, really? Who, praytell, did you dance with, Lord Waldron?"

"A certain sparrow that you've had your eye on." He stabbed a sausage, biting off the end of it before continuing. "She's a lovely dancer. I'm not surprised that she has your attention. Frankly, though, I didn't expect you to find someone so soon. You've only been out for two weeks, after all. You weren't fooling around when you wrote that you wanted to try your luck at finding a bride this year."

Of all the- "Corbin, I am *not* in love with Miss Sparrow." The replied 'mhm' sent his eyes rolling. "It was one dance, that's all. At a masquerade ball of all things. How do you even know if she gave me her name?"

"Because you're Bryant Wooldridge, duke of the sheep and master of solving mysteries." He paused for effect before adding, "You *did* dress as a detective last night, of all things. You wouldn't have thought of that costume if analyzing details didn't intrigue you even a bit."

He had a point there; Bryant was fairly analytical. He didn't like to act without knowing the cards, and didn't like to show his hand until he knew what was at stake. "That doesn't mean I know who Miss Sparrow is."

"It doesn't, but you do."

He sighed dramatically, acknowledging his defeat. "Just because I might have an idea of her identity doesn't mean I'm falling in love. It was one dance."

"Shepherd didn't even need to dance to fall for Lady Ruth," he stated simply. Then, changed his tone. "That look on your face when she walked over told me everything, you know. You like her. There's no use in denying it."

"Not at all. That was worry you saw, Corbin. Worry that a certain suitor of hers will not treat her the way a lady should be treated. Fear that he might disrespect her or cause her harm."

Corbin's eyes darkened. "If that's the case, who is she? No, nevermind that; who is *he*? If you're so concerned that she's in danger of mistreatment, I should know so that I can be on the lookout. You don't have to shoulder the burden alone."

That might be a good idea. More eyes made for better surveillance. He wouldn't need to worry about her safety when he slept in a bit too late at a house party or felt the need to leave the common room before the end of an event. "Keep in mind, Corbin Entwistle, that not a word of this is to be breathed to a single soul until I have solid proof," he began, pulling Cor into a side room to avoid unnecessary ears.

"I swear it. You can trust me."

"Very well, then. It's Lady Olivia. Earl Alden Kegg—you remember him from Battenhold, don't you?—has his eye on her, and

I've got a rather bad feeling about it. Lyz and Cristyn share the same sentiment."

His eyes narrowed. "Cristyn. She's the young maid, isn't she? Barely seventeen?"

A smile tugged on his lips. "You say that as if we aren't barely out of our teens ourselves." His smile faded into a disheartened frown. "I haven't an idea of what her past entails, but it couldn't have been good if the skills she's earned from it are the tremor in her hand and the wary glances she gives every time she rounds a corner."

"She seems to get along well with your footman—the one who has cousins in seemingly every household."

"Eryi, yes. Mother suspects he'll propose soon enough. They've developed nicknames for each other, though they don't dare use them when they think someone is listening."

"How do you know of them, then?"

"I'm always listening these days," he replied simply. Thanks to Earl Kegg, he always kept an ear for anything out of place, such as whispering in the hallways when no one was around. "At any rate, she doesn't trust him. That's proof enough for me, but the authorities will want proper proof that he serves a threat to Lady Olivia."

Corbin nodded, thoughtfulness written into the lines of his face. "I'll keep an eye on him. Perhaps I'll invite him over for tea so that my servants can make of him what they will. No doubt that, given the chance to meet the snake, they'll be just as concerned."

He shook his head and rose to fetch his cap. "I'm going up to my room to rest before the game of croquet. As you can imagine, I didn't sleep restfully." He bid Corbin a farewell and made for the stairs, darkness and fear trailing close behind.

...

The rolling hills of Lady Goddard's estate proved quite useful when constructing a match of croquet. Hoops lined up, forming a trail for the brightly colored balls to pass through. Guests teemed about the lawn, mallets held perfectly in their hands as the teams were divided. Their hostess seemed to have a fairly good idea of who was friends with whom and divided the teams accordingly.

Bryant was placed on a team with Brigham, Shepherd, and Lady Ruth; Corbin was on a team with his own acquaintances.

He grabbed his team's mallet and ball and knocked the ball through the next hoop easily. They went in rounds with the other teams, waiting for each color to pass forward before switching team members and knocking their own ball towards the pole.

Brigham took it from Shepherd and aimed. This particular route hadn't been as long as many were, and they managed to be only a few feet away from the end in just seven turns. If Brig scored this, they'd be ahead of the other teams. He measured his swing and hit the ball. It rolled perfectly between the last two hoops and hit the pole with a little *plonk*. Brig whirled around to face his teammates, a bright beaming smile on his face.

"Way to go, Brig!" Shepherd cheered as he clapped a hand on Brigham's back. "I daresay you've the best aim of any of us," he said with a chuckle. "We might have a chance of winning this game."

Lord Jenherd jeered. "Beginner's luck, I say. Might as well quit while you're ahead, Pwyll! There's no chance that you're going to beat me with that clown of a baron you've got on your team." His teammates laughed with wicked grins.

Shepherd balled his hands into fists, about ready to punch the marquis. "This so-called "clown" just won us the round, Lord Jenherd. That's far more than your team can boast. You haven't made it through the first five hoops yet."

Brig extended a hand, clasping Shep's shoulder. "Don't. It's not worth it," he mumbled.

Shep turned to face him. "But, Brig—"

"*It's not worth it.* I'm used to it. It's mild in comparison with what some of the others have said. Really, Shep, it's fine." He let his gaze fall to the ground as he handed the mallet to Bryant. "Let's just move on to the next round."

They did, silently walking to the first hoop of the next trail. As the winners, they were able to begin first. "Brigham," Bryant started, "I'm sorry."

"Don't be, Bry. You're not the ones with permanent sneers whenever I enter a room. It's not your fault they act like this."

"But I could change it. I'm a duke, after all. They'll listen to me."

"Don't be so sure. They're only captivated with you because of your sudden appearance in society. Don't believe for a second that they respect your opinion outside of the House of Lords—even if they *do* want you as a son-in-law."

Bryant stared in shock, words escaping his tongue when he sought a response.

"I don't care, Bry. Really, I don't. Let them say what they will; I've already become immune to it. There's nothing they can say that I haven't heard before." He let out a sigh that proclaimed their words affected him more than he let on. "Go on, then. Take your first hit."

Bryant bit the inside of his lip in anger as he lined up his mallet. "What do you suppose, Brig? Think we can beat this one in four turns?"

With a melancholic tone, Brig replied, "I suppose we can try. No guarantees, though."

He hated the hollowness that Brig's expression held; he hated that the boy was accustomed to such harassment. Was there a way for him to actually change the stereotype that had engulfed the Roberts family? Brigham's words stabbed like a bee's sting. It couldn't be as helpless as he thought, could it?

"Bryant," Shep reminded, "it's your turn. Take a hit so the rest of us can."

Right. The mallet needed to line up just so for them to manage this one quicker than the last. If he swung it with mild power, the ball would go far enough without veering off to the side. Slowly, calculatingly, he prepared his shot and swung. The ball rolled a few feet forward, just barely making it inside the hoop.

"Good hit. I can work with that," Lady Ruth declared as she took the mallet and marched over to the ball.

Something nagged at Bryant as he took his place beside Shepherd. A thought that wasn't willing to vacate his mind. "Shep, what was it you said?"

He raised an eyebrow in confusion. "It's your turn?"

"No, after that."

"Take a hit so the rest of us can?"

Bryant nodded. "That's it. Do you suppose that's how we can help Brig's reputation? Taking our own down a few notches?"

The lines in his face deepened with a mix of concern and skepticism. "What do you propose, exactly?"

"I'm not sure yet. It's just that you and I are two of the most popular chaps among the *ton* right now, due to how "exciting" it is to have a bachelor duke out, along with your scandalous number of dances with Lady Ruth. We could use that to our advantage." The idea started taking shape. Put themselves in a situation that required a hero of sorts and instruct Brigham on what to do. Make sure the papers are there to capture the moment and declare Brig a hero on every headline in Braxden.

Shep grabbed the mallet from his darling and lined up his shot. He narrowly missed the next hoop, sighing as he handed it off to Brig. "I've got it," he mumbled. "There's a rather old stable on the edge of my property. We haven't used it in well over a decade. I can ask my father to let us dispose of it with a few matches. All we must do is have the media believe Brigham has saved us from its flames."

"Are you certain, Shep? That could turn out rather dangerous. I didn't mean that we ought to risk our lives in such an uncontrolled way." He could picture it now: the roof caving in as poor Brigham dives through the flames in search of his friends, getting trapped with no one able to save him. "I don't know that we should attempt that."

"It's old wood. It should take quickly."

Bryant shook his head. "That's exactly what I'm worried about. What if the roof caves in on us? I don't want to cause my mother another heartbreak. Your parents shouldn't lose their only son. And if Brigham gets trapped? What then?"

"It won't happen. We can wait by the door with soot on our faces to make it look like we were in the fire proper. Brigham goes in for a minute or two and drags us out as we're coughing and wheezing to make it look real. No one is in actual danger and Brig is marked a hero." He watched as the boy took his shot, beaming when he managed to both fix Shep's mistake and get them close enough that Bryant could take the final shot. "You're up, lad."

Bryant took the mallet from Brigham and glanced at the other teams. He took a deep breath, carefully lined up his shot, and swung, knocking the ball into the pole.

His friends cheered as he walked back. "Well done, Your Grace," Ruth congratulated. "That will give us quite an advantage against the other teams in the coming rounds."

Lady Goddard approached them, slowly clapping in congratulations. "Well done. I knew putting the four of you together was a good idea. You might be able to win this game entirely." She nodded for the other teams to start before turning her attention back to the four. "Are you aware of what the prize is?" She left no time for their response before exclaiming, "Your pick for what dessert is after supper tonight. Isn't that just splendid?" Brigham's face lit up, suddenly eager. Lady Goddard all but ignored him as she asked Bryant, "What would you pick, Your Grace?"

His eyes narrowed at her obvious exclusion of Brigham, but he gave the answer she sought. "Cider cake. It was my father's favorite, I'm told."

Her grin softened into a solemn smile. "Lovely it must be to share something—even something as simple as a favorite dessert—with one you must miss so dearly."

He couldn't take her seriously. Her simpering and inferred condolences were lost on him after she ignored one of his dearest friends. What else could it be but pretense to earn his favor? "Indeed."

Thankfully, the lady turned back to her other guests as he responded, leaving the rest of them to talk as equals. "I'm sorry, Brig."

Brigham sighed in that famous, signature way of his before shaking his head. "It's fine, Bryant. I'm used to it." He nodded to Shepherd and Lady Ruth before turning his gaze upon the other teams as they tried to score second place.

Ruth spoke up, unable to let the matter go. "Lord Grimes, you shouldn't have to put up with their endless tormenting. It's not right."

He pivoted just long enough to bark a reply. "Right or not, it's how the world is. They'll not respect me unless they are forced and that is a feat that no one—not even His Grace, the perfect bachelor of the season—can accomplish."

Bryant met Shepherd's wary gaze with one of his own. They needed to prove Brigham wrong, and quickly. Before the world lost another Roberts to its agony.

He gestured to a spot on the ivy-covered wall for them to chat just out of earshot. "As much as I don't enjoy your plan, given how entirely dangerous it is, it might be our only hope. My fears for Brigham outweigh my concerns for what might happen if your plan fails."

Shepherd hummed an agreement. "Thank you for seeing things my way. But, if I may say so, I think you misworded your statement. It isn't your fear for Brigham, but your love. Us four—you, Brigham, Corbin, and I—are brothers, are we not? I'd die for any of you, and I know you'd do the same. That bond that we have and the love that comes with it is what outweighs the fear of the dangerous and risky. After all, as the Son of the Most High says, "greater love hath no man than this; than to lay down one's life for his friends"."

Bryant chuckled. "Are you quite certain that *you* aren't the one who's supposed to be in a pulpit instead of in a ballroom? That was well said, Shep."

"While I'll do my best to advise you lot as often as I can, I must, at the end of the day, leave the ministering to those whom the Most High has called to the task."

A grin that fought his forced frown made its way onto his face. "I do wish He'd grant me some of that wisdom you seem to have an abundance of. Perhaps I wouldn't be quite so outspoken if He did. I'd understand when to keep quiet and let things be."

Shep's brows knit together. "What do you mean?"

He let out a long sigh. "You've missed out on a fair bit while wooing your lady. I'll need to catch you up on it some time soon.

Preferably not while we're in earshot of any random passerby in the middle of a croquet game."

"Tonight, then?"

He shook his head. "I've promised to spend tonight in prayer about all of this. Despite the 'resolute' answer I've come across, there's something nagging at me that I haven't been able to shake. I need to ask the Most High for guidance."

"A wise decision. Some other time; after the house party, perhaps."

"Until then." And yet, a stab in the middle of his gut told him that it would be quite some time before he'd have the chance to catch Shep up on his findings. Perhaps by then, he'd have a bit more clarity on what to do about it.

Chapter Eight: All in Good Time

November 21st

Pattermar loomed tall overhead as Eloise crossed the sidewalk towards the vast estate. Despite being a mere townhouse, the grounds were extensive. The architecture was ancient, finding its roots in history hundreds of years prior. Turrets and columns supported the structure as many windows and doors protruded from its vast exterior.

The landscape was no less extravagant, with various shrubs and winter flowers dotting the grounds. Evergreen trees cloaked with new snow gave the estate a Christmas-y look.

She climbed the cobbled steps, taking care to not slip on any potential ice, and knocked on the door. Mabyn strode close behind, catching up just as the door opened.

A withered old man greeted her with a "Your Grace" before opening the door further. "The Lady is expecting you in the drawing room."

"Thank you," she replied as she and Mabyn made their way inside. The interior was even grander than the exterior, with tapestries and paintings lining the walls. Beautiful rugs lined the entryway topping lovely marble tiles. "Breathtaking, isn't it, Mabyn?"

"Indeed, my lady. I don't know that I've seen such a decorated home in all my life." They stared at the ceiling, enchanted by the hand-painted tiles that created a mural of artistry. "I should inquire about the artist. Some of those tiles would look lovely in your room, my lady. Wouldn't you say?"

"Most definitely." Sensing the footman's impatience, however, she continued on towards the drawing room.

"With your permission, my lady, I'd like to go belowstairs to visit my cousin. We've been unable to catch up for so long."

A smile caught her lips. "Of course, Mabyn."

"Thank you, my lady." The petite woman disappeared down the hall.

Eloise produced one of her calling cards as the man opened the door and escorted the duchess inside.

"Your Grace, how lovely it is to see you. Please, have a seat." Lady Seylor gestured to the sofa perpendicular to her own. "It's a pleasure to have you in my humble home, Your Grace."

"Please, call me Eloise. We're friends enough, aren't we?"

A bright, almost fake smile lit up the viscountess's face as she replied, "Thank you, Eloise. Feel free to call me Nerys." She relaxed ever so slightly when a maid came in with tea. "Perfect timing. Do you take it strong or weak, Eloise?"

"Strong, please." She didn't quite understand why the question was asked. Never had she come across someone who drank weak tea. Except for Earl Kegg, of course, but he'd proven to be a bit of an oddity. And, apparently, Nerys—after handing the duchess her tea, she poured weak for herself. "Thank you, Nerys." She sipped her tea slowly, taking care to not burn her tongue. "How is your daughter?"

The fake smile was replaced with a genuine one, though it still held its tacky nature. "Doing well, thank you. I heard that she danced with your son at the masquerade the other night."

Eloise laughed in her polite, "in public" laugh. "Masquerade balls aren't exactly known for intentional dancing, my dear." Her expression softened though at seeing Nerys's awkward, slightly hurt expression. "That isn't to say, of course, that he might be opposed to dancing with Olivia. She is quite a lively girl."

Her fake smile arrived again, pressed firmly against her face. "Of course. Thank you for saying so, Eloise."

She didn't neglect to note the harsh vowels, or the 'Your Grace' that had almost slipped past the Viscountess's lips. "I hear, however, that Lord Arioch has become quite taken with her."

Though that was nothing new, her eyes lit up, indulging Eloise's gossip. "Is that so?"

"We had him for tea at the start of the season. He seemed determined to have your Olivia for his bride. Do you know her opinion of him?"

Nerys glanced up at the ceiling before shaking her head. "I daresay that daughter of mine has been mum entirely about where her heart lies. *I* was certainly hoping that she'd set her cap for that Marquis friend of His Grace's, Shepherd Whitley. We all know how that's turned out, however."

She drew her brows. Bryant hadn't mentioned anything new about Shepherd recently. Brigham had been the focus for the past several weeks. "Oh?"

"He's fallen for Lady Ruth, the daughter of the Marquis of Gili. A fine pair, even if it decreases my Olivia's chances of a good match."

She had heard of that before. From Bryant's report, Shepherd refused to dance with anyone else. "I've heard the name, but I have yet to meet the woman. She seems lovely, or my son says she is."

The older woman nodded. "The best kind, from what I've seen." Her voice dripped with jealousy. "Only half as pretty as my daughter, though their children won't be ugly."

Eloise rolled her eyes. "They've only met recently but you're certain that he's found the love of his life. Really, Nerys, surely you know that love isn't so simple with these young ones." Especially not Shep. He was an only child, meaning any and all responsibility to continue the Stuart Duchy fell to his shoulders alone.

"It's a practical marriage, if not a love one. Though, if he only wanted practical, he should have chosen my Olivia instead. There's a practical match, if you ask me."

She spared the woman a half-laugh. "What is your opinion of my son, if I might be so brazen to inquire?" She almost didn't want the answer. Lady Seylor had a voice unlike any she'd met before, or since.

"Your son, hm?" She tapped her chin in thought. "Besides the fact that he'd make a good—perhaps even the best—match for my darling daughter, I'd say he's a sweet lad. He offered you his first dance in society, didn't he? That's a rather bold move; one not gone unnoticed by the *ton*."

In all honesty, she expected something far harsher than 'he's sweet' from the woman before her. Perhaps she simply voiced what she heard others say—Carmen, for example, who had nothing but good things to say about Bryant following their reconnection at his debut. But her tone and expression seemed genuine. She could only hope and pray it was so. "Thank you, Nerys."

"And, if I might be the brazen one, Eloise, what is your opinion of my daughter?"

Despite her best efforts to keep herself to a standard of not thinking ill of people, Olivia was one of those women who got on her nerves. Everything about the girl set her on edge, likely learned from Lady Seylor. She did everything in her power to ignore it: chiding Bryant about *his* antics, praying for the woman whenever she caused a negative thought or feeling.

All the same, she did not much like Lady Olivia Mosstyn. Perhaps that would change in the future, particularly as she herself had caught Bryant dancing with her on more than one occasion. "She's a lovely girl," she replied simply, hoping that Nerys would take her short answer as a good one.

The older woman hummed in satisfaction. "Thank you, Eloise. She is lovely, isn't she?" A bright, girlish smile broke out over her face. "Speaking of, I wonder where my dear girl is. She ought to be in here, ready for a promenade or some such should a suitor decide to call on her today." She raised an eyebrow at Eloise with a silent prompt of "perhaps your son?" attached.

"How lovely for her that would be," she replied. "Bryant's out with a friend today, I'm afraid, or I would have brought him along. It'd be good for him to socialize with our generation, if only to learn the proper course of drawing room conversation. He's missed his chances over the past few years."

"Indeed. Feel free to bring him next time you visit. It would be a delight." Still caught up in the idea that Olivia should be present, she whispered to the girl standing in the corner waiting for the tea service. The girl disappeared, showing up a few minutes later with the lady in question. "Olivia, there you are. You've met the Duchess of Whittaker, haven't you?"

A subtle shade of wariness formed on Olivia's face. "How do you do," she greeted.

"Come join us, dear. There's plenty of tea for you to partake in." She gestured to the seat beside her as her daughter crossed the room. "Strong with milk, correct?" Olivia nodded absentmindedly, all the confirmation her mother required. "Here you are, dear."

"Thank you," she responded shortly.

With a slight huff aimed at her daughter, she turned to the duchess. "Your Grace, have you had a chance to tour the grounds? We've the most beautiful winter flowers in bloom right now. I'm sure you'd love them. Perhaps I can arrange for our gardener to pick a bouquet for you to take home."

What a gracious host the woman had become now that her daughter was present. "That *would* be lovely," she replied, keeping the sneer off her face. "Perhaps another time. I should be heading—" A scream interrupted her.

The viscountess's brows raised in alarm. "That sounded like Morgaine."

"I'll peek through the door to see what the matter is," Eloise offered as she stood. The walk to the door felt eternal, soaking up the premonition through her toes, into her legs, pooling in her gut as it made its way to her heart. The latch undid with a *click* and the door opened. She pulled it just a crack to see into the hallway. A dark, long shadow fell across the tile. One that did not speak of a maid who'd taken a misstep on her way to the room.

Close the door, close the door, close the door the single thought rang in her head. Just as her eyes made contact with the figure—a tall, brooding figure of a man—she slammed the door shut. "Nerys, where is the key?"

"Why do you need the key?" Her voice was breathy, not at all confident as it wavered and petered.

"Just give me the key!" She half-shouted, exasperated with this silly woman and her stupidity. "We need to lock the door."

"This door only locks from the outside. I haven't a key for the inside of it."

Stupid woman, she mused again, hardly able to keep the rage from her face. "Then we need a barricade. Help me move this couch, Olivia."

Once again, the viscountess voiced her questions. "Why do we need to move the couch? What is out there, Elosie—" Her voice cut off as the door swung open.

The man now stood before them, gun drawn and ready to shoot. His grisly beard and unkempt clothes only enhanced his intimidation. Shoulders too thin for an assassin hid under his distressed shirt. His dark eyes held hatred, and determination lined the marks of something more. Something *hungry*.

Eloise spared a glance to the others, whose faces now drained of all color. The viscountess had all but passed out on the couch. "Sir, please, put the gun down."

He huffed, breath seeping in a steady, angry stream through his nostrils. "Don't tell me what to do. No one needs to get hurt." His eyes wandered the room, examining faces and counting heads. "Where is the master of the house?" A moment of silence passed before he cursed and aimed the gun at Olivia. "I'll burn this whole house to the ground with all of you inside if you don't tell me now!"

All eyes turned to the viscountess, who stammered, "In his office. It's upstairs. The servants can direct you there." She yelped when he took a step closer.

"No need to bother those hardworking souls," he mumbled. "I'll just have you guide me there." He grabbed Nerys's arm with a grip of steel, dragging her to her feet. "Lead the way, pretty face." Turning his attention to the other two, he muttered, "Don't try to get help. This will all be over soon enough." He held Eloise's gaze until she slowly nodded. Then, in a moment, he and the viscountess were out of the room.

She turned to Olivia, suspecting the girl to be in tears from distress. She herself felt like crying. Would the Mosstyns survive? Their daughter held her gaze to the door with an unexpected calm. Her hands betrayed her thoughts, shaking and trembling as they fought to find the embroidery hidden in the low table.

In a moment, the duchess crossed the room to the girl's side, pulling her close. "All is well, dear. Everything is going to be fine." She prayed her voice didn't waiver as she spoke the words her heart sought to believe. The chances of either Mosstyn parent surviving seemed impossibly low. Then, it had been a few minutes and no screaming sounded, so perhaps they had managed to break free of the intruder's grasp. What of Mabyn, who now could be unconscious or dead from the man's efforts to enter their home? How many servants had he killed to gain access to the house? "It is going to be all well." She rubbed her hand softly across the girl's back as she whispered comforts.

Her eyes caught on a book set on a side table: a collection of the sacred scriptures of the Most High. "Come, dear. Let us read and pray together. The Most High will surely hear our cries and send one of His angels to rescue us." She gently picked up the tome and turned to a page very dear to her own heart. "'I will lead the blind in a way that they do not know, in paths that they have not known I will guide them. I will turn the darkness before them into light, the rough places into level ground. These are the things I do, and I do not forsake them.'" She took a deep breath. "The Most High is here with us, dear. He has not left, nor will He ever. He is our light in this darkness."

Olivia did not speak, only nodded her head and leaned against Eloise's motherly embrace. They sat in silence as the minutes passed. Muffled shouting echoed overhead, accompanied by a single gunshot. Something heavy thudded onto the floor. That couldn't be a good sign. More shouting, louder this time, broke out. Words here and there became clear to them. "That was... warning. Now..." Definitely the voice of their captor.

Eloise ignored it, pulling Olivia's head to her shoulder, and softly sang old Deravailian lullabies. "Just past mid-morning light shines the star of Mardeli fair. Her golden beams send streams of rain to nourish the air. And just as everything seems too bright, her sister comes to block out the light."

"My mother used to sing that when I was young. I wonder where it's from," Olivia mumbled. Her voice kept a monotone rhythm, as if the dear girl didn't dare speak louder than she must.

"I suppose it's as old as Braxden itself."

The girl sat up. "We can go. We don't need to stay here. What will he do to us if we leave? It isn't as though he can see the street from my father's study." She stood, crossing to the door without a second thought.

"Olivia, wait." The duchess extended her hand to stop the girl. "I wouldn't."

"Why not?"

"It isn't what he could do to *us* that I'm worried about, dear. He may harm your parents if we leave." She fought against the chill that threatened her. A blanket, that's what she needed. Quickly scanning the room revealed a supply of them in the corner. "Here, dear. Let's just huddle together until this passes."

For a moment, it appeared as though the girl would listen to her. She pivoted away from the door, eyed the warm blanket extended to her with envy. Her hand dropped from the doorknob for a moment before her fingers regained their grip. "I can't. I need to protect my family."

A single second later, the second gunshot rang out. Olivia screamed and dove for the sofa, all manner of courage set aside. No thud followed. No one, she prayed, died today.

Eloise set a comforting hand on her shoulder. "It's alright. I believe that was meant to be a warning shot. Your father is well." She prayed it was so for all of their sakes. "It'll all blow over in a few minutes, I'm sure of it." The words sprang form a place of unusual peace within her. The flip-flopping of her stomach settled and the fog in her head cleared. They would be alright. She was sure of it.

Minutes ticked by with no sign of peace in the house. Shouting continued above them, followed by the sound of breaking glass.

A loud caw echoed around the home. Her blood ran cold as she tried to ignore the deafening tone. She gathered a shaky breath, blocking out the implications from her mind. Once before had she heard that sound, at her husband's deathbed. An old legend, she had thought; a wives tale. One did not easily forget the cry of Thanatos, defender of the recently deceased.

Someone pounded on the front door. "I'm going to see who it is," Eloise mumbled to the girl beside her. "Only when they must shall your feet leave this room. Is that understood?" She didn't wait for an answer before crossing to the door and checking the hallway. No one, to her relief, stood nearby.

She hurried down the hall and found her way through the maze of the estate to the front door, opening it. There, standing before her, was the constable. "Thank Heaven you're here. The intruder is upstairs, in the viscount's study."

"Lead the way."

She nodded and stepped back into the hallways. Shadows cast from the afternoon light sent shivers down her spine. She hadn't realized just how garish the decor made the rooms; how unwelcoming it felt now to stand there with all of the paintings and tiles staring at her. They passed a staircase with a thin iron railing that felt every bit as fragile as Olivia Mosstyn had looked. This house didn't seem like the grand manor she assumed it to be just hours ago.

Her thoughts recollected themselves the moment the open door to the study entered her line of sight. She gestured to it, ushering the constable inside and gasping at the sight.

Only two people stood in there: the constable and the intruder. Wynn swiftly grabbed the man, who had been distracted by the winged creature across the room, handcuffed him, and forced him to his knees. Her eyes wandered from the man to his captives. The gunshots had not missed their intended targets. Lady Olivia was now Lady Seylor, mistress of Pattermar, an orphan.

She trembled like never before as she stared. How desperately she wanted to look away, but found herself unable to withdraw her attention from the scene. It shocked her very core and sent the worst chill down her spine. Bile rose up in her stomach and she fought to keep it down. She was thankful that Thanatos's shadowy form covered most of the view.

Constable Smith turned to her. "How close are you to the daughter?"

"Not particularly, though she knows my son," she responded, feeling as though cotton had been stuffed into her throat. "This is horrible."

"Would you mind telling her what has happened? She should hear it from someone she knows."

Eloise nodded solemnly and clung to the iron railing as she descended the stairs. Stepping into a side room, she emptied the contents of her stomach. The words of a hymn sprang to mind. She uttered them quietly to calm her spirit and ease the trembling in her legs.

The doors to the drawing room were still closed. She took that as a good sign. Sure and certain, the poor girl sat shaking on the sofa, messy embroidery in her hands.

She looked up when Eloise entered the room, a relieved expression on her face. "Who was at the door?"

"The constable. A neighbor heard the gunshots and sent a telegraph. Praise to the Most High, he wasn't out attending someone at the time." She took in a deep breath and sat beside Olivia. "He asked me to let you know what has happened."

Olivia's eyebrows scrunched together in confusion. "What do you mean? I *know* what has happened. A man broke into my house."

"There's more."

Her tone brought Olivia's hands to still. "No. No, it can't be. It's not true." She all but slammed the embroidery hoop onto the cushion beside her. "They're fine. I'm going to go up there and see my parents." She rose to her feet, anger obvious in her gait. "Bring me to them."

"Olivia, I know this is hard to take in. I promise you, I understand how you feel. But you must believe me when I say you do not want to see them. It isn't a sight you'll ever forget."

For a moment, it seemed like Olivia would disregard her words. Her hand hovered over the door handle until finally, she relented and returned to the sofa in tears. "What am I going to do?"

Eloise took the child into her arms, providing her with all of the comfort a mother could. "I'll be right by your side, dearover. There are many things you need to know now. I will teach you, as I did my son. We'll get through this together."

Chapter Nine: Without Warning

November 22nd

Coffee splattered the front of a newspaper as the natural consequence of Bryant's shock. He turned to Brigham and showed him the headline. "My mother was there yesterday." He jumped from his chair, rushing to organize his breakfast dishes.

In his haste, he spilled his glass, fueling his heightened state with even more chaos. "My apologies, Brig," he hurried to clean the spill. "I've got to get home."

Brig rose from his seat. "Shall I call the coach?"

"If you could, yes. It would be faster than calling for my own." He meant the retort in some sarcasm, trying to keep the mood light, but the adrenaline stealing his breath kept his voice monotone.

"Bryant, take a moment to breathe. Your mother is fine. The papers say nothing about additional victims; only Lord and Lady Seylor." He pressed a hand to Bryant's back. "Slow down."

He couldn't slow down. What if the papers lied? What if they were targeting him through withheld information? It had happened before, in the territory. Could he have been followed home? His breath heaved as he tried to make sense of his racing mind. He needed to be sure Mother was safe. He hurried to the door, but Brigham blocked it, a stern expression fixed on his face.

"Brigham, let me pass."

"Respectfully, Your Grace, I cannot. Until you have settled down, I will not move." Brig gestured for Bryant to sit at the table.

He wanted to be angry. Brigham, of all people, should understand his desperation. Brigham, of all people, *did* understand him. Perhaps that was why his response was so unorthodox. He had been here before.

Slowly, he turned back to the table, his legs shaking with every step. A servant pulled out his chair and he sat with a *thump*. "I'm sorry, Brig. I forgot myself."

"There is no need to apologize, Bryant. You've done nothing wrong." He poured fresh tea for them. "Your mother is likely in a state of distress herself. There is no need to add yours to it." A pause as he sipped his tea. "Count to sixty for me."

Heat rose in his cheeks as he repeated the numbers aloud. Despite their relative privacy, he still felt embarrassed at the "childish" activity. All the same, he felt better. The ache in his heart slowly eased. His muscles relaxed and he could breathe again. He still felt that sting of panic, but his thoughts were clearer.

"Better?"

"Much." He downed the rest of his tea and rose. "Thank you, Brigham. I'll send a telegram once I am able." He made his way to the front while Brigham called for the carriage.

A footman opened the door and he stepped inside, glad for the solitude of the car. He rubbed his thumb against the rim of the window, tracing it again and again. If only he had agreed to join Mother for tea. Perhaps he could have done something.

Maybe then the Seylors would still be alive.

He stared at the city outside, noting just how empty the roads were. Newspapers littered the ground, picked up by the scant passerby. No doubt they were all hiding away, worried that they might be next. One carriage, Lord Jenherd's, approached them on the road. He rapped his knuckles on the roof and shouted, "Call them over, if you would. I'd like to have a word."

The coachman waved the carriage over and slowly came to a halt beside it. Bryant jumped out of the cabin and walked up to Lord Jenherd. "My lord, haven't you heard the news?"

The man glared at him. "Your Grace, surely you know by now to not address someone below you as "my lord." It isn't proper for someone of your standing." He huffed and continued. "To answer your question, I have. Unlike most of these buffoons, I don't need to worry."

"Why might that be?" He thought back to the conversation he overheard at Lady Goddard's masquerade. *I'm not as stupid as some of the others.*

"Because, Your Grace, unlike the others, I have played my cards well. My family can rest well tonight, knowing that I have protected them like a good father does." Irk filled his tone as he gestured for Bryant to back up. "If you're wise, and I know you are, your family will be safe as well." He called for the coachman to go on, leaving Bryant to cough on the dust.

If you're wise...

The sentiment gave him pause, even as he hastened back into his own carriage. During the masquerade, he and Lord Gregsay had argued about someone "following suit." Could that have been himself? Could they have bet that he would join whatever book had everyone in such a state?

That didn't quite make sense, did it? He shook his head, determined to sort it out later. Angarth soon pulled into view and he had far more pressing matters to attend to.

The minute the carriage stopped, he dashed up the stairs to find his mother. Mrs. Kendrick stopped him in the hall to take his coat and hat, at her insistence, before directing him to the conservatory. Without giving mind to the room itself, he shouted, "Mother! I've seen the news! Are you well? You aren't hurt, are you-" He stopped short at seeing one person in the corner. "Lady Olivia? What are you-"

Mother pulled him close, enveloping him in a tight hug. "I'm glad to see you, my son." She heaved a sigh of relief and kissed his forehead. "I am well, my dear, as is my companion." She smiled as she let him go. Her gentle face gave him some peace.

"Good. I cannot believe you had to witness such a thing." He shuddered. "Tell me what happened, please. I need to know."

She gestured to a set of garden chairs and relayed the events, careful to mention explicitly that the gunman did not threaten her. "As you can see, we are safe and sound. All will be made right in its own time."

"Mother, may I ask why *she* is here?" He attempted to keep his tone light. The woman's parents had just been murdered, after all. Despite his feelings against her, she deserved that dignity.

"I've offered to care for her in the coming weeks. She will need my assistance as she navigates everything that comes with a new title, just as you did once. Besides, she isn't safe in her own home. That was proven long ago. She is safer here, where Lukas is outside brooding at passersby. She can rest." Mother cupped his cheek with her hand, looking gently into his eyes. Whenever she did, he felt as though she could read his soul. "You could use some of that yourself, my darling. You look exhausted."

He chuckled, in spite of himself. "I'm not, Mother. I went to bed only a tad later than normal. Brigham wanted to show me the new star chart he made. It was restful to spend the night there instead of here, but I do wish I had agreed to accompany you yesterday instead."

Mother watched him in that pitiful way she did and shook her head. "You wouldn't have changed the outcome."

"But I-"

"No," she interrupted. "If you had come with me yesterday and tried some daring do, do you know what we would have today?" He shook his head as she concluded, "Two deceased Mosstyns and one son. My son."

Her words stilled him. Surely she couldn't be right. If anything, he could have been a distraction while the police sprinted there. Then, at least the Mosstyn parents would have survived, even if he had not. "Mother-" He couldn't get past that word. He didn't know what to say that could express this longing he had.

"You do not need to continue, darling. I understand." She smiled softly. "Duty has been fostered so deeply within you. The duchy has forced it upon your young heart. As your father would say, it is a good thing to carry, but you must be careful to not let it overtake you. You are only one person, Bryant. You cannot save the whole world."

Corbin had said something similar at the start of the month. And yet, he felt this desire for greatness deep within his soul. He was here for a purpose. The duchy wasn't his just because of his birth; heaven forbid he believed such a thing was truly up to chance. He was meant to do something with it, or with the opportunities it gave him.

"Get some rest, Bryant. The world is still for the moment. You can take up your cross this afternoon."

He agreed, after much internal debate, to dawdle on to his room and spend the morning in respite. On his desk, a copy of a novel sat, begging to be finished. Anguish in his heart, he picked it up and plopped into an armchair. His leg bounced as his eyes sought to settle on the page. The words, though definitely in his own language, flitted around the page, refusing to form their typical pattern. Perhaps he was more tired than he initially thought.

"May I be of any service, Your Grace?" Lyz asked, stepping in from the other room. "You seem out of sorts."

A loose sigh slipped from him. "Is it truly that bad? Or is it that both you and Mother know me well enough to see that I am on edge?"

Lyz smiled in an impish way and gestured to his still-bouncing knee. "Respectfully, Your Grace, the signs are quite obvious that something is on your mind."

"Could you call for tea? That should help." He vaguely tracked Lyz as the man rang the bell pull. "I assume you've seen this morning's headline?" Lyz nodded. "Then surely you understand my anxiety. My mother could have been killed." He rose from the chair and paced the room. "What if that man hadn't been there with a purpose? What if his only intention was to kill?"

His valet stopped his pacing with a touch. "Your Grace, take a seat. Shall I send a telegram to your friends that they might calm your mind?"

He shook his head, settling, if for a moment. "No, that's not necessary. I don't need to disturb them; not when the world is so fragile." His eyes flickered to the window and the street below. Was this life? Was he doomed to constantly watch over his shoulder for the next attack? It wasn't easy while in the territory, even with his band of armed personnel. It was almost suffocating now, when his life wasn't the only one at risk.

Cristyn knocked and walked in with the tea tray, setting it down promptly and leaving. She didn't shake this time. He stared at Lyz and wondered if he thought the same. It *must* have been Kegg's presence, then, that caused her disturbance.

"Perhaps I shall move to my study after tea. I have some things to investigate," he announced, pouring himself a cup and resting on the edge of his chair. "Thank you, Lyz. This has been enlightening."

...

Two days had Lady Olivia stayed with them, and she'd hardly spoken a word. He wanted to harbor resentment, wanted to pull from the part of him that despised her and add this to his list of reasons why she wasn't to be liked, but he couldn't. Not now. Not when she'd lost more than he had and was so new to this world of loneliness.

She kept her distance from him, which was to be expected. No doubt she needed the space to gather herself and get through the grief.

He didn't remember much from when he'd lost his own father. It happened so long ago. What he did remember, however, was dreading leaving the house, or going anywhere without Mother. He feared she would get sick and leave him as well. As an adult, he knew those fears were naught. And yet, as an adult, his fears took the same thought in a different form. What had happened to Lady Olivia only confirmed those deep-seated fears. Life was short, despite their efforts to prolong it.

At breakfast that morning, Mother handed him an altered schedule of events for the next few weeks. Their next event was scheduled for mid December- several weeks ahead. Over half of the events between now and then had the word "canceled" underneath. The others simply had a line through them.

She didn't want him to go out. Despite her previous displayed confidence, she worried, too. For Lady Olivia's sake, she refused to attend anything for the next month, offering instead to stay home with the girl, doing whatever women do when they have a free evening. For her own peace of mind, she refused to allow Bryant to go alone.

Her worry soothed the anxiety within him, making him feel both justified and more worried. It served as a reminder that he hadn't explained to her all that took place during his time overseas. He *could* handle himself; for two years, he had needed to defend himself from assassins and stray soldiers. All the same, it put him at ease that he could rest in the safety of his own home, and that Mother would as well.

He strode into the library, hoping to find one book in particular: his diary from school. His child self insisted it be placed here, among the greatest works of time itself. Now, he sought the information it had about one particular Alden Kegg. They were friends once, and perhaps stories of Kegg's own escapades had made it into the detailed book.

Perhaps in that book, there was a hint of how Kegg had changed so drastically.

The guilt he felt about his uneasiness around the man strengthened with Olivia's presence, as he was ever reminded of his mother's schemes. He needed to put facts behind his feelings. He wanted to believe Kegg was more innocent than he appeared. He wanted to hope that this feeling was baseless, yet every sign pointed otherwise. Every sign but the one he held most dear.

Though he dreaded admitting it, he learned in the territory that sentimental notions would get him killed. He needed to look at the objective facts before him. Unfortunately for his mother, all of the facts were against Kegg having the moral high ground.

Somewhere across the room, a book thudded to the ground. He jumped and whirled on his heels to face his observer. In the opposite corner, arm extended to keep others from falling, stood Lady Olivia.

"My apologies, my lady. I didn't notice you were here." He kept his tone reverent, but knew from the way his heart skipped that his face was twisted in shock. "Are you searching for a specific novel?"

It took her a moment to respond, eyes wide and cheeks red in embarrassment. "No, Your Grace. I was simply browsing." She turned away from him and steadied the shelf before plucking the book off of the floor.

He watched her carefully, unsure of what to do with himself. Should he attempt conversation? She would be staying with them for some time, after all. It would be good to have some sort of mutual understanding, even if that understanding was as brief as his condolences. Several times, he opened and closed his mouth, searching for something to say.

She spoke first. "Your Grace, can I help you?"

His muscles stiffened as he racked his mind for words. How could he close the gap between them and make her feel at ease here? This was her home, for the time being, and she had every right to be comfortable here. Her dark hair caught the light and he found his answer. "No, Miss Sparrow. I merely wanted to ensure you were all right after your ordeal."

Now it was her turn to tense. "What did you call me?"

His cheeks burned as he answered, "Miss Sparrow. That is your name, is it not?" The book fell from her hands and hit the floor a second time. If his heart did not pound so heavily, he would have felt pity for the poor thing.

It took her a moment to respond, but her surprise quickly turned to rage. "Sir Detective, I take it. I should have *known* that it was you behind that mask." She paced in her spot for a moment before verbally flying at him again. "I do hope you know that the goal of a masquerade is for one's identity to be kept *secret*."

"It still is, Lady Olivia," he hastened to assure her, "for we are alone in this room, and my servants do not eavesdrop."

She huffed before reconsidering her stance. Slowly, her shoulders dropped from their soldier's height and her withdrawal changed into scorn. "Surely you did not stop me only to reveal my identity to me. What do you want?"

Oh dear. He had not made the right decision. "My apologies, my lady. I only hoped to make you feel a bit more at home here, but it appears my words had the opposite effect."

Her scorn softened into a scowl. "Indeed they did. What are you going to do to fix it?"

"I'd like to formally offer my condolences. I didn't know your parents very well, but I know what that loss does to a person." He took a breath, calming the jittering in his hands. "As I told my mother the other day, I wish I had been there to stop it. We have had our spats, but you don't deserve that pain. No one does."

His words seemed to still her. "Thank you, Your Grace." She again picked up the book. "I should be going before anyone grows suspicious, but I'd like to thank you for opening your home to me."

"Of course, my lady. You are free to stay as long as you like." She left the room and he returned to his search.

It took a bit of digging, but he did find the journal. He made himself comfortable amidst a pile of cushions in the corner and opened the tales of his childhood. Scanning through them for any mentions of Alden, he stopped on one particular page.

May 25th, 1826

Today, the second to last day of school, Alden told us that he is not coming back next year. His father died last month and his mother wants to keep him at home with tutors, like my mother plans to do in a few years. I know we will see each other at some point, because we are both lords, but I will miss him here.

He was angry today. He even yelled at Brigham. He hasn't yelled at Brigham all year; none of us have. I am kind of glad he won't be here next year, if he keeps this up. Brigham has been through enough. He won't talk about all of it, or at least not to me. He cried when Alden yelled at him.

Headmaster did punish him for bullying, but his consequence wasn't bad. I think Headmaster pities him, since he just lost his father. I do too, but it wasn't okay for him to yell at Brigham. He hasn't apologized yet, either.

I have to go, but I'll write later.

Yrs,

Bryant

He didn't remember this page. Granted, he had written the words almost ten years ago. The words offered him very little in terms of new information, but it gave him perspective. Perhaps, for the moment, that would be enough.

Chapter Ten: Catching Butterflies

December 17th

Bright lights accompanied soft music in what was the largest party of the winter months: the Remdwell Ball. Nearly every regent in town was given an invitation—gentlemen and commonfolk besides—and the room was packed to the seams. Bryant glanced about the room, searching for anyone he might recognize. His mother decided to spend the evening with her cousin, making this the first ball where he was truly on his own.

For about five minutes.

Out of the corner of his eye, he spotted Corbin and Shepherd, both with champagne glasses in hand. "I'm glad I found you."

"It's good to see you too, Your Grace," Corbin greeted as he craned his neck around to see the area where Bryant had just stood. "Is your mother here tonight?"

"Not this time, no. I'll fill you in on the details when we're out of the public eye. Much has happened since Lady Goddard's house party." He turned from them, surveying the rest of the room. With the crowd, finding people he recognized proved tricky. Lady Anwyn took up her usual spot beside the piano, a few wallflowers laughing with her over some bit of gossip. Lady Ruth and her father stood opposite them near the door to the trellis. “Shep, your lady friend is here.”

“I know—” he began to say, interrupted by Corbin.

“He’s already danced with her twice, Bryant. Any more and he’ll be causing a proper scandal. He hasn’t even proposed yet.” Corbin’s grin gleamed in the warm candlelight that filled the room. “I say he should pop the question already and get it over with.”

Shep shot him a glare. “In time, Corbin. I’ve only been courting her for a month. Love takes longer to develop than a mere six weeks, you know.” All the same, his gaze returned to the spot where his beloved conversed with her father and a warm blush heated his cheeks.

“I’m happy for you, Shepherd; truly, I am,” Bryant offered, knowing that his tone fell short of the sentiment he truly did mean.

His friend’s brows furrowed. “Perhaps we should go find that place out of the public eye now so you can get whatever’s bothering you off your chest.”

He nodded, making his way out of the room and down the hall. “If I’m not mistaken, there’s a drawing room a few paces down this way. I don’t believe Lord Remdwell will mind if we use it for our conversation.” Sure enough, the muted redwood doors appeared in sight. An old set, for such a style hadn’t been common for some time. Dark oaks and spruces were in these days, giving houses a dark, gothic look to them. The room very well may have been abandoned long ago, save for the time or two that Mother had taken him here to get a bit of energy out when he was a babe. He pushed the heavy doors open, revealing an empty drawing room covered in a proper layer of dust.

“How did you know about this room? It seems as if Lord Remdwell himself doesn’t even know it is here,” Shep commented.

"This was my makeshift playroom when Mother took me to the Remdwell Ball eons ago. Anytime I got a bit too squealy or antsy, she took me in here to run around." He gestured to the floor, where they promptly sat in a makeshift circle. "Right, then. Where should I start?"

Corbin spoke up, that ever-teasing grin on his face. "The day you left the party seems the most reasonable to me; when you were all but convinced that you *didn't* like Lady Olivia."

"This isn't about her," he replied sharply; harsher than he meant to, of course, but all the same, he wasn't about to lay his own heart before them. "I mean, it is, but not in that sense."

Shepherd's eyes darkened. "Is that what you were going to talk about at the croquet game? Or, rather, what you mentioned but weren't going to divulge at the croquet game?"

"Not exactly; I had meant to discuss Marjorie with you, as Brigham is struggling with what to do in her regards. She's safe, as far as I am aware, for the time being. A lot has happened since then." He took a deep breath, preparing himself for the rather unpleasant details that even now weighed on his mind. "Just so you are aware, I have permission from the lady to talk about this. That *does not* mean you may share it with anyone else. This is to remain between us." Both of his peers gave their promises before he continued.

"Surely you are well aware of the headlines from a few weeks ago," he began slowly.

Corbin rushed to agree. "Naturally. My uncle hired extra security around the clock. As he put it, that idiot was bold enough to attack in broad daylight. He didn't want anything happening to Aunt Rosealie. I don't suppose your mother let you out of the house for weeks, given how little we've seen of you."

"Exactly right. The only thing is that she was there. Mother and Lady Seylor were having tea when the intruder broke in. For the moment, Lady Olivia is residing with us. Mother is teaching her what she can about managing an estate, in the event that she inherits everything. The attorney general will be investigating, of course, to discover Lord Seylor's plans. In the meantime, however, our house is her haven, away from the threat of death."

Both boys stared at him in shock. Shep cleared his throat and spoke first, tone heavy with grief. "Is there anything we can do to help?"

"I don't believe so. She's well taken care of at Angarth, as you can imagine. We're waiting to hear back from the attorney general and the constable on what the next steps will be."

"What will that involve?" Corbin inquired next. "Will the title pass onto her? If not, will the next Lord Seylor allow her to stay?" His voice trailed off as he sighed. "Should we set up a place in the country for her? Surely she'd be safer at one of our country estates, and perhaps more comfortable without the city noise."

Bryant shook his head. "No, moving her out of the city would only put her in more danger, I fear. Not to mention that it could socially compromise her. We don't want the public thinking one of us has acted improperly towards her."

Shep nodded in agreement. "Exactly. Are you certain, though, that Angarth is the best for her? You, in particular, have spent dance after dance with her this season. Wouldn't others begin to question her presence?"

"We have been very cautious about it. Mother has requested that she arrive before five at night and leave after ten in the morrow, to ensure that no eye is suspicious." His gaze drew to the light under the doorway. It flickered as though someone stood in front of it. He hushed the others and stared at the light until the shadows vanished.

"I thought you said Lord Remdwell wouldn't mind us using the room," Corbin whispered hesitantly, a mixture of confusion and annoyance in his tone.

"I don't believe that was Lord Remdwell. Whisper, please. I don't want to take chances. The briefest rumor and this entire operation is over." He met Shepherd's gaze. "We need to avert the gaze of the public. Do you suppose we should follow through?"

Corbin looked between them with utter bewilderment. "What do you mean?"

Shep nodded. "I think we should. It'll be risky, but this could be what saves us all."

"What are you talking about?" Corbin raised his voice ever slightly, begging to be noticed.

"Agreed. However risky, this could bring about the best rewards for them. I can see it now: "Baron Saves Marquis and Duke From Fire" the caption will say."

Corbin scooted forward and raised a hand. "Wait. Fire? What on Kestia are the two of you going on about? What are you planning?"

Shep cast a tentative glance to Bryant—who promptly nodded—before sharing their plan. "We were discussing at Lady Goddard's house party that we ought to do something to raise Brigham's self esteem, as well as the overall opinion of his family among the *ton*. Through a bit of discussion, we determined that he could save us from a fire.

"There's an abandoned barn at the edge of my property, see, and the wood is old enough that fire would cling to it easily. We smear some soot on our faces to make it look like we were caught in the blaze, stand just inside the doorway, and carefully arrange for Brigham to pull us out. If we play our cards right, it makes him look like a hero."

"We figured," Bryant picked up, "that the risk was low enough for this to be a viable option. We all walk away safe and sound and the press goes wild with Brigham's name in every paper across the kingdom. A brilliant plan, providing we can work out the details."

"And if the reporters are suspicious? How would such a fire even start without someone actually lighting it? They'd look into such an incident once someone made that connection."

"It's old wood. The chances of it catching fire must be astronomically high," Bryant countered.

"Not in the middle of winter! The air isn't hot enough. Even if the sun *is* shining directly onto the wood, it's far too cold for it to simply ignite. You need a better cover story than just 'it randomly burst into flames because of the *freezing cold* sunlight' to make this work."

They sat in silence for a few moments, considering the various scenarios and outcomes for what excuses they could come up with. "I've got it," Shep stated. "It's sure to be dark in there. I'll have a lantern and "accidentally" drop it onto some of the hay. I'll tell the press that I tripped and fell, and the flame from the lantern caught."

"Will that work?" Corbin's voice dripped with skepticism.

"It must," Bryant replied. "We've little other choice. The Roberts family needs a boost in morale and fast, before this world claims another tragedy upon their name."

...

With a plan firmly set in place, Bryant strolled around the ball in search of which young ladies he ought to dance with. The choices were abundant, given how many invitations were handed out. He could dance until the very end of the party and have hardly met even a handful. Should he, just for tonight, forget about the fact that his title draws attention to his presence no matter where he goes and dance with whomever he pleases?

He wanted to, but he wasn't sure he should. The press would be everywhere, lurking in every corner and behind each attendee. If he meant to break his pattern, they'd surely notice.

Then again, his presence in a ballroom at all was sure to cause a stir, given his absence for the past two weeks. Rumors that he'd gone back to the country already started to circulate. Why not choose his own dance partner based on whom he wanted to dance with instead of the algorithm that he'd created?

His eyes flitted over the faces of the various patrons, noting one in particular. Lady Olivia. Mother suggested she go tonight, if only to prove she hadn't died as well. The lady had hardly spoken a word to him since arriving at Angarth. Perhaps now was the time to see if she might spare a conversation.

Slowly, he worked up the courage to walk over to her and ask her to dance, hoping that she'd entertain Bryant Wooldridge after her exchange with Sir Detective. "Lady Olivia, might I have this next set?"

She turned, carefully, calculatingly, and awkwardly smiled. Not her genuine, 'I'm actually enjoying myself' smile, but at least she hadn't grimaced. "I would be delighted to, Your Grace." She took his arm when he offered it and followed him out to the midst of the dancers.

They started the dance—a waltz—and Bryant offered his first bit of commentary. "I hope the evening is of some cheer to you." He left it at that, hoping that she'd pick up the conversation of her own volition. If she held any interest in him at all, she'd be willing to talk.

"Is that so, Your Grace? In what way?"

He chose his next words carefully, not wanting to appear pushy. "You deserve the chance to smile again," He sent a prayer heavenward that she would accept it.

She frowned. "You're rather dense if you believe I want to smile. I wouldn't have come at all had it not been for your mother's insistence."

"My apologies, my lady. It is only that..." he hesitated, searching for the right thing to say. Grief, however he knew it, was unfamiliar to his adult self. The closest experience he had was with Brigham, and heaven knows that man experienced far more than grief. Then, a memory sprang to mind. His adult self repeated to Brigham what Brigham himself had said a decade ago, when Bryant was grieving his father. Surely it could apply here. "I do not wish you to drown in your grief. It is an unrelenting force, Lady-"

"Stop," she interrupted. Her hair flicked against her shoulders as she shook her head. "'My lady' is far more preferable. It keeps my identity innocuous. I wouldn't want any of these gents figuring out that I carry far more to my name than a few larks." A fair point, given that many of the men in this room were far poorer than she was. Any whisper of a title would draw their attention faster than a moth to a flame.

"Very well. My lady you shall remain."

She pressed her lips into a thin line. "Why are you dancing with me? I rather thought you hated me."

"I have never hated you. We had our differences, for sure and certain, but I cannot hold those against you. Not now. Too much has happened."

"You didn't answer the question." She glared.

He glanced around the room at all of the eyes watching the dancing, praying none of them were listening. "I wanted to protect you." Stuffy air made its way through his lungs as he took in a deep breath. "Your inheritance is your own now and, as far as we know, so is your title. Too many men here know that, and desperately want it themselves."

Her expression shifted from her glare as she hesitantly smiled. "That is sweet of you. Perhaps you aren't quite as dense as I presumed."

Women were going to be the death of him. They insulted him, ignored him, and pretended to enjoy his company when in love with another. This one stabbed with her words like a dagger and stung like a nest of wasps.

And yet.

And yet his heart fluttered as she spoke. Heat rose up in his cheeks when she teased. And beneath the mask of perfection that she'd put up, he could see it in her too. She enjoyed his company, however much she tried to ignore the fact.

Somewhere along the line, the music had dimmed into the light tunes that played between sets. Here they stood, hand in hand, staring into each other's eyes. "My lady, might I accompany you to the refreshments table? Perhaps to the garden afterwards?"

She nodded in a slow, dazed way that he'd never seen her do before. "That sounds nice." Her hand rested in the crook of his elbow as he led her away.

"The night is quite lovely, isn't it?" He didn't exactly want to talk about the weather, of all things, but it seemed the most reasonable topic for the moment. Such things had to be handled delicately, no matter the witty banter they'd exchanged previously.

"Indeed. Though, I don't appreciate just how cold Braxden gets in the winter. If I had my way, we'd be staying at our holiday home near the Alcastair Mountains. It's much warmer there in comparison." A pause. "I would, that is. I'd be staying there. At my holiday home." He could hear the heaviness in her breath.

She downed a glass of champagne and dragged Bryant by the arm out to the gardens. "It is really a lovely evening. Not as cold as it has been, and not a cloud in the sky to suggest snow on the way. A beautiful night to have a ball." With a grin, she added, "I shall have to ask Lady Remdwell how she always manages to have her balls on such clear nights. I can't remember a single one where the weather has been poor."

"So then," Bryant stated, trying to lift her spirits, "clearly, she must have some sort of mystical powers to ensure that her night is never ruined. Perhaps she's familiar with one of the fae who has the ability to keep the clouds away." That earned him an eye roll as they turned to waltz down the pathways through the maze-like hedges; they were the only thing that dared to grow in the harsher temperatures. A rather pleasant sight that would make for a lovely backdrop someday. Perhaps he'd recommend it to Shepherd for that day when he finally proposed to Lady Ruth. The moonlight provided a wonderful air of mystery.

Come to think of it, the light shone on Olivia's hair differently out here. While the candlelight turned her hair to a lighter brown, this dark moonlight made it look almost blue. It looked lovely against the pale blue of her dress, as if it were the sky and her hair the ocean. The ringlets of her coiffure framed her face just so and highlighted the rosy blush in her cheeks. His breath left him as he stared at her face. Had he ever seen something more radiant? If he had, the memories refused to surface. The very world around them seemed to disappear as he took a step closer.

The illusion shattered as her brows furrowed. "Your Grace, did you hear me?"

Oh no.

"I'm sorry," he apologized as he chuckled sheepishly. "I've a lot on my mind tonight." A true enough statement, though she was the only thing currently on his mind. Heaven help him, he was spoony for her.

"Hm. I suppose that's excusable. All the same, I expect you to focus on my words in the future. Now, I'll ask again. Do you plan to stay in Braxden for the entirety of the season?"

He nodded. "I do. Mother wants to ensure that I can experience my first season in full; I've also a duty to stay informed on our government's current affairs and to be present when I am needed. So, yes, I do believe I shall be in Braxden for the next few months."

She smiled warmly. "I'm glad of it. Perhaps the season will acclimate you to the culture of nobility."

His heart pounded at what she could mean by that. Did she expect him to act the same as his peers, particularly towards his friends? Did she think him ignorant for going to serve the territory?

The worry in his face must have been obvious, for she laughed at him. "Your Grace, it's rather simple. Noblemen, even ones of your age, don't walk around with dust on their uniform."

Flames licked his cheeks as he chuckled sheepishly at himself. "My apologies, Miss Sparrow." He could still feel his heartbeat in his chest, but relief flooded him if dust was her main concern. "I shall attempt to do better next time."

She gently cupped his jaw with her hand, staring deep into his eyes as her thumb rubbed across his cheek. "There is no need to apologize. Not here, where the moonlight hides any trace of imperfection."

He took her hand in his, pressing it to his lips. Her eyes sparkled in the pale moon. They stood in silence, neither daring to move until a voice from inside called out for Olivia. "Shall I see you in?"

"By all means," she whispered, clinging to his arm.

A few days ago, the idea of staying in town terrified him. Now, however, it didn't seem so terrible a fate.

Chapter Eleven: Elevenses

December 19th

Breakfast was scrumptious, as always. Aneira had nearly outdone herself, claiming their resident house guest as her excuse to cook whatever she could. It was a small enough gesture; nothing too grand or out of character for Aneira. Here at the breakfast table, Bryant could see Olivia's tension slowly resolve as she savored the meal.

Today, however, her usual tension was ever present, accompanied by stormy eyes. Eyes that, Bryant observed, stared at his mother as her fluttery voice spoke of an invitation to tea extended to Alden Kegg.

"Lord Arioch wanted to ensure he had the afternoon free to call, so I extended an invitation to elevenses instead. It would be lovely for you both to join us."

Bryant spared a glance at Olivia, noting that her lips were pressed into a thin line. "It should be lovely, providing our company gets along well." He could hardly believe that his mother was yet trying to play matchmaker for the couple.

Granted, he didn't know if his feelings were from his disdain for Kegg, or his butterflies for Olivia.

Emotionlessly, the girl stood. "I believe I'll go out for a walk through the gardens this morning. Breakfast was lovely, Your

Grace; so lovely that I believe I shall be too full for morning tea. Give my compliments to your cook." Then, she was gone.

Once he was sure she couldn't hear him, he mumbled, "Mother, I don't believe this is a good idea."

She waved a dismissive hand. "Bryant, I'm certain her unease is due to her situation. She's been having nightmares, you know."

He did know; the whole household knew. It was hard to be oblivious to such things when she awoke in the middle of the night screaming. He also knew that her eyes never held the darkness of them when brought before Aneira's outstanding meals. "She only seemed nervous after you mentioned Lord Arioch. I don't think she's comfortable with him."

Her brows furrowed as she analyzed what he said. He knew that look well; she was seriously considering his words and comparing them to her memory. "I suppose you're right," she began slowly, sighing. "I should have assumed that it wasn't yet time to have guests in the house. The poor girl must be frightened out of her mind at the prospect. All the same, I've already extended the invitation. Perhaps I can convince her to join us. It isn't as though she will be alone with him."

"Or, perhaps I could take tea in my study, Olivia in the conservatory, and you could entertain Lord Arioch." He didn't quite fancy watching Alden fawn over Lady Olivia for the entirety of morning tea, especially after their exchange at Remdwell. "I do believe that would be the most pleasant turn of events." He attempted to use the voice she did when she planned events with her friends, using her words rather than her title to set details in stone.

Her piercing look told him that his suggestion wasn't going to be heeded. "You should be among your peers, Bryant. They'll enjoy your company far more than they will mine."

"Lord Arioch might argue otherwise," he countered. "According to him, I'm rather boring and need to lighten up."

She bore a look of disdain now. "I do hope you haven't been trying to upend his hopes of courting Lady Olivia, dear. Despite your grievances against them both, the match would suit them well. He's gone long enough without a proper family around him. Surely this can only do him good."

Or, it could harm her. He couldn't stand for that. Neither would Mother, given the fact that she's done nothing but dote on Olivia in the time that she has spent with them. He would hardly be able to fathom why she was pushing for the marriage, except that she hadn't been there when Alden had "joked" about Bryant being dishonorable. She hadn't heard the words of ungodliness that spilled from the earl's mouth; hadn't seen the wicked grin on his face or the glint of mischief in his eyes that spelled out the heartbreak of an unfortunate maiden.

"Quite the reason, then, for me to take up tea alone. I'd rather spend the morning with my papers than attempting to foil Lord Arioch's hopes for marriage." As much as he thought to watch out for the woman, Alden couldn't get his claws on her in his own home. No one would dare be so disrespectful. His mother's presence was enough.

After all, Lady Olivia was no fool. She didn't have feelings for Kegg. No amount of his charms would stir her heart if she already set it against him. She'd see right through his plans on her own.

"I cannot make you come, but you should consider it. Perhaps it shall change your mind." She rose from the table, indicating that the conversation was indeed finished.

Dread pooled in his stomach. This day was going to be a challenge.

He sent a silent prayer to the Most High as he walked to his room for the strength to resist making quips about Alden, for the constitution to avoid gagging at any flirtatious comment the earl made towards Lady Olivia. His stomach refused to settle even as he opened the door to his room. "Lyz, my best coat, if you will."

Lyz's eyebrows rose in question. "Your best coat at nine in the morning? Whatever for?"

Normally, he would have made a snarky, lighthearted comment about politics or some such thing, but at the moment, he needed Lyz as a friend. "Mother decided to invite Alden Kegg over for elevenses."

His brows dropped as he let out a winded sigh. "That should be... *interesting*, to say the least."

"She's taken it upon herself to connive his engagement to Lady Olivia. I don't know how I'll be able to stand it. Everything he has done shows that he is a reprobate, unworthy of her hand. I doubt that his desire for her is anything genuine."

"Beg pardon for inquiring, Your Grace; do you have any intentions regarding Lady Olivia? I have heard the name quite often between you and Her Grace."

He could have sworn that the thick walls of his home prevented eavesdropping. "I currently harbor no plans to court her. She isn't the type for me to fall for."

And yet, he'd felt butterflies when she was Olivia, not just when she was Miss Sparrow. They'd had easy banter and got along quite well. For heaven's sake, he'd almost *kissed* her in the Remdwells' gardens. He could deny any current plans to court the woman, but he couldn't deny that he felt *something* for the lady.

Their banter. Surely that was going to occur again; perhaps even today. That would irritate Kegg, wouldn't it? With his determination to win the girl over, seeing someone else laugh and speak with her in such a friendly manner would irritate him. The thought brought a ghost of a grin to his face.

"Actually, Lyz, I believe that elevenses might not go as badly as I thought."

...

Anticipation crawled like a spider in his stomach. Kegg was set to arrive any minute now. Mrs. Kendrick stood just around the corner from the drawing room with a tray of sweets, ready to bring them forth once the guests settled in. Portencia was ready with the tea tray.

He let out a sigh as he noticed the sound of footsteps coming in from the gardens. Mother, with Olivia in tow, entered the hall.

Deep green eyes lifted from the floor to greet him. "Good morning, Your Grace."

"Good morning, Lady Olivia. Did you find the ride through town pleasant?" The best question he knew to offer as his stomach did somersaults. Start the banter now and he might not need to worry about it later.

She nodded, a soft smile on her face as opposed to the bright, fake one. "It was quite nice, given the pleasant smell of rain in the air after the storm last night." She took the arm he offered and followed him to the drawing room. "I don't believe I've ever had the privilege of visiting Angarth before. It is rather lovely." A pause. "The decor is a tad strange, however."

"How do you mean?"

She glanced at the wall behind her. "Photographs, but not of the occupants. Shepherd Whitley, Corbin Entwistle, and... Brigham Roberts? The two of you are friends?"

"Is that a surprise to you, Lady Olivia?" He vehemently stepped back, tense now at what she would say.

A low hum echoed in the room. "Perhaps not. It is only, I had assumed your association with the Roberts household was out of obligation, or pity. I did not expect it to be genuine friendship. Particularly at the beginning of the season. Then, I expected that your association with them stemmed from ignorance of their standing."

"Ignorance?" He repeated, attempting to calm himself. His blood boiled, but he could not allow himself to lose his temper. The scolding he would receive alone held back his tongue. "I am not ignorant of my friend, or of the reputation his family has. Yet, I know that reputations can be deceptive." He took a deep breath. "Was there anything else?"

Somewhat more withdrawn, she replied, "I like the addition of the photographs. It provides the house a homely feel." Silence fell between them for a brief moment as she found her voice. "The roses at the back of the house were lovely."

"Our gardener will be quite happy to hear of your approval. In the meantime, I shall thank you in his stead." He offered the banter between them, hoping it would inspire her to follow suit before Kegg arrived to ruin it all. As irritated as he was at the moment, he couldn't bear to let Kegg manipulate her.

"Thank you. I don't give out compliments to just anyone, you know." A hint of an uneasy grin tugged at the corners of her mouth.

The trio stepped into the drawing room to settle in. Mid-morning light shone in from the bay windows, illuminating the silver table and bright furniture. A small clock ticked on the mantle of the fireplace, already lit to warm their guest from the blustery morning.

Bryant took a seat opposite the door and fidgeted with his hands. "Are you quite certain, Mother, that you cannot entertain him alone?"

She shot him a glare from the sofa. "Bryant, truly, you must learn to keep company that you disagree with. You don't wish to be expelled from the House of Lords for misconduct. This is not Battenhold, and you are not a child. Keep still, be polite. I don't require that you say a word."

Heavy air left his lungs as he forced himself to relax. "Very well, Mother. I trust your judgment. I shall say no more." He crossed his arms and stared at the entrance. "You don't suppose there's a chance the wind prevented his arrival-"

The front door's loud *creak* cut off his words; Lord Arioch appeared in the doorway to the drawing room a moment later. "Good morning, Your Grace, Lady Olivia," he greeted the women. Daggers from his eyes dug into Bryant as he continued. "And Your Grace. Apologies for being a tad late. I'm flattered that you waited to have tea until I arrived." He took a seat beside Olivia and relaxed into the linen fabric.

"Good day to you, Lord Arioch," Olivia greeted, disdain all but dripping from her coldly polite words. "Did you find the ride through town pleasant?"

A whisper of a grin lit up Bryant's face as his own words echoed back. The words lost themselves on Kegg, but it gave Bryant hope. She would stand her ground against him.

"Quite pleasant indeed, Lady Olivia. How did you find your own journey?"

"Enjoyable, thank you." Her lips pressed together in a firm line as Mrs. Kendrick entered with the tray of sweets, Portencia trailing behind her with the tea tray. Both were set on the low table before the women left the room. "Weak or strong, Your Grace?"

"Strong, please. No cream or sugar, I like it plain. Mrs. Kendrick's sweets are enough for me." He took one of the plates along with two pieces of shortbread—the best shortbread in all of Braxden, he'd forever claim—as Olivia poured the tea. "Thank you, my lady." A liberty he shouldn't have taken, he knew, but it was worth it if it annoyed Kegg. Olivia certainly didn't seem to mind.

His heart jumped into his throat. Those cursed butterflies. He needed to make conversation, not be rendered speechless. Of course, the thought made him wonder. Shepherd had become mute with Lady Ruth, stuttering and stammering like never before. If speech had become difficult for him as well, did that mean...?

But, no. It wouldn't work, no matter their banter. He knew that well before. Lady Olivia was not his type, despite his mother's interest in the woman. She'd like a softer-spoken, gentler woman like Lady Ruth just as well, surely.

"I suppose I shall try strong this time, with cream and sugar of course." Alden took his cup from the table and sipped. Though Olivia couldn't see for pouring tea, his eyes widened and he attempted to hide his grimace. "Thank you, Lady Olivia. It is a splendid cup." He eyed the remainder warily.

The gesture brought a small smile to Bryant's lips for a brief moment.

In the next, it was wiped right off.

"Lord Arioch, what do you think of the season so far?" Mother's silvery voice spoke. It sent chills down his spine.

Alden smiled widely. "Oh, it has been marvelous. The best I've attended thus far." His glances fell towards Olivia. "My plan is to wed before the end of the season."

"Marvelous." Mother watched the two from the rim of her glass, a twinkle in her eye. "And you, Lady Olivia, from the time you have spent out? What is your opinion?"

The younger woman stared at her with veiled shock. "The beginning of the season was pleasant. I enjoyed the Remdwell Ball last Tuesday eve." Heat bloomed in her cheeks as she fixed her sight on her tea.

"A delightful ball indeed," Kegg agreed with a bolster in his voice. "A shame it wasn't a masquerade, where title and name are meaningless." Bold of him to say so. "All the same, it was a lovely evening. If only I had the chance to find you there, Your Grace. His Grace arrived alone, and was missing for half of the night."

Bryant began elevenses with anger simmering. No longer could he keep it from boiling over. "Am I a child that must be supervised all evening, Lord Arioch? I wasn't aware that I was forbidden from ducking into a card room."

"No need to ruffle your feathers, Your Grace. I mean no harm in it. There are a multitude of reasons for your absence." His eyes betrayed his sour expression, revealing just how much he delighted in causing the conflict. Why on Kestia was that?

"We both know what you meant." He could sort out Kegg's confusing motives later. Right now, his present threat was protecting his honor from this rascal.

Kegg rose to his feet with a sigh. It might have been a typical deep sigh, but Bryant's ears heard a pretentious, overdramatic exhale. "Perhaps it's destined for the both of us to remain acquaintances, Your Grace, for it seems I'm never welcomed in your presence. I can't imagine what I've done to make you dislike me, but it seems clear to me that I've pinched a nerve that isn't able to settle. Therefore, I shall respectfully take my leave. Good day, Your Grace, my lady." He tipped his cap to Mother and Olivia before strutting out of the room.

Bryant gestured for Portencia to see him to the door. He didn't trust Kegg to not wander the house looking for anything he wanted to take in revenge. "Apologies, my lady." He noticed that Kegg had uttered the words. Kegg probably thought of him a rival now and had only been nice to appease the lady, as if she hadn't taken to using direct, brutal conversation before.

"No need, Your Grace. He spoke out of line. He's rather dimwitted about respectable tea conversation and could hardly tell social graces from table manners. I almost feel the need to apologize on his behalf."

Had the situation been more lighthearted, he would have desired to laugh at her statement. After all, she'd been discussing rumors just moments before Kegg entered. "I shall accept your apology on his behalf and thank you." He really wasn't in the mood to joke just now, but he wasn't of the mind to let her slip from his grasp either.

"Mother-" he began, wanting to right the claim.

She put a hand up and with her soft, silvery voice, comforted. "There is no need, Bryant. I know where you were."

Guilt flashed in Olivia's face a moment later. "I suppose, Your Grace, that I ought to apologize for myself. My own talk of rumors wasn't much different from his." Her voice dipped into a mumble as she rambled. "Granted, I wasn't so direct or prone to believing them as he was, but I had been curious, and that's quite nearly the same."

She took a short, deep breath before concluding with, "I'm sorry, Your Grace. I should have known better than to speak ill of your friends, even if it was only in asking after rumors. They are, after all, just rumors. I should have known not to lend an ear to them in the first place." The look that she offered him didn't hold arrogance. Rather, it showed a bit of hope.

A soft smile graced him. He hummed. "I suppose I can forgive you. *If*, that is, you'd be willing to tour the gardens with me after tea?"

Heaven help him. Just weeks ago, he would have been sorely put out even after an apology. Now, however, he was willing to put aside his anger and accept her apology wholeheartedly. Nevermind the fact that he offered to spend more time with her besides. She was doing something to him that he didn't understand whatsoever. Out of the corner of his eye, he spotted an odd look on Mother's face. He couldn't begin to imagine what she was thinking, after the verbal crossfire he sparred in.

He really, desperately, needed to have a long conversation with Shepherd.

Chapter Twelve: Morning Papers

December 20th

On His Grace's orders, Eryi strutted down the streets towards Selcomb Estate to meet his cousin. If there was one person of the entire staff of Selcomb that knew what was going on under the surface, it'd be Jerid Bowen. The Bowen family was famous for sticking their noses where they didn't belong. Usually, such a reputation got them into trouble. Today, however, it was the very thing that would help solve a mystery.

Cristyn's sweet face that morning brought a smile to his own, but her concern only hastened his steps. His Grace was smart to heed her fears; even more so to enlist his help. If Lord Arioch was up to something fishy, he could find it out.

He strode up the drive, making his way around the back to the servants' door and knocking heartily. The manor's housekeeper greeted him with a bright smile that failed to mask her irritation and let him inside. "Jerid's waiting in the kitchen. You remember where it is, don't you?"

"Of course, Mrs. Whiteford. Thank you." He darted past her, making his way down the hall to the warm kitchen. "Jerid! Good to see you again." The cousins embraced, patting each other on the back in greeting. "I take it you've got my telegram, then?"

"Indeed I did, Eryi. A fancy thing, that." He extended the small piece of paper.

A grin flickered at the corner of Eryi's mouth. "His Grace's idea. He insisted that we ought to inform you of what we needed before I stopped by. Have you found out anything just yet?"

Jerid shook his head. "I've done a bit of snooping, but I've seen nothing yet. Perfect timing, by the way," he mumbled as they made their way up the servants' stairs. "Lord Arioch has stepped out for his afternoon calls. I don't believe that he'll be back for several hours."

"Wonderful, that. The Most High's doing, no doubt. He must see that we're not meaning any harm, only trying to protect a friend." He shared Jerid's smile as they approached the study. The doorknob wasn't as lenient as he'd expected. It didn't so much as wobble as he tried to turn it.

"Lord Arioch only allows the maids in here to clean, and only once a week. He keeps it locked when he is away. If there's any sort of information on his affairs, it'll be in here where he can keep an eye on it." He pulled a genuine Bowen grin as he lifted a small, shiny object from his pocket. "Fortunately, we Bowens have never been good at leaving well enough alone." The key fit perfectly in the lock, clicking as he turned it. "And away we go," Jerid whispered as he turned the now-pliable doorknob. They entered swiftly, closing and locking the door behind.

The desk was lined with a veritable storm of papers, mismatched in piles stacked higher than the shelved back of the desk itself. "How does Lord Arioch find anything in this mess? How are *we* supposed to find anything in this mess?"

"You forget, Eryi, that I managed to steal the gradebook from our teacher in primary school without her notice. If anyone is well-tasked for the job, it would be me." Jerid kept his grin affixed as he sorted through the first stack. "Take that stack over there. Make sure to keep the pages in line but don't make it look too pretty. Lord Arioch keeps it a mess for a reason. He, no doubt, knows where everything goes." He flipped through the pages, taking only a second to glance at each one as Eryi picked up his first stack.

The pages in his hands bore so much information. He couldn't fathom how Jerid could sort through them so easily when their words contained complex numbers and figures that related to anything from the state of his estate to the taxes owed to the king for last year's harvest. All the same, he did his best to scan each page and move on to the next as quickly as he could manage. "What exactly are we looking for, Jerid?"

"Anything that could suggest immorality. A court order, risque letters, a written plot against someone; it could be anything."

His eyes flickered in search of the words 'jail' or 'court' or even 'wife' and 'child'. A report about the financial state of Selcomb fell across his gaze. Interesting, to be certain, how much red ink soaked the page, but nothing of use right now.

"I found something," Jerid exclaimed as heavy footsteps bound down the hallway. He cursed sharply and dropped his voice to a whisper, shoving the other papers back where they belonged. "I could have sworn he'd be gone all afternoon. He must have only stepped out to greet a guest. Come on, then. Up into the ceiling we go."

Eryi's brows furrowed. "Into the ceiling? How?"

"The tiles are removable. There's a crawl space up there large enough for us to get through to the other side of the wall." He hoisted himself up through the gap, reaching a hand down to pull Eryi up. The door slowly swung open just as he slid the tile back into place. "Keep absolutely still," he whispered. "Any movement will be heard."

Eryi nodded silently, focusing on the voices beneath. One was decidedly Lord Arioch. He'd only heard the voice a handful of times, but the raspiness was unmistakable. The other was unknown, though it was clear by Jerid's wide-eyed expression that he knew vaguely who it was.

In the muddled air of the crawl space, discerning the whispered words proved difficult. He only managed to pick up on a select handful; 'Jetlis', 'benefactor', and 'collect' being among them. It was possible that Lord Arioch had borrowed money to keep his estates, given how much he owed to about every service in Braxden. He wondered why the man didn't just sell the estate and move to the country permanently. He could always stay at an inn when visiting town, anyways.

For a single moment, Lord Arioch dared to raise his voice above the whisper. "Jetlis, have you gone mad?" Jetlis must be the other person, then. Strange that he'd be consulting this Jetlis about his estate's finances when Eryi hadn't ever heard of the man before. He knew all of the members on Selcomb's staff *including* Lord Arioch's financial advisor and his name wasn't Jetlis.

He could be a barrister helping Alden ward off legal bankruptcy, given how many businesses the man was indebted to. Surely Jerid knew.

"I suppose I'll have Tarvin look into it. It seems to be our only option, providing that he can follow through. Have a good day, Jetlis. Take the servants' entrance when you leave. I'll not have anyone seeing you by the road."

Did he hear him correctly? Most barristers were respectable gentlemen who would be appalled at taking a servants' entrance instead of the main door. Most lords were respectable gentlemen who wouldn't dare offer such a thing to a barrister. There were too many missing pieces, too many parts of the conversation he had missed. All the same, he followed Jerid through the crawl space to the other side of the room, dropping down into the hallway before Jerid secured the loose tile back into place.

"Who is that? I mean, he's Jetlis, obviously, but what does he do? I thought Lord Arioch's advisor was a man named Skinner, not whoever that man is."

"I don't quite know who he is; just that he comes around every now and then to chat in the study with His Lordship. All the same, we shouldn't linger here. Let's meet up in the kitchen—going separate routes to avoid His Lordship's watchful eyes—and then we can discuss everything."

A plan as good as any, providing they didn't get caught. But then, what was life without a little risk? Not a proper Bowen life, for sure and certain.

He hopped from room to room, using the connecting doors as a shield to get to the servants' stairs. Shuffling down them as quietly as the crumbling stone would allow, he snuck into the kitchen and waited until Jerid's dark head popped into view. "Good, he didn't catch you." He paused for a moment. "Why is your ear red?"

"Arioch didn't find me, but the housekeeper certainly did. Boxed my ear for slacking off." He chuckled. "She's tenacious, that one." The paper fell to the table with a soft scrape. "Let's see what's on this, shall we?"

"Of course." Eyri peered over the letter. "'To the esteemed Earl Arioch, from the desk of William Newman, on account of his finances and estates in this event requiring your critical attention.' What do you suppose that is about?" he muttered.

"Hush. We can't have someone hearing us." Nevertheless, Jerid picked up at the spot. "'These, my instructions to you, shall be enacted exactly as is declared. Your presence is requested in my court on next Friday, dated October 15th, 1832, for a matter of honor and propriety. Should you have further questions, contact my secretary's office.' Rather brief, isn't it?"

"And old. At the very least, we have cause to assume he has been improper. Perhaps I can have Lyz take a look at this and-" Jerid snatched the paper from the table. "Whyever did you do that? We need to understand what is going on here."

"If Lord Arioch finds that this paper is missing, he will have my head, and likely yours as well, and who knows how many others. I need to put this back at the earliest chance I am given." He avoided Eryi's eyes, knowing the persuasive thought within them. "I will examine it when time allows, but I cannot allow this page to leave these halls. I do not trust Lord Arioch to act benevolently towards theft."

Eryi's shoulders fell, but he nodded. "You are right, of course. We must take the necessary precautions." He stepped back from the table, urging Jerid to go on his way. "I'll report to His Grace what we have discovered, and wait patiently for word from you."

"Godspeed, cousin."

...

"You've sent the telegram, haven't you?" Bryant questioned for the fifth time that day as he waited with a box of matches for Shepherd's cue. They'd already poured oil in discreet places around the barn to aid in the fire's spread. Patches of soot covered the contours of his face and smeared across his forehead to match Shepherd in his 'I was just in a fire' look. It had to be believable, after all.

"Of course I sent the telegram," Shep answered aggravatedly. "He should be coming up the drive at any minute. You trust me, don't you?"

Bryant loosed a sigh as he double-checked the oil. They'd already disposed of the can, not willing anyone to discover that the entire fire had been a set up. "Of course I do, Shep. I'm just nervous. I haven't exactly set a barn on fire before." His stomach crawled with a mixture of fear and anticipation. "What will your father say when he finds out?"

"I've already spoken with him. He thinks I'm burning it to save time in dismantling this old thing and has already informed the servants to stand by with water buckets. We have his complete permission to do this." He gasped and took his place by the door, signaling to Bryant to light the match and toss it over to the farthest corner. "He's coming up the drive now."

With a deep breath, Bryant struck the match and watched as the flame traveled across the oil, catching fire to the ancient wood. Shep had been right; the wood was indeed old and dry enough to catch the flames quickly. He joined Shepherd by the door, waiting for Brigham to notice the flames that climbed up the walls of the old barn.

"Wait, Bryant, I forgot." Panic coated Shep's tone.

"Now isn't exactly the time, Shepherd!" He stared as the flames grew ever closer. Smoke poured into his lungs and stung his eyes. Whatever Shepherd had left would have to be dug out from the ashes.

He turned his attention back to the window. Brigham was sprinting towards them now, fear written into every line of his face. He shouted something as he began to run, terrified tears dripping from his eyes as he dashed towards the barn. "Shepherd! Bryant!" He called out as he drew near.

Their plan was going well, all things considered. They didn't want to give Brigham too much information on what they were doing, out of worry that he'd have rejected it. He hadn't known that they were going to burn the barn down. The only thing they had to sacrifice was a little bit of his time and stability. The only thing wounded was Brig's assurances that they were safe. After this, they would be.

Until, of course, Bryant glanced from the window back to where Shepherd was supposed to be. The man wasn't there. "Shep, where did you go?" His heartbeat picked up as he scanned the area.

"Up in the loft. I'll be down in a few seconds. I just need to grab— here!" He held up a small wooden box triumphantly. "I'm making my way down now."

His eyes darted around the loft, noting how the fire climbed up the walls, edging ever closer to the roof. "Shep, the fire's getting closer!" He could only watch in panic as Shepherd crawled to the edge of the loft and stole down the ladder.

Shepherd walked over to the door, coughing. "See? No harm done. Now we just wait for Brigham and—" A large creak cut him off.

Bryant spared a glance up, eyes glowing as they reflected the red-orange that consumed the wood above them. "How close is Brigham?"

"Not close enough. He needs to be in here, remember? To make it look believable, he needs to stand inside for a minute or two so that the papers believe that he was trying to find us before he pulls us out." The roof gave another *crack* as the wood shifted and burned. Ashes and chunks of charred wood fell from the roof as the flames engulfed the beams.

"I fear we don't have that sort of time, Shep." He counted his heartbeats as he watched the roof warily, deeming what moment would be the best to call off the ruse and flee. When close was far too close for comfort.

Brigham stepped inside the barn, all but screaming their names. "What on earth are you two doing?"

"Count to sixty for me, Brig," Bryant commanded, feigning a sense of calm as smoke filled his lungs. It stung his eyes and burned in his throat, but the need to make their scheme convincing took precedence over any discomfort.

He coughed from the smoke before replying, shock and anger bursting in his eyes. "What? Why? Bryant, if you weren't aware, this building is *on fire*. We need to get out of here before the roof caves in on us!"

"Count to sixty. Then we'll go," Shepherd echoed. "One, two, three..." They stood in a sort of triangle, counting out each number as the flames rose higher and higher. Just after they hit fourty-two, a large beam from the ceiling fell, shattering and sending charred bits of wood everywhere. One such piece flung itself into Bryant's pant-leg, burning his skin. He yelped as he jumped back and swatted out the bit of flame that had caught on the fabric.

"Bryant, we need to go!" Brigham urged, coughing all the while. "Before either of you get hurt further. We need to go!" He grabbed Shepherd's sleeve and tugged as he strutted towards the door.

Bryant nodded and followed behind, only to find himself pinned to the ground a moment later, his back in searing pain. One of the heavy boards from the roof fell, trapping him underneath it. Shep and Brig darted to pull it up, struggling with the weight of it. Bryant scooted out from underneath as quickly as he could, taking Shepherd's hand to pull himself back up. They ran, barely making it out as several other boards fell and poured smoke into the air.

"Are you okay, Bry?" Shepherd spoke hesitantly, his words catching as the soreness of his throat became evident.

He stammered a response as his knees buckled. Adrenaline pooled in his veins, causing his hands to shake. "I— I don't know. I think so." He spared a glance back at the barn. Only a husk of the original wood remained, orange-red still consuming the structure. "That was too close."

"Not just "too close"," Brigham mumbled angrily. "What on *Kestia* was that about? You could have died! Yet you just stood there until the roof all but caved in on us!" He turned his tirade on Shepherd, leaving Bryant to suffer through the overwhelming anxiety that coursed through him.

Breathing was almost impossible. If they had waited ten seconds longer, they'd be goners, dead where they stood. His back burned with an unceasing fire. He shrugged out of his jacket and laid down in the grass, hoping that the snow would soothe the burning.

"Bryant, no; don't do that. The ice will only make it worse." Shepherd appeared at his side in an instant, lifting him up onto his feet. "Don't you remember from school? With burns like yours, ice only helps to kill the nerve. I know it's painful, but you have to wait."

The servants appeared in the yard a moment later, buckets of water in hand. Far too late for him, unfortunately. "Shep, I need to sit down. I— I don't feel well." Nausea rolled through him in waves as dizziness clung to his head. He swayed, all but falling onto Shepherd.

"The kitchen. You can sit down in the kitchen. It's too cold out here; you'll get hypothermia." He lifted an arm across Bryant's shoulders and led him inside. Brigham trailed behind with a string of curses.

"Brig, not right now. I'll explain everything when we can, but Bryant needs our attention." He called to the housekeeper to send for the family physician and then motioned to a maid to bring a wet towel.

Bryant shuddered as Shep placed the towel over his back. It scratched and soothed in a conflicting manner that stressed his system. He wasn't entirely sure that he wouldn't pass out. It helped, though, that he was now sitting down instead of relying on his wobbly knees to carry him.

A moment later, the duke entered the room, darkness spread across his face. "I knew I should have never let you boys dismantle the barn in such a way. It wasn't safe." He wrapped his arms around Shepherd. "I thank the Most High that you're safe. Who knows what could have happened if Brigham hadn't been there?"

Shep and Bryant exchanged a look before turning back to the duke. "I owe him my life," Shep mumbled as he nodded towards Brigham. If the boy hadn't tugged at his sleeve and pulled him away from Bryant, he'd be the one with scorch marks across his back, moaning in agony as his skin burned.

"It's good that it hurts," one of the maids stated. "That means the nerves aren't dead. It'll take a while to heal, for sure and certain, but it will be on the mend." The physician confirmed as much after he arrived. Severe burns, and several bruised ribs (perhaps a fracture, but he wasn't certain), but nothing further. No permanent damage had been done, but Bryant wouldn't be stepping out onto the ballroom floor for quite a while.

The chaos slowly calmed down. Bryant's head cleared of the fog that had taken over. His stomach settled as the adrenaline declined, leaving him with the odd combination of being emotionally drained while experiencing a veritable fire across his back. Explaining this to his mother wasn't going to be easy.

"I believe I'm owed an explanation," Brigham barked once everyone was out of earshot.

Shepherd spoke up, allowing Bry to disconnect from the conversation and gain some semblance of emotional stability. "It all started at the croquet game, with the other gents jeering the way they do. We thought it was unfair, so we hatched a plan to boost your reputation. I just so happened to think of this old barn that stood a hundred or so feet from the house. Father gave me permission to dismantle it and gave no qualms about me electing to burn it. So, we decided that we'd invite you over, light the barn on fire, and pretend that you saved us from the flames. But, of course, it isn't exactly pretend anymore."

Brig shook his head slowly, eyes wide in disbelief. "I don't believe it. I never thought I'd see the day when Shepherd Whitley did something stupid. You idiots could have died!"

"I know. It was an idiodic thing to do and I see that now. We should have told you beforehand so you weren't going in blind—"

"*You shouldn't have done this at all*!" He shouted, tears streaming down his face. Never had Bryant heard the boy shout as he just had. They'd done more damage than repair, he feared, no matter what the papers would say tomorrow.

"I— I'm sorry, Brig," Bryant offered feebly. It wasn't enough to repair what they'd destroyed, he knew, but it was all he could offer.

"You had better be," he spat. "Good night, Your Grace, Lord Pwyll." He left through the servants' door, not daring to meet their eyes as he turned away.

Bryant met Shepherd's gaze with weary eyes. "What have we *done*?"

What, indeed.

Chapter Thirteen: To Be Or Not To Be

January 10th, 1836

Silence weighed heavily on Bryant's heart as he looked out the window of his carriage. The argument with Brigham still held his thoughts captive. He'd found no way to mend the gap he'd created. Just another example of him never knowing when to keep his mouth shut.

Being stuck in bed for three weeks had been torture. Though he enjoyed the company of Mother, Lyz, and Eryi, it wasn't the same as interacting with a human being that he didn't live with.

Lady Olivia had departed for home the day after the incident. Mother insisted, as it wouldn't be proper for her to stay while he took up primary residence for this accursed house arrest. He was almost sad to see her go. Following their exchange at the Remdwell Ball, he had begun to enjoy her company.

Corbin had visited a time or two, sharing his stories and jokes in an attempt to cheer him. Every time, he left with sad eyes and a downtrodden heart. Bryant informed him on the first visit about the argument he and Shep had with Brigham. He'd simply nodded his head and made a comment about how Brigham must be as hurting and lonely as Bryant and Shepherd were. When asked for any advice, he shrugged, unsure of a solution.

He'd almost expected Shepherd to visit on occasion, but his presence at Angarth was lacking. For good reason, he supposed, given that Shep always claimed he did his best thinking when out in the country. It was smart to assume, then, that Shep wasn't in Braxden anymore.

How had something so simple fallen apart at his feet?

It wasn't supposed to be dangerous. Brigham would arrive, they'd stay for a minute or two, and then he'd play hero and pretend to pull them out of the flames.

He hadn't expected Brigham to be upset that they'd even attempted the idea. Upset about being left in the dark, surely, but not at their proposed solution. This ended all of the bullying—he assumed, given the headline of the following day being in Brig's favor—but he turned on them for even risking it.

Brigham had always been independent, relying on himself to get everything done that was under his care. His sister's respites from home, holding the weight of his family's burdens, and everything else that came with a father torn away from his family. Could it be pride in someone else trying to ease the burden that caused his outrage? Potentially, but his emotion didn't match anything from before. That show of ego was a far cry from the pure *fury* on his face.

They all hated lying, so that could play a part in it, but Brigham had nothing to do with their lies. He didn't know what was going on, nor did he fake anything. The headlines spoke only truth. He saved Bryant's life that day.

Brig's words echoed in his head. *You shouldn't have done this at all*! He was mad that they'd even attempted the barn-fire, but why?

Then he remembered the tears that had streamed down Brigham's face; the look of pure terror in his eyes. It wasn't anger—not exactly—that had torn the hole in their bond. It was fear. He was afraid of losing them. He had been scared of losing his friends because of something risky they did to help him; as if they'd almost died *because* of him. Correlation and causation were different things, of course, but Brigham had blurred that line several times before. Who's to say he wouldn't do it again?

Right, then. As soon as he was able, he'd visit Cargan to apologize and to explain everything properly, now that tensions have been given time to calm. For the moment, however, he traveled to the theater. After three weeks in what was essentially luxurious house arrest, the physician gave his permission for Bryant to see a play, citing that such an event wasn't likely to put strain on his back and halt his healing, so he gave in to the temptation.

He wasn't entirely sure that he would enjoy it, regardless of the quality of the show.

It was nice, though, to be out of the house. The whole world seemed brighter because of its newness.

His eyes caught on a man lurking down the road. Due to the crowds making their way up and down the cobble, he couldn't quite determine the look of him. A tan cap was all that really defined him, and even that was not fanciful by any means. Just clean and proper, like a gentleman's cap. He only really stood out because he'd been taking the same path as them for at least ten minutes. How the man could walk at the same pace as trotting horses remained to be seen.

Before he could note anything further about him, the carriage pulled to a stop. Pedr hopped off the driver's seat and opened the door. Bryant took a deep breath to prepare himself for the excursion before exiting the carriage. "Thank you, Pedr. Come 'round in about two hours, I should think." He nodded a goodbye before making his way inside the building.

People swarmed around the halls, purchasing tickets and finding their seats, most of whom he didn't recognize. They were peers, as far as he knew, but he hadn't been out long enough to match names with faces. Others were of the upper class, or of the upper fringe of the middle class; those wealthy enough to eat fulfilling meals and heat their homes all winter long. Bankers, estate managers, barristers, and the like. He knew those men even less than he did his peers, making him feel quite out of place. The Remdwell Ball may have been his first excursion without his mother accompanying him, but this was his first event where he was truly on his own—no band of brothers to see him through with enjoyable, lighthearted conversation.

A pang of guilt struck through him as he purchased his singular ticket. If only he hadn't agreed to Shep's plan. He should have argued more about the risks of it, should have understood that Brigham wouldn't want them in harm's way just to boost his reputation.

"Should have" wouldn't get him anywhere. There was no changing the past. He could only pray that it wasn't too late to mend what he'd broken.

He took a seat in his box—the ticket seller insisted that he have a good spot—and sighed. If he were being entirely honest, he didn't even know what the play was about. It was eons better than sitting around at home, though, and for that he was thankful. As an additional bonus, it would provide some surface level conversation for his dance partners at the Mortimer Ball in a week. A reasonably smaller event than the Remdwells', but one that his mother insisted he attend. Iver Mortimer was a friend of Corbin's, so he was certain to have at least one friend in attendance.

The candlelight dimmed as the show began. Characters and costumes blurred in his eyesight as he stared, blankly registering what was going on. He paid enough attention to determine the basic plot and the quality of the play, but it didn't draw him in enough for him to try to focus on the details. Nothing did anymore, it seemed.

An hour—or two, perhaps; he wasn't entirely sure—passed before the candles shone again and lit the main house. He rose from his box and waltzed his way down to the lobby. Patrons bustled about as they filed their way to the door, blocking his way and overshadowing his sight.

"Your Grace?" A feminine voice greeted him.

He turned to face her and found himself staring at Lady Olivia. "Hello there. Did you enjoy the play?"

She nodded, replying with, "It was an interesting story. I think the lead could have done a better job with his character, though. It must have been one of his first performances, for his voice wobbled quite a bit and his hands held a tremor throughout the entirety of the play. The plot had a few holes in it as well, but I enjoyed it on the whole."

He hummed in agreement, scanning his mind for what he could say next. A shame that he really hadn't paid much attention to the show, but other things held his mind captive. Fortunately, she opened her mouth to comment again.

"Lord Grimes was in the headline of the news a fortnight or so ago."

Or, perhaps not so fortunately. "He was, indeed. My valet secured a copy of it for me while I was stuck at home." If she'd read the article, he wouldn't need to explain further. The reporter had been thorough in his examination of the incident, including everything; Shep's father giving them permission to burn the barn; Bryant's second-degree burns keeping him abed for days; Brigham's heroic rescue.

Of course, if the reporter had been thorougher than thorough, he would have noted that the entire incident was a set up. But, naturally, only three people knew that, providing Brigham or Shepherd hadn't told anyone. Or, rather, providing that Brigham hadn't blabbed about the entire thing after feeling guilty.

It wouldn't surprise him if he had.

"How have you been? With your burns, I mean. Are they painful?" Her brows knit with a mixture of curiosity and worry that he hadn't seen on her before. It felt odd to see her concerned, even in spite of recent developments. In his subconscious, he mused, she was still the obnoxious girl he once knew her to be.

"I've been on the mend. Mother has finally let me outside the house, though I'm not allowed to dance until Lord Tristan's ball next week. The physician doesn't want me to accidentally damage any nerves. I believe that it shall be quite some time yet before I'm allowed to ride."

He quite missed his morning rides on Verse, fleeting across the grounds with the wind in his hair. He did his best thinking while on the back of his trusted steed, as it gave him the opportunity to think and focus on things other than the path he took. If he ever gave in to simply thinking at his desk, he was certain that the servants would think him insane for just sitting there, lost in thought.

"You should know that I've put in a request for you at the chapel. Our congregation is praying for your recovery."

Would this woman ever cease to surprise him? First at her creativity, then at her wit, and now at her compassion. She'd done well to prove that she was far more than the mask she'd put on. "Are you here alone, Miss Sparrow?"

A hint of a grin sparked across her face at the nickname. "Indeed so. I was supposed to be coming with my cousin, but her duties as a mother called her away. Given that I live a mere three streets over, I chose to walk the distance here."

She said it in such a tone that it prompted him to ask, "Might I see you home? It's rather late, after all, and the streets get rowdy after hours. Pedr should be bringing the carriage 'round within the next quarter hour or so." It *was* rather late at that. Drat. He'd planned to visit with Brigham right after the play, but that would have to wait until the morning. It would be a long night, then, if tonight was anything like the past few weeks. Perhaps dead eyes with dark rings abounding would help his case in convincing Brig of his repentance being real.

Olivia met his stormy eyes with curious ones. "That would be lovely," she concluded as she placed a hand on the crook of his arm. "I take it that Pedr is your coachman, then?"

Mother would have chided him, had she been here. His peers rarely referred to their servants by first names, and never to those that didn't know them. "Indeed. He's been on staff at Angarth for almost as long as I can remember. He started as a footman just after my father's passing." He remembered so very little of those days. The grief muddled everything else. "He and Lukas, our gardener, did well to protect Angarth against relatives looking to pound a few larks out of me, given that I was just a child at the time and therefore gullible to their manipulation." Was he over-sharing? He couldn't be certain. Though, it couldn't have mattered to his lady, for she took his arm and led him outside.

The chilly night air greeted his lungs with a friendly embrace, relieving him of the emotion that had coated his throat. "If I might ask, why do you wear a mask when you're in public? Why not show the *ton* who you really are?"

She raised an eyebrow. "And just who am I?"

He hummed in thought for a moment, not quite having the foresight to anticipate that she might ask him for an explanation. "You are... elegant, witty, and bright. Your smile is like the first ray of sunshine as dawn breaks across the horizon. You've shown me your heart, the depth of your emotions and thoughts. I don't really understand why you'd want to hide all of that under a layer of crass comments and frowns."

"Perhaps it's because I have a reason. I'm sure you're aware of my substantial dowry. My attitude keeps men away from it, until someone willing to look past it comes along. They are not quite romantics, unlike a certain duke I know." Her ghostly smile returned just as Pedr pulled the carriage up, greeting the pair.

"Pedr, there's been a bit of a change in our plans. We're dropping Lady Olivia off at Pattermar before returning home. The lady has no one to accompany her safely home, so I've volunteered our carriage." He extended a hand to help Olivia up the single step. Chills went down his spine as she took his offered hand and climbed into the cabin. They'd touched hands when dancing, of course, but never had it shocked his very core. He tried to keep the smile off his face as the shiver settled.

Pedr noticed, however, and caught a grin that spread widely. "How very kind of you, Your Grace." He disappeared up to the driver's seat before Bryant could toss a glare his way.

His servants were starting to notice the ideas that he shouldn't be having. And yet here he was, sitting across from Lady Olivia while his heart fluttered and his stomach churned with beautiful fears. "I suppose I ought to catch up on the latest gossip, given my complete absence. Has one of your friends set her cap for Lord Waldron?"

Both eyebrows raised, then. "Lord Waldron? The Earl?" Shock dissipated into her muddled, almost-angry expression of thought.

"I don't believe I've heard the name on any of their lips. Why do you ask?"

"With Lord Pwyll courting Lady Ruth Watton and Lord Grimes essentially disappearing from society, that leaves Lord Waldron to ask after."

A look that could either be smug or curious crossed her face. "Why not ask about yourself?"

Why not, indeed. Because he feared what he would hear. Because he was entirely certain that the woman he was meant to settle down with was sitting right in front of him, and the thought set him on edge the way *she* set him on edge. Because he knew deep down that he wasn't sure he could settle for the practicality of picking someone gentle as his bride. "Alright, then. Have you heard *my* name among your friends?"

"As a matter of fact, I have," she stated haughtily. "Would you like to know which of them was talking about you?"

He barely registered the carriage wheels coming to rest as he responded. "If you're willing to give me that information, certainly." Hope and fear mingled in his heart, buzzing his heartbeat in his ears and nearly drowning out her voice.

"It may or may not have been a certain viscount's daughter that you know extensively well." Just at that very moment, Pedr opened the carriage door. Her composure shifted entirely back into the emotionless, arrogant shadow of herself, intent on concealing her nature from the world.

Bryant jumped out and offered a hand to Olivia. Her fingers felt like fire and ice against his skin. "Shall I see you to the door?"

"That would be lovely, Your Grace." Her smile held none of the genuinity that he knew she possessed. Given that the only people present were himself and Pedr, he had to wonder why she took her act to such great lengths. Did her heart truly need such extreme conservation?

Upon reaching the doorstep, she stated, "I enjoyed our ride, however short it might have been. Perhaps I shall see you again soon." For a single moment, he saw her left cheek divot into a dimple, a reminder that she found him trustworthy with who she really was.

He brought her hand to his lips, giving it only a quick peck, afraid that a proper kiss would linger longer than it should. "Until then."

...

The moment he closed his bedroom door behind him, Bryant let out a rather heavy sigh. His head swam with thoughts and emotions, all of them relating to Olivia. It drained him rather quickly, leading him to splash water on his face and find a novel to read in order to calm his racing heart. The words on the page barely registered as *her* words jumped out at him. She'd talked about him to her friends. Was it possible that she felt the same butterflies that he did? That her own breath caught every time she noticed him from across the room?

If he pursued a courtship, would it end up the way he'd always imagined it would? With a charming, righteous wife at his side as they experienced life together, the Most High as their guide?

Lyz popped his head in from Bryant's private parlor. "Your Grace, might I be of assistance? You had quite the puzzled look on your face as you came in from the hall."

He thanked the Most High for such a valet as Lyz. The man never failed to be there when he was needed, asking exactly the right questions to help Bryant sort through the fog that cloaked his mind. On the days when his father's face was just a distant memory, he could manage to admit that Lyz had very much taken the role of father-figure to the struggling young duke. "Not unless you understand women of high society, Lyz."

The valet visibly shuddered. "That is a breed that I haven't been able to comprehend, Your Grace. Aside from Her Grace, of course, but I have Mabyn's help, there. Perhaps Lord Pwyll will be able to assist you once he returns from the country."

That's what he was afraid of. Even if Shepherd *did* return within the next few days, he wasn't all that certain that Shep would be willing to have such a conversation with him. Their friend group was still in shattered pieces, and that brought him too many fears to count. What if he wasn't able to patch things up with everyone? Would they hate him forever for the scheme that had gone too far?

One thing was certain. He needed to speak with Brigham first thing tomorrow. "Lyz, make sure that the carriage is ready to leave directly after breakfast. I've a very important call to make at Cargan Estate."

Chapter Fourteen: Brigham, Alone

January 11th

Brigham really didn't want to be here. The house choked him with its silence as the days passed. It'd been nearly two weeks since the incident and he missed his friends, missed going out, and missed enjoying the sunshine. They must still think him ungrateful, for the only people knocking at his door had been reporters asking for his side of the story—which he turned away as soon as he could—and peers who sang his praises for "rescuing" his friends. So, not wanting to cause any unnecessary gossip, he forced himself into a sort of isolation to avoid conflict with those whom he cared for most.

He hated every minute of it. Being alone stabbed him to his very soul. Before this, he thought that he liked being alone. He enjoyed being able to sneak away from the fuss and stress of events and parties into the quieter chapels or libraries. Books had once welcomed him with open arms. Now, he couldn't stomach a single word.

Hadn't Shep and Bry realized just how dangerous their plan had been? Even *if* their scheme had gone exactly as they expected it to, they were still in danger of being burned alive and Bryant had the scars to prove it.

They shouldn't have risked their lives for his reputation. He'd dealt with bullies for years before his debut. What made this any different that they'd felt the need to risk their very lives to make it stop?

Day and night had blurred together as he'd searched for an answer. He went over the situation with his mother, his sister, even his valet, yet he had no solid answer. It could have been the last straw in their tolerance of letting him handle it, but then that begged the question of 'why now' when it could have been better back when they were at Battenhold? What made this situation different?

The one thing he did have to be thankful for was his sister. She reported that many matrons had visited her in the past few weeks, to either gossip about his "heroic rescue" or to simply get to know her. She seemed happier than she ever had been, despite still having the occasional bruise on her face.

Another insufferable knock hit his front door. He'd directed Benneit to man the door at all sane hours to ensure that he didn't need to face any solicitors. When his own door felt a few thumps, his brows furrowed. Clearly this was not another reporter.

He crossed to the door and opened it, finding himself face to face with Bryant. "Your Grace," he greeted hesitantly. "What brings you by?"

"I thought we might be able to talk," he answered with the same amount of premonition. "I wanted to explain everything."

They could do that, couldn't they? He could allow a simple conversation. Bryant wouldn't be here, after all, if he despised him. "Of course. My parlor is just through that door. We can talk there." A great deal of dread stole through him as he walked the short distance between the hall and the parlor. What if this conversation proved that he ruined any chance of being close with his friends?

They were nearly brothers. That sort of separation would kill him. "What is it?"

"I'm sorry, Brig." Bryant was apologizing? Bryant, who even now had burn marks on his back, was apologizing. He thought that the distance kept between them meant that His Grace was stewing in anger or resentment, not that he'd felt guilty and wanted time to let things settle.

"What we did was dumb. You were right. We shouldn't have taken such drastic measures to accomplish what we did. There were other ways to go about it that we simply didn't consider. Shepherd had planned everything out and it sounded like a good idea." He took a deep breath before continuing. Brig noticed a tremor in his hands.

"At the end of the day, we did it because we wanted to help you. It's not fair that you should have to put up with teasing and bullying every time you show your face in public. We wanted to give you something better and this is what we came up with." He ran a hand through his hair. "I'm sorry, Brig. We should have run our idea past you. I assumed that you would object to any idea we came up with, though, and I couldn't stand to see them bully you for something that isn't your fault. Will you forgive me?"

His voice was shaky as he replied, "Of course, Bry. All is forgiven. But why—" he tried to steady his tone. "Why would you risk your life just for my reputation? I mean, yes, if things had gone exactly as you wanted, there was little risk, but it didn't. You almost *died*. Why would you do that for me?"

A soft smile lit up Bryant's face as he responded. "As Shep said, quoting the Most High, "no greater love has a man than this: than to lay down his life for his friends." You're worth it, Brig. We all think so."

Tears welled in his eyes as he hugged Bryant. They were friends, regardless of the despair that had clung to him, regardless of the thoughts that told him that they hated him. "Thank you, Bryant. Just— Never do this again, okay? Promise me that you'll never do this again."

"I promise. I won't go around burning Shep's barns down anymore. That kind of *backfired*, anyway," he said with a hint of a grin.

"Bryant, I swear, if you attempt that pun again, I am going to punch you."

Laughter burst forth from Bryant and in a moment he was gasping for air. It felt good to hear it after so many weeks. Relief flooded him and he managed a smile back. He missed this. Words simply could not express how deeply he missed this. As Bryant looked back at him, he noticed a subtle shift in the wells of his eyes; a burden lifted in them, the heaviness no longer there. He wasn't sure if Bry even noticed the change himself.

It stretched to the man's smile and he straightened himself out. "Alright, alright. No more terrible puns. Give me just a moment to make sure my gait is *stable*."

Even as he fought off the grin that tempted his mouth, he sent Bryant a glare. "Come on, Bry. Let's send for tea before heading out for a game of cricket."

...

With one thing off today's to-do list, Bryant's heart already felt lighter. Cricket with Brigham had mended the crack put between them. Another weight off his shoulders.

Hopefully, Shep had sent a telegram while he was out to inform him that he'd arrived back in Braxden. Then, the marquis would be able to patch up his side of things and their friend group was back together again. They needed a win after so many things going wrong.

He stared at the sky as he plodded along the street home from Cargan. With careful word choice, he'd insisted to Pedr that he walk the distance by himself. "I want to ensure that I can handle such a distance without assistance," he'd stated. It was enough to convince the coachman to go home without him.

Truthfully, he needed the time to sort through the new emotions that had taken hold in place of despair. Peace filled the holes in his heart, having spent much of his time alone reading and praying. His prayers had been heard and answered, if the conversation he'd just had was any indication. Uncertain joy accompanied it, fueled by the aftermath of the play.

Perhaps he was finding his own happily ever after, just like Shepherd.

A noise behind him cut his thoughts short. He glanced over his shoulder, noting that no one stood behind him. Still, he walked with unease, sparing looks every few minutes to not draw suspicion. There it was again-a sort of shuffling coming from a few feet behind him. He turned to face it, again seeing no one. His brow furrowed as he continued down the path, keeping the hatpin he'd borrowed from his mother in his grip. The small makeshift weapon was sharp enough to stab.

"How do you do, Your Grace?"

He shifted his expression into a frown. It didn't surprise him that Kegg would trail him, given the man's character, but it was curious all the same. "Lord Arioch. A pleasure to see you. Though, granted, I find it a bit odd that you felt the need to track me instead of speaking to me outright. The latter makes for far better communication, so I've heard." He kept a friendly, warm grin on his face to ease the tension rising through him.

"I saw you last night. You were chatting with a mutual acquaintance of ours."

Oh no. He was referring to Lady Olivia. He had to be, for there was no one else whom he stopped to talk to beyond a simple "hello" or "how do you do" to the occasional marquis or earl. This conversation was not about to go very well. A jealous man never made for safe, simple conversation. Shepherd knew that full well, and had relayed such stories in passing.

"I wasn't aware that you were at the play last night. If I had, you can be sure that I would have stopped to say hello." Best to deflect the daggers being sent his way instead of replying to his statement directly. "Back to my question, if you will; why are you following me?"

"The crowds don't make for good privacy, as I'm sure you can understand. I had to be certain that no one else would hear what I have to say."

He raised an eyebrow. "Just what is it that you want to tell me?"

"As I said before, you were speaking with a mutual acquaintance of ours."

Where was he going with this? "And if I was?"

"You also gave her a ride home."

"I did. She'd come alone—walked from her manor, mind you—and I didn't want her traveling on her own in the dark. There are people lurking around the streets, if you weren't aware." A silent jab to appease the growing urge to punch him in the face. He mentally shook his head, unable to deny that there wasn't just one jealous man in this conversation.

When had he let his guard down enough to actually catch feelings for the woman?

"I also know that as you dropped her off at home; you kissed her hand."

Was Kegg ever going to say more than the simple 'matter-of-fact' statements that he already knew? "As is customary for a duke to do when calling upon a young lady. It wasn't as though we were unsupervised. My driver was there to witness the whole thing. And you were as well, apparently." He threw his hands up in defeat, sighing loudly. Hopefully, it would deter him. "Lord Arioch, I don't quite understand what you are trying to accomplish by simply stating what I already know."

"Stay away from her," he said with that same 'matter-of-fact' tone, as if the earl could command a duke in any sort of legitimate way. "She will be *my* bride, Your Grace, and no one else's. Lady Olivia is mine. I know what you're playing at. You're too good to actually want her. How did you put it when we first met? "She is known for her loud, distasteful opinions," I believe you said. There's no chance that you've changed your mind after a mere month and a half.

"You must be after her dowry. What else would you want? You obviously dislike her, after your colorful depiction of her attitude. You couldn't love her. Not like I do, at least. You want the land and the money that she is set to inherit." He leaned forward in such a threatening way that Bryant couldn't help but back off. If he wasn't sure that Kegg had changed before, nothing could convince him otherwise now.

"I was being polite, that's all. Nothing more to it. After all, as you said, I couldn't entirely change my mind after just two months. I saw a woman in need and I offered what I could to help. You can understand that, can't you?"

He growled before taking a few steps back. "I suppose so. Keep your distance, Your Grace, or this might not go over well for you. I can't have you changing your mind about her."

Bryant could manage that. It wasn't a change of mind that he'd had—far from it. It was a change of heart.

...

By the time he'd returned to Angarth, Bryant's back ached in pain. Perhaps allowing Pedr to go on without him was a bad idea after all. At least then he wouldn't consciously face Kegg's glares whenever he tried to talk to Lady Olivia, and his back wouldn't feel the searing pain of a hundred suns.

Eryi was waiting for him the moment he entered, a telegram in hand. "Shepherd Whitley, Your Grace."

A smile lit Bryant's face as he took it. Despite feeling like bugs were crawling around in his stomach, today had gone pretty well. He glanced through the telegram to get the general idea before making his way to his study. If Shep had sent anything about what he'd been thinking, it was best to read it in a place where he could keep a firm head on his shoulders.

He'd always imagined his father sitting at this very desk, answering correspondence and doing paperwork before a long day checking on tenants and attending government meetings. Those sorts of thoughts draped him in warmth like an old blanket and a roaring fire. It made him feel safe and, reading this unexpected, potentially uncomfortable telegram, he needed to feel safe.

With trepidation, he took a deep breath and began to read the telegram. And, upon reading the last word, let it out in a relieved sigh. Shep had come to the same conclusion that he himself had and would be apologizing to Brigham as soon as he could. He also suggested that they should meet up to chat soon. That was good; he needed someone to talk about Kegg's antics with and Shepherd seemed the best option.

He quickly penned a reply, along with a time to meet the following day, before bolting from the study and back to the front door. "Eryi, take this to the telegraph office and have it sent to Shepherd's estate post haste. I want to be sure that he gets it before making other plans."

"I'll be off right away, Your Grace." Eryi doffed his hat and closed the heavy doors behind him.

He savored a moment of silence until a gentle voice called out, "You were out for quite a while, Bryant."

He turned to face his mother, who half-smiled as hope twinkled in her eyes. "Things went well. We played a game of cricket. I walked home. I didn't want Pedr to be out for so long when I didn't know when I'd be finished with things at Cargan. Brig accepted my apology for my foolishness. Shep is going over to talk it out with him as well." He winced as the adrenaline from Shep's telegram faded, leaving him with the flaming pain across his back.

"That's good. I was praying for you, you know."

She was, because she was his mother and she cared immensely for him and his friends. His mother, who kept the Most High in mind through everything she went through. He'd never met a single person outside of the clergy who kept to the steady, disciplined life of a Follower like his mother had, and he was eternally grateful for her dedication. "Thank you, Mother. I appreciate it greatly."

"Have there been any new developments that I should know about?"

He almost laughed at the timeliness of her question. "Over tea. Quite a bit has happened, I think, and I need to sit down with a nice cup of tea." Before he could say a word, one of the maids left the room to get a tray. "Your parlor?"

"Of course, dear." That brought a soft, thoughtful smile to her face. "That was always your favorite room when you were a boy, back before your father passed. He'd be working in his study and you always wanted to interrupt him, but you stopped your shenanigans whenever I brought you there. The large windows kept you captivated for hours as you watched the passersby."

They walked hand in hand as she continued, "Your father would read to you whenever he had a break, not wanting to tear you away from the room lest you attempt to barge into his study again." She gestured to the long settee against the large, central window. "Those were my favorite days. But now... now, I think we've a new beginning ahead of us." Her dark brown eyes bore into his, piercing right through to his soul. "Tell me about Lady Olivia."

"How did you know?"

A proper grin spread across her face. "Mothers always know these things, love. Do you plan to ask permission to court her?"

"I haven't decided yet. I'm still quite new to my feelings for her. I was convinced that she was harsh and demeaning, but she's shown me a part of who she really is. She's witty and kind when she wants to be."

"When she wants to be?"

His eyes dropped to a corner of the patterned fabric of the worn settee. "She feels the need to hide who she is from the world. When I dropped her off after the play, she claimed that society would leave her dowry alone if she bore brashness, protecting her until a man willing to look past it comes along."

Mother smiled gently, warmth like rays of light shining from her eyes. "And here you are."

Heat bloomed in Bryant's cheeks. "I'm not planning to court her just yet, Mother. I'm still undecided about this. She's not the type of bride I had in mind at the start of the season."

"Bryant, dearest, allow me to be your voice of reason. By all that I understand, you care for her deeply. Why not pursue the relationship? If it's not meant to be, you can end the courtship. If she really is as you say, she'd be a lovely wife for you."

His brow furrowed. "I thought you liked her. Why do you say "if she is" as though you didn't already believe the best in her? You always do, from what I've noticed." She'd even gone so far as to shush his snide comments about the lady.

"Lady Olivia isn't the only one who puts on a mask for society, dear. I have my own opinions about people, but I've learned to keep such things to myself. Good thing I did, for the moment she stepped into our home, she was nothing but kind." She pressed a kiss to Bryant's forehead. "Anything else I should know about?"

"I had a run in with Alden. He followed me for a few blocks on my way home before attempting conversation. While you might think it's good for me to pursue Lady Olivia, *he* didn't. He was at the play and noticed me chatting with the lady. He *also* saw her go into my carriage and followed us then. He was especially outraged when I kissed Olivia's hand—as is customary, mind you." He sighed, shaking his head. "He all but threatened me to stay away from her."

Mother stared in shock. "Truly? He seemed so kind at first. And to think I disregarded your words against him as harsh criticism." She sighed. "I'm sorry, Bryant. I should have listened."

"It's alright, Mother. You didn't know him enough to understand that he'd changed, and I didn't have proof enough to show for it. All that matters now is making sure that this doesn't end in tragedy."

"Is that likely to happen?"

He met her eyes with his weary ones. "I don't know."

Chapter Fifteen: Open Wounds

January 14th

A loud, desperate knock on the door to Angarth startled its inhabitants from their slumber. Eryi reached the door first, swinging it open and revealing a young woman, sopping wet from the rain. Her red eyes spoke to more than rain soaking her cheeks. "Who are you? What brings you to Angarth at such an hour?"

She let out a strangled sob as she tried to speak, taking several seconds to find her tongue. "I'm Marjorie, Marjorie Morris. His—His Grace offered a room if I needed it." Her startled, ghastly look said she needed it. "At least, that's what my brother told me. If I am mistaken, I can—"

"No, stay! Of course His Grace has a room for you," he replied as he gestured for her to come in. "Please, make yourself comfortable in the drawing room. I'll prepare some tea while one of the maids readies the room for you." He was hesitant to leave her side when she was in such a state, but she'd never have a warm bed if he didn't call for Cristyn or Margred to fix one up. "I'll only be gone a minute."

She nodded with a gaze that held distant even when it looked his way. What on Kestia had happened to the poor woman? With such sunken eyes and pale face, he almost feared he'd allowed a ghost into the house. It'd be best to not take long getting what he must.

The hallways seemed longer than usual as he made his way to the kitchen. Shadows hung to them in unnatural ways, ready to leap out and grab him any moment they wanted. He paid them no mind; this was too important for him to get hung up on faerie tales and ghost stories.

No fire lit the kitchen hearth, unfortunately. That would delay him a few minutes more. He ought to wake both Cristyn *and* Margred, then. Perhaps even Portencia or Tels besides, just to ensure that the girl did not go without companionship. Taking care to not wake Aneira, the cook and kitchen matron, he crept into the girls' room and nudged the three of them awake.

"His Grace requires your assistance in the kitchen." He whispered to each of them individually so as to not disturb the others. Each nodded her head before going out to the kitchen to await further instruction. He joined them a moment later. "Portencia, go to the drawing room. A Mrs. Marjorie Morris needs a woman's comfort." The girl boasted a confused look but nodded and swiftly left.

"Margred, fix up one of the rooms in Her Grace's wing for the lady. Take as much care as you would for a house guest, but be quick. We've a limited amount of time." At last, he turned to Cristyn. "Cristyn, my dear, could you help me get the fire started? I'd like to have tea for the lady."

"I shall have the hearth blazing within a minute," she replied as she grabbed the matches off the mantle. The flame caught on to the sticks easily enough, taking to the larger logs after a time. She set a pot overtop with water enough to make all of them tea after serving Marjorie.

"Eryi, if I may ask," she started, hesitation filling her voice, "why is she here at such an unnatural hour? Has something happened to her?"

His shoulders rose and fell as he took a deep breath, preparing his answer. "In a word: yes. While she hasn't confessed to me her situation (I didn't take the time to ask) she mentioned that His Grace invited her to a room here if she needed it. I wouldn't push the subject. She was in quite a state of distress when I met her at the door." He spared a glance at the pot, counting the seconds until it bubbled. "Will you bring it in?"

She huffed. "I dare say, Eryi, that you're trying to shrug all duty onto us girls; I ought to tell you to bring it to her yourself." Her annoyed expression hardly passed as a mask for her worry. "I'll be back in a minute." She took the tea tray, loaded it with sweets and cream and sugar—everything necessary for a good cup, she insisted—and swung the kitchen door open before disappearing.

Eryi's shoulders hung heavy. This whole situation was riddled with disorder. What woman of society showed up at a duke's house at three in the morning? What duke offered a woman not his relative a room 'if she needed it'? His eyes clouded as he sorted out the possibilities. His Grace was far too sensible and much too godly a man to make a mistress of any woman—and this woman's distress upon arriving was a solid sign that she wasn't there for that anyway—and he knew that she was no cousin, even a distant one. Why, then, had Mrs. Marjorie Morris shown up at the threshold?

He recalled her gaunt frame and hollow eyes. Could her husband be ill? Disabled? Involved in some sort of carriage accident? But then, why would His Grace offer a room in advance when she'd likely want to remain at her husband's bedside during his recovery?

Cristyn entered with an empty tray in her trembling hands. "I've never seen such a sight, Eryi. After Portencia shows her to her room for the night, I'm going to ask if she knows the cause of the lady's distress. I'll bully the answer out of her if I must." She shook her head and sighed. "I do wonder why she went here instead of to her brother's home. Though, I suppose Angarth is a fair bit closer than Lord Grimes's estate."

Lord Grimes. That was the missing connection. "What do you suppose is the matter?"

"If I had to guess, trouble at home. Seems to be common among ladies of her standing. You do know her story, don't you?" She tilted her head in a way that would have been adorable if the context was not so disheartening.

He didn't, to what would be the surprise of every woman on the estate. He'd never been a gossiper—unless, of course, the gossip involved treason, spies, and murder, but that didn't count. Not here. "I'm afraid not. Don't suppose you could tell me, Goldie?" Her nickname, for her brilliant golden hair.

"I don't know why I asked," she mumbled. "She was engaged to an earl during the war. Around that time, her father was thrown into the sanatorium for speaking out against the king. Her fiancé broke off the engagement. Hardly anyone cared to talk to her. She became isolated entirely, excepting one particularly wealthy merchant who thought that their marriage would be to his benefit. She accepted his proposal, if only in her grief. They've been living unhappily ever after since." Her eyes spoke of quiet disbelief. They spoke tales of her wrath at the cads who dared treat a woman with such disrespect; anger that would be directed at him in a moment's notice if he didn't respond the way she anticipated.

"Is he the violent type?"

That caught her attention and pulled the anger forward as her eyes lit with fury. "If he is, I'll kill him myself. What kind of *monster* would hurt such a lovely girl?" She was ranting now, pacing the room in quiet, seething rage. Pausing her tirade, she whirled on her heels to face him, pointed a finger and hissed, "Eryi, I pray you're wrong about this," before continuing on.

He could fill in the rest on his own. He knew by her tone, by the very way one eyebrow stood on edge to the other, that she feared he was right. The churning in his stomach didn't attest only to nerves either. Something was terribly wrong. Once they got proof enough, the police must be called. No lady should endure such abuse. "Care for some tea, Goldie? It'll settle your nerves."

She paused mid-sentence, pivoting to stare into his eyes. He could get lost in those eyes if she ever stood still long enough to give him the chance. Deep as the sea, bright as a summer's day. "I don't know that I can stomach tea right now, thank you."

He shrugged and poured a cup for himself. "I don't suppose getting worked up is going to help anything." With a solemn grin, he added, "I hope you know I'm saying that to myself as well. Don't think for a single minute that I'd sooner spend my days tormenting you than assisting the inconsolable young woman in our drawing room."

Her silence was more than enough of a reply for him. "Goldie, she's safe now. I doubt whomever she's running from suspects that she's at Angarth. If they do and they show up here, I'll fight them off."

That, of all things, brought a smile to her lips. "You? Really. Eryi, you screamed like a child at the sight of a snake in the cupboard last summer. You expect yourself to be able to stand up to a man twice your strength without backing out at the first punch?"

Her amusement would be the death of him, he was sure. Only at his pain did she smile with those mocking eyes and all too beautiful lips. "This is different, Goldie."

She hummed in agreement. "I suppose it is."

The fire crackled as the only sound between their labored breaths. No matter any jokes or memories shared between them, the stress of their circumstances weighed heavy on the air. Marjorie Morris was in some kind of serious trouble and they needed to help her in whatever way they could.

Footsteps creaked overhead. Good. Portencia and Margred would return soon. He might ask one of them to stay in the girl's room overnight just to be sure no one tried to break in. He had half a mind to do it himself if it wouldn't scare the woman half out of her wits. Not in her room, then. Just outside the door.

"I know what you're thinking." Cristyn's angelic voice interrupted. "You should heed some of your own words and recognize that she is safe here at Angarth. No one would dare harm her here. Not with Lukas waking in the next hour or two."

Lukas, their gardener, was nearly nocturnal, preferring to wake well before dawn and sleep just as the last of the day's light dwindled away from the world. Despite his rather domestic career not requiring much physical labor beyond moving the occasional plant, the man had enough muscle for the both of them.

Alright then. He'd guard the door until Lukas could. That should satisfy the rolling in his stomach.

"Eryi, you deserve to rest just as much as the rest of us." He expected her to continue on about making his way to the men's quarters once he finished his tea, but she instead said, "You should ask His Grace to allow you the day off once he wakes. Being awakened in the middle of the night for such a stressful situation can damage your health." She huffed at his eye-roll. "You'd better get on with it, then. Hurry up to her room before someone breaks in." A faint blush accompanied her look of disdain as she finished with, "Goodnight, my dearest."

He spared a smile for her before downing the last of his tea. "I'll see you in the morning, Goldie." His arms enveloped her in an embrace as his eyes fixed on the golden firelight. "Sweet dreams, my beloved." He pressed a kiss to the top of her head and walked to the door, looking back into the room at his beautiful lady as she tended the firelogs.

Taking care to avoid the squeaky steps, he dashed up to the second floor and crossed to the women's wing. Soft sobs echoed from one of the rooms. He sat just outside, leaning against the door to support his back. If anyone wanted to enter, they'd have to get through him.

What was precious had to be protected.

...

A nudge and a kick awoke Eryi in a blur. He rubbed his eyes, fully aware of the dim hallway not yet lit with blessed sunlight. The kick hadn't been sharp; just hard enough to wake him. A gruff voice attached itself to syllables that resembled his name. His bleary eyes caught sight of a cotton shirt and speckled beard. Lukas.

"Lukas, I can watch over the lady until His Grace is able to handle the situation. I'm perfectly—" he yawned—"perfectly comfortable where I am. Never mind my stiff legs and achy back. Cristyn has promised to speak with His Grace about allowing me a day off for handling this." Not Cristyn's exact words, but she had suggested it. "Go on to your gardening."

His leg wobbled in reverb to another kick. "His Grace insisted that I take your place."

"His Grace is awake, then?"

"Yes, and he's specifically asking for you in his sitting room. I suggest you hurry. Wouldn't want to make His Grace wait."

That was all that needed to be said for him to be on his feet. "Thank you for informing me, Lukas. I'll be off, then." He bounded down the hallway, shaking the night's drearies from his legs and shoulders. Something must have happened for His Grace to be up so early.

Swiftly, he rapped his knuckles across the door of His Grace's room. A quiet 'come in' pulled him past the doorway. "Your Grace, you asked for me?"

Bryant stood intimidatingly beside his valet. "Yes. Margred thought to inform Lyz of Lady Morris's presence here. What exactly happened last night?"

"I don't know much, Your Grace. She simply showed up at our doorstep and said you'd offered her a room. I directed her to the drawing room and instructed some of the maids to see to her needs. Any conversation would have been between them, not me."

If that was the truth—which it was; there was hardly a reason to lie—why did His Grace's expression fill with even more torment? "Send a telegram, if you will, to Lord Grimes. He'll want to know that his sister is here."

"Of course, Your Grace." He stayed for only a moment, just long enough to ask, "Will I be needed afterwards?"

The duke shook his head. "No. Take the day off, please. Cristyn's attested to your weariness in dealing with this. You have my thanks, Eryi. Who knows what could have happened if you hadn't heard her knock and allowed her in?"

He didn't want to imagine. Surely whomever—or whatever—she fled from would have found her in the rain and taken her back. That was unlikely to end well for the lady. A shudder stole through him as he thought of the possibilities of what might await the woman at home. "I'll have the telegram out posthaste, Your Grace."

...

If there was one thing Duchess Eloise Wooldridge disliked, it was dissonance in her own home. Today had her puzzled. Just last night, everything had been calm. No one acted out of the ordinary or kept themselves to any standard lower than usual. Today, however, the servants buzzed about with a worry to them and had some uncontrollable urge to whisper and glance about.

It started with Mabyn, of all people. While setting out a walking dress for the morning, she'd been startled by a bug flying into the window. Mabyn wasn't scared of bugs.

Then it had been Portencia, who nearly dropped the breakfast tray when taking it back to the kitchen.

Now, it was Cristyn, who was even now mumbling and whispering to herself all sorts of phrases as she brushed the tangles out of the duchess's coiffure.

She set a hand on the girl's arm to halt her movement. "Cristyn, what is going on within the walls of my manor? I know something is amiss. I can see it written across everyone's faces but my own. Has something happened that I need to be aware of?"

The girl froze. Set the brush down. Pulled a strand of loose hair behind her ear. "I assumed His Grace had told you after he awoke. I suppose, then, that he hasn't."

"No, he hasn't; that wasn't the question. What is going on that I don't know about?"

She spared a glance to the doors, almost searching for hidden eyes and ears. "Lady Marjorie Morris, the sister of Baron Grimes is, here. She arrived in the middle of the night asking for a room."

It'd happened, then. What the dowager had feared finally came to pass. "I see. What room is she staying in?"

"Three doors down on the left, m'lady, though she's currently taking her tea with His Grace in the drawing room downstairs.

Eryi has taken to commanding all of us to ensure that there's someone with her at all times."

"Good. It wouldn't do for her to be alone." Her next question came with hesitation, unsure if she really wanted to find out the truth of the matter here or from the girl herself. Best to go in with all the cards in her hand, she determined. "How much does Eryi know of her situation?"

"Right little, m'lady. She hasn't told him anything that I'm aware of, and she hasn't breathed a word of it to any of us maids. All he knows is that she showed up at the door last night, looking more distraught than Aneira when something new she's made turned out wrong, and said His Grace had offered her a room." She picked up the brush again and finished detangling the pale locks. "All done," she whispered with trembling hands.

What caused her maid's hands to tremble? Not fear of *her*, for sure and certain. She did well to make sure that her iron fist of rules was softened with grace and generosity in her dealings with them. "Cristyn, what is the matter?"

She didn't speak right away, pacing a few steps and clinging to the brush with white knuckles. When at last she did respond, it was through a series of syllables that blurred together, stringing her words in a nearly-incoherent statement. "I'm worried that whoever the lady is running from has ears everywhere and is spying on us to find the perfect opportunity to capture the lady."

That certainly couldn't happen with Lukas out front working on the roses or his lowers working on the rest of the grounds. Not with Eryi and Lyz ever about the property. Not when Bryant himself sat with Marjorie to ensure her safety. All the same, a familiar stab of worry captured her own stomach. "She's safe here, Cristyn. No one would dare hurt her here." A truth she prayed would stay true. Angarth was a fortress of a manor, for sure and certain, but it wasn't invincible, even if her own son would sooner take a bullet than allow the lady to be put in harm's way.

"I pray you are right, m'lady." She took a step back. "I believe I should be going. Aneira likely needs help in the kitchen." Then she was gone, only the brush back on the counter in her place.

She prayed a silent prayer for Marjorie as she dressed in her day gown. No sense in calling for Mabyn when she was perfectly capable and when time was ever so important. She reached for a shawl to battle the cold January afternoon and made her way down to the drawing room.

Quiet, gentle laughter filled her ears as she approached—both feminine and masculine. Bryant seemed to make good company for the lady. Perhaps she should keep her time elsewhere and not ruin the moment with her all too necessary questions. Questions could always be had later.

But, alas, Marjorie's eyes met her own and she beckoned the duchess in. She stepped into the room and greeted them. "Welcome to Angarth, Marjorie. Though, I daresay you've already met quite the warm reception."

She responded with a warm smile. "Indeed. The people on your staff are incredibly nice. It's a lovely change from what I'm used to."

A distinct yellow-purple bruise showed on her left cheek. On her right, a line of reddish skin showed proof to a cut that hadn't burst all the way through. Her eyes, though now sparkling, held a darkness that she hadn't noticed before. "It's so kind of you to allow me a room in this difficult time. I appreciate it ever so much."

'Difficult time'. She said that as though this were something simple—like being unable to chat with a friend who was on holiday or her favorite maid getting married and moving on from the household. Not as though her skin bore proof of a marriage that should have never been. Not like her very soul spoke to the trauma and heartache she'd endured.

"It's our greatest pleasure, Marjorie. You are always welcome at Angarth." She took her seat beside the lady.

Not a moment passed before Eryi appeared in the doorway. "Your Grace!" Both duke and duchess turned to face him. He passed a sheepish grin before turning to Bryant. "*His* Grace," he clarified, "Lord Grimes is here. You wished to speak with him."

"Ah, yes. Thank you, Eryi." He turned to Marjorie. "Farewell, my lady. I shall return with your brother within the hour."

"Until then," she said with a ghost of a smile. A smile that held so much pain for a girl not even thirty.

Chapter Sixteen: Closure

Brigham and Bryant strolled into his office quickly, eyes darting to every window and door in search of eavesdroppers. "Lyz, could you perhaps wait belowstairs for the constable?" He hated shoving Lyz from his very room of duty, but the matter was far too private at this time for ears not their own. As much as he trusted his staff, there could be some with alliances unknown.

"Of course, Your Grace." He left in post haste, disappearing down the hallway.

"Bryant, why is my sister here?" Brigham's voice almost held insinuation, though he couldn't determine its aim.

"She panicked. Brig, he almost killed her."

All tone of accusation fell. "What?"

"I don't know all the details. I didn't want to push. But she has so many scratches, and bruises besides. I fear she could have died had she not run here."

The accusation replaced itself with rage; this time clearly aimed at Mr. Morris. "Has the constable been called?"

"Not yet. I didn't want to overstep my place in all this. I figured you'd want to know what happened before making any sort of decisions." Though, now that he was hearing the words himself, the constable should have been called hours ago. Brig having more authority over the situation or not, that man needed to be arrested for what he'd done.

Brig, however, only nodded in agreement. "Thank you, Bry—for all of this. I know I wanted to handle it myself, but she might not be here if it weren't for you stepping in. I am indebted to you."

"I'll hear none of that, Brig, and you know it. Let's get this settled before it gets worse." He called for Eryi. "I know I gave you the day off, but this is urgent. A telegram to the constable post haste."

Eryi cracked a shy grin. "I've already sent it, Your Grace."

His brow furrowed. "You did?"

The lad nodded. "I figured you'd call for him by the end of your visit with the baron so I sent one out. Even if you didn't call for him, his presence is clearly necessary here."

The words his mother would have for Eryi if she knew. All the same, he was grateful. The sooner Wynn arrived, the better. They hadn't much time to spare now that the day had risen in full. Morris could be asking around at any time for his missing wife and it seemed unlikely that he'd take a simple 'she's not here' for an answer. Their ability to hide her presence here diminished with every minute that passed.

"Thank you, Eryi. That is all." He turned back to Brig. "What do you suppose we do while we wait?"

"I'd like to have tea, if I may. No need to bother the servants with making it, though; I know how to make it myself. Just lead the way. As Cook has taught me, kitchen conversations are the best kind."

...

"Marjorie, dear, could you explain what happened? The constable will be here soon and he needs to know." She wrapped gentle arms around the girl once she was sure that such an action wouldn't frighten her. "It's alright, dear. You're safe here."

The girl nodded slowly and let out a long breath. "He was out with his friends—at a race or some such thing—and he'd been drinking. When he got home, the meal was ready so we ate. He didn't like what Chef made for one reason or another and decided in his drunken stupor to break apart his chair by slamming it against the wall. When that wasn't enough, he threw the pieces at me like daggers." She lifted her sleeve to reveal a cut that used to hold a large splinter. "His aim was terrible, but he still managed to land a few pieces."

She shuddered as she continued. "He decided that wasn't quite enough either and grabbed me by the throat, thinking to choke me to death. That's when our maid, Lizbet, came in. She managed to drag him back enough for me to get free. We ran out together. She disappeared somewhere between there and here, presumably going to her family. I doubt she'll be back, not that I blame her. I don't know if I want to go back." Then the tears started streaming and her tone became filled with pain and anger instead of melancholic numbness.

"He's broken our marriage vows. I knew he never loved me, but he didn't have to. Hardly a love match is found in society anyway. But this—" her sobs cut her off as she leaned into Eloise's comforting arms. "What am I to make of this? What do I do now?"

"You can stay here with us for as long as you need to, dear. He's crossed a line and will pay for his actions, rest assured. There's no need to worry about him anymore. Bryant's called for the constable. You are safe."

Instead of replying, she only nodded with half-heartedness. It would take quite a while before the girl stopped looking over her shoulder in fear and years longer before she could let herself put her guard down enough to heal from the betrayal that gripped her so deeply. How tragic that this girl who had already endured so much heartache needed to deal with a broken marriage on top of it all. She was just thankful that Marjorie had found the courage to run when she had. Who knows what could have happened if she stayed at home?

A knock echoed from the door. "Come in," Eloise called. Bryant stepped inside.

"Brig is wondering if he could speak with his sister in private," he explained as Brigham entered the room.

"Of course." She stood and offered her seat to the baron before joining Bryant out in the hallway. "I am so thankful for you, my son."

"Why is that, Mother?"

"Because if it weren't for you, she might not be here." She walked down the hallway, searching for a servant to catch. "Portencia, please inform Aneira that I'd like her to make orange cake for our dessert tonight."

Bryant's cheeks flushed. "Mother, you don't need to have Aneira make my favorite dessert."

"Why not? You're a right hero, Bryant Fintan, and we should celebrate."

"I wasn't doing it to be a hero. I didn't even think it would help. I was overstepping my bounds *again* and it just happened to turn out well. That's all." He sighed, turning away from her to look out the window. "I'm no hero."

Eloise paused for a long minute. Bryant never had been one to take attention, despite his heritage all but foistering it upon him from the moment he was born. She met him at the window and pivoted his shoulders so that he faced the now-distant drawing room. "They would think otherwise." She watched as his gaze melted from the hardness of self-criticism into the warmth of understanding.

"I suppose they would," he said shortly, a hint of a smile on his face. He'd done the right thing, whether society would accept it or not.

A moment later, the front door sounded off. Eryi quietly greeted the lawman standing outside. "She's in the drawing room. Please, follow me." He led the constable past the duke and duchess and to the drawing room.

"Shall we see how this story ends, my son?"

"Indeed." Her son offered his arm and led her to the group, taking their seats across from the baron and his sister.

The constable took his time in both asking questions and writing down their answers. He examined the nasty cut on her arm and the bruises that dotted her neck, as well as matching her story with Eryi's tale of her arrival.

Brigham looked entirely uncomfortable during the ordeal. Understandable, given that his sister was recounting again the horrors that she'd endured at the hands of her husband. His face was a revolving door of anger, fear, and dismay as Marjorie answered the questions without so much as a tear to attest to her sorrow.

How sad it was that the horrors barely phased her anymore. She thanked the Most High that, somewhere along the line, the poor girl realized that her husband didn't intend to leave it at a simple bruise here or there but that he was trying to kill her.

A shiver ran down her spine as she heard the words for the second time. The very idea that such things *had* to be taken this far to be looked into wasn't fair. Wives ought to be respected for their positions, not seen as another piece of property. *Hardly a love match is found in society*, Marjorie had stated. It was true; men preferred to look at dowries and ladies at titles rather than at the people behind them. Who would respect someone they saw only as a means to an end?

Not Mr. Morris. That much had become clear.

The constable rose from his seat as he declared, "Thank you all for your time. If you'll just give me the address of your maid, Lady Morris, I shall confirm with her what transpired last night and get word to the court justice." He wrote down the address that Marjorie gave him and gave his thanks. "I'll be in contact. Good day, Lady Morris, Lord Grimes. Your Grace and Your Grace." He doffed his cap to them before walking out.

Bryant broke the silence first. "What do we do now?"

"We all tidy up for a nice parlor game before supper," Eloise responded. A parlor game would surely break the tension and ease Marjorie into her temporary home. Perhaps they'd invite the servants—those who could be spared from dinner preparations—to ensure that the lady would feel safe, knowing who it was that waltzed the halls of Angarth. "Eryi, if you would gather some of your fellows and meet us in the parlor, that would be most appreciated."

Eryi was off in a second, barely allowing her to finish her sentence before he'd risen, uttering a short "Of course, Your Grace" as he left.

"Thank you so much for all of this. You have no idea how thankful I am," Brigham stated. "I only wish that I'd stepped in sooner. Perhaps then this situation could have been stopped well before it came to this." The steely glint in his eyes spoke of the sentiments pouring into his head.

She couldn't stand for that; she had to intervene before the thoughts took over the truth. "It's our pleasure, Brigham. Thank *you* for letting us know of her situation so we could extend the invitation." He lifted his gaze to meet her own, shock writing itself into the lines of his face. "A valiant effort all around, wouldn't you say?" She forced a smile that she hoped said *you did what you could.*

To have Marjorie stay with him would have left her exposed. Mr. Morris would no doubt invade Cargan without a second thought, but Angarth? The fortress of a manor was guarded by a team of servants that were well versed in fighting off thieves before their time on staff. Getting past Lukas would be a feat in and of itself, but if he met the others, they'd have him locked in a room long before the constable showed up to take him away. It was better for her to reside here, where she was safer.

Brigham did what he could and it was enough.

...

Lord Grimes was no fool; he knew exactly what Her Grace's smile meant, but he couldn't shake the pang of guilt that overwhelmed him. He stood and followed as they made their way to the parlor for whatever game Her Grace had in mind, but the movement didn't cause his gut to settle. No matter what Her Grace claimed, he hadn't done enough. He didn't attempt to remove his sister from her near-fatal marriage, nor did he offer a place for her to stay. He even told Bryant to stay out of it and let him handle it.

His friend had been right, as ever. He'd handled it by *not* handling it and his sister almost died because of his inaction. He mentally cursed and took a seat beside Marjorie as Her Grace explained the game. The words were almost incomprehensible to him as his own thoughts took over. He'd failed as a brother. The one thing—the *only* thing—his father asked him to do in that final letter was to take care of Marjorie and he'd utterly failed to do so.

Someone nudged him, bringing his focus back to the game. "Brig, you've got to stand up for this game." Bryant extended a hand to pull him up before whispering in his ear, "Your sister is safe and that's all that matters. Let yourself relax a little, hm?"

He meant well; Brigham knew he did. And yet, he was wrong. So much more mattered. All the same, he stood with the others and allowed Eryi to pose them in their game of 'The Sculptor'. A harmless parlor game often meant for relatives at a holiday party, but it would serve its purpose in breaking the tension all the same—for Marjorie, at least.

If only there were some way that he could make up what he lacked. Perhaps some other event would show itself as needing his assistance. He'd prove that he was responsible, not just to his father, but to his peers who teased him mercilessly. He could prove to the world that the Roberts family was one of diligence and kind-heartedness and ought to be respected.

The room around him fell quiet as he noticed that everyone was staring at him. "What is it?"

"You're the last one standing, Brig. You've won this round and are the new sculptor," Bryant informed him as he stood back up. "But, I can understand if you'd prefer one of us take up the role. Library's open if you want to get away."

He shook his head. "I'll stay. I feel I should be here right now." He didn't add the "physically, not mentally" but knew he didn't need to for Bryant to understand. This situation had clung to him and refused to give him up.

What if he couldn't earn back his worth? What if an opportunity never came to make up for what he'd forsaken? Would his father forever be disappointed in him?

Word of the divorce—providing that the constable took it to that step—was unlikely to reach the sanatorium in which the former Baron Grimes lived. He'd never know that Brigham had failed him in so great a way. It shouldn't matter then, but it did. Because that was his father. Because his mistake almost cost his sister her life. When- *if* his father was released from the prison of an institution, he'd see Brigham in all of his shortcomings and he'd understand that his son had let him down.

Would he, in turn, think himself a terrible father for not being there for them? Brigham couldn't allow that. The only reason the elder Roberts was *in* the sanatorium was because the king thought him daft for disagreeing with him. A far better fate than execution but harsh all the same. His father was only trying to protect the lives of those across the sea. The king hadn't understood such compassion and they all paid the price for it.

Brigham sighed as he finished adjusting his last statue (Marjorie, coincidentally) who immediately laughed at the awkward position she was in. She, at least, volunteered to play the game straight on. According to Eryi, some of the maids were more hesitant. Cristyn, in particular, though he couldn't fathom why. She seemed to be Eryi's lady friend, of sorts. He'd assumed that meant she'd be as outgoing and wild as her beau of a footman.

Why was he so dreadfully terrible at judging people's character?

He turned back to the remaining statues: Bryant, Eryi, and Mabyn. He wasn't surprised at the two servants easily being able to school their expressions. Their jobs all but depended on it. Bryant, however, shocked him. The boy had always laid his heart out on his sleeve; he was even more transparent about his feelings than Shepherd.

Carefully, he turned and twisted Bryant's arms and torso to form somewhat of a cupid shooting an arrow at Eryi. Humorous, or so he thought, given that His Grace mentioned frequently the blooming romance between Eryi and Cristyn. Bryant must have thought so too, for he soon joined his mother in the 'we laughed' corner.

Eryi was much harder to crack. His usual grin fixed flat to his face, void of other humor. Brig took a moment to study him before moving his limbs to resemble a ballerina.

At that very moment, Cristyn stepped in to call them for dinner. She took one look at Eryi and couldn't hide the laughter that spluttered forth. In a moment of weakness, he caught her laugh and lost his balance, tumbling to the floor.

Mabyn cracked a grin as she declared, "I've won, then."

"Your Grace, the meal is ready," Cristyn informed as she took Eryi's arm and pulled him up. "Come on then, love," she mumbled to him as they exited the room with the other servants. Marjorie took Her Grace's hand and they followed suit, leaving Bryant and Brigham alone.

"Brigham—"

"I know what you're going to say, Bry, and I can't. She could have died if you hadn't stepped in—probably *would have* if she hadn't had the thought to run to Angarth instead of Cargan, and then her husband would have been able to find her easily and she'd be right back in his conniving hands. If it weren't for *you*, she wouldn't be here. But it should have been me." He ignored the raise in Bryant's eyebrows as he continued. "I should have stepped in sooner. She needed me, Bry, and I did *nothing*."

"You told me what you feared. That led me to making the offer. I may have been the one to step in, but I never would have if you hadn't been honest with me. When Mother says this was a team effort, it was, through and through. You're not as much of a failure as you think."

He shook his head as he stepped out of the room, following the smell of food to the dining room. "I wish I could believe you."

Chapter Seventeen: Under The Cover Of Night

January 17th

The morning dawned with a knock at the door- this one, bright and cheery. Brigham strode into the manor with a beaming—albeit tired—smile. Bryant was at his side in a moment to welcome him.

"What brings you by?" He was almost giddy seeing Brigham so pleased, and could guess quite accurately the cause for his delight.

"Morris has been arrested. I'm here to bring Marjorie to Cargan." Tears of the truest joy brimmed in his eyes. "She's safe, Bry. My sister is safe and she's coming home." He laughed, and it was the deepest, most heartfelt laugh Bryant had ever heard.

Within the span of an hour, Marjorie's few belongings had been packed up, along with several gifts from Her Grace, and the siblings were on their way home together. Whatever the rest of the day brought, Bryant felt lighter than he had in a long, long time.

...

The door to Kegg's study shook as Jetlis barged in. He spoke steadily, though his body language suggested trouble. "Morris has been arrested." He clenched his jaw as he closed the door.

"That blasted idiot," Kegg muttered. "He had a direct order to guard his anger, to keep his threats empty." He hated to think of the ramifications of this. "The attorney general will have someone look into this, not to mention the law. We must be on the defensive, covering up anything we can." He let out a heavy sigh and leaned back in his swivel chair. This was far from simple. Ledgers must be rewritten, meetings done in complete secrecy. He could only make calls to houses with eligible young women to avoid suspicion himself, and to give purpose to his visit.

"What would you have me do first?"

His head snapped back up. That was so like Jetlis; quiet, obedient. "Disguise yourself as my servant. We can't have you running back and forth between contacts without an official uniform."

He grunted, eyebrows raised. "Do you believe that wise? It would tie my name to yours without doubt if I am caught."

"Exactly. That is your cover. You can easily say that you are on errand if you are caught speaking with the merchants. I can supply a list for you to take if they press further. We will all be safe." He stood and rushed to the door. "Come. We don't have time to lose."

...

Bryant stood on the front steps of Pattermar Manor, poised to knock on the mahogany door. It opened abruptly and he lost his balance. He scrambled to grab the door frame, catching himself at the last second. Straightening himself out and brushing the dust off his suit, he greeted, "Good day. I'm here to call upon Lady Seylor, if she'll see me." He handed the man his calling card, catching the man's unimpressed look.

The butler mulled over the card before gesturing into the house. "Very good. If Your Grace will follow me to the drawing room where the lady is waiting, I shall have you introduced." The grim elder took his coat and led him down a series of hallways. "His Grace, the Duke of Whittaker."

One look at Lady Olivia sent off alarms in his head. She fidgeted with her embroidery as she set it aside. Her hands, now free of the needle, shook fiercely. "Your Grace." Her eyes went immediately to his empty hands. He groaned inwardly. In the hastiness of his trip, he'd forgotten the customary gift of flowers.

Mother had assured him that calling on a lady wouldn't be daunting. The lady herself wasn't, for sure and certain, but the situation he was calling upon certainly was. The maid glaring at him from the corner was no help.

"Please forgive me, my lady, for the lack of a bouquet. I didn't want to bring flowers and risk giving you a variety you disliked." Had it been just the two of them, he would have admitted his err of memory. Standing in this parlor, with her maid's eyes not leaving his person, he suddenly felt the need to do what he could to impress them both, regardless of the truth.

She took in a deep breath, eyes narrowed. "All is forgiven, Your Grace." If her tone was anything to go by, the rest of his call would not go well. "You brought your card so we know who you are, at least," she retorted. "What is the reason for your visit, Your Grace?" Her eyelashes batted slowly. Under normal circumstances, that was meant to be flirtatious. The rest of her expression declared it was anything but.

"I meant to see if you were well, my lady." He eyed the maid in the corner, unsure if he was able to speak freely.

Her facade cracked, if only the slightest bit. The cattiness she displayed regularly swapped with genuine wonder for a single second. "How kind of you. I am well. Thank you for your visit." He half expected her to shoo him out of the room with how brief her sentences were. When his feet refused to move, she narrowed her eyes. "Was there anything else, Your Grace?"

He sucked in a breath as he prepared his question. "Would the lady care to accompany me on a walk?"

Olivia cast a glance at her maid. She glared in disapproval, but Olivia seemed to take that as assurance. "Yes, I should think so." She rose from the settee, gesturing for the maid to follow. Bryant offered her his elbow.

As they stepped outside, Olivia's facade fell completely. The tightly strung girl melted away into the wild, emotional woman that begged to be noticed. "I apologize for my cattiness. The servants expect me to act like my mother. You cannot imagine how heavy that is."

He faced her and replied, "I can. I'm not a duke because I'm the son of a prince, after all."

Her lips parted in a gasp of embarrassment. "I apologize again, Your Grace. I'd forgotten that the title wasn't yours from birth."

"'Tis alright. I forgot to bring you flowers, after all. Now we're even." He dared to breathe a smile in the hopes of cheering the gloom.

"I don't mind that you forgot a bouquet, just so you're aware," she responded warily. "There's no need to dwell on it. I'm not so shallow to be worried about that just now. You may want to remedy that, for the press's sake, however."

He grinned. "I believe I'll hasten to do just that. Shall we go to Outrey Park? Various vendors have set up market booths with hothouse flowers. You can have your pick of the best flora Braxden has to offer."

Olivia smiled—a win that made his heart soar in victory. "I'll take you up on that."

The pair strode towards the entrance to the park with linked arms. To any passersby, they looked like a happy courting couple on a simple stroll. Perhaps it could have been, if Bryant's heart didn't pound so as he rehearsed the questions he wanted to ask. The witty banter between them was fun, but it distracted from the real issue he came to address. Still, he waited patiently for her to select her flowers, not desiring to ask at the wrong moment.

Before long, they noticed the tents and tables of marketmen selling flowers on anything they could bring—benches, tables, tablecloths, wagons, etc. The line stood impressively at half a mile long, with vendors on both sides calling out to customers.

He followed behind Olivia as she approached several sellers, picking out a flower or two (which Bryant paid for) before moving on to the next table.

In a hushed voice, the lady picked up conversation again. "Are you actually here to check up on me? Were you truly so concerned for my welfare?" Her voice hung with a heaviness that wrought his heart.

"Lady Olivia, if I may be candid, I lost my father as well. I remember how empty our home felt, how cold and painful living there was; I hoped to provide a distraction, however brief." He attempted the voice that Shepherd always used when he wanted to squeeze information out of someone.

"You're calling me a liar, then."

"It would seem so." He kept a straight gaze, meeting her green eyes with the kind of confidence he'd seen so many times in his life.

Her eyes flashed with insecurity as she took a step back and whispered. "Not here. Not where everyone can see us." She raised her voice enough to where those closest would be able to hear her clearly. "Care for a promenade through the gardens of Pattermar? I can drop off this lovely bouquet on our way there."

He had to give her points for acting. Not a trace of her pain shone through as she spoke. "You've a shrub display throughout the cooler months, do you not? I'd greatly enjoy seeing it." If he were lucky, the press would take notice of their outing and write an article about it in the gossip column. If providence would have it his way, Alden Kegg would read about it in the papers tomorrow and decide to leave Olivia alone.

Of course, anything he knew about the man suggested that he'd only take it as a challenge to pursue the woman further.

"Your Grace, you wanted to see the shrubbery?"

A sheepish grin spread across his face as he realized he hadn't followed her beyond the park's gate. "Coming, my lady." He extended his arm to her again as they walked around to her family's land. She let go of his elbow upon reaching the steps. She ascended quickly, handing off her bouquet to a servant in the foyer before returning to Bryant's side.

"I dare not go inside. That house is suffocating."

Here, safely among the trees, she could no longer hold back. She glanced at the windows for any disproving faces before collapsing to the ground in tears. Bryant took a seat across from her, allowing her the moment to grieve. Had they been in the country, with miles of distance, she would have wailed and screamed. In this garden, with servants not ten yards away, the sobs wracked her body silently.

Bryant's gaze did not leave her, waiting for an invitation to provide comfort. They sat together as the minutes ticked by, her tears easing steadily. Finally, with a shaky voice, she spoke.

"How did you know?"

"As I mentioned before, I've also lost my father. I understand what that feels like. It wasn't hard to reason how much anguish you must truly be in."

"It's not polite to call a woman a liar," she spouted.

He hesitated, unsure if she was attempting to be humorous or crass. "Pardon me, my lady. I must have forgotten."

"For a duke, you are rather dense sometimes, aren't you?" She sniffled and wiped her tears with a handkerchief, sitting up a little taller. "Shall we go look at the bushes, or am I to sit here miserable like a helpless babe?"

Bryant stood and offered his hand to her, hoisting her back onto her feet. "It would be nice to see the gardens, if you are willing to show me."

She took his arm and strutted on. "If you're so interested in our shrub display, this is our gardener's favorite. If His Grace the Dunce is unable to tell, it is a rather elegant depiction of a ceasg."

"Elegant indeed," he responded absentmindedly, as an image of Marjorie's bruised face appeared. Her injuries wouldn't leave his mind, and it made him wonder if the intruder had been so gracious that his targets were the sole bearers of violence."Lady Olivia, did the intruder harm you? A scratch, a bruise, something worse?"

She hesitated, still desiring to deflect from the topic. Ultimately, she shook her head. "No. Not me directly, at least. He did enough damage to my parents." She shivered; from the wind or the memory, he couldn't say. "He was so very angry with Father. Threatened to burn the whole house down if he didn't get what he wanted. I assume he was delirious, but who's to say?"

Bryant took a step closer, hoping the proximity would lead her to feel secure in such an exposed area of the grounds. "He won't get to you now; not while I'm here." His heartbeat roared in his ears. Words like those weren't said lightly. They spoke of promise; the promise of a future together, of hidden feelings, of romance. Guilt pooled in his gut as he hesitated to say more. He wasn't here to romance her. He'd only come because he wanted to check up on her. Mother's words were getting to him.

He gently took hold of her arms to comfort her but found himself shocked instead. She was freezing. "We should get you inside soon, my lady."

"Your Grace," she started, "not a word of this to anyone. Not the conversations, nor your romance, nor the incident itself. I don't want a single word on the lips of anyone; the *ton* could easily turn this into a scandal. I know my parents weren't perfect, but they deserve better than to have their deaths used as gossip."

"Not a word," he vowed.

"You must understand, Your Grace, that I've quite the reputation to uphold. Nothing—and I mean *nothing*—must taint it. No more talk of guns or madmen or promenades through the gardens." Her voice trailed off as her eyes fixed onto one point. "Do you see that? There, in the bushes. Something is glinting in the sunlight."

He only had a moment to look across the steep-banked creek to the shining object before Olivia was dashing across the gravelly slope. "Take care, my lady. The ground isn't stable." An instinct crept up in him to place his hands around her waist to steady her. The thought startled him as he stepped back, slipping on the rocks and falling onto his bottom.

"I'm alright," he rushed to assure her, cheeks blooming with embarrassment as he stood himself back up and dusting himself off.

"Well, now we know that the greatest harm these pebbles can do is cause one to get a bruise on their bum," she retorted as she hopped the creek and walked up to the bush. "It's some sort of scale, I think. It is quite pretty. Rather large for a fish, but then, I'm not particularly familiar." It was about the size of her palm, with pale streaks of color across the silvery surface. The edges were brittle and sharp. She scanned the area for any others, but could find no more like it. "I'd be given to assume one of the servants caught a fish here, but there's no other signs of life." She handed it to Bryant, who tucked it away, and began stalking back down the banks. He extended a hand to assist her across, but she shooed it away and insisted she could manage on her own.

The pebbles, however, had a different idea in mind. In a single moment, Lady Olivia tumbled down into the muddy water. She pulled herself upright, rolling her eyes and scolding the rocks before turning to Bryant. "Forgive me, Your Grace, for appearing in such a state. The creek did not appreciate my perfection and chose to redo my coiffure." She sighed and attempted to stand, yelping when she put pressure on her left foot. "Oh goodness, I hope it's not sprained." Scolding the creek again did little to ease the pain and frustration written across her face.

"If I might be of assistance, my lady," he offered as he stepped closer. They linked arms as he pulled her up from the grime. "Rest your arm across my shoulders. I'll do the same with mine and yours and support you on the way back." An uncomfortable position for them to be in, but her household would understand once he explained. People had a way of respecting a duke's word regardless of how it appears otherwise.

He looked up at the tree-line, looking for the tall spire of the atrium. "My lady, I don't see the manor." He spoke hesitantly, still scanning the leaves for any sign of cobble and spackle. "How vast are your grounds?"

"Not as great as our dear gardener would like. All the same, I didn't think we'd wandered off so far. Do you see the ceasg shrub?"

A moment spent scanning the area proved what he already knew. "Negative. No fantastical bushes in sight." He searched for anything that might be familiar to her; anything that could be considered a landmark. "Do you recognize the creek?"

"Come to think of it, I don't. While I've no doubt that this travels along our property, our creek isn't lined with gravel; only sand

and dirt." She took a step forward, wincing in pain and clinging to Bryant's coat. "At least this venture couldn't get any worse."

"I don't suppose that's just wishful thinking, is it?" She asked what he meant and he gestured to the horizon. "That, o wise one, is what we call the sun. It provides light. When we don't have it, we don't have light."

Olivia sighed, convincing him to follow the creek until they could find something of interest to follow instead. "Promise me you'll not breathe a word of this to anyone. Having a sore ankle is bad enough."

"On my honor, my lady." They hobbled along together as the light dwindled from the sky. Spots of yellow-orange dotted from behind the trees ahead. "Do you see that, my lady? Street lamps." He hurried their pace, all the while making sure Olivia could keep up on her one foot. He didn't fancy dragging her back home, as entertaining as that image might be.

Soon, the dirt and mud changed to cobble and slate. They stood on a solid, firm road. "At last," Bryant declared as he took stock of their new location. "I'd say we happened to traverse into Outrey Park, given the vast meadows either side of our makeshift path. I'm thankful we have walked this path before. It will be easier to find Pattermar from here." They continued on in relative silence as Olivia's pain, given the increase in her winces and squeaks, grew worse.

Footsteps joined theirs, marching in time down the pathway. He spared a glance behind to see who—or what—was following them, but saw nothing. Odd, given the clearness of the footfalls. All the same, he turned back and kept his gaze on the path ahead. Not a moment later, the footsteps began again. "My lady, do you hear footsteps?"

"Yes. I don't suppose it's anything other than someone out for an evening stroll." Her voice wavered, betraying her confidence.

"I dare say I didn't see anyone behind us. You don't suppose we're imagining the same sound, do you?" He glanced again over his shoulder, finding now an old man standing where he had not before. A pale blue wisp floated around the figure, giving him an unnatural glow. "My lady, keep walking. There *is* someone behind us." He kept an eye on the figure as they walked. The man didn't seem like a threat, but his face contorted oddly, like the muscles refused to conform into a single likeness.

All at once, the man broke out into a run. Bryant didn't dare waste another second in returning to the manor, scooping Olivia into his arms so they had a chance at outrunning the stranger. "Forgive me, my lady, but this is necessary." He ran as fast as he dared, not bothering to look at the man behind him. Wasting even a moment could end in tragedy.

The manor steps lay just a few yards ahead now but the footsteps thudded louder as the stranger gained. Panic rose in his chest as he ran onto the property of Pattermar. He'd no sooner crossed the threshold that the footsteps stopped. He turned to face the stranger with confusion, ready to fight if need be, only to find that the man glowing blue had vanished. Gently, he set Olivia back on her feet. They stared at the path. "He was there only a minute ago."

"I know. I saw him. He had such a strange, ghastly face; almost inhuman." She paused only a moment before turning towards the mansion. "I should head inside." Her hesitancy suggested that she didn't really want to. Or, perhaps, that was his own inner voice begging her to stay. Not that he *needed* her to stay, but they'd had a rather good, honest time before she tripped in the creek and the sun set and a grisly old man scared half his life away. "Thank you for the walk, Your Grace. Goodnight."

His heart fell at her words. "Goodnight," he repeated, watching as she walked inside. Despite the scare, a whisper of a grin sat on his face. Today had been a good day.

...

The oak doors of Angarth closed behind him as he stepped into the foyer. "Eryi, can you send a series of telegrams?"

"The usual, my lord?"

"Indeed. Two o'clock tea on the morrow in the drawing room. It's urgent."

Chapter Eighteen: To Wager A Life

January 18th

Bryant's pulse ticked loudly in his throat as he strolled towards the drawing room. The events of the past few days weighed heavy on his mind, confusing as they were, and he needed to know how to proceed. The situation was difficult enough with Kegg's threats aimed at him, but the man chasing them last night only caused more worry.

Could he have been sent by Kegg as a means of intimidating Bryant away, or had he been hired by the murderer who invaded Pattermar? Did he truly disappear? Why was he blue? Surely it was not due to the lighting.

"Lyz, what should I do? There's no way of knowing who that man was, with it being so dark. What if he tried to break into the home after I left? Would he harm Lady Olivia?"

"I wouldn't presume to know, Your Grace." Despite the troubling circumstances, Lyz held the pretense of a half-grin. "Beg pardon, but if you're throwing your questions at me, is there a need for the meeting downstairs?"

A whisper of a frown tugged at his mouth as he replied, "Apologies, Lyz, but my mind is frazzled. I haven't the slightest idea of what to do. Any advice you might have beforehand would be greatly appreciated. Granted, you've admitted to not knowing more than I do. If you *do* have anything more, you'll let me know?"

Lyz interrupted him with a short "Your Grace" before opening the door to the drawing room.

Bryant took a moment to collect his thoughts before stepping inside. "It's good to see you all again. I'm glad you could make it on such short notice."

"Naturally we'd all show up," Corbin replied, fighting a grin. "It's been too long since we've seen each other."

Shepherd made a snide comment and turned his attention to Bryant. "What's on your mind? You wouldn't call a meeting to simply make conversation. Is there something wrong?"

He found a seat across from the group and took a shallow, raggedy breath before responding. "I paid a call to Lady Olivia last week." The others teased him for a moment, quieting when he raised a hand. "*Not* because I'm interested in her. You all know of her situation, and my family's involvement in it. Do not tease me for having a heart." He paused for a moment to let the commotion settle. "We strolled in the gardens, where she could speak freely.

"Upon our return trip, we were followed by an old man whose skin seemed to glow blue. When I called out, he didn't respond; only started to chase us until we reached the manor. I looked over my shoulder as we ascended the steps only to see that the man had disappeared. My fear is that the man was sent to harm Lady Olivia." Or, that he'd been sent by Kegg, but he didn't want to admit that; he didn't want to believe that his peer was so vengeful that he'd make good on his threats. "What should I do?"

Brig and Corbin simultaneously turned to face Shep. He glanced at them. "What? Corbin could know what to do for once. Brigham, have you got any ideas? Why am I always the one giving advice?"

"Are you asking for an explanation of your own qualifications?" Corbin inquired.

Shepherd sighed, his gaze drifting to the corner of the room. "Give me a moment. There's a fair bit of detail that I need to sort through."

"Wait," Brigham piped up. "Describe the man again, Bryant."

"He was old, stumpy, wore ragged clothes, and glowed blue. Supposedly, anyway. It could have been a trick of the light."

He strode to the door. "I'll be back in a few minutes. There's a book I need to reference that might be in your library." He disappeared down the corridor, leaving the three to stare after him.

Corbin pierced the silence that followed with a bold suggestion. "You should call on her more often to protect her. If her family wasn't safe within their own house, she'd be safer with you than at home."

"If I did that, she might take it the wrong way," he argued.

"Not if you informed her of your plan beforehand. Keeping her out in public is a good way to protect her. No one would dare attack her where there are witnesses. What easier way to ensure her safety than by accompanying her on strolls and promenading around town?"

"Around town. You realize, then, that the media would publicize our every move, all but announcing our courtship before we've started it." His eyes shifted, glancing around the room as the idea came together.

"The media. If they wrote in the newspapers that I was courting Lady Olivia, she'd be safe. I could probably afford to hire ten different private investigators and detectives if something did happen to her. Not a man alive could compete against that amount of sleuthing."

Shepherd spoke up. "All of that is true. Why, then, haven't you?"

Bryant looked at him quizzically. "How do you mean?"

"You should launch an investigation into her parents' deaths."

He thought for several minutes, running the calculations in his head. Yes, Constable Smith had taken in the murderer, but why was the man there in the first place? What debt did Lord Seylor owe? "I could do that," he voiced quietly.

Turning to Corbin, he added, "your plan is wonderful. There's only one issue."

"What might that be?"

"This could scare off any potential suitors. I don't want to take away from her season. Once word spreads of our fake courtship, her entire list of prospects—save for the most persistent—will drop their attentions, thinking the matter settled. What if the threat proved to be naught and the rest of her life is set up for ruin because of *me*?" He shook his head. "I couldn't do that to her."

Shep and Corbin exchanged a knowing look.

"What?"

"For someone who is definitely *not* interested in Lady Olivia, you sound like someone who is head-over-heels in *love* with the woman. Why, you're worse than Shepherd is when he's going on about Lady Ruth," Corbin stated.

He sighed and shook his head as Brig entered the room holding a large, fanciful tome. "It took me a few minutes to find it, but this has a creature similar to what you described."

"What book is that?"

"*Hopewell's Guide to the Daoine Sidhe and Other Magical Creatures*. My mother gifted my sister a copy some time ago. I've read it in its entirety, just as I have with every *other* novel in our library." He flipped through the charcoal pages until he reached one. Holding it out so that the rest could see, he read from the page.

"'Muirch men often appear on roads or along fences. They most commonly take the form of old, haggard men with bent-over backs and unkempt clothing. Muirch men are most notable for their lack of speech and faint blue glow.' That describes your mystery man to the letter." He paused a moment before continuing in the passage. "'While generally harmless, these old men send fear into the hearts of those they come across by chasing them down in the darkness until the victim steps into the light.'"

Bryant nodded thoughtfully, recalling the lampposts just outside Olivia's home. "I'm glad we got that sorted before I ended up driving away all of Lady Olivia's future suitors," he replied. "Good find, Brig."

"Thank you." Brigham plopped himself down beside Shepherd. "Now what? We've solved the issue of the man. Is there anything else we need to discuss?"

Shep spoke up. "There *is* one detail that has caught my attention. You mentioned that you didn't arrive at her home until after dusk. How late, exactly?"

He paled at the thought. "I'm not entirely sure. It couldn't have been particularly late, given that we left well before sunset." His brow furrowed as he scanned his memories, particularly those of the large clock tower stationed inside the nearby park. The clock rang out two o'clock on the hour when they stood in front of the ceasg shrub. "Six, I'm sure of it. The clock tower rang when we left and I heard it ring four times subsequently before we arrived back."

"That's good. Rather long for a call, but there should be no qualms about it." At Bryant's indignant look, he clarified, "I know you would never behave improperly but her servants and neighbors might not."

"Believe me, Shep, I would sooner risk Corbin's torment than act inappropriately with a woman," he stated with total seriousness. Then, a thought came to him, bringing with it a subdued grin. "Besides, Brig's promised to punch me should I ever hurt a woman and I don't plan on letting him any time soon. He's been practicing, you know."

Brigham held back a grin of his own as he flexed his twiggish arms. "I doubt my punch would even hurt you, Your Grace."

"Shep will punch me in your stead, then. He's got enough muscle for the both of you."

A comfortable silence fell between the group as they put away the topic of murich men and late soirees. Brigham set the heavy book on the low table as Shepherd fiddled with something in his pocket.

"Since we're all here," Shep started, "I suppose I should discuss my love life as well." He paused, eyes scanning the room "I plan to propose to Lady Ruth at Lady Tristan's ball amongst the rose bushes. Ruth loves roses, so I thought it'd be the perfect opportunity." The room went silent as Shep unearthed the ring from his pocket. "My mother selected this for me. It's been passed down through her family for generations."

The three stared at him in awe. "It's a beautiful ring, Shep," Brigham offered. "I'm just a bit taken aback. The season's hardly over. You've been courting her for a matter of weeks and you're already proposing?"

"I don't see the point in waiting longer. We've developed a proper kinship, I think. My family adores her and her family respects me." He took a deep breath, muscles relaxing as he exhaled. "I've never felt this way about anyone. She lights up my day in a way no one else ever has. I can't imagine the rest of my life without her." Silence followed his words as he met the eyes of his friends.

Corbin spoke next, a respectful whisper of a grin on his face. "I told you that you'd be the first of us to fall in love. Lord Tristan owes me eight larks." All eyes turned to him as his grin spread.

"You bet on which of us would find a wife first?" Brig nearly shouted the question.

"It was only eight larks! That's hardly anything at all considering the bounty my tenants have provided. When all is said and paid for, eight larks is nothing," Corbin defended.

"That's not the point!"

Shep raised a hand to silence them. "Brig, I don't mind. In truth, I've been of mind to court Lady Ruth for some time now. It's only that I was unable to until her debut at the end of October. The ball was our first dance, of course, but I've been pinning after her for months. Corbin picked up on this, naturally—he is Corbin, after all—and questioned me about it before the end of last year's season. He knew to bet on me because I'm the only one who had said anything about being sweet on a girl."

Brigham held his gaze for a moment before muttering an apology to Corbin. "I'm happy for you, Shep; all of us are." His voice held a sadness, the cause of which was uneasily fixed. "You must work hard to make sure she knows you love her, even after you've married."

"You can trust me, Brig. I've been as loving and faithful as I can be in this courtship and I don't intend to stop after the wedding." He rose from his seat. "I hate to go, but I've a proposal to plan and a house party to pack for. I bid you all good day and respectfully take my leave." The door opened before he managed to cross to it—Eryi's doing, no doubt—and stayed steadily open as Corbin followed.

Brig, however, stayed behind, a question on his lips. "Bryant, what do you think of Lady Olivia?"

He took only a moment to respond. "I'm not planning on proposing at Lady Tristan's ball, if that gives you any clue." Realizing the sharpness of his words, he winced and apologized. "Honestly, Brig, I'm not sure. She always seemed the prickly type; stubborn, hoity-toity, rude. After all of this, though, I know that's just a facade meant to hide what she determines unloved by the *ton*.

"All the same, she's hesitant to be honest with who she is. Her prickly nature comes back at a moment's notice. It's possible, even, that she has yet to show me who she truly is."

Were those the marks to show that their relationship wasn't meant to be? If she didn't trust him with the worst of herself, shouldn't he move on and pursue someone more along the lines of what he'd expected in his future wife?

And yet, he remembered the buzz of her fingers touching his; the warmth of her knuckles against his lips when he'd kissed her hand. Despite his uncertainties that their pairing would be convenient or fortuitous, the thought of courting her grew ever more appealing. The thought of courting anyone else made his stomach twist in unease.

"Would you jump in front of a bullet to save her?"

The question brought a smile to his lips as he answered, "I'd jump in front of a bullet to save *anyone*, Brig. Friend or otherwise. I'm not in love with her; not even infatuated. My affections are simply for her as a human being created by the Most High and nothing more. I'm worried for her safety; that's all." Was his lie obvious to Brigham or had it fallen shallow on his ears alone? All he needed to worry about, for the moment. If she was alive, all was well.

Brig didn't let the matter settle. "And in your spare time this season, have you thought of anything but?"

His eyes widened as he scanned the last few days for so much as a passing thought for anyone else, beyond that which called his immediate attention. "Oh."

"I need to leave," he continued as he stood, "but you should really ponder why you care so much. None of these lads have dared to become so involved in the lady's life; few have even now that the title is her own. Why are you an exception?" The door opened as he walked, closing with a *thud* behind him just as Eryi slipped inside.

"A house party at Lady Tristan's." Eryi took Brig's place in the room, settling in as fluidly as ever. "Strange things have been going on over there, so I've heard. The lord of the house is going batty with wagers and bets, not daring to spend his time on something that won't get him more money."

"An interesting assessment," he mumbled back. "Greed getting to him, or is there something more to it?"

"*That*, I don't know. Peligro hasn't found out yet. Given the estimates of his wagers, though, it's nothing too serious. They're rather small, each of them under a kej in worth. The amount of bets is what bothers me." Before Bryant could ask, he continued, "He's got over three dozen bets with various men; half of whom I didn't even recognize the names of. It's the strangest thing."

His brows knit together in subtle concern. "This was on a ledger, yes?" Eryi nodded. "You didn't happen to see Entwistle on that list, did you? He mentioned he had a bet with the man."

"I don't recall seeing that one, Your Grace. It's possible I missed it, given that I only had a few minutes to read through the list, but I would think that I'd remember seeing the name of one of your friends." He paused for a moment before shaking his head. "No Entwistle on that one."

Bryant frowned. "More than one ledger?"

"Just the one that Peligro knows. It's the strangest thing. Just a few weeks ago, while at Selcomb, I noticed that Lord Arioch's ledger has been in the red for quite some time."

"Kegg? Alden mentioned once that his estate was in disrepair but I hadn't expected the ledger to reflect that as well." He shook his head, rising to his feet. "Thank you for informing me, Eryi. Now, I'd best be off. I've a house party and a proposal tomorrow and I'm hardly prepared for it."

Eryi cracked a grin. "Who's the lucky girl, Your Grace?"

"*I'm* not proposing, you dolt. Shepherd is."

"Of course. My mistake," he replied with a grin that stated his lack of belief. "Until tomorrow, Your Grace."

"We leave just after breakfast. Don't forget, Eryi. It's imperative that we aren't late." His thoughts swirled around his head as he hurried back to his room. Olivia wasn't in danger at the hands of the blue man—that much had been made clear enough—but the threat of the break in lingered like a new wound. Someone found the need to bring a gun into her house and the very idea sent chills down his spine. Chills he wouldn't be able to shake easily.

...

Cold rain dotted the hazy horizon as Bryant dressed the next morning. "Charcoal, if you will," he muttered to Lyz, who promptly held up the garment. He shrugged into it easily enough, noting that he might need to get it tailored soon. "Is my mother joining us for the party?"

"No, Your Grace. She thought it best to spend the evening with Lady Marjorie and Lady Roberts at Cargan."

His hair stood up on end at the mention of her name. She was safe, yes. Her husband had been arrested. The staff were instructed to keep watch of her at all times. Bryant had even spared some expense to hire a night patrol guard for the home, to ensure there were no intruders.

Marjorie was safe, and he was thankful for that. Yet he couldn't help but worry; for her, and for others in his care whose livelihood was under threat.

The incident with Olivia still sent shivers down his spine. He struggled to sleep last night, knowing full well that she could be in danger at any given moment. If the threatener was so bold as to walk into their house in full daylight with a gun, he would be brazen enough to hurt her while she slept. He really shouldn't be losing sleep over it like he had. Something else happening was unlikely. Still, he couldn't shake the image of Olivia's trembling hands. She was terrified that something else would happen.

Why was *he*?

A sharp knock disrupted his thoughts followed by a bright and urgent "Your Grace." Eryi popped his head into the room. "A telegram just came for you. It's from the constable."

Bryant's brows knit together in worry. A telegram this early? "Thank you, Eryi." He scanned the lines for any indication that something was wrong. With all that he'd seen in the past few days, it wouldn't surprise him if someone had taken an illegal sort of shine to his property.

Nothing was wrong, however, if the telegram's words were to be believed. "The Mosstyn assassin has received his sentence. He has been jailed for life, with a possible consideration for the death penalty." Relief swept through him. The danger had been put to rest and, hopefully, his sleepless nights wouldn't be far behind. Lady Olivia was safe from those who threatened her wellbeing.

"There is still a bit of time before the house party for me to check in on the matter, if you wish. Perhaps he confessed a motive, or accomplices. Either could help in our search for the mastermind behind all of this."

"No need, Eryi. You may ask about it at a more convenient time. After the house party, that is. Could you set this on my desk?" The matter was as settled as it needed to be until he returned. No sense in forcing his friends to wait for him because he got curious about an issue currently put to rest. The telegram would wait in his study until an appropriate time.

"Of course, Your Grace."

"Lyz, is everything prepared for our departure?"

"Of course, my lord. We should be going if we are to make the party at the designated time. The rain last night did quite a number on the roads. Eryi, you are ready as well, I presume?"

"As always, Lyz," he responded with a grin. "I say, house parties are the most fun when it comes to snooping. Never know what information I could happen upon for the gossip columns while looking for the study."

"Don't get into trouble, Eryi," Bryant warned.

He feigned indignation. "Your Grace, I would never."

Chapter Nineteen: All Things In Their Season

January 19th

Carriages rolled up to the Mortimers' country estate in quick succession, each taking only the amount of time required to unload their passengers before leaving the drive. Guests made their way indoors to the simple first ball whilst their valets, lady's maids, and footmen took care of their belongings. Eryi was one such footman, bringing Bryant's suitcase up alongside Lyz. "You don't mind if I stop by the kitchens to chat with Peligro, do you?"

"Not at all. I can handle unpacking His Grace's things in the meantime."

With permission in mind, Eryi hastened down the servant's staircase and into the kitchen. He scanned the room briefly. Some of the servants eyed him with wariness, unsure if this house party meant that they'd be required to eat with the staff of their employer's guests. The others donned grins and smiles at his presence, relishing in someone to share gossip with. Only two were of interest, sitting in the corner: tall, tan-skinned Jerid and lanky Peligro. He took a seat beside them. "If you've some time to spare, I have a few questions."

Peligro nodded and downed the rest of his soup. "Let me finish up and we can go out to the stable. It's quieter there."

"Of course." The trio waited in silence as the others partook in gossip and food, each rising from the table when their duties led them elsewhere.

At last, Peligro finished off his bread and cheese and stood, putting his dishes with the others. "Come on, then. There's much to discuss." He led them off towards the stables, grabbing a pitchfork to sort through the hay as they spoke, adding another layer of sound to keep their secrets hidden from the world.

Jerid stepped forward. "Lord Arioch has borrowed funds to continue his spending. *Who* he borrowed the money from is another story. I haven't any idea from the ledgers. The name was abbreviated, see; even if those are the man's real initials, we haven't enough of a clue to bother tracking him down. It isn't a normal debtor, or he would have put the man's name. He wants his identity to remain a secret."

Peligro spoke up next. "If the same man is in Lord Tristan's papers, I'll bet it's for the same purpose. Who knows? Maybe the marquis isn't as stingy about who he writes into his ledger and has put the chap's full name."

"Or, perhaps neither of them even know this benefactor's full name. It's probable that he'd want to remain anonymous."

"That is a fair point," Jerid acknowledged. "All the same, it couldn't hurt to ask. The more information we have, the better."

"If Parks is worried about this and Lord Tristan continues to bet with borrowed funds, it can't end well," Peligro added. "I don't intend to let my employer sack me to the curb over his betting habits." Not to mention that he could lose the estate, or worse.

Eryi held a hand up. "Jerid, you don't suppose it could be the same man who ordered the deaths of the Seylors, do you? The murderer shouted about a debt owed before the incident."

"It's possible," he agreed, stabbing some of the hay and tossing it into a stall. "Does Wynn know if the man had any connections?"

"I'm not sure," Eryi replied. "His Grace received a telegram that he received a sentencing, so Wynn would know if a sort of confession had been made. We haven't had time to look into it yet." His gut churned as he looked around them, unable to shake the sudden feeling that they were being watched. He shivered, certain that it was just paranoia.

Hopefully the telegram would answer their questions. They needed that information before the world had the chance to cave in on them all.

...

Bryant hushed Corbin as they darted out into the gardens. Brigham stood just opposite them, hidden in the bushes on the other side of the path. Twenty feet ahead of them, staring out at the water fountain, waited Shepherd beside his lady. Apprehension hung thick in the air even as a chill breeze swept through the brush.

"Moment of truth," Corbin whispered. "Will shy Shepherd propose to the lady he talks non-stop about? Will he chicken out and walk back inside, leaving the lady on her own out in the cold?"

"Don't ruin the moment," Bryant whispered. "Let them be."

He rolled his eyes but muttered, "Fine," before shutting his mouth, watching as Shepherd and Ruth chatted.

As annoying as it would have been if Corbin's antics had ruined the proposal, he was right about something. If Ruth accepted his proposal, they would live the rest of their lives together in romantic bliss. If she did not, Shepherd would live with a broken heart, perhaps even settling for a virtuous marriage to carry on the duchy rather than a love match.

Would the reality of the season crash down on them? It had only been a few months, after all. What if they married but Ruth determined afterwards that she hadn't truly been in love? He couldn't bear the thought of Shepherd, through no fault of his, spending the rest of his life with a woman who was his wife in name only.

Shepherd paused the conversation. Bryant quickly hushed his thoughts and shooed away the worry and fear. "Lady Ruth, from the moment I met you, you have captured me, heart, mind, and soul. It would be the deepest honor if you agreed to be my wife. Will you accept my proposal?" Tears poured down her cheeks as she nodded. "Are you alright, love?" He asked timidly, not wanting to cause her further distress.

A laugh burst forth, "Yes, dear. I'm just—I've always dreamed of this moment, never really sure that I'd find it in this society. So many of those men are worried about dowries and lineage and I was worried that; but then, our Most High sent me you."

For a moment, they stared at each other in blissful silence. Lady Ruth abruptly stepped back, worry on her face as the tears and sniffling stopped. "You asked my father, didn't you?"

Shepherd mocked offense and splayed a hand over his heart in faux pain. "As if I'd be so ninny-headed to forget that, love." She laughed, assuring that his joke had the effect he intended. "I asked him last week. He said, and I quote, "It took you long enough" and then proceeded to blast me with questions to ensure I knew that you are the most precious jewel in the world, worth far more than any diamond or any piece of silver imaginable."

Corbin gagged at the flowery words and nudged Bryant with his elbow, inviting him to join in the jeer. He wouldn't. Nothing could possibly make him want to shatter Shepherd's moment.

The couple shared a kiss, for which Bryant promptly turned away, directing his gaze inside at the ball. People crowded around one corner as footmen darted around the room. Bryant's brows bushed together, displaying his confusion as he tried to make sense of it. A tall man emerged from the chaos, stepping into the shadowed gardens.

Then, in a flash, the man ran past them. Despite the shadows of night, Bryant could make out the long object in his hand that glinted in the moonlight. A knife. As if on cue, a feminine scream erupted from inside, drawing Bryant's attention to the ballroom for a brief moment as the three escaped their hiding spots in the bushes to join the couple.

A large raven flew past them, gliding into the room. It took on the form of a shadowed entity, separating the crowd. People were no longer crowding around a solitary corner but were instead turned away from it, horror on their faces as wispy smoke billowed into the room.

"What on Kestia-" Bryant started.

"Bryant, you're the fastest of us. Can you catch up with him?" Corbin sent a questioning look his way, nudging him forward. "If you hurry, you might nab him before he gets off the grounds."

Shepherd shook his head. "He has a knife, Corbin. It wouldn't be safe. Best we find someone who has a description of the man and give it to the constable when the situation can be dealt with properly."

"He's going to get away," Corbin argued.

"Better that than one of you ending up dead!" They fell silent, knowing that Shep was right. "This might have been an isolated incident, perhaps even a planned attack. The chance of him killing again only rises if someone gets in his way. Mark my words *on my life*, it isn't going to be one of you." He set his mouth into a firm line and offered his arm to his new fiancee. "Let's all go inside and see what happened."

Brigham nodded, taking the lead as they went inside. The night had gone so beautifully—so perfectly—up until this point. At least Ruth agreed to marry Shep, but even the happiness of that news didn't shake the fear and dread of the evening's most recent event.

The party-goers stood around the room; some stood alone in corners crying, others gathered around one spot; likely the location of the body. Bryant stood on his tiptoes, trying to see over the shoulders of the men.

"Do you see anything?" Brigham whispered.

"Not yet. I can't see through all of these people," he mumbled back, searching for a glimpse of what might have happened. Catching a glimpse of Thanatos's shadowed form, he knew he didn't need to guess. Eryi stared at him from across the room. If the paleness of his face and red tint to his eyes were any indication, he knew exactly who the victim was. "I'll be back in a moment, Brig."

He strode to the side of the room, standing just beside the stairway. "Eryi, do you know the man that did this?"

"Not the murderer," he muttered, rage filling his tone. "Only the victim. Jerid." His eyes went cold and glassy. "We were talking out in the stables. It had started out as simple gossip, Your Grace, but clearly it meant much more to someone else. I don't— that is, I—" His breath quickened.

"Easy, Eryi. Take as much time as you need."

He took a deep breath, voice shaking as he spoke. "We were discussing the ledgers again. Peligro noted that Lord Tristan had borrowed some money from an unknown man. While he didn't borrow much, this apparently upset Parks—Tristan's valet, that is—and so this must have been quite serious." A slow sigh hissed from his teeth as he shook his head. "Someone must have overheard us talking of it—otherwise, why would he have killed Jerid?—and thought that, for whatever reason, we knew too much to be left alone." His eyes widened. "You don't suppose it's the same bloke who attacked the Seylors, do you?"

"An accomplice is a possibility. But then, that begs the question of motive. Why are ledgers and bets so dangerous that people must be killed over them?"

Eryi shook his head. "Not the ledgers themselves, Your Grace, but what those men have done to get their money back. Someone doesn't want us finding out what has happened, and what will should this operation continue."

...

Hours passed before the police could round everyone up for proper interrogation. Eryi gave one man his eyewitness account, as well as recounting the possible connection between that and the conversation they'd had in the stables. That merely earned him a dismissive wave and a "I'll look into it" before the man turned to other sources of information. Bryant offered his account of the man rushing past them in the garden; after which, the officers took their search to the garden for evidence.

Bryant took a seat in the corner of the room, listening to the soft piano music that flowed through the room now that the chaos had died down. Lord and Lady Tristan stood with ashen faces, gazes watching the constable like twin hawks as he made his way around the room.

"Your Grace, I didn't expect to see you here." A shaking voice greeted his ears. He turned to see Lady Olivia walking towards him, trembling as much as her voice suggested.

"Lady Seylor," he greeted, "a pleasure to see you." He patted the seat beside him, gesturing for her to join him. "Are you well? The man didn't harm you in his escape, did he?"

She gave him an odd look. "None of the nobility were harmed. The only body is the servant boy."

"And to think that if I hadn't accepted the invitation, none of this would have happened. Jerid might still be alive." Olivia paled at his statement. He blushed upon recognizing his error. "Eryi believes he was murdered because of the conversation the two were having beforehand."

"That couldn't be your fault, Your Grace. How were you to know?"

He brushed her statement aside and responded tonelessly, "Shepherd Whitley, the Marquis of Pwyll, proposed to Lady Ruth tonight. She accepted." With a sigh, he added, "He proposed a mere minute before that monster ran through the gardens. A right shame that this all happened on the same night, so close in time. For *this* night to be seared in their minds forever." He shivered at the image. Poor Eryi; poor Jerid.

"Something else we've been discussing, my lady, is the possibility of this being related to the man who broke into your estate. While crime isn't exactly a rarity, it isn't often that the nobility are threatened so directly." He spoke carefully, hesitantly, not wanting to scare her further. Though, in all honesty, he probably should have left the matter alone if he intended not to scare her.

"I suppose such things must be brought into consideration. There's only one thing. Didn't Braxden police already arrest the man who murdered my family? What could this have to do with that?"

Bryant shook his head slowly, gathering his thoughts together. "I'm not sure." They were still missing so many of the pieces. "Only that neither event was an accident, nor did it intend to appear as one." He shuddered. Jerid's murder was hardly systematic. There'd been no planning, no orderly escape. Just an overheard conversation and a stab in the back from a kitchen knife. Yet it couldn't have possibly been a mistake.

Heavy footsteps approached them. "Excuse me, my lady. Would you care to dance?" That voice could only belong to Kegg. It reeked of indignation and bitter concern.

"Dance? Lord Arioch, how can you think of dancing at a time like this? The officers are still interviewing witnesses; there is still blood on the floor in the corner." Her own voice dripped with indignation. "I will not dance with you again; not today or any other day. Do I make myself clear?"

Alden's eyes darkened, turned flinty, as they focused on Bryant. "Perfectly." He promptly wandered off into one of the side rooms, presumably to sulk.

"If you'll excuse me, my lady, I need a moment away from the madness." Bryant stood and wandered the hallways as he attempted to clear his mind of Jerid's face. The poor lad was only a few short years older than himself; two and twenty, if he remembered correctly.

He bumped into several of his peers, all of which held ashen faces and a facade of joviality to mask their concern. Servants too wore a deep fear, not knowing that this incident was intentional, scared to bits that they might be next. Nature itself seemed uneasy. The wind did not disturb the trees where the songless birds nested for the winter.

The manor held the architecture of an old abbey. By proxy, it had a private chapel somewhere on the first floor. If peace could be had anywhere, he would find it there.

The halls felt uninviting as he wove through them, certain he was lost. Moonlight shone through stained panels, twisting and reveling in their colors upon the tile floor. The candles lighting the way cast long shadows across the walls that seemed to leap and jump as he walked. Down the first hallway, left. Half that hallway, right. Another right and he stood before magnificent mahogany doors. The wood nearly rattled as they opened. He was met with angry shouting from within.

"How *dare* You be silent to me, after all You have put me through! If You do even exist, in all of Your cruelty, fix this baidch mess for me! It's the least Your Holiness could do, to pay the debt that You owe me." The voice, though angry, hinted at true madness.

His eyes darted around the room, adjusting to the light while he looked for the voice's source. There, hidden between pews and shadows, sat one Alden Kegg. "Alden?"

His former friend turned to face him so vehemently that he must have not heard the door open. "Your Grace! I didn't see you there. How- how long have you been standing by the doorway?"

"Not long, Kegg. No need to worry about my hearing any confession." His brows knit together. Rather odd that Alden would be in here after being out dancing not ten minutes ago. "Is there something amiss?"

His voice rang darkly. "Beg pardon, Your Grace, but it's nothing I can disclose. Not even to you."

"I can respect that." He rushed his next sentence, barely able to form the words before they slid off his tongue. "How will you break the news to your staff?"

"How do you mean?"

"Eryi informed me that the body is Jerid's."

Horror splashed between his eyes. "That was... Jerid?" His head fell into his hands as he rubbed his temples. "I can't believe it. *Jerid*." His lips pressed into a firm line.

Odd reaction for the man in front of him, with few social graces and a superiority complex. A mere servant shouldn't have caused more than a sniffle. "You didn't know?"

"No." He took a ragged breath, running his hands through his hair. "If I *had*..." He didn't bother to finish his sentence. A sinking feeling in Bryant's stomach said he didn't need to.

"You didn't. Kegg, tell me you didn't."

"I didn't," he mumbled, sounding far more as if he were trying to convince his own baidch self than anyone else. His head swiveled as he rose to his feet, pacing and muttering incoherently.

"What *did* you do?" Bryant rose to match his height. "Kegg, are you the reason my footman's cousin was murdered?"

"No, no; I promise- I *swear* I didn't mean for any of this to happen."

"That doesn't sound any different." He grabbed Alden's arm, gripping it tightly, nails digging into the fabric sleeve. "The police are just out in the ballroom. You can answer to them just as soon as we get there." Not before he landed a few square punches, for Eryi's sake. Just as he wound up to take the first hit, a figure appeared behind him and grabbed him by the elbow. He struggled for a moment, flailing as he wrestled against his surprise attacker before a familiar voice reached his ears.

"Bryant, I'm not trying to fight you."

It was only Shepherd. No knife. Just Shep. He sighed and let his arms rest as all manner of rage and horror drained from his expression. "What is it, Shepherd?" His own voice was unfamiliar to him, full of bitterness. "Shouldn't you be off with your new bride-to-be?"

He responded with annoyance, a single eyebrow raised at his peer. "I should be. Clearly, however, I need to be here, preventing you from doing something you'd easily regret. I thought you'd grown up from your days of pummeling your peers, Bryant. What's going on?"

Bryant sent a dark glare in Kegg's direction, hoping that it could actually pierce skin. "He's responsible for Jerid's death."

Shepherd's brow furrowed. "Jerid?"

"Eryi's cousin. The servant who was murdered." His lips pressed into a firm line as he turned away from Shep. "I was going to bring this disgusting excuse for an earl out to the police when you found us."

"Those aren't the words I would use, Bryant," he muttered. "Justice is not ours to deliver. The constable will deal with him should he be guilty. Now let's *go*." He grabbed both Alden and Bryant by the arms, dragging them out into the hallway. "Not another word about what happened in there until all of this is settled. Is that clear, gentlemen?"

"Technically, we both outrank you, given that your title is simply a courtesy title and—"

Shep pulled harder on Kegg's shoulder, silencing him as he leaned in. "Not. Another. Word. Do I make myself *clear*?"

Alden swallowed audibly. "Crystal."

Chapter Twenty: Hunting A Dead Man

Eryi raced through the upper halls of the Mortimers' estate. If Jerid's killer didn't want them to know about the bets, he'd do everything in his power to learn everything about them and bring the man down. Rage burned through his skin, fueling every furious glare he sent those he passed, slipping down hallways in search of the study.

At long last, he reached the study, bursting through the doors without care for who might be inside. No one would dare bother him; not today. Not while Jerid lay in cloth, his body cruelly ready for inspection. He sorted through the stacks of documents as his vision tinted red. His eyes flitted over each one, looking only at the title to know what pages held the information he sought.

Someone appeared in the doorway. "Eryi? What are you doing in here?"

He jumped in surprise and turned to face the intruder. "Oh. It's only you, Parks. I'm searching for what Jerid was going to find before—" He shook the cobwebs of thought that poured into his mind—and the image of the corpse along with it—before diving into the stack again. "I need the information about who Lord Tristan is borrowing from."

Parks rested a hand on the stack to pause his work. "Surely Peligro can get that in a few days' time. You shouldn't be here, Eryi."

"Jerid is dead," he seethed, not stopping his rant to let Parks process the statement. "A man in a cloak killed him right in front of me. I need to find this information now, to avenge him." He pressed his lips into a thin line, determined to focus all of his attention on the stack in his hands until he sorted through it all. "Why does your blasted lord keep so many baidch papers?" He flipped through them, growing more than impatient.

Parks stopped him. "Eryi. Take a breath. Lord Tristan doesn't keep his financial reports on his desk. They're in a locked drawer where they belong. If you'll be nice and explain to me why you need this so badly, I'll let you look at them. If not, I expect you to go home with Lyz and Mabyn and Their Graces when the party is over. Is that understood?"

Eryi met his eyes for a long moment as Parks eased the papers away from him, at long last letting go of the stack in his hands. "Fine." He took a deep breath. "Fine. This started so simple, you know. We were just boys snooping where we oughtn't have. But now..." his voice dropped to a breath as tears pricked his eyes. "In the stables, Jerid, Peligro, and I were discussing Lord Tristan's financial state. See, Lord Waldron had mentioned once in passing to His Grace that he'd made a series of bets, some of which with Lord Tristan.

"I thought "oh, what a bit of fun gossip to pass along" as any right-headed boy would. Peligro thought to sneak up here and check the ledgers to see if Lord Tristan had any more information about what these bets might be about. That's when he noticed: not only was Entwistle not in any of those ledgers, but Lord Tristan was borrowing money from a benefactor. Nothing great, as well you know, but just enough to raise a few questions.

"Peligro got to talking with Jerid, who works for Lord Arioch, because his employer's name *had* been listed there. He and I discovered earlier that the earl's ledger was entirely in the red and that he was borrowing massive amounts to make up for it. Suspiciously large deposits were being made from an unnamed benefactor, as well. With the threats from the Mosstyn murderer, we thought it might be all connected. Lord Seylor owed a debt and lost his life to it," His mouth pressed into a thin, angry line as he continued, "and now, so has Jerid. I'm to tell his betrothed that he loved her." His hands formed fists as he looked around the study for something—anything—he could punch without causing lasting damage.

Parks shook his head and stepped in front of the boy. "Take a hit at me, if you must. Heaven knows I've more than enough training to take it."

All sense of rage dropped from his expression as a tormented sense of peace washed over him. He couldn't hurt Parks. "No, thank you. Enough people have been hurt tonight." Except one, and he suspected Parks filled in the silent sentence for himself. "I need to see these ledgers to try to figure out who this benefactor is. If we can do that, we can trace him to the murderer and call the police on him."

"Figured all that on your own, did you?"

He filled in the silent 'you and Jerid' as the sentiment stung his heart. Never again would he and Jerid dare to risk a jaunt up to this lord's office or that lady's drawing room. No more games of cat and mouse. Not until the Most High saw fit to call him home as well.

"I know that look in your eyes, Eryi. If you so much as think that you'll be taking a bullet after this money, think again. His Grace is too kind to allow it. If he knew what danger you're getting yourself into—"

"He's offered to help, Parks."

Parks met his eyes, defeat mingling with worry before a disbelieving smile mixed in with the bunch. "His Grace's headstrong mother is allowing him to risk his life over a few pounds?"

"I don't believe Her Grace is aware of the situation. She is spending the week at Cargan. A pity, for she missed Lord Pwyll's proposal to Lady Watton. It was lovely, if the plans I've heard are true. A small event in the rose gardens."

Parks held up a hand to give him pause. "What did you say?"

"That he proposed in the rose gardens?" That couldn't be the object of Parks's interest.

He shook his head. "Before that."

"That Lord Pwyll proposed to Lord Watton's daughter?"

"Give me just a moment." He dug around the desk for a key, producing it before shoving it into the locked drawer. "How widespread was news of his proposal?"

"It couldn't have been well known. He only just told his closest friends yesterday. You don't exactly proclaim something like that to the world before you tell your closest friends."

A suspicious look crept across his face. "And if someone were listening to that conversation?"

"Parks, if you're about to suggest that there's a baidch spy in my own company—"

He shook his head. "Not at all. An unacknowledged visitor or two, perhaps, but no spy. What if the proposal was meant to be a distraction?"

"What do you mean?"

"Lord Pwyll's proposal was a quiet affair in the gardens. Our overhearer might have mistaken the marquis to be the loud sort; the type to propose in a grand, public setting. So, while everyone fawned over the newly engaged couple, he could stalk around the house doing whatever he wished."

"Such as?"

"Such as threatening Lord Tristan about some borrowed money gone missing. Clearly, whoever threatened the Mosstyns is fearless in the face of potential scandal, unafraid to act in the middle of the day. The middle of a ball should hardly suit him less."

"It's a wonderful theory, Parks. Only one issue though: they caught the man who killed Lord and Lady Seylor. He's in prison serving time."

Parks's eyes dropped into a disappointed glare. "Honestly, Eryi, if this is as intertwined with things that should have nothing to do with it as we think, they can have more than one man to threaten people. It isn't as though there's a limit to how many criminals you can have in your organized crime ring."

"Then this entire endeavor could have been for naught. We might never find his murderer."

A short knock sounded at the door, followed a moment later by one of the stable boys. "They think they've found Jerid's murderer!" The boy was gone in a single second, hopping back down the steps from whence he came.

If he weren't about to kill somebody, Eryi might find such irony hilarious.

"There'll be plenty of time to interrogate him on your own time once the constable's finished with him," Parks warned as they descended the steps. "You've spent your whole life getting into trouble, Eryi. Now is the one time you had better stay out of it."

...

Kegg had gotten himself into quite a pickle this time, for sure and certain. He stared down the constable with pitiful eyes that both screamed "I'm guilty" and "I swear, it's not me!" His heartbeat ticked in his throat as more people surrounded him. Despite what he expected, the officers did not send them away.

"What time did you arrive, Lord Arioch?"

He noticed that, despite the lawman doing so for everyone else, he didn't give the customary "this is just a precaution" speech. A lump formed in his throat as he realized that he might not make it out of this one. The investigator's question repeated in his head. With Tarvin out of commission, Jetlis had needed to serve as the coach. He'd been late, as well; almost all the other guests had arrived before him. "Half past two, if I recall correctly."

"Have you left the premises since then?" He kept that same cold tone, watching Kegg's every movement like a hawk.

"No, sir. I've kept to the grounds." Jetlis hadn't, though. He'd gone back to the manor for something he'd apparently forgotten.

A pair of men stepped into the room. He recognized one of them as a footman at Angarth but the other was unfamiliar. "Is this him?" The footman spoke with a rage that seeped into every letter.

Shepherd answered him. "Yes; he is the current suspect. Eryi, please do try to restrain yourself. We have a lot of questions to get through."

"I know. I'm doing my best." The fury in the man's eyes never left.

"See to it that you keep yourself under control," the constable retorted. "I don't fancy having to report two murders. You understand?" At Eryi's nod, he turned back to Kegg. "Where were you at the time of the murder?"

He cleared his throat and replied, "I was dancing with Lady Cordelia Edmondton, I believe. Either her or Lady Caitlyn Pryce. You may ask either and they will confirm that I danced with them around that time." He silently sighed in relief, knowing his alibi had proof; that he didn't need to lie his way out of this particular trouble. He got so irritated when he had to lie to keep his innocence.

The lawman called the women into the room and asked them a few brief questions—adding that "this is all standard procedure" to his statements that he'd entirely misplaced for Kegg. Ultimately, he let them go without further question.

"Well, officer, you heard their answers. May I go?"

"Not quite yet, Lord Arioch. Clearly, you were engaged at the time of the murder. Still, the question remains as to why you were in the library, looking every bit as guilty when His Grace found you. Care to explain that?"

He didn't want to; he hated with every fiber of his being that he had to. This whole situation was humiliating. "It's Selcomb, my estate. I was praying because our funds have gotten dangerously low. Low at the *end* of the harvest season. So, I thought to ask of our Most High for help, if only wisdom in what to do."

Miracles never cease, it seems, for the constable accepted his explanation and let him go. He breathed a sigh of relief as he exited the room—still watching over his shoulder at Eryi, who was being held back by a valet—and walked up to his room.

"Evening, sir," Jetlis greeted as he gingerly removed a fake beard. "How was the night?"

Kegg growled and shut the door loudly. "Jetlis, how could you be so foolish? I was almost arrested because of your little stunt. Do you want to blow this for all of us?"

"It had to be done," he responded, rising to his full height. "They were getting too close."

"There are other ways to take care of things! We would have had more time if you let them figure it out on their own. But *no.* You have directly drawn attention to us. Your interference could cost us everything!" He scowled and stalked to the window. "Why couldn't you leave well enough alone?"

In the window's reflection, he saw Jetlis set his things down and move towards him. "Kegg, you don't understand."

The audacity. Nothing could possibly make such a compromise valid. "What don't I understand? *You* weren't the one they accosted!"

"They know about the ledgers. The bets. That servant—Jerid?—knew everything. He and his friends were going to track down Morris's name. They weren't *getting* too close. They *were* too close."

Kegg met his gaze. "What? How could— but they were just footmen. Footmen shouldn't have access to the financial records." Unless the others were valets getting information, chatting amongst themselves away from their employers. But, no, he'd met Bryant's valet and the man was ancient. Why did boys have access to such important documents?

"However they got them, they know. We must inform our employer and warn him to hire more discreet policy men to handle his transactions. Tarvin's approach yielded nothing but miserable consequences." Jetlis waved his hands and turned to face the door.

This wasn't going to be easy.

"You know as well as I that Tarvin acted because he had to, not because of his own desires. Of course, he didn't need to take it so far. Regardless, our funds are running out, what with our supplier in prison. Lord Seylor was the obvious first choice because of how much he owes us." Going after him, demanding an ultimatum so that they could continue supplying *stable* bank accounts with betting funds—at interest, of course—would have been smart if Tarvin hadn't been so baidch stupid.

"Not because his daughter is all but engaged to the duke?"

Jealousy flashed in his eyes; he could feel it rise from somewhere deep within his chest, surfacing and streaming through his veins.

"He hasn't proposed yet. Until he does, Lady Seylor's debts are her own, to be covered by no one else. The late Lord's debts have passed on to her, and I have my ways of getting that money back, even if it means threatening her beloved Lord Whittaker." He hated that; he resented Bryant for all the good fortune he'd come across. He was the one to have a stable home life, despite losing his father. He had the riches, the estates, the friends, the education. And now, the girl. Their marriage could be used, still. The duke, out of the kindness of his heart, would pay back anything her family owed.

More, if they demanded it.

The scene played out in his head like a dream; dark and shadowed and beautiful. Newlywed Olivia Wooldridge kidnapped and held for ransom. He'd hold a pistol to her throat, that all familiar *click* shouting as Bryant walks up with the money. Worry writing itself into the duke's brow as he watches his bride squirm against the gun.

He'd never hurt her; he couldn't bring himself to that. The duke didn't need to know that, though.

"Jetlis, prepare the carriage, and the suitcases. We have a house call we need to make. After that, we're going home." He paused as his gaze fell on the window. Dark clouds stormed overhead. "And pack an umbrella, to protect the list of our beneficiaries. Wouldn't want to lose track of who we must speak to today."

"Of course, Kegg. What do you have in mind, exactly?" His tone spoke of a will that matched Kegg's imagination, only *his* likely ended with a lot more blood.

...

Bryant stared at the crowd around him, each dressed in their finest black. Rain poured as thunder sounded, covering the minister's solemn words. Few of those present at the party had bothered to attend Jerid's funeral. Most in attendance were servants of Kegg's, or family. Jerid had a multitude of cousins, given the variety of appearances in the people before him. He recognized a few from the various events he'd attended over the season. One in particular stood out: Trent Smith, who worked for intelligence as an agent. In this time of peace, as an operative on the lookout for whispers of war from their enemies.

His heart weighed heavy as the day before played over and over in his head. Alden, for all intents and purposes, had nothing to do with Jerid's death. He breezed through the questions with a valid alibi, one that Lady Caitlyn had confirmed when questioned.

Yet Bryant had been ready to kill him for being in the wrong place at the wrong time. What was wrong with him?

He'd lost his kindness, misplaced his compassion. His time in society hardened his heart to the point where he'd been entirely ready to kill a man for seeking the solace of the Most High.

The minister's words barely registered in his mind as the darkness settled, taking hold of his thoughts with its blank noise. A shiver ran down his spine as pain took over his senses. He was no better than the man who killed Jerid, threatening an innocent man for supposed involvement.

Something within him tugged at his heart, something that spoke truth and light and hope. A tug that said *there is more than you know*. But the darkness tried to shove it down.

He let it.

Chapter Twenty-One: Consumed

February 8th

Eryi stepped up to the Braxden police station and knocked. Promptly, Constable Wynn opened the door and let him in. "I'm here on behalf of His Grace. We received this telegram," he presented the piece of paper, "and are hoping you have more news for us. Perhaps a confession? Accomplices?"

"Unfortunately," Wynn began, "the man said almost nothing. He did state that there *are* accomplices, but did not provide any further information, even when we offered him a lighter sentence. He has devoted himself to the death penalty."

"A tragedy on both counts." He paused. "May I speak to him?"

"I-" He hesitated.

"As a friendly visit," Eryi assured him. "Not as an interrogation."

Wynn grabbed his key to unlock the ward door. "You may. Keep things civil, don't badger him, and don't provoke him to anger. You have five minutes."

He strolled into the cell block and looked through the bars. Fury wrote itself into his brow as his eyes fell upon John Morris. As desperately as he wanted to thrash the man, this wasn't the time. Finally, he found the man of the hour. "Tarvin, I take it," he muttered. "I have a few questions for you."

The man grinned, an insatiable kind of thirst in his eyes. "You can't get anything out of me. They've already tried. I've done well."

"Very well, I have one question."

"Name it."

"What was in it for you?"

His eyes narrowed into a suspicious glare. "Isn't it obvious? Money. They promised me ten percent, as long as I could help them."

Eryi's lips curled up in a smirk. "Surely you don't trust a band of thieves and murderers. If a drifting pirate demands part of the treasure, do you know what happens? He is promised a fair share for his labor, and when the time comes, they kill him and divide his portion among themselves."

"My accomplices aren't the type to do that."

"It's something to think about," he said, turning on his heels. Lord willing, Wynn would be able to get a bit more out of him.

...

Hollow, dead eyes stared around at the too-familiar ballroom. Skirts and suits swirled around as musicians played lively music that used to cheer him. Not anymore; not since Jerid died. He could barely stomach the ball as it was, finding his gut churning with every moment that passed.

Twice had he seen young women eye him, as if wondering why there were such dark circles under his eyes and wrinkles in his brow. Thrice had women looked at him, wondering why he didn't ask one of them to dance. His own mother tried to pry him away from the wall and convince him to take up a set.

Her pleading didn't change the state of things. He knew who he was, what he'd become. There could be no turning back; not now that he knew where his heart really gave its allegiance.

Brigham had attempted to lure him away with talk of the court justice approving a longer sentence. Marjorie's step of justice did not cheer him like it should have.

What could, when he was a monster?

Jerid's funeral had been over two weeks ago—the day after his murder. That was good, at least. The constable hadn't the need to keep the man's body for further examination. His family could give him a proper burial. Good for Eryi, he mused, given that the two were close family. No doubt that the lad would have bullied the lawman into allowing a funeral if he had denied it.

Eryi. He'd seen that raging, murderous look in Eryi's eyes too. The boy sought revenge as much as he did, though *he* could probably get away with it. A duke killing a man would cause a great scandal indeed, but a footman? He could slip away into the night given a strong enough alibi. Given the chance, he probably would. Ask Cristyn to marry him, finish his business in town, and leave for good. No one would be any the wiser.

Why, then, did he not feel this rage towards Eryi, only to himself? What made him different?

One answer, one that said *nothing* was quelled as another one sprang up. Eryi hadn't actually tried to kill Kegg. He'd wanted to, at the interrogation. For goodness sakes, Shepherd had told him to restrain himself. What was it Eryi had replied with?

I'm trying my best.

If he didn't have more self control, he'd have attacked Kegg just as Bryant had. There would be no Shepherd to keep him from following through, either; no one attempting to pull him back before he ruined not just Alden's life, but his own.

"Bryant, people are starting to stare." Mother's quiet, gentle voice broke the rattling thoughts choking his mind. "Are you quite certain that you can't dance tonight? Not even one set?" He shook his head. He couldn't stomach anything that could be mistaken for cheer; not now. "Lady Olivia is over there. I know the two of you have taken to each other nicely." This statement, too, was met with silence.

She let out a long sigh. "Bryant, I know Jerid's death has struck you, but there are better ways to handle situations like these. From what Eryi has told me of him, he'd want you to take action and find the killer; to move on with your life once everything is set right. You can do that, surely; can't you?"

He glanced at her, shaking his head. "You don't understand, Mother." He let out a breath that told of his dissociation but said nothing more. Now wasn't the time for such heavy conversations; not in the middle of a ball where over a hundred people danced and laughed and cheered. Not where he could make a scene of himself.

His mother took his answer and the silence that followed with understanding. "Very well. I don't suppose, then, that you'll want to dance with Lady Olivia before Lord Arioch can." Her words struck him, as well she knew they would.

He pulled his gaze up from the floor and allowed his eyes to focus, following to the corner where the lady stood. Sure enough, Alden was making his way down the stairs, stare aimed directly at her. "I suppose *one* dance couldn't hurt anything."

Forcing his feet to move took what little strength he had left. The pain striking his heart roared in his ears, increasing with every step he took. He didn't want to be here; he *shouldn't* be here, when he could prove himself better than the rage that overtook him. Or, if it seemed he'd never achieve worthiness again, return to the solace of his room until he fell victim to his agony.

Despite the protests of his warring mind, he kept his feet moving. "My lady, might I have this dance?"

She turned to face him, surprise written all over her face and mischief sparking in her eyes as she teased, "He speaks at last! The great recluse speaks!" Her joy muted when she noticed his exhausted, dreary expression. "Your Grace?"

"May I have this dance?" He repeated, keeping no mirth in his tone. It wouldn't do to be happy, even when he felt he was doing *something* right by protecting Olivia from Kegg's clutches.

Clutches that might be cleaner than he assumed.

Lyz could have been wrong.

Cristyn could have been nervous about having a new guest, nothing more.

The hair on his arms still stood on edge when his gaze met Kegg's, however. Despite his doubts, his instincts didn't dare assume the man was innocent simply because he was legally righteous. Taking care to keep Kegg in sight as the musicians began to play, he led Olivia away from the corner. He offered the shallow bow customary to the start of the dance and led her through the steps with the same monotonous care that she always gave to her tread.

"Your Grace." It came forcefully this time. Not a question. A demand. "What is on your mind?" He couldn't quite place the emotion. He didn't want to try. After all, he was only here to protect her from Kegg; nothing more.

Kegg, who wasn't as psychotic as he thought, only lacking respectable morals amongst his peers. What a mess he'd made of things.

"It's nothing you need to concern yourself with, Lady Olivia." He kept his tone monotonous and steady, void of the roiling emotion in his chest.

She glared with that glare she'd given as Miss Sparrow. The glare that pierced him to his very core. "If it's nothing of concern, why is it written into your face? Why do the shadows in your eyes not flee when you look into mine? If you don't want someone to know the story, why do you not hide the grief?"

Exhaustion, mainly. It clung to him as emptiness ripped his heart apart. There was no point in using the only energy he had to hide his grief. "This isn't the place for talk of what has happened."

"It's Jerid, isn't it? The servant who was friends with your footman?" At his silence, she assumed she was right and continued on with a softer tone. "The fact that his murderer is still at large, or something else?"

He didn't want to correct her; he could hardly bring himself to shed his darkness with the truth. All the same, he stopped the set as a verse from the Scriptures came to him. *There is nothing hidden that will not be revealed.* Despite his conviction that he deserved the punishing anguish he felt, his soul desperately wanted to be free.

With trepidation, he walked to one of the side rooms and sat in a large armchair, gesturing for her to join him. "It involves Jerid's murder, but that isn't the issue I face." He took a breath heavy with anguish, praying he wouldn't hyperventilate. "Just after I left you, I sought out the chapel in hopes of finding some solace in the Most High. What I found instead, however, was Alden Kegg."

The bitter words he spoke but a fortnight ago sprang forth like new, just as they had a hundred times over since that night. "He was rambling on about how he 'didn't mean for this to happen'. I had assumed he meant Jerid. That, for whatever reason, he'd been the one to take the lad's life."

His jaw clenched as the darkness spoke to him. *You're a monster*, it whispered. *A murderer.* "As you well know, the constable interrogated him and found him clean, a perfect alibi to match." *Don't tell her. She'll hate you. They all will.*

"What happened before the constable interrogated him?" She stretched her vowels with deep concern and reached for his hand. "What happened to cause your grief?"

Don't tell— "I wanted to kill him; I would have, if Shepherd hadn't been there to grab a hold of me and stop it all. I almost killed an innocent man because he wept and prayed for guidance in the spot where I had wanted to do that exact thing." He shook his head and let out a sigh that wreaked of disgust. How could he have been so hot headed? How could he have let himself go so far as to attempt to murder someone?

"Bryant," her tone was soft. She called him *Bryant*; not Your Grace, or Sir Detective, or anything else she'd taken to calling him in recent weeks. She called him *Bryant*—that symbol of familiarity, of closeness.

She didn't hate him.

"Bryant, I don't blame you. Not that I condone such rash behavior, but I don't blame you. If I suspected someone of killing my maid's cousin, I'd be downright furious. If I didn't have more restraint, I could have been in the same spot as you."

Her words were lost on him. The willingness to drown in his despair swallowed his soul's cries for freedom and he retreated into the stoic pillar of a person he was before. "As I said before, my lady, it's nothing that you need to concern yourself with."

She glared in that way that said *I think otherwise*. "You were doing what you thought was right."

That was quite the problem, though. He was doing what *he* thought was right, not what the Most High commanded of him. He gave Kegg no time to explain, no compassion or empathy, no calm discussion before he threw that first punch. "You're right, and I'm all the worse off for it."

She huffed, speaking with a tone that mixed softness with a growl; a tone he suspected only she knew how to perfect. "Bryant, the very fact that you're so remorseful over this shows your heart. If you had truly been as merciless as Jerid's murderer, you wouldn't be so pained. You care. He didn't."

For a moment, it seemed like her words would stick. He could feel his heart reaching for truth to coat it; craving to feel something beyond the bitterness and anger.

But that didn't seem right. He was gone, just as he ought to be. Why would he deserve any less than to pay for his sins with his grief? The light had been snuffed out by pain and regret and he felt no hope of recovery. Just as it ought to be.

"I should go."

Her hand should have stopped him. Her reach should have held him back. But it didn't. His eyes were hollow and he was consumed.

He stepped back into the ballroom, determining that he ought to go up to his room for the night. Leave the party altogether, perhaps. He needn't stay here; not when he could just send the carriage back around for his mother at the party's end. His feet found the stairs and plodded up them as he reflected on Olivia's words.

You did what you thought you should. Continuing to do so—to rely on what *he* knew—wouldn't fix anything. He needed to seek wisdom outside of himself. What was the Spirit of the Most High murmuring to him through the despair?

Shepherd's face appeared through the fog with a memory from their school days. Battenhold was where Shep had gotten most of his endless wisdom. Peace sorted its way through the turbulence of his thoughts at the sight of the memory and forced him to settle. He'd get advice from Shepherd, as he always did.

He scanned the area, searching faces and suits to find his dearest friend. Shep stood near the edge of the room, once again dancing with Lady Ruth. Hoping his oldest friend wouldn't mind the interruption, he darted his way along the walls.

Shepherd, it seemed, noticed him approaching; as he muttered something to Lady Ruth before making his way over. "What's the matter?

"Could we go up to the library? I hate to take you away from your fiancèe, but it's rather urgent, I think." He was grateful that Shepherd didn't ask for further explanation. Instead, his dear friend simply nodded and followed him up the stairs and into the library. "I'm not exactly sure how to put this or what to say; all I know is that the Most High is directing me here."

"That explains it, then," Shep responded. Noting the furrow in Bryant's brow, he continued. "Maybe fifteen minutes ago, I got the strangest feeling that you needed me. I tried looking for you, but you must have been off somewhere, so I took to my lady instead."

He stared, calculating through the muck where he'd been fifteen minutes ago. "I must have been with Lady Olivia then." Hope spurted in a small crack of his heart. Surely he couldn't be too despicable if the Most High thought him worthy of such grace.

He took a seat at one of the large mahogany tables, gesturing for Shep to join him. "I almost killed Alden." The words seemed easier to say the second time around.

"I know. I was there with you, remember? I held back your punches. There wasn't a doubt in my mind that you'd try to take revenge for Eryi and Jerid by killing whomever you thought was his murderer. The tenseness of your arms told me everything your words didn't." He took a deep breath. "You made a mistake; that's all. I was there to keep you from making it."

"We both know it was more than a mistake, Shep. Mistakes can be fixed—however easily. What I was going to do could never be undone."

Shep nodded, a deeply thoughtful expression on his face. "There is no excuse, I know. Explanation of cause is not justification of reason. All the same, I know *you* too. Your anger got to you for a moment because of how much you care for these people. That's more than most of these lords can boast."

Bryant kept silent, unable to bring himself to respond. Shep was incredibly kind for taking the time to speak with him, but this was his own battle. He was caught up in this mess because of his actions—both what he did do and what he should have done. Jerid wasn't dead simply because of a few misplaced words or because he was in the wrong place at the wrong time.

"There's more to the story, isn't there?"

He struggled to speak. To tell the truth meant he would have to surrender his guilt. To surrender his guilt meant that he couldn't torture himself for what he should have done differently. "I don't want to say."

Shep sighed, taking a moment to meet Bryant's eyes. "If we don't have it out now, it's only going to hurt you later. You can tell me what's going on."

He tore his gaze away, unwilling to let Shep see the tears that continued to brim like liquid glass. They sat in silence for several moments before he spoke, a ragged breath adding sharp edges to his words. "It's my fault."

There. He'd said it. Now he waited for the moment when Shepherd realized how horribly dark his mind truly was. He couldn't forgive a man who caused a murder—whether the man meant it or not. Shep was kind, but even he had to draw a standard of judgment.

But when he met Shepherd's eyes again, it was not scorn that he saw, but compassion. "How do you mean?"

The unexpected reaction spurred his confidence, enabling his voice. "Jerid's death. It's my fault." His expression *had* to waver—to shift into disgust or betrayal or *something* other than grace, but it didn't.

"How could that be your fault?"

"I was the one who asked Eryi to go snooping around with his cousins. If I had kept my mouth shut, or gone about this a different way, or simply had Eryi stay home that day, Jerid would still be alive. But he isn't. Jerid is dead because of me." He glared at Shepherd. "Go on. Ridicule me. Shout or scream or yell or run off to the country again—just do *something* that I deserve."

"Bryant, none of that was your fault. Did you give his murderer the knife?"

"I might as well have," he retorted.

Shep shook his head. "That sort of talk won't do any of us good. You did *not* enable his murderer. Sure, your instructions for *Eryi* were underhanded, but you aren't responsible for this man's actions. Unless you directly ordered his death, you are not responsible for what happened to Jerid any more than you're responsible for what happened to Marjorie."

Blast it all, this wouldn't have happened if he had stayed home, wallowing in his own self-hatred. Life was easier when he could swim down and drown in his guilt. Returning to the surface would take far more work and far more love than he deserved. "But I—"

"No, Bryant. You did exactly what you were supposed to do. Eryi was already snooping when he spoke to you, correct?"

"Yes, but if you're about to insinuate that this is somehow *his*—"

"I'm not. All I'm trying to do is show you how it isn't yours. Eryi was already sticking his nose in everyone's business when he spoke to you. You wouldn't have asked if he hadn't brought it up. He had the choice to say no. Your words only *influenced* his choices. Similarly, his choices influenced Jerid's choices, and that culminated into being near the stables during the proposal. None of that—*none of that*—caused his death because none of that forced his murderer to pull out a knife. There is only one person at fault here and it isn't you."

Bryant pressed his handkerchief against his damp eyes. "I didn't think about it like that." Silence again fell between them, more pleasant and calm than the last.

"Tell me what's going on in your head, Bry." The words were gentle, the tone steady and reassuring. Like a crackling fire on a cold night or a warm cup of tea during a rainstorm.

He loosed a sigh and frowned. "I'm frustrated. Angry with myself for even considering snapping his neck. His alibi was backed but I let a few misplaced sentences color my view so terribly that I thought him a murderer and was about to become one myself." Tears again blurred his vision. His voice wavered as he spoke. The last of his walls broke down. "I don't understand what's happening to me, Shep. I've lost something, I think, but I don't know what, or how to get it back."

The words felt as hollow as he did, even though they came with tears that stung his eyes and wet his cheeks. Their hollowness took some of the bite away. As the sounds left him, so too did some of that emptiness. His burden lifted, if only slightly.

Shepherd laid a hand on his shoulder. "Bryant, I know few of my words will be able to pierce the darkness holding you captive, so I'll keep my words few. Have you repented of your hatred?"

"Yes." Several times, each with bitter tears that left him feeling more empty than before.

"Then you are forgiven. Nothing can change that; the slate has been wiped clean. You are restored, so wake up and realize that the Most High will not hold against you that which you have turned from. Wake up, Bryant, and notice that ours is not a calling to guilt and shame but to freedom and life."

Shepherd was right. He had been redeemed. His thoughts still bombarded him—he suspected they wouldn't stop from one inspirational moment—but the weight of them seemed lighter than before.

"Thank you, Shep." He coughed to clear the emotion from his voice, surprised that it held gratitude instead of the emptiness it once professed. "It's going to take some time, I think, to heal from all of this, but I don't walk this path by myself. The Most High has sent me the best confidant and the dearest friends."

Shep met his gaze, sincerity and kindness in the wells of his eyes. "Don't forget, Bryant. There is a Friend who sticks closer than a brother."

He almost managed a smile as he repeated, "Thank you again, Shep. It means a lot to me."

"I'll be praying for you." He smiled briefly before clearing his throat. "Now, if you'll excuse me, I believe I have a dance to finish. Wouldn't want to keep my lady waiting." He strode out of the library, leaving Bryant to his lonesome.

"I suppose I have a dance to finish as well," he muttered to himself. Though he still didn't feel up to participating in the party belowstairs, Shepherd's words had brought sense to what Mother said earlier. As painful and as difficult as it would be to move on, he owed it to Eryi, to Jerid, to find out who *actually* murdered the man. He needed to ease his heart away from its suffering one step at a time.

The first step would be concluding his dance with Lady Olivia. She deserved it for his sharp, curt behavior earlier. Perhaps he'd even manage to offer an explanation worthy of her forgiveness.

Making his way to the ballroom, he scanned the faces for his intended. Her dark hair stood out amongst the blondes and fair brunettes, making spotting his lady all the easier.

His feet stopped when he noticed her talking with his mother. "What is she..." he mumbled to himself as he crossed the room. "Lady Olivia, pleasant to see you again."

She met his gaze with a smile that said *you seem different*. "A pleasure, certainly, Your Grace. I was just speaking with Her Grace about how your footman is doing. I know it's only been a fortnight since the incident, but I was curious to hear how he'd been getting along."

Bryant nodded his head. "Thank you for inquiring after him. He's devastated, to say the least, but he and Cristyn are finding a new sort of peace together as they grieve." Eryi had even promised to propose to the girl once his year of grieving had passed. A spring wedding, they'd most likely have. Yet another wedding he'd have the honor of attending. The thought brought a bit of a smile to his face even through the gloom. He extended a hand, nodded towards the other couples. "Care to dance, Lady Olivia?"

She caught his smile and took his hand. "I would be delighted, Your Grace."

As he led her away from his mother, he mumbled, "I don't suppose we could put aside the pleasantries, Lady Olivia? You did, after all, use my first name during our conversation earlier, and I quite miss hearing it in your voice."

The statement made her laugh just as it brought a blush to her cheeks. His heart fluttered at the sight. "I wasn't aware that you were such a flirt, Your Grace." Neither did he, but she apparently brought out a side of him that he'd never known before. "Very well, then. I shall call you Bryant so long as you call me Olivia. It's only fair that you use my given name as well."

"I could be made to honor that request, Olivia." Something that felt an awful lot like hope buzzed in his chest as her laugh filled the air. "Could I call on you tomorrow, Olivia? I should like to better make your acquaintance."

She hummed in thought, but the grin on her lips spoke miles into her mind, saying that she only postponed her answer to keep him waiting. "I *suppose* I have a free slot in my schedule around afternoon tea. We could take it in town, if that is to your fancy, Bryant."

"That sounds lovely." He pressed a kiss to her hand as the music swelled and the dancers took their places in line. "Afternoon tea tomorrow. I shall count down the hours."

Chapter Twenty-Two: Spilling Tea

February 9th

Nerves churned his stomach as Bryant looked in the mirror. "Are you certain that I look alright, Lyz? Is my cravat too poofy? Any hairs sticking up where they shouldn't?"

"Your Grace, there's no need to fuss. You've taken tea with the lady before, haven't you?"

He snorted a laugh. "Only because of my mother's iron will to see her wed Lord Arioch. Of course, that's changed between then and now." He took a deep breath, allowing the air to swirl in his lungs before exhaling. The sensation calmed him somewhat, but the newfound peace did little to still the cacophony of thoughts running through his head. "This is something entirely different; far more personal than the balls and house parties and card rooms. It will be just the two of us. No one around who will interrupt, no reason for us to step away from the moment."

A shiver ran down his spine as the immensity of the moment hit him. Providing this went well, he'd ask for permission to court her. Providing *that* went well, he'd ask for her hand in marriage. That *was* what he was supposed to do in this situation, right?

"Perhaps this is happening too quickly. Then again, if she felt uncomfortable by my offer, she wouldn't have suggested tea in town." His head hurt as the various factors swam around in his head, choking all other thoughts with their weight. "This could be the moment that defines the rest of my life."

Lyz held up a thick winter coat. "This is the part where you trust that the Most High has brought the two of you together for a reason. Perhaps that reason *is* just to protect her from Lord Arioch, or to comfort her through the trauma of the invader, but it could be that He has brought you to the woman you will spend your life with."

"I do believe that is quite my point," he responded solemnly as he shrugged into the coat. "This could be everything or it could be nothing. What if today goes poorly? Or, what if it goes right but we find out later that we're incompatible as a match?"

"Take a deep breath, Your Grace. This doesn't need to be as difficult as you're making it out to be. Are you sure of your feelings for her?"

"Yes."

"Do you doubt that you might want to marry her in a few months' time?"

He bit his lip. Was he sure that this was the right choice? Olivia *was*, after all, the opposite of what he'd been looking for. Even if she wasn't as curt and sharp as she showed herself to be, she retreated into that nature in public at a moment's notice.

Which would he be marrying? The witty, compassionate Olivia or the snarky, obnoxious Olivia? If his proposal was successful, would he be willing to risk unhappiness at the hand of the latter because he fell in love with the former?

"I don't know yet. There's too many things to consider. I suppose I'd want to marry her by the end of the season. Providing, of course, that things progress as they have. What I can't figure out is if it would be the right decision." The weight of potential rejection brought a tremor to his hands and sagged his heart. He had questions; far too many questions to be certain of his heart's loyalty. "What if she doesn't feel the same? What if *I* think today goes well, but she doesn't?"

Lyz gave him a small smile as he opened the door leading to the hallway. "If that's the case, Your Grace, then I'll say this. You've only just entered society. Many bachelors wait to marry until their late twenties. Some wait even longer. There will be time to move on. Don't forget your title, either. That's a bargaining tool worth much more than you might think. There *will* be other women willing to marry you."

"I don't want her to simply be able to put up with me because of my name or my wealth. If that were the case, I could have been married long before now. My debut would have been unnecessary. I could have wed in the territory or on a brief trip home. Blast it all, I could have had a bride lined up before my eighteenth birthday if I cared that much about finding someone *willing* to marry me."

He sighed, a feeling of dread crawling along his spine. "Apologies, Lyz. I don't mean to be curt. It's only that… Lady Olivia has stolen my heart. Will she give me hers in return?"

Lyz's smile broadened as he led Bryant out to the drive, where the carriage awaited him. "That, Your Grace, will only be answered in time."

He strolled into the carriage, staring out the window to get a new perspective on the tumultuous emotions stirring his soul. Despite his concerns, he couldn't imagine marrying someone other than the woman who stole the very breath from his lungs with a single glance.

If she didn't love him as well, he'd be at a loss as to how to move on. If this didn't go according to his heart's desires, he might as well pack up his estate and return to the country.

The words he'd uttered to Shep in the garden so long ago echoed back at him. *I suppose that you know you're in love when living a single day without that person feels like it could kill you.* He was in love, plain and simple, and he knew that he'd give away his entire fortune if it meant that she loved him too.

...

"Shall we sit at this table here, Lady Olivia?" He gestured to one beside a large street-facing window, through which one could see snow-covered trees and couples walking about the marketplace. "I confess that I've not taken tea in town before. Have you?"

She nodded. "A time or two, but never to simply sit and enjoy the company." She took a seat across from him and stared into his eyes. To any onlooker, it was a friendly, casual glance.

That friendly, casual glance, however, made his insides churn in fear. What if this didn't go the way he wanted it to? "What would you recommend? Of the sweets, that is. Do you have a favorite?"

She pursed her lips as her eyes wandered in thought. "Their honeycakes are quite nice, but a tad too sweet for my taste. My personal favorite, however, is their tiramisu. I've not found another tearoom in Braxden that serves it."

His brows knit together as he sounded out the unfamiliar word. "I don't think I've ever heard of that before. What is it?"

"Ladyfingers dipped in coffee, layered into a cake with chocolate and cream. It's a lovely combination of flavors that provides a balanced sweetness."

She paused the conversation to give their order to a waiting steward. The man disappeared for several moments, returning with a teapot and a tray of sweets. "Thank you," she said to the waiter before turning her attention back to Bryant. "Strong or weak?"

"Strong, please."

"Your Grace," Olivia began as she handed him his cup, "I've a question for you. I don't believe it's one that I've heard among the *ton*—at least, not among my acquaintances. Everyone knows that His Grace, the Duke of Whittaker, has decided to spend his season dancing with the less popular women; the second daughters; the baronesses, the gentlemen's daughters. Why did you choose them?" He could almost hear the silent '*why did you choose me?*' in her tone.

Her grey-green eyes pierced his soul with their deep color and thoughtful gaze. His heart pounded in his ears as he searched for a response to her statement. He knew full well what his answer was. Forming it into words was a different matter. "To put it simply, Olivia, my title comes with both great responsibility and great publicity. People notice my every action and—usually—respect my decisions. My peers especially keep a watchful eye on me, simply because they know I could upend their own plans for marriage with my title alone."

"What does that have to do with the wallflowers? You'd hardly be ruining a match by giving them your attention. Not many of your peers plan to marry the quieter, less-endowed women. Younger daughters and those with poorly titled fathers aren't sought out for marriage."

"My point exactly. The *ton* notices what I do and fawns over it. So, when I draw my attention to the women that they ignore, I'm bringing *their* attention to them as well. Men will notice whom they never would have otherwise.

"Take Lady Cordelia Edmondton, for example. Her mother is invited over for tea with my mother near-weekly. She's often spelled her worries over her daughter marrying, which is why Lady

Cordelia was one of my first choices in dance partners. Just last week, her engagement was announced in the papers to an esteemed viscount; the very same viscount that she danced with directly after my set with her on the night of my debut."

Her brows furrowed rather than relaxing; something that perplexed him. Wasn't it a good thing that he was helping the wallflowers in finding matches when they'd otherwise go unnoticed? "And what, if I may be so bold to ask, when a lady doesn't want such attention? Not all wallflowers are that way because they have a more humble lot in life. Some of us have chosen the walls because we don't care for the attention."

Was she referring to herself or to a friend? Either way, she brought up a fair point. He hadn't considered that the women might not prefer the attention garnered by the *ton*; or that they were fine with a lesser match if it meant having a good one.

"Admittedly, I may have been presumptuous in thinking they didn't want the attention."

"Don't forget to mention arrogant. While you might be the only eligible duke this season, the *ton* has its eyes on other highly titled men as well. Yours isn't the only enviable name, Bryant. Even if it were, not every woman is interested in being spotlighted as a duchess or marchioness or countess. They simply want the best match that they can get; one that suits their personalities and desires. Sometimes a lesser title *is* the best match."

Marjorie had believed that. A shudder went down his spine at the thought. It wouldn't be too long before all of Deravail knew how that marriage had turned out. The approved divorce would, once known, cause even more of a scandal than news of her incarcerated husband would.

Her eyes narrowed. "You haven't given me the whole story. This isn't just about titles, is it?"

There was more, but he couldn't tell her. Not in such a public place, at least. Even if they *were* in a private setting, however, Brigham wouldn't want him sharing the details of his sister's horrible marriage. Not when it was just one more thing to mar the Roberts name. The best way to keep the secret was to simply not share it, no matter how trustworthy Olivia might be.

"I'm not at liberty to discuss my reasons further. It's not my story to share." When it *would* be, though, he didn't know.

Any day now, the press could figure out why Marjorie hadn't accepted any invitations or why Mr. Morris hadn't been seen around town. When that day came, he'd explain to her his true motivations. He didn't want women to be neglected by society. Shunning was what led Marjorie to accepting the match in the first place. No matter how much attention the wallflowers did or didn't want, they couldn't want a marriage like that one.

"You will tell me someday, won't you?" Her tone nearly sounded like worry, but it held a chord that rang of hope.

He took a deep breath, glancing away from her deep gaze. "Someday. If I am allowed."

"Very well, then. I shall remain content with the knowledge you've given me until you have permission to share." She took a sip of her tea before asking, "Bryant, if I may be so bold, what happened between our two exchanges last night? Your demeanor changed when you asked to finish our set; not to mention that you seem rather cheerful today—a stark contrast to the beginning of the night. What caused the change?"

A slow smile rose across his face as he answered. "Lord Pwyll got a hold of me and reminded me of the Most High's forgiveness." The cheer hadn't come right away. In fact, he had spent the entire night in prayer, weeping. And then, after a while, he slowly began to come to reason. He rose that morning with a lightened spirit and a far more sensible heart.

Whispers of that darkness still lingered, as he suspected they would, but it seemed to him bearable, knowing whom he could turn towards.

"I must say that I'm quite jealous of the friendships you share with your peers. Such closeness isn't common amongst the ladies of the *ton*. They prefer envy and arrogance to compassion and vulnerability. Kindness may be a virtue in writing, but it takes second fiddle in practice."

"You don't have any friends? I thought Lady Anwyn—"

Olivia snorted a laugh. "I have *acquaintances*. People who tolerate my presence because of my father's- because of *my* wealth. Lady Anwyn is such a person." She took a sip of her tea. "Do you prefer your time in Braxden, or are you more suited to the quiet, peaceful life of the country?"

Bryant responded tentatively, "I like being able to meet with my friends at a moment's notice as I can in the city, but I prefer my country estate. It reminds me of my time overseas, seeing to the needs of the people that the Most High has placed in my care. I wouldn't give that up for anything."

The shadows in her eyes shifted as she tilted her head. "You wouldn't prefer the galavanting of an heir or a second son to the responsibilities given to you?"

He shook his head. "Not at all." Memories from an age long passed poured into his mind. His father, before his passing, did well to train him in the responsibilities of his title, knowing that it wouldn't be long before the boy inherited his position.

The responsibility on your shoulders is a great burden to bear. Many people will depend on you. Think clearly, act wisely. That is your duty.

His father's last words to him, excepting the goodbyes and teary 'I love you's.

He coughed to clear his voice of emotion before continuing. "The Most High has seen fit to give me this duty and I'm content to follow through. I wouldn't give up what I've gained for a bit of freetime or a bit less responsibility."

A hint of a smile poked through her curious expression. "You, Bryant, are the first man that has responded to that question in a humble, noble way. I'm incredibly pleased." The smile broadened as she downed the last of her tea. "Shall we be off, then?"

He glanced at the clock on the mantle. It read a quarter past three; rather late for them to remain in the tearoom. "Ah, of course." He took out his pocketbook and placed the correct number of miths and larks on the table. "Shall I escort you home?"

"I was actually thinking that we might peruse some of the nearby shops, if that's alright with you. It's not as though anyone will oppose my staying out longer, and your mother is too much a dear to protest."

His brow furrowed. He couldn't recall 'perusing shops' on his mother's list of things to do in the preliminary stages of a courtship. Was such a thing normal? Was she testing if he was willing to spend more time with her?

Well. Spending time with her *was* enjoyable. "That would be lovely. There's a bookshop a block over. Perhaps we can start there."

Olivia rose from her seat. "Perfect. I've been meaning to see what new novels are out. Book clubs and things, you know."

"Do you enjoy reading, my lady?" He hoped she wouldn't mind the nickname, especially since she seemed to think him interesting enough to keep around.

"On occasion. Very few have ever captured my interest, but there are some I find enjoyable." She took his arm as they strolled out the doors and down towards the shop. "Do you suppose that—" Her voice cut off with a scream as Bryant felt himself being pulled away from her.

A rough voice reached his ears as he felt something cold and sharp touch his neck. "Empty your pockets," his attacker barked.

"Give me just a moment." He dug his hands into his pockets and pulled out his pocketbook. "I don't carry much on me, but I hope this will suffice." He took out the few notes that remained and held them out. Even as the man took the money from him, the blade dug deeper into his skin, nicking the first layer and sending a trickle of blood down his neck.

Adrenaline poured into his veins as he met Olivia's gaze. She trembled in fear, shadows pouring into her eyes as she watched the scene unfold. With shaking hands, she pulled out her own pocket money and held it out to the man. "Take this if you must. Don't hurt him." Her voice held a strength and a depth even as it wavered and trembled.

The man narrowed his eyes and took the extra larks from her before tearing his knife hand away and colliding his foot with Bryant's leg to temporarily immobilize him. "Thank you kindly, m'lord, m'lady." He doffed an invisible cap. All at once, his ragged form disappeared back into the shadows as if he'd never been there at all.

Bryant's heartbeat roared in his ears, silencing the world as he took a brief moment to collect himself and find his footing. "Are you well, Olivia?"

She looked at him in disbelief. "Am *I* well? You're the one that has blood streaking down your neck! We should abandon the bookstore—it's not like either of us could purchase something anyway—and take you back to Angarth."

"It's not that bad of a cut. The blade only just broke skin. It should heal up within a few days." He wiped at the cut, wincing as it stung. "I've had worse, believe me."

"All the same, we should go. The carriage will be safer than walking out on the roads." She took his hand and tugged him towards his carriage as if to emphasize that she wasn't going to argue about the matter. "Are you sure you're alright?"

He nodded slowly as he helped her up into the carriage's cabin. "Really, Olivia, it isn't as bad as you might think. Not much worse than a papercut." He sat opposite of her as the horses started trotting towards Angarth. "I enjoyed our outing—other than the mugging, of course. Perhaps I could get a raincheck on the bookstore?"

A ghost of a smile appeared. "Certainly; my schedule is rather full for the next few days. Perhaps on Friday? We could take tea again and then be off. It would do us well to have one of your footmen with us; or your valet."

Bryant chuckled at the thought of Lyz trailing them as a maid usually did. "I'm afraid Lyz won't be much help against an attacker. Lukas, our gardener, would, but I wouldn't want to tear him away from his work. All the same, I don't believe that the man will harm us again. It wasn't as though he targeted us specifically. He was a desperate man looking for a few larks to make ends meet." His eyes narrowed in thought. "If he tries robbing me again, I might offer him a job."

"You cannot be serious."

"Entirely. Did you notice his clothes? How dirty and torn they were? He looked as though he could use the money. Besides, most don't steal for the fun of it; they do out of desperation. There are always positions at my estate that can be filled." He took her hand

and gave her a hopeful smile. "Some of which are higher than others."

...

Jetlis sauntered into Selcomb with a few larks in hand and a wicked grin on his face. "Kegg, you'll be glad to see what I've found," he said as he bolted up to Alden's study and swung open the door. "You'll never guess who I ran into while out for a stroll." He thrust the paper notes onto the desk with a *whack*. "I may or may not have come across His Grace walking hand in hand with Lady Olivia Mosstyn."

Jealousy flickered in Alden's eyes as he met Jetlis's steely gaze. "What of it?"

"Their marriage is the answer to all of our problems, is it not? See them married by the end of the season, her debts become his. His fortune falls upon the newly married duchess's shoulders to fill her grave of debt."

"You're going to have to explain more than that, Jetlis." He kept his voice monotone as he counted the notes. His brow furrowed as he set the bills down and narrowed his eyes. "Did you *rob* him?" He took in a sharp breath and pushed away from his desk. "You have been reckless as of late. One of these days, it's going to backfire on you."

"It was necessary, believe me. Cause a bit of chaos, he realizes that life isn't eternal, she realizes that she loves him, he proposes in a few weeks' time. Life-threatening situations cause feelings to emerge quicker than usual—or so I've heard."

Kegg's pulse ticked in his veins as quiet rage filled his senses. "Very well. It isn't as though they can trace cash back to you." He paused as his eyes narrowed further. "They didn't get a good look at you, did they?"

"I was wearing a mask, let me assure you. I'm not stupid enough to give them anything to go off of. I even disguised my voice. There is no way that they could know I robbed them."

Kegg pressed his lips into a firm line. "I just hope you're right about this, Jetlis. If you aren't, there will be consequences for us all later down the line."

"I am well aware. Believe it or not, I'm not stupid like Tarvin." He allowed a moment of silence to let the words settle before sighing. "There is one thing. Our funds are, shall we say, gone. With Morris's accounts frozen and the merchants on edge, we have no one to borrow from. We *must* collect soon, lest we all starve. Lady Seylor owes us the most, but there are others we can take from that will not draw suspicion. Who would you recommend?"

He shook his head. "No. You've done all you can for the time being. I'll stop by Lord Gregsay this afternoon and see what I can get from him. If that fails, however, we may need to consider an alternative." He stared at the money on his desk. "Perhaps something similar to your methods."

Chapter Twenty-Three: Options

February 11th

Brigham stood at the door to Pattermar, not quite sure of why he was there. Just hours earlier, whilst securing some winter fruits as a surprise for his sister, he'd run into Lady Olivia. They exchanged pleasantries and he thought that would be the end of it. That was normally where such things stopped, providing they even got to that point. One could never tell these days. Not even the front page story about his "heroic rescue" could inspire all of his peers to treat him well.

That wasn't, however, where things ended. Instead, the lady continued the conversation: asking after his sister and mother, inquiring about his purchase, and about his own health. What followed, however, was what surprised him the most.

She asked him to call upon on her that afternoon.

He'd been taken aback, for sure and certain. A young woman simply didn't demand that a gentleman—even one of his lower standing—call on her. That led him to believe that something else was going on, and he was going to find out what it was. A Roberts was nothing if not a tad too curious.

He rapped his knuckles on the door thrice in quick succession, ensuring that his presence would be known to the staff inside. Feet shuffled from inside as the door swung open. "Greetings. I am here to call on Lady Seylor, if she'll see me." He repeated the words Bryant had told him to say; what Bryant himself had said when he called before.

The image of Bryant's shocked expression when he asked for advice about calling on the lady didn't easily leave his mind. While Corbin had suggested Bryant keep an eye on the lady, Brig didn't expect his friend to develop feelings for her. He hadn't thought Olivia Mosstyn to be his type.

Though, many a night, her name had been on his lips as the four of them discussed the progression of the season. He'd thought it an odd coincidence that she kept interrupting his life. By pure chance, his mother had taken tea with them at the same time as the intrusion. Out of respect, Bryant had visited later to check up on her. That level of grace was all Bryant kept his stories as, so Brigham had never thought to read into it. Bryant didn't lie, nor did he—usually—tell half-truths. He hadn't expected there to be anything more to Bryant's feelings than what he freely spoke of.

All the same, pure jealousy crept onto His Grace's face as he instructed what to bring and what to say. Brig stood in the foyer, now; a bouquet of alstroemeria and chrysanthemums in one hand, his calling card in the other. The footman let him into the drawing room, where he promptly greeted Olivia and the lady of the house. "For you, my lady," he offered the flowers. "His Grace, the duke of Whittaker, mentioned these were your favorite."

That seemed to appease her. "Thank you, Lord Grimes. His Grace was correct." She smiled coyly at him and suggested they take a walk through the park across the way. She glanced at her maid, who did not seem willing to leave the room with them. He sighed mentally, completely aware that his family name no doubt clouded her judgment.

The maid rose to her feet, but Brig could hear her silent hesitation. No doubt she was wondering *what if someone sees us with him* and similar questions he'd heard whispered over the years. Most of the lower classes were sympathetic. Not this one, so it seemed.

Accepting that as his cue, he offered an arm to Olivia and strolled out into the hallway. The maid joined them at a moment's notice, sauntering a few feet behind them as they walked out to the street.

Crossing the cobble road to the park—and giving the maid ample time to keep a distance behind them—he asked, "Lady Olivia, if I may be so candid, why did you ask me to call on you? It isn't exactly conventional by any means. Was His Grace not what you expected?"

She sucked in a breath. "I appreciate the direct nature of your question, so I shall answer directly. I am not interested in setting my cap for anyone other than His Grace. However, I am uncertain as to if His Grace harbors similar feelings. We went for tea the other day and everything seemed to go well, but I need to be certain. I thought perhaps that by strolling with you..." her voice trailed off, the silence filling the end of her sentence.

"I can assure you, my lady, that Bryant is as committed to you as you are him. He isn't the type to call on a lady without intention." He spoke with a steady voice even as his thoughts whirled around him. Guilt stabbed his gut as he reminded himself that he didn't really *know* what Bryant thought of Lady Olivia. He only knew Bryant.

"Does his mother approve of me?"

"I don't presume to know the thoughts of Her Grace but, from what His Grace has told me, she is quite fond of you. At the very least, she is fond of hearing Bryant's stories of you." He hoped that was true. Given what he knew of the duchess, it was likely that she adored hearing of Bryant's tales as he fell in love with the woman.

Providing, of course, that he hadn't kept her in the dark.

"He talks about me?"

Another blow to his pride. "Frequently." Though, hardly ever to him. The conversations, he'd noticed, were with Shepherd or Corbin at the fringes of cardrooms or balls. All the same, he'd heard her name a fair few times on Bryant's voice. He dropped his gaze to the ground ahead as they traversed through the park. "Why all of the questions, my lady? Have you a need to doubt his affections?"

She didn't answer right away, only glanced about. "I— If you must know," she stammered, "I overheard him speaking with your other friend. Shepherd Whitley, is it? They had a conversation at Lady Tristan's house party. He claimed that his interest was only to ensure that I was safe and that he only called on me because your mutual friend, the earl of Waldron, believed it would keep unwanted visitors at bay."

Brig's eyes betrayed him; he knew it even before her expression twisted. "That was how it started," he began, choosing his words with utmost care, hoping they were correct. Bryant's feelings had started *after* the intrusion, hadn't they? Granted, he'd mentioned her frequently before in hushed conversations to Shepherd or Corbin, but something as big as a crush would have been announced to their little group, surely. Then again, he'd seen the jealousy on Bryant's face as Brigham had explained his predicament. He'd seen them dancing in ballrooms with love-stricken grins.

Clearly, Bryant had neglected to inform him of a few important goings-on.

"Allow me to assure you, my lady, that his intentions are far different now." His hands began to itch as he spoke only what he could assume. Bryant had never left him out of a conversation for something so public before, yet that was twice now that Bryant had coordinated something with Shepherd or Corbin and neglected to tell him about it. Of course, he himself had a great deal going on between his sister and brother-in-law, but to be excluded from something as important as Bryant's first potential courtship stung worse than any of his bullies' snide comments.

"His Grace has affection for you." He didn't dare say more lest his voice betray him.

The single statement didn't soothe her worries. "How can you be so sure? Perhaps he's heard of my lofty inheritance and thinks himself to play my affections for his own profit."

Brigham snapped to attention, rushing to say, "His Grace would never do that." Never would Bryant take advantage of a woman's standing. Never.

Thoughts of the past several weeks poured into his head; times when Bryant outright cursed because of Marjorie's godless husband. He'd done everything he could to make sure that she was comfortable in her situation, even having her over for tea now and again. If ever Bryant had an opportunity to pressure someone into owing him, this was it. And yet, he hadn't asked for so much as a lark in return.

"He's a good man, my lady. He wouldn't dare hurt you." If he ever did, he'd get a punch to the face as Brig had promised so many years ago.

"How do you know?"

His expression softened at the sound of her desperation. "You know of my family's reputation, my lady, and I don't think I need to tell you that the rumors are false. All the same, my sister accepted a loveless marriage with a heartless coward because of those rumors. Since returning to the capital, Bryant has done everything in his power to change her situation. When I say everything, I mean it. He danced with her to provide her some friends, called on her; he even opened his home to her so she didn't need to stay with her husband. On the night her husband almost murdered her, he was there to be her fortress.

"When I say that Bryant Wooldridge, Duke of Whittaker is the most honorable, noble, and gracious man on this planet, I mean it." He observed her expression then, studying the lines written in her forehead in an attempt to read her thoughts.

"I'm so sorry about your sister. I had no idea." Her muted, quiet tone reflected her thoughtful dark eyes. "That's it, then, isn't it?"

"I don't follow."

She nodded her head in realization. "At tea the other day, I asked His Grace why he kept to dancing with the wallflowers. While he gave me one reason, there was more that he refused to share, claiming it wasn't his place. Your sister is the reason, isn't she? He wants to make sure that no other woman has to endure what she did."

Brigham nodded, swallowing his anger and hurt as guilt rose up in his gut. Here he was, upset at being left out when his oldest friend had saved his sister from death itself.

Bryant had his reasons for everything, even for leaving one of his friends out of his personal life.

That realization didn't take away the sting of knowing he *had* been left out.

"I suppose His Grace is a true gentleman-sort, isn't he?" She stepped back, straightened her dress, and nodded. "I don't suppose I doubt him much now. It's back home then, I believe. Thank you, Lord Grimes, for putting up with my antics."

"A pleasure, my lady." He offered his arm and she took it as they strolled back to Pattermar. Bidding Olivia farewell at the steps, he took his leave.

...

Olivia waved goodbye to Lord Grimes from a window, feeling rather pleased with all that had transpired. She was relieved for the reprieve from the house. Its grand, echoey walls felt far too empty. Perhaps she would host a party of her own here, to liven up the space. It had been dead for too long.

She turned and came face-to-face with her estate manager. She jumped at his sudden presence, chiding him not to scare her. "What do you need, Prat?"

"Just a moment of your time, my lady. Who was that at the door?"

Her eyes narrowed. Prat had never asked about her social life before. It could be something new that she would need to adjust to as the Marchioness, but she somehow doubted that he was merely curious. "Lord Grimes, a dear friend of His Grace, the duke of Whittaker. Why?" She forced a commanding tone to intimidate him. It didn't work.

The old, grizzly man frowned. "Lord Whittaker practically proposes and yet you accept solicitations from men like him? He has no prospects. What will His Grace think when this is plastered all over the papers tomorrow?"

She glared. "Who I allow to court me is none of your business. You'd do well to remember that."

"Actually, my lady, it is. The attorney general stopped in to inform us that your father was severely in debt; far more than our estate can make in a year. Furthermore, after discussion with the king, it was decided the title would pass to you, given that you have no close male relatives. The king does not wish to put such debts on an innocent man." He leaned closer, his withered gaze more intense. "We are destitute. Lives are at stake, my lady. His Grace is the perfect match, the end to our problem. There must be no discussion."

She stared at him in shock before remembering herself. "I will marry whom I choose. You will not have influence over that. You are not my father, Prat, and you do not have the ability to act as he would." Her heart pounded in her jaw. There was no dowry, no security; only a hope that Bryant did love her as she suspected. How could her father have been so careless? So foolish? He couldn't have predicted his death, or so she hoped, but he surely knew that the bride price had to be paid eventually.

"You are right, my lady, but time is ticking. You must make a choice eventually, or your tenants will suffer. There is more at stake than yourself." Prat's eyes narrowed into a piercing gaze. Olivia suspected he used it on her father many a night. "If you do not marry the duke, you will lose everything. This house, your title, your tenants; everything."

She shuddered. "I will pray that the Most High protects us."

He scoffed. "The Most High wouldn't care; not about families like your own who gamble with what they have been given. Here you are, living in luxury while your tenants go hungry. He will not care. Your prayers will fall on empty ears. This is your only hope. Marry the duke and all of your problems disappear."

"You," she stuttered, "you're wrong. He will listen, and He will answer."

"Doubtful. All the same, your plans to involve yourself with Lord Grimes are unsavory. His family is comprised of lunatics. For your own safety, Madame, consider His Grace instead."

Her hands curled into fists as she tried to keep her tone rational. "The baron is one of His Grace's closest friends. They have known each other for years. I wasn't accepting solicitation; I was asking him a few questions about the duke. Regardless, it *is* none of your business. I will consider all you have said, but I make no promises. Remember, I am the master of this house, not you."

He sighed, resigned to her words. "It is as you say, my lady." The air fell silent for a moment as he pulled a note from his pocket. "This, my lady, might be convincing."

She took the note, scanning the words. Her hands trembled. "Where did you get this?"

"It was on my desk this morning. You are in danger, my lady, if you do not find a way to pay these men. They have given you five days. Do with that what you will." The door closed behind him with a *thud*.

With a storm brewing in her chest, she broke into a run and made for her room. Morlais, her lady's maid, waited with a look of expectation on her face. "How may I be of assistance, my lady?"

"Morlais, we need to make a plan." She sat at the desk and rolled the top up. "I have just discovered that I am penniless. Further than penniless, actually. The attorney general stopped in and I am without even a living wage."

The maid smiled softly. "The duke-"

"I cannot," she breathed. "He has been too kind to me, too gentle. I can't burden him with this. I'll marry someone else, someone whose heart is not so tender. Someone whose heart is in his appearance and not in me."

"You have tea with the duke in four days. What do you plan to do?"

She stared at the desk, littered now with papers she barely understood. "I don't know. I think he loves me. I don't wish to break his heart, but I don't know what else to do. He deserves better than this."

The clock chimed five, beginning the dinner hour. Morlais grabbed pins from her coiffure to style it for the meal. "He loves you, my lady, and any man in love is willing to do crazy things. Say the word, and he will give you whatever you desire."

"I desire to not trick him like this. I must tell him, and expect heartbreak." Her voice wavered. It wasn't loving to lie; certainly not to lie about something so important. Yet this was all so confusing. Perhaps after the tea, she might have a better understanding of what she should do.

"If heartbreak is what you expect, perhaps we should wait until you can be certain of his affections." She picked up a horsehair brush and began undoing the curls. "Be sure, my lady, that His Grace is not one to run from adversity."

She knew that, now more than ever. In fact, His Grace seemed to flock to adversity like a moth to a flame. Perhaps she was a flame to draw him in.

Chapter Twenty-Four: Bringing To Light

February 15th

As soon as he returned to Angarth, Eryi would need to thank Mrs. Kendrick for the parcel of food she'd insisted he take with him to Selcomb. It had proved rather useful in convincing Lord Arioch's butler to let him into the earl's study. More useful than sneaking around with Jerid, at least, since the threat of prison didn't loom over his head.

A sharp pang struck the chords of his heart as he looked through the papers for anything concerning the debts. The last time he'd been here, Jerid was still alive. In fact, their very last conversation was concerning these debts and their significance.

He was snooping for the exact same thing that had gotten Jerid murdered.

Shivers trailed down his spine as he searched the room. Unlike before, he had it on good word that Lord Arioch wasn't set to return for several hours, giving him the perfect opportunity to be careful and thorough in his search for any ledger containing betting information.

He sorted through the numerous stacks, setting aside any document that didn't match his criteria until his eyes fell upon the folder of records he required. Carefully, he slipped each page out and glanced through it. Most of them were written in red ink. Not quite what he was looking for, given that most of them were about the fields in the country and the staff's payments.

At the back of the folder, however, lay a very interesting piece of paperwork. One he had seen before, but ignored. Accounts with various lords' names with a variety of deposits and withdrawals. Lord Tristan, Lord Gregsay, Lord Jenherd; even Lord Seylor's name was listed, though it had been crossed out and replaced with Olivia. Those were the most concerning, given that her father's withdrawals outweighed the others by a great deal. His Grace would want to know the debt he was marrying into.

"Looking for information without me?" Peligro's sudden voice behind him made him jump. "Don't think that you shouldn't have asked me to tag along just because you can bribe Steffan on your own. I don't want to miss out on this." He glanced at the paper in Eryi's hand. "What have you got there?"

"This is the betting that I mentioned before. You remember, right? An entire list of the borrowers. Look at this account here, though. A deposit *into* his account, not out of it." He looked up, hands shaking.

"I take it that name means something to you?"

He took a deep breath to steady his voice. "It means more than *something*. That man is in prison for attempting to murder his wife. He's a drunk and a criminal." He rubbed his eyes to ensure that he was seeing properly. For sure and certain, clear as day, Mr. Morris's name was written in black ink across the bottom of the page. "Mr. Morris is supplying money so that Lord Arioch can distribute it and they both get rich off of the interest."

With wide eyes, Peligro stated, "But this means that Lord Arioch could be behind the break in at Pattermar, and—"

"And Jerid's murder. Come to think of it, the man that did it looked familiar. I can't quite place where I've seen him before." The thick beard could have been fake, but even so, it was difficult to imagine the man's other features. The darkness was to the murderer's benefit. They had once thought it their own, as they discussed secrets and gossip.

"It could be someone on staff here, or perhaps an acquaintance." He clenched his jaw. "Why do all of this, though? None of the lords have paid him back. He can't earn interest if he doesn't demand payment."

"He's biding time, waiting for the interest to make this all worth it. Not that any of it is worth it, or truly ever was. They'll hardly make pennies on the dollar." He stared at the desk, eyes catching on a document on the desk. "What's that?"

Peligro picked it up. "A letter, of sorts. It's from Morris, but it's dated recently. You don't suppose Lord Arioch has been asking for money, do you?"

Eryi reminded him, "He's in prison. Kegg wouldn't dare tie their names together. I doubt Wynn will allow visitors either, given that he almost murdered someone."

Peligro's eyes darkened. "Someone out there *is* a murderer, and I suspect that it's because of His Lordship. It doesn't make sense. Why would he risk innocent lives in the name of money?"

"Lord Arioch doesn't have a sterling reputation for respecting human life." His mind flitted to the numerous confrontations Bryant had regaled him with during long evenings. "I doubt he'd care that keeping his life of luxury cost a few souls."

Peligro stared at the paper in his hands. "This is enough evidence to take to Wynn, isn't it? We can have Lord Arioch arrested for murder and then the matter is solved and put to rest."

Eryi shook his head. "We know that there is a connection, but Lord Arioch is in the clear by legal standards. There's nothing wrong with loaning money to his peers, and he had a solid alibi at the time of Jerid's murder. If we had a record of payment for a hitman, or some such thing, that would be notable. What we have now is circumstantial at best. We need to find more to put all of the pieces together."

With wary eyes, Peligro glanced around the room. "That will have to wait. Lord Arioch will know at a single glance that someone was snooping through his things."

"We should take this one with us as proof."

"No, we shouldn't. This document isn't an old one. You take it and Lord Arioch will know beyond a shadow of a doubt that his operation isn't safe." He tucked the paper back into the folder and began setting the room to rights. "Come on, Eryi. The truth will show itself in time."

Eryi's eyes fell upon a wad of cash on the desk. His Grace had mentioned being robbed of a few larks that seemed to match the amount in the pile. The two couldn't be connected, could they? Why would Lord Arioch need to send someone out to rob the duke when it would only cause more problems for him? Nothing made sense anymore; not the ledger, not the murder, not the motivations. All the same, they needed to figure it out, and quick.

First things first, he needed to tell His Grace. They had a meeting scheduled in two days' time, and he prayed that was soon enough. His Grace's schedule was too compact to have it anytime else.

"I'm afraid time is the one thing we're running out of."

...

Tea. That's all it was. Tea.

She had taken it with Bryant before. Multiple times, even. Why did this single secret threaten to ruin the day?

Olivia knew why. She elected to ignore it. Things were going exceedingly well with Bryant, especially considering that he didn't even *like* her at the start of the season. She had won the elusive duke. Her mother would have been impressed, were she here to see it.

She should have been saddened by the thought. If she were honest with herself, however, her mother only used her as a trophy to be upheld. She was the perfect angel, the diamond her mother wanted for her own gain and glory.

What mattered much more were the debts, and how they would affect her life now. Regardless of Prat's concerns, she could hardly consider marrying the duke. It would be too much to ask him to pay her debts. Perhaps she was too proud, but she would rather die an old maid than ask him for his help. He was generous as it was. There was no need to push him further. Besides, the debts her father had accumulated weren't simply a lark or two over what their income was. They were extensive. It would take years of good harvests to pay them back. *If* she asked Bryant, would he even be able to pay?

She didn't need to ask that question. She would keep her mouth shut. Bryant had been a dear gentleman to her. The press would eat him alive if he involved himself in her scandal.

"Begging your pardon, Olivia, but you seem a touch distracted. Is the tea not to your liking?"

Her heart ached at the blissful innocence sitting across from her. "Yes, it is. I apologize, Bryant. I was... trying to savor the moment, is all."

His worry dissolved and broke into a smile, striking a chord within. "Shall we be off to the bookstore, then? I promise that I have money to pay this time. Pedr is watching should anything happen." He extended a calloused hand to help her up. She accepted, however hesitantly, and followed him outside. He was so genuine, so heartfelt.

And she was not.

...

Taking elevenses with Mother was always a delight. Her smile never failed to cheer him—certainly so when he remembered the days she hardly smiled at all. To see it was a ray of hope to pierce his heart.

Today, he needed that hope.

His outing with Olivia had gone smoothly the day before—she felt the need to grip his hand a little tighter as they passed the alley—yet he couldn't help but feel that something was wrong. She had seemed so distant. While he could, understandably, brush it off as despair over her situation, a rolling feeling in his gut suggested her hesitancy was caused by something much different.

Her eyes didn't speak of sorrow. They spoke of conflict.

Perhaps that is why he welcomed today's tea with open arms, instead of making an excuse and playing detective in his study. He needed his mother's wisdom.

"Bryant, dear, I've never witnessed you stare so intently at a piece of fruit in all your life. What is eating your thoughts, my darling?"

He chuckled. Mother knew him well. "I confess, there is something."

"Your smile tells me that this isn't about the mysteries awaiting you upstairs. Indeed, this must be some quandary of love or laughter."

"Right again, Mother. It's about Lady Olivia." He paused long enough to see the look of intrigue on her face. "How do you know if a lady has lost interest?"

Mother's smile fell instantly. "It should be fairly obvious, especially with Lady Olivia. She won't give you the time of day if she does not wish. Do you mean to say that she has?"

"That is what I am trying to figure out. We went to tea yesterday, as you well know, and she was lost in thought for most of our outing. If I thought it were flashbacks or grief or fear, I would drop the issue. But, when I looked into her eyes, I saw concern. Hesitancy. She was not comfortable being there with me. What I don't understand is *why*."

A smile met his question. Mother took in a breath so calm, she may as well have been soaking in sunshine and music. "Ask her, darling. If you wish to torment your heart then by all means, keep silent. Should you talk to her, instead, you'll find that you build bridges from your torment to hers. She trusts you, Bryant. If she would tell anyone what lies so heavily on her heart, it is you."

Bryant caught her smile as he downed the last of his tea. "With your permission, Mother, I'd like to journey to check on her now."

"I'll call for the horses."

"No need to bother the groomsmen. It snowed last night, and the trip might be nearly as slow with horses. I can walk just fine on my own."

Mother looked skeptical. "I suppose. Be sure to layer up well. I don't want you catching your death from being underdressed for the walk. Boots, coat, all of it. Make sure Mrs. Kendrick approves of your ensemble before you step out."

"I will, Mother." He rose from the table, darted up to his room to fulfill her request, and received said approval. Flowers in hand, he stepped out.

The snow, though not terrible, was heavy for Braxden. His ankles felt the bitter chill as he walked, despite his boots and thick stockings. He hoped Olivia had a roaring fire in the drawing room when he arrived.

He should have taken up his mother's offer of the carriage, but the carriage would have had as much difficulty getting through the snow as he did. It was better for him to go alone and not risk anyone else suffering in this weather.

Stately, he sauntered up to the front door and knocked. A minute or two passed before anyone answered. The staff likely assumed no one would attempt to traverse through town after such a snowfall. Reasonable, by all means; with soaked socks, snowy boots, and freezing hands, he'd almost abandoned the endeavor.

"Greetings, Your Grace. Here to call on Lady Olivia?" The butler smiled softly and ushered him inside. "I'll send for some tea. This weather is terrible."

"Thank you, Gregory. I'll see myself to the drawing room." He didn't offer up his coat, wanting something to keep him reasonably warm until the tea could arrive. A moment later, he sat in the middle of the drawing room, staring at the various embroidered pillows that dotted the couches. One by one, he counted the seconds until Olivia joined him.

"Hello again, Bryant. Why the unexpected call?" A smirk lit up her face. "Did you miss me so desperately that you couldn't wait until the masquerade on Tuesday?"

He shook his head. "I'm not entirely sure why I'm here. I just got this feeling that I needed to be here, that perhaps you needed something." At that moment, one of the maids stepped in with a tray of tea. She set it down swiftly, routinely, before curtseying and leaving the room. Bryant took the teapot. "How will you take your tea?"

"Strong with milk, if you will." She took the cup poured for her and sipped. "I do wonder what led you here. I am in no great distress; neither is anyone in the household. Are you quite certain that you didn't miss me?"

Her teasing statement pulled a ghost of a grin as he shook his head. "As much as I do truly enjoy our time together, it wasn't your absence that pulled me here." Even being here hadn't settled the nerves in his stomach that warned him of danger. He couldn't shake the feeling that something was—or was about to be—dreadfully wrong.

"Perhaps you came to promenade in the gardens, then."

The intention in her statement couldn't have been more obvious. "I'll have you know that I *am* planning to offer, but not today. I've another day in mind for it, Miss Sparrow." He spoke her nickname in hopes that his unease would settle. Hours ago, he'd ruled out that the nervousness was because of their relationship. Their being together seemed the correct path forward. Many hours were spent on his knees asking for guidance in handling the intended courtship. He had peace when he thought of them together.

Thinking of this house, alternatively, gave him only unease.

He lifted his eyes to meet hers, noticing that hope had sparked in the beautiful grey-green. That spread a smile across his face, to know how much she anticipated the moment he officially asked for courtship. "Could it be, perhaps, that you missed my company?" His heart pounded as her expression stiffened.

He could see the struggle in her eyes as she forced her mouth to a cheery disposition. "Not at all, Your Grace. I simply thought that you might have sought after my attention, given that this is the third time you've called on me this week alone." She took a slow sip of her tea as if to emphasize her point. "Now that you're here, of course, we might as well do something. This room is dreadfully chilly. Movement will get the blood flowing. Tour the gardens again, perhaps?"

"That would sound lovely, my lady, but the snow has built up quite substantially since yesterday. I'm afraid we wouldn't be able to get very far."

Her brows furrowed. "How deep is it?"

He gestured to the defined line of soaked linen on his trousers. "Enough for me to almost consider turning back whilst on my way here. It's a bit too frigid outside for a promenade."

Olivia opened her mouth to speak when a sudden scream permeated the air. "Not again," she exhaled as she clamored for the door. "This can't be happening again; it just can't!" She flung the doors open and ran for the foyer.

Moments later, the sound of shattered glass joined the cacophony. A large shadow fell across the foyer as a dark form took shape. Bryant's breath stopped in his throat at the sight, remembering the creature at the Mortimer Ball. There could only be one reason for its presence.

The footfalls of Olivia's heels brought him back to reality. He reached out and grabbed her wrist, pulling her away from the hallway. "Olivia, if there is a man who has broken into your home, *don't run towards him.* Please, stay here, where you're safe."

She growled. "I'm not some damsel, Your Grace, for you to act as though I don't know what I'm doing. I know what risks are out there. I'm simply doing what I can to keep my people safe. Why would you want to keep me back from that?"

He met her gaze. "You do not know what you're about to run into. That man likely has a gun, for which you would have no defense, or a knife, for which you have no training. Let the staff handle it." His eyes pleaded with hers to go back into the drawing room.

"If the staff could handle it, my parents would still be alive."

The sudden sound of a gunshot drew their attention back. Olivia attempted to rush towards it, but Bryant insisted he go first. Whatever the issue be, he had spent two years of his life dodging assassinations and angry mobs; he could handle a hitman far easier than she could.

He turned a corner and came face to face with a man too familiar. "You! You're the one that—" his voice stopped as he saw the blood pooling on the ground. The man held a gun. A round-casing lay beside his foot. Next to that, a servant with an ashen face and lifeless eyes. "Who- who are you?"

"Your Grace, what a pleasure to see you again. I hadn't heard that you were in the neighborhood. If I'd known, of course, I might have changed my trajectory for the day. It's much easier to rob a man's house when he isn't home." He loosed a low laugh that only aided his terrifying demeanor.

Bryant swallowed his fear and took a step forward, noting that Olivia was no longer behind him. He briefly glanced at the door, hoping, *praying* someone had escaped to get help. "Why have you broken into Pattermar?"

His eyes turned flinty, losing any sense of humor or joy. "I'm here to have a little chat with Lady Seylor and then I'll be on my way."

"What sort of chat?"

He stroked his beard. "That, Your Grace, is no one's business but my own." Bryant took another step forward, outstretching his arms as the man attempted to slide past him and leave the room. He held a hand out, halting him from proceeding. The man shook his head. "Your Grace, why would you do that? I can promise you that it won't end well."

"Perhaps it won't end well for me, but I will have served the purpose for which I was called." Even if the situation demanded his very life, he would give it.

"You're a fool, boy. I'm giving you a chance to run free." He flinched at the statement, unsure why he would be allowed to live as a witness to the event. Perhaps the man didn't wish to spill more blood and risk being caught. Perhaps, until caught by surprise, the gun was meant as a threat, not a weapon. "You have until I count to three to step aside and let me go on my way. One."

His mother's face flashed before his eyes. He pictured her red eyes and damp handkerchief after hearing of his death. She would miss him, but that wasn't enough to force him to move; not if his death could provide enough time to save the lives of the others.

"Two."

The laughter of his friends met his ears. They would understand why he left them. While they wouldn't be pleased that he'd sacrificed himself, they would understand. They might even spare a story or two for future generations about his heroism. Shep, at least, would know the weight of the love that had taken hold of his very soul.

"Three."

The sound of a bullet pierced the air and shattered his hearing. He braced himself for the impact even as Lady Olivia's face filled his sight. Concern wrote its way into her brow as she said something he couldn't hear. Only when a policeman's face joined hers in his peripheral did he realize that no bullet had pierced his flesh. Blood did not pool down his side. The man that had been standing before him a moment ago now sat crouched down on the floor, hands clutching a bloody shoulder.

"On your feet. You're coming with me." Officer Northwood grabbed the man by his non-wounded arm and dragged him to his feet before addressing Bryant and Olivia. "Officer Hitchens will meet with you in a few minutes to ask questions. Until then, wait in a comfortable place. The drawing room, perhaps." He nodded a farewell and pushed his captive onward.

"How did they get here so quickly?"

"One of the servants ran for the jail the very moment Morgaine screamed," she responded with ragged breaths.

Bryant grasped Olivia's hand and led her to the drawing room. Her pulse ticked rapidly against his own and a sound like a strangled sob echoed from her lips. He chose a settee for them to wait upon, holding Olivia tightly while he slowly swayed back and forth. "Take a deep breath, love. I'm here." He kept his grip tight, as though he feared a breeze could sweep her out of his arms. "The police will take care of everything."

"He won't be able to stop them all," she whispered. "There will always be another one lurking around the next corner, waiting for the moment to strike." Tears streamed down her face. "Why do they care so little about human life? Why don't they care that they prioritize money over someone's soul? Why do they want the money *so badly*-" She stopped herself. "I didn't mean to-" Unable to finish her sentence, she stared at the wall across from them, hyperventilating.

It clicked in his mind that, while he knew about the debts, she wasn't aware of his knowledge. Suddenly, her hesitation made sense. With the title passing to her, she had access to all of the financial records. Only recently would she know the debts she had. Debts that, clearly, she wasn't able to pay for.

"Olivia." The single word, spoken with the deepest love, caught her attention. "I know."

The color drained from her face. "No. No, you can't. It's my burden to bear. It's-" Her voice stilled as he gently grabbed her hand. "What are you doing?"

"Your life is worth far more to me than any price. Whatever they are asking, I will pay it."

She shook her head. "I can't let you do that, Your Grace. You've been incredibly generous with me, but I cannot allow you to cover my expenses. It is too much to ask."

"From a suiter, perhaps, but from a man that loves you? Not at all." She opened her mouth to speak, but nothing came out. He held her in silence as they waited for Northwood to return.

It felt strange to hold her so closely. He supposed it ought to send shivers down his spine like touching her hand had, but this felt different. It didn't sear his skin with warmth or give him peace beyond measure, but it gave him a sense of purpose. This was where he was meant to spend the rest of his life; side by side with the woman he loved, through the most difficult times.

The minutes ticked by like eternal waves of anguish as he anticipated the moment when Olivia's breathing regulated and her pulse slowed to normal. Witnessing two break-ins, fearing that those she loved would die, couldn't have been easy. He struggled to comprehend her level of fear until he recognized the agony that had held her eyes so intensely.

It was something that he had seen in his own eyes time and time again. Not just the fear of losing those you love, but the fear of not being able to stop whatever forces threaten them. He couldn't count how many times he'd felt that exact emotion; when his father died, when Brigham faced the bullies in school, when he'd been forbidden from offering help in Marjorie's situation. How could a person survive so much fear?

He'd asked himself that question a handful of times throughout his life. The one he remembered most clearly happened when he was eight. His father had recently passed and he was struggling to cope with his grief. He asked Brigham what he did when he was scared. The answer was simple.

Brigham had pulled out his copy of the sacred scriptures and turned to a page. "'In times I am afraid, I will put my trust in Thee. In the Most High, I will praise His word. In Him have I put my trust. I will not fear what flesh can do unto me.'" He had no reason to fear. His trust was in the Most High, who raised men from the dead and healed the sick and injured.

Bryant placed a soft kiss on the top of Olivia's head and whispered, "There is no reason to fear. The Most High is with us."

A sudden noise at the door startled him. Bryant locked eyes with the constable before pulling away from Olivia. She made a noise of protest before noticing that they weren't alone. A dark blush lit her cheeks as she righted herself. "Officer Hitchens. You have questions for us?"

"Right." He took a seat across from them and started down the list. Half an hour ticked by before his pen stopped gliding across the paper. "Do you know where to inquire about arrangements for the funeral?"

Olivia shook her head. "You'll need to ask the housekeeper about her family. I haven't met them." She scooted a little closer to Bryant. "I feel miserable about this entire thing. If I'd mentioned the debts to someone before—"

"That wouldn't have helped the situation, m'lady. A possible motive would have only applied to the convicted man, who did not confess the names of his associates. We had no way to perceive an additional threat." He set his notepad down on the low table. "Is there anything else either of you know?"

Olivia shook her head but Bryant spoke up. "One of my servants, Eryi, has been looking into the betting. He has family and friends in various households and connections to the information about their financial states. There's a fairly long list of nobles that are involved in this. I couldn't give you all of the names, but he could."

He hummed in thought. "I'll stop by Angarth later today. Thank you both for your time. Someone will stop by to speak with your housekeeper about the funeral and contacting the victim's family. I'll be keeping you all in my prayers."

"Thank you, Officer. You'll keep us updated?"

"Of course, Your Grace." With that, he dipped out the door and left.

Olivia waited for the soft *click* of the latch before letting out a breath and relaxing into her seat. "Your servant was looking into it? The one whose cousin was killed?"

"Yes," he replied, his stiff tone now solemn. "He's determined now more than ever to expose these men for their treachery."

"Whose idea was it to investigate? His? Or yours?"

"For this matter, mine." He poured himself a cup of cold tea and took a sip. "Do you recall the tea with Lord Arioch that my mother arranged?"

She smiled. "How could I forget?"

"His demeanor set off an alarm in my head. I didn't know what to make of it, so I asked Eryi to investigate, to determine if there was a rational cause to doubt his character. That's when he first learned of the debts. Neither of them thought that paper was important until later, after Jerid's murder."

A short silence fell between them, uneasy and loud. His heart raced as he thought of what Olivia would ask him next. Her response surprised him.

"Don't you feel guilty about it?"

"How do you mean?"

"The way I see it, and I don't mean to offend, your action indirectly caused that man's death. I cannot begin to describe the guilt I feel about Morgaine; and you, so much more tender-hearted than I, surely feel the same."

In spite of himself, he smiled. "I did, once, until Lord Pwyll got a hold of me."

"What did he tell you? What words could possibly make this agony go away?" He could hear the desperation in her voice. His heart softened as he recalled the hours he spent with that same tone, crying out for the flames of guilt to dissipate. Shepherd had brought him some semblance of comfort. Perhaps he could do the same.

"He asked me a question, to begin with, and I'll ask you one likewise. Did you give him the gun?"

Her eyes narrowed. "Well, no. I didn't."

"Did you give him the bullets? Did you let him inside the manor?" She shook her head. "Then you are not responsible for Morgaine's death. That man and his comrades are."

"You might be right, but I could have prevented it. My estates manager warned me about this. There was even a notice, ordering me to pay immediately. Perhaps if I had applied for special license and married someone quickly I might have-"

"Stop. This won't help you. All of these 'what if's can't change what has happened. Nor should they change what will." Bryant took her hand, gently brushing the surface with his thumb. "You couldn't have predicted this outcome. Neither could I, that day. If I had known, I would have kept Eryi at home. I didn't, on either counts. That doesn't make Jerid's death my fault, anymore than Morgaine's death is yours."

Tears burned her eyes. "I wish I could undo all of the damage that this has done; but, of course, I can't. Perhaps I could do something for Morgaine's family. They'll need a bit of extra money now that... now that they don't have the income her service provided. I have *some* pocket-money I could offer them, but it's the last of what we have."

He wasn't quite sure what else to say. The glazed-over look to her eyes made him wonder if she was even still talking to him. So, he let her air out her thoughts, content to listen and ponder as she worked out the ideas in her head.

"Can we go to Angarth, Bryant? I need to get out of this house, whether the snow permits it or not. I'm willing to traverse its frigidity if it means not being *here*."

"Of course, my lady. Whatever you need." He took her hand and slowly plodded to the door. "Are you okay, love?"

She took a deep breath. "I don't know, but... I'm thankful it wasn't worse." Her feet halted as she looked into his eyes. "I keep thinking about the moment that I returned and saw *you*. You, standing in front of that man knowing full well that you would die. Yet, you stood with a pistol pointed at your chest to protect my household; to protect *me*. What have I done to deserve you?"

He didn't have an answer; he suspected that she wouldn't take one anyway. Instead, he pressed a kiss to her forehead. "Before his death, my father taught me about the responsibility on my shoulders as a duke. It is my duty to protect my people; to defend those I love."

Chapter Twenty-Five: Words Like Poison

February 16th

Red dotted her vision and refused to leave it. Her afternoon at Angarth didn't change that, either. Nothing rid her of the bloody memory. It burned against her eyelids, forcing sleep to be elusive and unwelcoming.

Her eyes stung from the hundreds of tears she'd shed. Pain wafted in and out of her heart as she grieved. It had struck an odd chord with her because she hadn't truly developed friendships with her servants. Her understanding since childhood was that the servants were below her. And yet, here she sat with burning eyes, feeling completely lost at the death of the maid.

She felt dizzy and put a hand on the vanity to support herself. Never in her life had she needed to feel so *much*. It flowed out of her at a moment's notice, and rarely did her heart cease its cries. In her weariness, she could only ponder why.

Her thoughts were interrupted by a loud knock at her door. She sighed and rose to answer it, surprised when Prat's face appeared in the doorway. Rage wrote its way into every detail in his face, from the narrowed eyes to the deep creases in his forehead. "What is the matter? Why do you disturb me?" He wouldn't be upset at her visiting Angarth, was he? That wouldn't make any sense, given that he wanted her to marry Bryant. Then again, stranger things have upset him before.

"You spoke with the police yesterday." Accusation filled his voice. Odd. She was only doing her duty as a citizen and as a witness to the crime.

"I did. To not cooperate would have been wrong and make me look as though I'd been an accomplice. I was honest."

Her reply did little to soothe his expression. "You didn't need to mention the debts."

She matched his anger. "Yes, I did. I had to explain the reason behind the ambush. The previous intrusion wasn't just a stupid fool's attempt at earning a few larks! There's an entire conspiracy of men attempting to rob Braxden's nobles and ruin its families. If the police didn't know the whole truth of the matter, they would be even more blind as to whom they are looking for. I doubt that man has been willing to admit anything." She took a deep breath, trying to calm her tone. "I had to tell them. To keep what I knew away would only do us more damage."

"The benefactor isn't going to be happy."

Indeed not; though he clearly wasn't happy as it was. She rolled her eyes at his statement and responded with, "I do believe his feathers were ruffled without my assistance."

A growl echoed from his throat, guttural and vengeful. "It wasn't your place. You should have called me down from my study. I would have handled the matter—"

"Yes, by lying through your teeth!" She shouted, taking a step towards him. "Do you honestly want these men to continue hunting us down? That is what will happen if the police aren't able to find them! To be entirely honest, Prat, it looks to me far more like you're on their side instead of mine." Emotion stirred within her.

Had she not cried the entire night, tears would have brimmed her eyes. "Do you want these men to hurt me?"

The man took a step back, bumping into the wall. "Of course I don't want that. All the same, it can't be helped. They would have murdered you today if your precious duke hadn't defended you. To betray them now will only mean the worst for you. If they hear that *you* told the police about their operation, they will send someone in under the cover of night to dispose of us all. Do you want *that* to happen?"

She glowered in silence.

"I didn't think so." He rested a hand against the doorpost and released a heavy sigh. "You've been spending quite a bit of time with His Grace. Do you think he will propose soon?"

"I cannot be sure. He mentioned yesterday that he wanted to discuss something with me in a few days' time, but he did not specify what about." She hated this. Words could not express how deeply she hated this.

"That's good, at least. You should put a bit more pressure on him to hurry it up. The sooner you are married, the better for everyone involved."

"I can't do what you're asking of me. While he's convinced he loves me, I'm not entirely sure yet that marriage is the best path for us. Even *if* I am certain that we ought to marry, I won't force him to propose. I'm not some obscene, pretentious girl who thinks that the whole world ought to be at her feet."

The deep *timbre* of his voice that she once found comforting now shattered what little respect she still held for him. "Society thinks otherwise."

Regardless of how true those words were, he had no right to speak to her so. "Leave me be."

"You were born to be a societal diamond. Everyone expected you to marry well and are surprised it has taken this long. You are in your fourth year. The options for you are running out. At this point, your peers and mine alike expect you to marry His Grace. Do not disappoint them."

She stared incredulously at the man who was supposed to have an overview of her *finances* and ignore her personal life; yet here he was, acting as some kind of authority figure. "You can't possibly expect me to organize some sort of... *situation* that would require a quick marriage."

He shook his head but replied, "I'm not asking you to risk your reputation. All I require is that you convince him to marry you by the end of the season. That is the timeline I was given. You'll do well to stick to it."

"I can't do this to him. He deserves better than some conniving girl out to steal his fortune." She shook her head, certain now that it was best they didn't marry. The moment she got married, her debt would transfer to her husband. Bryant deserved far better than a marriage that brought only obscene amounts of debt and a sparse bit of land.

"You said he thinks himself in love with you. Surely, then, getting married is all he desires of you. It won't matter to him that there is debt attached to your name. If he's truly in love with you, he won't object to paying for it as part of the terms of your marriage."

Olivia shook her head again, determined to stand for justice. "I won't ask that of him, even if it means that the men in charge of this scheme will design to kill me. I'd rather sacrifice myself than force such disgrace upon him."

His eyes narrowed. "Why would you do that?"

"Because it's what Bryant would do."

...

Dark. That was the only way that Portencia could describe Selcomb. Even after meeting with Eryi's friend Peligro, the cathedral-style manor felt incredibly dark. If she were the superstitious type, she'd believe a ghost or two resided here. She pressed on through the various stairwells and hallways as she made her way to Lord Arioch's study.

A shiver made its way down her spine as the memory of her last visit filled her mind. He was a rather unruly fellow. It didn't surprise her to hear that Cristyn despised the man or that Lyz thought him the dangerous sort. Of course, that was *after* she'd entangled herself in the web that was Lord Arioch's business.

That one night would forever sear itself into her memory. She'd just received a letter from her older brother, telling her that they were going to lose the farm if they couldn't keep a steady income. Tears had blurred her eyes as she read the letter over and over again to ensure she wasn't seeing things. The words failed to change.

She had run off into the night, trembling as the cold air soaked her skin with its needles. Blinded by her tears, she failed to see the man in front of her, accidentally slamming into him.

He'd taken compassion on her wary state and offered to pay half of her income if she promised to gather information about the various households. Little things; the salaries of employees, work hours, how often certain purchases were made. It was odd, but she wasn't about to object. They'd needed the money.

Then, three months ago, he'd changed his request. It was no longer financial information he wanted, but information that only she could provide: the state of affairs at Angarth. He wanted to know the goings-on, the thoughts of His Grace regarding certain persons, and, later, inquired of His Grace's relationship to

Marjorie. Lord Arioch hadn't bothered to explain his reasons; he claimed that her knowing too much was dangerous. She would become a liability that would ruin the whole operation.

She was tempted to run to His Grace and explain everything, but that would only end in her going to prison along with them. With her brother still struggling at the farm, that wasn't an option. He needed the money she was providing both as a servant to His Grace *and* as an operative for Lord Arioch. She'd get neither if she told anyone about the goings-on at Selcomb Manor.

The door to the study stood before her. All she needed to do was step inside to receive her new mission. It was a simple act; one that she'd done a few dozen times before. Why, then, did her hand tremble so much as it grasped the doorknob?

She managed to swallow her fear and thrust the door open. "Lord Arioch, you asked to meet with me?"

"Yes. Thank you for joining me, sweet Portencia." His wicked grin was only enhanced by the pale moonlight. "Care for a drink? I shan't be able to finish this bottle of rosé on my own." He extended a glass but Portencia couldn't bring herself to take it. "Oh, come on now, luv. There's no harm in accepting it. Call it a gift." His voice slipped into a street accent.

She hadn't yet been able to determine if it was a facade he'd mastered to appear on the same level as his accomplices, or if it was the result of growing up without parents and peers to teach his voice the noble tongue. Cristyn would have known in an instant.

"I shouldn't. It wouldn't do for me to be stumbling my way back home; the others would be suspicious." She stepped back, angling herself beside the door for a quick getaway if need be.

While his eyes flickered resentment, he kept his grin affixed to his face and stalked closer, cupping her jaw with his hand. "There's no need to be so tightly strung, my dear. Surely a room can be prepared for you if you aren't comfortable with going out." Something dastardly filled his eyes that spoke volumes as to *which* room would be prepared.

"What is my mission, Lord Arioch?"

He rolled his eyes. "Such a righteous woman. So focused on business and morals that you've hardly any time to enjoy yourself." He sat straight and set the glass down, voice dropping to a near-whisper. "I've an associate that needs a vital word from me. There is no doubt in my mind that he has heard of some recent goings-on. I need you, dear one, to visit him. My cook will give you a meal to take to him so that you don't look out of place. Once there, tell him that His Lordship is well taken care of."

She eyed him warily. "Are you referring to yourself or...?"

"That," he snapped, "is none of your business. Once you have finished giving him that message, return here. There's a second part to this mission that I need you for. Don't worry, my sweet. It's nothing that will compromise your precious morals."

If this were her first visit to the study, she'd be hesitant to believe him. After so many missions, however, she knew otherwise. Lord Arioch was many things, but he was no liar. That knowledge, however, did little to settle the stormy unease in her gut that raged as she left the manor, basket of food in hand.

...

John Morris. The associate of Kegg's that she was supposed to visit was John Morris. She'd almost told him no, but that would cause problems that she couldn't afford to create.

Now, she stood in front of the jailhouse, preparing herself to face the man who had caused such deep terror and trauma in the heart of dear Marjorie and trying to *not* remember how distraught the girl looked on that night weeks ago. It was bad enough that she needed to run errands for Kegg to help her brother; that was morally gray enough on its own. But to give food and a message to a man who attempted to murder his own wife pushed the limits of her conscience.

She wasn't sure if she could do it. She knew that she *shouldn't*. It would be easy enough to walk away—to simply leave the basket at the door and knock before running off into the night. There were jobs to be found in every city, so sending money back home wouldn't be difficult—if a bit more complicated. In an hour, she could be on a wagon leaving the city. She could leave in two shakes of a butter churner.

The question still remained of *should*. Could she leave with little repercussions to herself? Without a doubt. But what would it mean to her brother, who would go weeks without money and months more without the kind of money she brought in now? What would it do to Lady Olivia, who was no doubt being targeted so Lord Arioch's pockets could be lined with gold?

Would His Grace suspect her death if she left without a word? No body would be found regardless of any search. And of the servants, who took her in off of the streets and brought her up in a loving community? She couldn't leave them and simply let them think she suffered a tragic end. It wouldn't be right.

She could leave, but she wouldn't. She'd play the part of a worried cousin like Kegg told her and finish her mission; once again, shutting down her conscience to help those she loved.

When could she draw the line?

With her story well-versed upon her weary soul, Portencia stepped into the frigid jailhouse. "Wynn, hello."

The constable met her eyes, concern written into his brow. "Miss Hymn. What brings you by? Is something wrong at Angarth?"

She shook her head. "I'm here to visit John Morris. He's a distant cousin, see, and I thought it'd be best for me to bring him some food; per my mum's request."

Wynn pursed his lips for a moment before sighing and letting her pass. "I don't usually allow visitors for violent convicts, but I'll make an exception for you, Miss Hymn. Keep your visit short, though. I'll be right here if you need anything."

"Thank you, Wynn. I won't be long."

Her heart beat loud in her chest, pounding against her lungs and stealing her breath. The hefty man sat cross-legged on the floor alone in the cramped cell, with a displeased expression on his face that faded once he saw her.

"John Morris?"

"I might be. Who are you, pretty thing?"

His voice sent shivers down her spine. Not daring to give her name, she answered with, "Lord Arioch sent me. I'm to give you this along with the message "His Lordship is well taken care of,' whatever that means." She extended the basket, hoping her fear was not reflected in her hands.

"I see. Thank you for telling me, Miss Nobody." His grin twitched but didn't turn from its fixed place. "Was there anything else?"

"No- no, there wasn't. That was all." She thanked heaven that Cristyn hadn't been the one to find Alden Kegg that night. With a deep breath for courage, she left the basket on the ground and hurried out.

"Find everything alright?" Wynn's eyes sparked worry but he didn't voice his concern.

"Yes. Thank you, Wynn."

...

"What's the second part, Lord Arioch?"

He tapped his chin. "Oh, how to put this. I need you to convince the duchess to host a ball at Angarth. It doesn't matter how big the guest list is so long as I am on it."

She narrowed her eyes. "I don't have the power to speak so with Her Grace. I'm a servant, remember? Why would she listen to me about hosting a ball?"

"She trusts you, does she not?"

"Yes, she does," Portencia replied. The duchess really shouldn't—not after the past few months—but she did, because she had reason to before. "That doesn't mean that she will trust my advice when it comes to her social image. A maid doesn't suggest such a thing."

Lord Arioch gave her a wicked, sweet smile that soured her stomach. "She does *now*. I trust you can figure out the perfect opportunity to slip a mention of it. You've proved yourself rather good at that."

The poison. Her stomach churned as the memory lit her vision. "Lord Arioch, I can't hurt them. The guilt of it almost killed me before. I can't— I *won't* hurt them."

"There's no need to hurt them, my dear. All I ask is that you arrange a ball and ensure that I am on the guest list. Nothing more, nothing less. There will be plenty of other men who can handle the details from there. You have a clean conscience and I get what I want."

He opened a desk drawer and pulled out a gun, fiddling with the barrel as he holstered it. "Now, I've a meeting to get to. My accomplices have proved themselves idiotic for the last time." He met her eyes with a snarl of devilry as he stood. "If you don't fancy going back to Angarth so late at night, my offer of a room still stands. Remember to report back to me as soon as you can get away. I'll give you the payment then." He sidestepped past her, slipping through the door.

Her hands trembled as she closed the door behind her and fled to Angarth, knocking furiously after realizing the kitchen door had been locked. Eryi opened it cautiously, eyes widening at seeing the disheveled woman behind it.

"Portencia? Why were you out so late? Curfew was hours ago," he stated bluntly, ushering her inside and pressing a cup of tea into her hands.

"I had to make a call. Urgent family business," she offered. That was all the truth he'd need to accept her reason. No mention of the details would be necessary, thank heaven. She wouldn't be able to handle any sort of scrutiny tonight.

"Is your brother alright?"

Blast Eryi and his stupid questions. "Larn is fine. At least, he will be now." She sent him a look that she prayed he could read. She couldn't deal with his questions tonight; not when guilt still crawled in her gut like a hellspawned spider.

"I'm glad to hear it. Get some rest, alright? We've a long day tomorrow." He yawned as he set his own cup of tea in the washtub.

"Eryi, why are *you* awake at this hour?"

He shrugged. "Couldn't sleep. His Grace and I are discussing a few matters tomorrow and it's keeping me up."

"You're not in trouble, are you?"

Her statement pulled a grin. "You wouldn't be surprised if I was, hm? Unfortunately, I'm not the one in trouble this time. The situation would be so much easier to figure out if that were the case." He sent her a soft, sad sort of smile. "Good night, Portencia. I'm praying for you and yours."

"Thank you, Eryi."

Chapter Twenty-Six: Biding Time

February 17th

Morning greeted Bryant all too quickly. With the early sun came a knock at his bedroom door. He groaned, threw a shirt on, and opened the door. Eryi stood face to face with him. "Come in, please. I apologize that this is the first time we've had a chance to go over your information." He ushered him into his parlor. "What have you found out?"

"Lord Arioch has been receiving funds from John Morris to distribute to the other lords. Of course, it doesn't appear that way in the ledgers. Morris's name was labeled with "debtor" to cover it up. We need a confession to prove their connection." he sighed heavily. "Lord Arioch is the current mastermind, and the one who must have ordered the deaths of Jerid and the Seylors."

Bryant grasped the armrest on his chair as a way to soothe his reeling mind. He hadn't imagined all of this when he had a "bad feeling" back in November. "Have you thought of any strategies to pull a confession?"

Eryi nodded. "Spent most of the night pondering what we can do. I've considered as many contingencies as I could imagine. As far as I see it, there's one clear option."

"Here, let's talk in the parlor where we can sit down." He strode into the side room and plopped into a chair, gesturing for Eryi to do the same. "Alright. Let me hear it."

"I'm sure you're familiar with the saying about catching flies with honey?"

"Of course."

"Arioch is a fly—in more ways than one. All we need to do, then, is to offer some honey to draw him out."

Bryant narrowed his eyes. "I don't quite follow."

"You, Your Grace. You'll approach him during a formal event and inquire about placing a few bets. From there, it should be simple. He agrees to talk it out with you, you place a few strategic questions, and we've got all we need to charge him for conspiracy to murder."

Bryant nodded hesitantly. "Essentially, then, I need to figure out the right phrasing to squeeze out any sort of confession that he's the mastermind. Right?"

"Right. Providing we can get that, this entire operation is finished. We should meet with Wynn to confirm that he can be a witness. Of course, in order to involve him, we'll need an extra invitation. I don't suppose you know how to procure a plus one for an event?"

He could manage that, if only he were the one to handle their correspondence. His mother had taken it upon herself to sort through the invitations and determine which ones were the best options for his first season. "I'll need to chat with my mother, but I'm sure we can figure something out."

"Great. Any questions before we go to meet with Wynn?"

"Just one, that I can think of. What if Kegg asks how I found out about the bets? I can't very well admit that my main source of knowledge is from a few sneaky servants." He'd claim that Corbin was his primary source of information, but Eryi had already mentioned that he hadn't been on the ledger.

He realized now just how good it was that Corbin had kept his bets few and far between instead of falling into the trap of gambling that so many of their peers had gotten into. It could have been Corbin fearing for his life instead of Olivia. Not that the one was much better than the other, but the man was careless about his own safety. Olivia at least had the sense to keep a maid with her.

"Lord Tristan. Lord Waldron is an acquaintance of his, is he not? You could establish a connection through their association. Just claim that he mentioned it in passing conversation and that it caught your attention."

"Alright. I think we have enough to talk to Wynn. If we get his approval, I'll speak to my mother about getting that plus one." A knock on the door nearly made him jump.

Eryi bounced to his feet and opened it. "Portencia? What brings you here?"

The woman stepped into the room, a tray in hand. "I thought you both might want some tea. It's a rather chilly morning, after all." She plastered on a bright smile as she set the tray down onto the low table. "What seems to be the discussion at hand?" Her voice cracked as she spoke. The tremor in her hands only amplified the obvious: she was incredibly nervous about something.

"We were simply discussing an upcoming event." Best to keep his staff as in the dark as possible, just in case Kegg was the type to take his staff hostage for what they knew. "Could you send word to my mother? I'd like to ask her about our recent invitations to ensure that I can secure an invitation for my... friend."

"Of course, Your Grace." She bit her lip, which only confused him further. Something was bothering her, quite clearly, but what?

"Is something the matter, Portencia?"

She gave a half-hearted laugh and shook her head. "It's only that, if you're concerned over the guest list, why not ask Her Grace to host a ball of her own? She's yet to do so this season, and it might bring some life back into this manor. It hasn't been the same since Lady Morris left, you know."

That couldn't have been what was on her mind, could it? Surely the idea of making a suggestion wouldn't cause her hands to shake. Unless, that is, he'd completely underestimated his presence here at Angarth. Never before had he been the master of the house. Everyone followed his mother's orders above all else until this fall. It could be the nerves of making a suggestion to (what could be considered as) a new employer.

Of course, Portencia hadn't been nervous when speaking with him before.

His servants and their secrets were going to be the death of him.

"I hadn't thought of that. It's a fairly good suggestion. Thank you, Portencia." He nodded to dismiss her before taking a cup of tea and turning to Eryi. "Wynn can wait long enough for a cup to be had, right?"

"Don't forget, Your Grace. You promised Lady Olivia that you'd call on her later today," Eryi reminded.

"Ah, yes. Of course. A quick cup of tea, then." The way Portencia shivered as she stepped out into the hall didn't go unnoticed.

One of these days, he was going to call for a staff meeting and order everyone to spill what on Kestia it was that made them such a unique set of staff. Portencia with her sudden nervousness, Eryi with his endless list of contacts, Cristyn with her incredible ability to read people. They all had stories and he felt awkward and out of place by not knowing them.

"Eryi, how is it that you have so many family members spread across different households?" He supposed it was wasting time to ask such questions in the present moment, but they had tea to finish before heading out. Wynn could wait a few minutes longer.

"Grandmum wanted us to be central, in the same city, but knew that we wouldn't last more than a fortnight working together. She raised most of us, you know. My parents died to disease when I was ten. Peligro's parents, too. She kept us—and a few of our other cousins—off the streets long enough for us to get decent work."

He smiled softly. "If it weren't for her, I wouldn't be here. *We* wouldn't be here, piecing this case together once and for all. Without her, we wouldn't have access to Lord Arioch's documents. Marjorie would have been left in the cold." His eyes narrowed as his voice trailed off. "Your Grace, there's someone lingering by the door."

"Probably Portencia, waiting for a reasonable time to take the tea tray back." It wouldn't surprise him, what with the maid acting so strangely this morning. "Eryi, has she mentioned anything to you lately? Anything that would strike you as odd or strange."

He pursed his lips. "She may have knocked at the kitchen door several hours past curfew last night; said there was some family issue that had come up. I didn't think to press further. Should I have?"

"I don't know. It just seems rather odd to me that she acts on edge. I've never seen her like this."

"Perhaps it's the morning chill getting to her." Eryi's tone didn't agree with his words, confirming the suspicion that something *was* off today.

He nodded half-heartedly. "Perhaps." His teacup clinked against the mahogany as he set it down. "We should get going. If we're going to set up an entire ball, we'll need to work quickly. Should we change the order of things and speak to my mother first? I'm sure the constable will be willing to show up no matter the day, if it'll provide invaluable evidence against Kegg."

"That might be best, yes. Time is running out if we want to catch him before something *else* happens." He shivered as he rose to his feet. "Shall I ring for breakfast in the drawing room, then?"

"Yes. Thank you, Eryi. I'll meet you down there just as soon as I'm dressed properly." He slipped back into his bedroom as Eryi stepped out into the hall. His heart thumped loudly in his chest as a sinking feeling formed in his gut. Time *was* running out, he feared and, one way or another, someone was going to pay for it.

...

Eloise strutted around the large, dusty ballroom, directing servants as she sized up the state of the room. Bryant's suggestion that she host a ball had warmed a side of her that she'd forgotten about entirely. She'd shuddered when he asked her to ensure that Alden was on the guest list, but she complied when he explained why.

The news of Alden being associated with the recent murders shocked her. Bryant had mentioned a few weeks ago that the man had threatened him over Lady Olivia, but she hadn't imagined that he would actually command his accomplices to *murder* to get what he wanted. If inviting him to a ball was the way to get evidence against him, she would gladly do her part. Even now, Mabyn had a guest list in hand and was compiling the invitations to send out.

With as much force as she could muster, Eloise pulled open the heavy curtains at each window, allowing glorious light to spill into the room. She took a broom in hand, determined to not leave all of the cleaning to the servants. Her closet held a linen apron for a reason, and it wasn't just for those years when baby Bryant was insistent on repelling any food she gave him.

"His Grace mentioned that I'd find you in here." A familiar, warm voice greeted her. "I'm only here for a visit, Your Grace, but when Bryant mentioned that you were cleaning, I thought I might help." Marjorie joined her side, a broom in one hand and a dust-pan in the other. "There's quite a bit of work to do to prepare this room for a party, wouldn't you say? We had better get started."

Eloise chuckled. "You don't need to help me, Marjorie. You're a guest here."

"The more hands there are, the lighter the work," she hummed as she waltzed around the room. "How have you been, Your Grace?"

"We've managed. The whole household misses having you around. I do too. It felt nice having another lady around to chat with. Not that I mind conversing with Bryant, mind you, but it isn't quite the same." A light grin spread across her face.

"I do quite understand. My growing up years were fairly lonely having only a brother for a friend; a brother that is nearly a decade younger than me, at that." She paused, overlooking the room. "Perhaps it would be best to divide and conquer. If we split up the room into different sections and assign one person to each, we can get the room clean much more efficiently."

"A splendid idea. I shall call everyone that can be spared from the kitchen to join us. Give me but a moment." Eloise stepped out into the hallway and made her way to the kitchen.

"Aneira, how many hands do you need to prepare the food for the ball?"

The older woman paused her task, putting her hands on her hips as she thought. "We have three days to prepare, correct? You may have Cristyn, Tels, Margred, and Portencia; the last, providing you can find her. No one has seen her all afternoon."

"That's rather odd. It isn't her afternoon off. And she isn't working on some other part of the manor?"

"Not that I can tell, Your Grace. I would check with Mrs. Kendrick to be certain, but I do know that not a hair of hers has been seen in my kitchen since lunch." She dismissed the three chosen women before turning back to the food before her.

Eloise ushered the girls into the hallway. "Marjorie is currently in the ballroom. She'll put you to work while I figure out where Portencia has gone off to." She walked off towards the foyer as the girls made their way down the hall.

Her target sat on the kneeler just shy of the front door. "Mrs. Kendrick, might I bother you for a moment?"

The woman sat upright. "Of course, Your Grace. How can I be of assistance?"

"Do you know where Portencia is?"

She squinted, as if the motion would allow her to see her memories more clearly. "I can't say that I recall seeing her anywhere. She slipped out for a short walk just after lunch, but promised she'd be back within the hour. That, of course, was a few hours ago now, so she should be back." Her head tilted as she asked, "Aneira hasn't seen her?"

"Not since lunch. It worries me. Portencia isn't the type to be late, or to contradict her word when she's given it."

"Do you suppose something happened to her?"

Eloise took a deep breath. "It's possible. I hate to think so, but it's far too odd that Portencia would break her own pattern. I'll have Eryi send a telegram to the constable. This worries me. It isn't like her to lie about where she's going or when she'll be back. I can't help but think that something *has* happened."

"Wynn will be able to take care of the details. No need to get your feathers ruffled, Your Grace. I'm sure she'll turn up."

"I hope you're right, Mrs. Kendrick." She added a silent *I just hope she doesn't turn up dead* as she made her way back to the ballroom, stopping on the way to snag Eryi and send him off.

In the few minutes that she'd been gone, the room had drastically changed. The years of dust and grime were almost removed from the floor. Tels held a bucket of water and a rag and had taken to scrubbing the swept areas to prepare it for shining.

Cristyn spotted her first and piped, "Does Mrs. Kendrick know anything about Portencia's disappearance?"

She shook her head and sighed. "She hasn't seen her since the girl stepped out for a walk after lunch. I've already had Eryi send a telegram to Wynn asking him to be on the lookout for her. Beyond that, I don't know that there is much we can do. I'd send a search party if so many of our people weren't stretched to their veritable limits because of this ball."

It was an interesting balancing act, for sure and certain. If she sent people out to look for Portencia, the house wouldn't be ready for the party. If she kept everyone here, the only thing being done for the dear girl was the collective praying of the household. While under any normal circumstance, she'd never risk a servant's life for her own gain, but these were hardly normal circumstances. If they didn't manage to prepare for the ball, Bryant wouldn't be able to speak with Alden about the debts and Wynn wouldn't be able to take him into custody, leaving him free to send more men after their peers and their families. Either way she turned the coin, lives were at stake.

Portencia would show up soon, wouldn't she?

"Your Grace, are you alright?" So captivated had she been by her thoughts that she didn't see Marjorie approach her. "Here, let's pause a moment," the young woman called to the others. "Let's pray for her right now. It's all we can do, isn't it? Surely, then, we ought to offer our time to this as a group before anything else happens. The Most High might operate outside of time itself, but that doesn't mean we should neglect our responsibility."

"You're quite right, Lady Marjorie," Tels offered as she gestured for the other two to join them in a circle. "Portencia could be in trouble. We need to offer up our prayers for her before it's too late."

Eloise noticed Cristyn's shiver as the girl joined them. Due to her story, no doubt. A sad tale, that one, that would likely leave scars on the dear girl's heart for years to come. "Let's hold hands, then, to unite us." She took Cristyn's hand and Marjorie's before bowing her head and opening her heart to the Most High. Years of memories spent studying the ancient texts flooded her mind; each verse a reminder of the Most High's calling, of His love and protection. She prayed that He would offer Portencia that same protection despite the precarious and unknown circumstances the woman might be in at this very moment. "I ask that You remind her of Your protection and Your light, Dear One; wherever she may be."

Each of the girls around her voiced a similar statement before Cristyn, with a shaking voice, offered the final sentiment. "Lord, You who brings peace to each and every soul, be with her. Keep her in the path of Your light. Keep harm far from her as she travels down this dangerous path. Teach her the ways of Your truth and honesty. We ask this in the name of Your precious Son. Amen."

"Amen," Eloise echoed, the word's translation clear in her mind. *Let it be.*

Chapter Twenty-Seven: Pieces

February 19th

Anticipation hung like a heavy blanket over each soul at Angarth. Even now, Constable Wynn and Eryi waited as guests began to arrive, milling about the grounds. They'd determined it was best not to approach the situation quickly, giving the guests time to settle into the familiar rhythm of evening functions before breaking the silence. It was best to make the scenario look as genuine as possible to avoid Kegg's suspicions.

Bryant stared at the door, waiting and watching for anyone he knew. Shepherd, Brigham, or Corbin, preferably, so that he could air out the unease settling in his gut. This wasn't going to be easy to pull off. If he so much as said one wrong thing, Kegg would know what he was playing at and their whole operation would be ruined.

He felt a tap on his shoulder, nearly jumping out of his skin at the touch. "Your Grace, I was hoping to have a word."

So much for their plan of *waiting*. He turned to face the man, fixing a warm smile on his face. "Evening, Lord Arioch. I'm glad you found me. I have some business I'd like to go over with you. Are you enjoying the party?"

"Of course. I know Her Grace hasn't hosted a ball in some time, but this is exactly as I imagined it would be. The food and music is up to an impeccable standard. I'd expect nothing less from Her Grace." He pressed his lips into a firm line. "Now, Your Grace, about that business. Care to drop a hint as to the topic?"

He shook his head. "A hint might not be enough. Here, follow me. It's not the sort of conversation I'd prefer to have in a crowd. I'm sure you can understand."

"Of course, Your Grace." He followed as Bryant walked into a small side room. "What is it?"

He spoke hesitantly, repeating the words that had swirled around in his head for hours before. "I have it on good word that if a gent needs money, he can go to you. Is that correct?" He took a moment to ensure that his breathing was steady, not willing to let anything reveal how nervous he was.

Kegg's eyes narrowed. "Where did you hear that?"

"Lord Tristan mentioned it when we were playing cards the other day." It was difficult to ignore the roar of his pulse in his ears. "What about it, then? Care to help a fellow out?"

"Apologies, Your Grace. I haven't got the funds for it at the moment," he answered, his tone filled with disdain and arrogance. "I do wonder though why Lord Tristan would dare mention it to someone when he knew it was a closed-door system. Only those involved are supposed to know."

"How do you get new people, then?"

"We have everyone we need, Your Grace. No sense in giving away more than I'm getting in." He emphasized his last words, whether he knew it or not. "I'm sorry, but I can be of no assistance to you." His eyes held a heaviness that came with unbearable grief. Bryant had seen the look in his mother's eyes a decade ago. It was odd to see it reflected in Kegg's eyes, given the apathy he'd reflected before.

Guilt pooled in Bryant's gut as his mind warred against his heart. If he questioned it, he might receive a curt response and be cut off from other potential conversation. Keeping quiet, however, would mean there was no chance at seeing a glimpse of Kegg's heart. For all appearances, the thing that brought such despair to his eyes could be the very same information Bryant was seeking.

With trepidation, he spoke up. "Is everything alright, Kegg? I don't mean to intrude on your personal life, but you seem rather distracted tonight."

Kegg met his gaze. "With all due respect, Your Grace, it's none of your business. I suggest, now, that you return to the party. I'm certain that your guests are missing their host."

"My mother is hosting, actually. My name didn't appear anywhere on the invitations so I doubt that most of them know to expect me." He gave a light grin in the hopes that it would soothe the tension between them. "Truly, is everything well?"

He relaxed into an armchair, shaking. "I shouldn't be telling you this. Not when you've so obviously made me your enemy. You have seemed... amenable, as of late; I suppose that counts for something. Jetlis, one of my employees, was arrested last week for the murder of a maid." As soon as the words left his mouth, his eyes shot open. "*Oh*," he breathed. "You were there. Wynn said as much when he interrogated- *ahem*- questioned my involvement. Jetlis was one of my closest friends. One of the few men I could trust in this world."

"May I ask who the others are?"

Kegg's glazed expression stiffened at once as his previous coldness returned. "It isn't for our borrowers to know." He gritted his teeth audibly before adding, "Your Grace, this feels more like an interrogation than a business deal. What are you playing at here?"

Bryant stood silent for a moment, stunned by the phrase. Quite simply, it wasn't used among the *ton*. Something to deal with later, when he had time.

"I'm stressed," he responded. "I'm sure you can understand the pressures dealt to us gents. Tenants to look after, business to take care of. On top of that, the woman who has my heart has been threatened with death twice and one of my servants is missing. My apologies if I'm being apathetic, but I have quite little control over it. I hope you can forgive me." He allowed rage to steadily build into his tone. Kegg would think him getting defensive and wouldn't hold his words against him any further.

"My apologies, Your Grace. I suppose I assumed that being a duke came with people to do your every bidding instead of the other way around." Something in his eyes shifted, but it certainly wasn't sympathy. Caution was more apt to describe the shadows that now poured into his pale eyes. "Allow me to speak with my associates and I'll see what we can offer you in loans. Providing, of course, that you pay us back as soon as you are able."

"Thank you, Alden. I greatly appreciate it." Their conversation was over. Kegg stood to move to the door. "Wait. I have a question, if I may."

"You may."

He opened and closed his mouth a few times, trying to gather his thoughts. His pulse ticked in his ears. "I just want to be sure everything will be above board. In the attack, Jetlis said he had business to take care of. I know what that business is. You know as well as I that he is in prison, and it is perhaps likely that his actions were his own, but I must be certain. He *was* your employee, after all. I need reassurance that the two aren't connected."

"I did not order Jetlis to murder that maid." His answer was quick; almost too quick.

"That isn't what I asked, Kegg."

"You wouldn't be here if it weren't for him. None of you would be. If Jetlis could have simply followed his *baidch orders* we would be out of the country by now." Alden seemed to tremble for a moment before collecting himself. "You will be fine, Your Grace. Your connection to Morris makes you far too suspicious of a target; not to mention your apparent distaste for me. You can rest safely at night knowing you will not be at risk."

"But others will be?"

He huffed. "Goodnight, Your Grace. Tell your mother that I enjoyed the party." As he reached for the handle, it jiggled. The door swung open and Wynn stepped inside.

"Hello, Lord Arioch. I couldn't help but overhear your conversation. If you don't mind, I have a few questions for you." He gestured to the chairs as he walked further into the room.

"Constable Wynn, a pleasure to see you," Kegg greeted joylessly. With all of his strength, he pushed Wynn, attempting to shrug past him. Bryant attempted to grab his coat but failed to latch on as the cloth slipped through his fingers. The man bolted from the room, leaving Bryant's line of sight within seconds.

By the time the pair managed to collect their wits and run after him, he had disappeared into the crowd. Bryant's motley crew spread out, searching in every part of the room before moving on to the side rooms and gardens.

Alden Kegg was gone.

...

"What do we do, Wynn?" Bryant interrupted his pacing to ask, glancing around at the others to gauge if they had any ideas or not. All eyes floated to Wynn, however, suggesting that they were at as much of a loss as he was.

They'd gathered as soon as the last of the guests had departed—a painful four in the morning. As soon as they could be certain that their conversations were safe from unwanted eavesdroppers.

The constable shook his head. "There isn't much we *can* do, unless we find him. I've sent out telegrams to the sheriffs and police of nearby cities and counties with instructions for his arrest. Every man of the law will be looking for him; they've put up wanted posters for civilians to identify the man as well."

Corbin sat up straight at that, a fascinated grin slowly creeping across his face. "There are wanted posters? He's a regular outlaw, then."

"Outlaws have actually committed crimes, Corbin," Brigham retorted. "At this point, Kegg is only wanted for questioning. Providing they can question him efficiently, they will then have sufficient evidence to say he has committed crimes. *Then*, he can be classified as an outlaw."

"All the same, he's an outlaw in some fashion." Corbin pushed his blond hair out of his eyes and turned back to Wynn. "Is there anything we can do beyond just searching for him?"

Wynn nodded. "I do have one lead. My men have interviewed the staff at Selcomb. Lord Arioch stopped there to gather a few supplies after leaving the party last night, taking a few hours to rest at that. From there, he set off towards the center of the city."

Shepherd spoke up. "He went north, then. Of course, that was several hours ago. He could be anywhere by now."

"Not true," the constable countered. "Lord Arioch is essentially bankrupt. He has no money save for what he has lent to others or has borrowed himself."

Bryant nodded, shadows darkening his eyes. "He'll be paying a visit to whomever he can to swindle some money for the trip."

"Exactly. I've a list here with names and addresses of the various men who have borrowed from His Lordship, courtesy of Eryi here. We'll split up into pairs—safety in numbers, after all—and take a few names each. With all of us working together, we should be able to investigate each household to determine which he visited and which he did not. That can help us plan a map of where he has traveled to understand where he is going next." He paired up everyone in the room—Bryant with Eryi, Brigham with Shepherd, and Corbin with himself—before passing out a paper to each coupling. "We'll reconvene here by ten to share what we have learned. Everyone, fan out."

The groups rose and left the room, talking amongst themselves to determine a plan of action. Bryant met up with Eryi, glancing over the list in his hand. "We have Pattermar on our list," he noted.

"A great deal of goings-on over there. I say we check it out first and foremost. Lady Seylor owes him the most, after all." With a hum of thought, he staggered out to the stable and readied two horses. "This makes for faster travel than if we bring a carriage."

"I do wish I'd spent more of my mornings on horseback since the incident. I'm afraid I'll be a bit behind." He mounted the steed—a beautiful chestnut Andalusian named Shandy—and followed close behind Eryi as the men made their way into the city.

...

Portencia could hardly remember being so hungry before. The only way she'd been able to tell time was by the light under the door, and even that proved difficult. Her throat stung from lack of water. If things continued like this, she'd die of dehydration within a few days. She cursed the closet for the hundredth time as she attempted to shove the door open once again.

Remaining calm proved more difficult by the minute. In fact, her heart hadn't beat normally since the moment she stepped out of Angarth the other day. That had been days ago and every second since had killed her a little bit more as she waited for the nightmare to end.

If the situation hadn't been so terrifying, she would have laughed at how similar the encounter had been to the night several months prior. So caught up in her thoughts was she that she hadn't been aware of her surroundings. Somewhere along the line, she'd run off the road and down an overgrown path through a beautiful field. The lovely scenery gave her an opportunity to retreat into herself and reflect as she walked, blissfully unaware of what went on around her.

Lord Arioch had nearly plowed her over on his horse.

And now she sat in the dark of an old closet at Selcomb, waiting for the moment that Lord Arioch freed her. Or, rather, the moment that he sent someone else to rid her of her bounds and set her free. He'd been quite clear when he left an hour ago that he wasn't to return, given that anyone could simply stumble across her hidey-hole of a new home and take her testimony. It didn't appear as if Lord Arioch ever intended to return to Selcomb, or to Braxden, again.

Her current situation proved to be rather confusing. She certainly hadn't expected him to kidnap her that afternoon, but what surprised her more is that he only bound her in this dingy closet.

Perhaps she was more of a liability than she thought.

Lord Arioch's last words as he left the manor still echoed in her head. *I'm going to reason with her even if it costs what I want most of all.* The last few months' worth of overhearing His Grace's conversations filled her head. The tea he'd hosted, in particular. Lord Arioch wanted to have Lady Seylor for a bride. Did he want that more than the money, however? Or, perhaps she'd gotten it backwards; he was going to reason for her hand by forgiving all of the debt.

That seemed unlikely. He was far too money-minded to be such a romantic. There were only so many Bryant Wooldridges in the world, after all, and Lord Arioch was not one of them.

For sure and certain, though, he was going to Pattermar. She could only hope and pray that someone got to him before he ruined any more lives; that of His Grace and Lady Seylor in particular. After so much heartache, they deserved a happy ending.

A scraping noise outside the door caused her heart to skip a beat. When a shadow blocked the light seeping in from under the door, she began to hope that maybe she'd get a happy ending of her own. The handle jiggled but did not turn—locked, most likely. A short little clang gave her a bit more hope that whomever was on the other side was determined to open the closet and find her there.

Light poured into the room as a familiar face peered in. Dark, ruffled hair fell over beautiful brown eyes that highlighted a spattering of freckles to make up the face of Peligro. "*There* you are. The housekeeper thought you might be on the grounds somewhere." He offered his hand and pulled her up. "You don't happen to know where he's going, do you?"He brought her out into the study before closing the closet door and locking it again.

"Not exactly, but I've a very strong feeling that he's gone to Pattermar. It's the only thing that makes sense with what he said."

"What *did* he say?"

She repeated the words and watched as his face turned ashen. "I don't know that they require such a strong reaction, Peligro," she stated hesitantly, trying to be optimistic. "I mean, it isn't as though he would—"

"Clearly, you don't know His Lordship very well." He grabbed her hand and ran to the stables, instructing her to saddle one of the horses. "We haven't a minute to lose."

"Where are we going?"

"You're going to find the constable. He should be at Angarth. If not, check with Eryi or Cristyn about where he is before heading out again. Once you find him, let him know that he needs to be at Pattermar."

"And where are you going while I do all of that?"

Peligro swung up onto his steed. "I'm going to Pattermar now, before it's too late."

Chapter Twenty-Eight: Consequences

February 20th

Olivia's gaze shifted from Prat to the new visitors. Her eyes locked with Bryant's deep gray ones as relief swept through her. If the duke had come at such an early hour, it was likely that the constable would be right behind him. They were saved.

The relief was short lived, however, as the blade pressed further against her skin. Sweat poured down her back as adrenaline pumped in her veins. Her vision blurred as the fear overtook her senses. The consequences of her father's stupidity had caught up with them and what she feared most was about to come true. She was about to die at the hands of his debtors. This is what it felt like to die in injustice.

Bryant stepped forward, blessed determination in his eyes. "Kegg, let her go."

His grip on the knife tightened as he turned to face her heroes. "You don't have the authority to demand that, Your Grace. I'll do as I please." He called to someone Olivia couldn't see. "Derwyn, tie them up. Don't let them out of your sight until I've gone." Steely ice-colored eyes studied Bryant's frame, sizing up the threat he posed. "If you try anything, Your Grace, she's dead. Keep that in mind as you deal with my associate here."

The man named Derwyn stalked towards the door, grabbing Bryant and Eryi and dragging them to the side of the room. He tied their wrists together and shoved them back to back.

Though her throat burned from the adrenaline, Olivia found her voice. “Lord Arioch, I’ve told you half a dozen times already. My father didn’t have the funds to repay you. Why on Kestia did you think *I* would?”

A sickly smile grew over his face. “Believe me, darling, that isn’t what I expect of you.” His flinty gaze turned to Bryant. “As you can see, Your Grace, your sweetheart is in a bit of a pickle. She has found herself in a mountain of debt—owed to me—that she cannot pay. I’m sure you can understand that I must take collateral.”

Bryant shook his head, horror glinting in his eyes. “Please, don’t kill her. You love her, I thought. This isn’t going to make things better.”

A growl vibrated from his chest, making its way forward as a bark. “Begging your pardon, *Your Grace*, my personal satisfaction isn’t exactly yours to judge. I must admit, however, that you are right.” He lowered the knife and held Olivia’s wrists up so that they were face to face. “There was a time where I could have sworn I loved you.”

If it wouldn’t end with more blood running down her neck, Olivia would have spat in his face. It would be amusing, but it was hardly worth the effort. Instead, her stomach churned with bile.

“Perhaps there can be a new change of plans,” he mused. “I was going to take advantage of your infatuation with His Grace to force *him* to pay your debts, but why should I bother with *him*? Why not marry you myself as I originally intended?”

The very idea of being married to the brute sent chills down her spine. The bile in her middle threatened to erupt. She almost wished it did.

Alden hummed in thought; the low, deep sound resonated against her skin. Her heart paced quicker at the feeling. Fear turned her knees limp and useless, unable to hold her up against her captor's arms. She hated this feeling, but what was she to do? He had a knife and clearly would stab her if she refused to cooperate.

"That is quite an idea, isn't it, lovely? A small country wedding should suit us just fine, love, don't you think so?"

"Don't call me that, you pig." As best as she was able, she slammed her weight into him to knock him off balance before kicking him in the shins.

He barely reacted, simply collecting himself and grabbing her arm, halting her attempt to make for the door. She silently cursed her body for failing her when she needed her strength most. "Dearest, you don't want to do that. You leave me and I'll murder Morlais, the servant boy, *and* your precious duke. Their blood will be on your hands. Surely you don't want that." His pale eyes pierced her soul, startling her as she relented, muscles going slack in defeat.

"I think you'll grow to love me, dearest. We'll live a quiet life in the country. I'll give you as many children as you wish to pass your days with and a household full of servants that you can order around however you wish. Doesn't that sound lovely?" He tightened his grip as he made for the door. "Derwyn, stay here until I send word that we're safe. If anyone comes to the door, shoot them."

Olivia caught a single glance at Bryant as Kegg dragged her to the door. Pure panic had spread across his face. His eyes said everything she needed to know. *I love you*, they cried. A thousand more statements were shared in that one moment, but they all resonated with that one phrase.

I love you.

Tears blurred her vision as, with one final tug from her captor, Bryant's face disappeared from sight. The door closed behind them and Kegg helped her into his carriage. Pattermar slowly left the edges of her vision. She was truly and utterly alone.

...

Anger rose up within Bryant as he watched through the window as the carriage left the premises. He had to get out of these ropes, but nothing could be done while Derwyn watched him. The gun was already aimed, poised to kill if he so much as moved the wrong way. He couldn't merely sit and do nothing, though. How could he? The love of his life had just been kidnapped. He needed to find a way to save her from Kegg's claws.

A clock sat on the mantle in the next room over, barely visible through the cracked door. They still had hours before ten, unfortunately. No one would know that he and Eryi were missing until Olivia and Kegg were far out of Braxden.

At least Wynn had sent out a warrant for Kegg's arrest. Every lawman in the nation would be looking for them before long. She would be found in time. Alive, if the desires of his heart were heard and acknowledged. For the moment, however, she was in the hands of the enemy and the only thing he knew to do was pray.

He'd been a man of the Faith for most of his life but never had it felt so entirely necessary. Naturally, he grew up in the Faith, under Mother's training, but his prayers had still felt hollow. Unattainable. Trying to grasp the wind.

This was different. His prayers were active and living, rooted in the hope that he'd had his whole life. What need did he have to fear? Olivia was very much alive and would remain so unless things went terribly wrong. The Most High would work things out in its time.

Eryi wriggled behind him, trying to discreetly free himself of the ropes that bound him. "Do you think Wynn will know to look for us?"

Bryant glanced at the clock again, agitated when he noted that only five minutes had passed. "Not for another few hours. No one will know we're missing until after the designated meeting time. Of course, by then..."

"By then it'll be too late," Eryi finished with a sigh. "It's hopeless, then. We've lost."

"It's not hopeless," he argued. "The Most High is still on our side. He can work through the muddled impossible to bring out a miracle."

"I sure hope He does, Your Grace. For her sake, and for yours."

...

Portencia dismounted just outside Angarth and dashed inside, running for the kitchen. She needed to find Eryi to ask after the constable. Why Peligro had known that the constable would be here, she didn't know. Asking that particular question hadn't seemed important at the time.

"Portencia?" A squeaky, feminine voice greeted her ear as Tels pulled her into an embrace. "Portencia, it's been three days! Where have you been?"

She took a deep breath before shrugging out of Tels's arms. "I'll explain everything when I can. For the moment, I need the constable. I was told he would be here."

Tels shook her head. "He *was* here; not an hour ago. He and His Grace formed a search party to find Lord Arioch. Why do you need him?"

"Again, I'll need to explain later. Do you know where he was going?" Her pulse ticked loudly in her ears as she analyzed their next options. What could be done without the constable? Peligro wouldn't be able to do much on his own and there was very little that she herself could do in aid. They needed Wynn if they were going to stop Lord Arioch in time.

"I don't. He handed out lists with the names of various members of the *ton* but he didn't leave them here. Even if he did, I don't know which one he took."

"Okay. Thank you, Tels. I'll be back when I can." She didn't say *I promise* like she had three days prior. Not because she believed the words a curse, but because she didn't want to make a promise that she couldn't keep. Without knowing exactly what Lord Arioch was planning, she could only expect the worst. If it came down to it, she'd give her life to save those currently under Lord Arioch's gaze.

She hurried back out the door and mounted her horse before taking to the streets. Fortunately, the *ton* had one thing in common: they all liked having grand estates, even when in town for the season. Finding the various lords on that list wouldn't be difficult. Choosing the *right* ones, however, would make the difference between life and death.

...

Peligro knocked twice on the servants' door before letting himself into the estate. Even a fool could have noticed the dangerous shadows lurking beyond the front windows and understand that taking a different door was best for all involved. He crept past the kitchen, past the adjacent hallway, making his way to the foyer. While in the storeroom, he picked up a pan for self-defense—and as a method of attack if pouncing on a man ever became an option.

Just outside of the foyer, he took stock of the situation. One man—who was certainly *not* His Lordship—sat on the floor, a gun pointed at the hostages. The one facing him made his mouth go dry. Eryi locked eyes with him before returning his gaze to the floor. He breathed a silent sigh of relief. His cousin was smart enough to pretend that he hadn't noticed.

The duke was there, of course, but he would have done better to leave it to Eryi. He was now just another person to keep track of if things went south. Every moment that wasn't carefully calculated would end up fatal for them all.

First up, he had to figure out how to get the gun away from the thug. How could he if he also needed to take him by surprise to knock him unconscious?

Eryi lifted his head again, meeting Peligro's gaze with a questioning expression. Peligro glanced at the thug tellingly before revealing the pan in his hand. With a slight nod, Eryi began to tease his captor. The usual boyish things of height, weight, attractiveness to the ladies.

If he wasn't family, Peligro would have disowned him for his stupidity.

All the same, it did the trick. The brute walked over to silence his captive and Peligro pounced, smacking the man's head with all of his might. He fell to the ground, unconscious.

As he helped his cousin with his binds, he muttered, "Why is it that your ideas are always stupid enough to work?"

"Because," Eryi responded as he freed his hands, "I'm a Bowen and that's what we Bowens are baidch known for." He knelt to untie His Grace before opening the door. "Come on. We don't have much time. We need to find them before they get too far. Peligro, stay here in case anyone arrives looking for us. We're headed to Lord Arioch's country estate."

...

Portencia rode up to the Mortimers' estate and knocked swiftly on the door. Her heart beat furiously in her chest as she rapped her knuckles on the door with as much force and urgency as she could muster, praying the inhabitants would hear her plea.

The butler answered, brow furrowing at the sight. "Can I help you, Miss?"

She nodded. "Is the constable within?"

He shook his head. "The constable left with the Earl of Waldron a quarter of an hour ago. He stated that he was off to Lord Gregsay's estate next, if that can help you. Good day, Miss." He closed the door just as Portencia scrambled back to her horse. Lord Gregsay's estate was nearly twenty minutes away. If she was going to catch up, she had better hurry.

The town of Braxden sped by in a blur as she counted down the moments and watched the street signs to find Lord Gregsay's manor. Shadows shifted slowly as the time passed, evident by the quarter chime from the great clock in the center of town.

Fortunately, the usual traffic that filled the streets was calm and quiet today. She suspected it was due to the early hour and the marketplace merchants still preparing their wares for the day, but she thanked the Most High anyway. Anything that could get her to the constable faster was a miracle in its own right.

She passed the town square, counting houses now until she reached the small manor. The two horses outside gave her hope. Diving now to the door, she turned the handle just as a party on the other side turned it, pushing it open. She stepped back, allowing the other person to exit. Wynn, thanks be; alongside Lord Waldron. "I've been looking everywhere for you."

Corbin's eyebrows rose in surprise. "Portencia? Where have you been? Her Grace was beside herself with worry when—"

"I'll explain everything in time, I promise. Right now, we need to leave. Lord Arioch is at Pattermar and I fear we won't be able to get there quick enough to stop him."

That was more than enough to get Wynn on the back of his horse. He didn't wait for them to do the same before he took off towards Pattermar, leaving the pair to scramble to catch up.

...

"You've missed them," Peligro informed them. "The duke and my cousin left just minutes ago. Eryi said that they were headed to Lord Arioch's country estate. Hopefully, that is where our missing couple are as well."

"His country estate. And, blast it all, that's nearly a day's ride away," Wynn responded. He called to a stray servant in the hall. "Look after this thug and make sure that he doesn't try anything. Take away any weapons on his person. Tie him up if you must." He turned back to Peligro, Corbin, and Portencia. "Come on, then. We haven't a moment to lose."

...

Night had fallen by the time that Bryant and Eryi rode up to Birkwood Manor, Kegg's estate in Pewitt County. Kegg's carriage was in the carriage-house, a definite sign that this was where he planned to hide—for the next few days, at least. He left his horse in the stable and ushered Eryi and himself inside through the servants' entrance.

The staff was fairly welcoming, thanks be, allowing them to stay for a cup of tea and a hot meal. While the thought of doing anything other than saving Olivia sent his stomach churning, he complied. They hadn't stopped all day, after all, and he needed the short respite before barging in to thwart Kegg's plans. He and Olivia, according to the housekeeper, were spending the night in separate rooms. No words had ever seemed sweeter, excepting the silent *I love you too* that his lady had uttered hours ago. However, the warning of three burly brutes protecting the lady soured the moment. How were they to fight against that with only the two of them?

He and Eryi ate in silence, understanding that the moments ahead of them were too serious to make lighthearted conversation or clever banter. They had to keep focused on the task at hand. The silence, however, gave his thoughts time to catch up with him. He was sitting in Kegg's house with his servant about to rescue the love of his life from a man that, not long ago, was attempting to murder the both of them.

His heartbeat had never been louder. It thudded in his ears, giving him quite the headache. Every ounce of his body felt the anxiety weighing on his shoulders. If they didn't pull this off...

A loud rap from the door caught his attention. He opened it, surprised to find Wynn, Corbin, and Portencia. "Thank heaven you're here. Come inside. We can plan a proper course of action now." In spite of himself, he let out a nervous chuckle, relieved that there were others to aid in their attempted rescue.

The task before them seemed less perilous now that they had aid. His heart seemed unfazed by the comforting fact, however, heaving waves of anxiety through his gut. As the previous months of laughing and dancing played through his mind, he found himself startled at how similarly he felt at the beginning of his first season. Speaking to strangers didn't appear so daunting now.

"Kegg is in the east wing of the house while Olivia is in the west," Eryi informed. "She's been put under heavy watch, though. Three of Kegg's strongest servants have been instructed to ensure that she doesn't escape. That leaves one for me, one for His Grace, and one for His Lordship. Peligro, you can help out our lords with theirs. I'm sure they aren't accustomed to fighting murderers. Portencia, you can sneak in while we have them distracted. Wynn can then go to the east wing and arrest Kegg."

Corbin spoke up. "Eryi, that sounds easy in wording, but how strong are these guys *exactly*? I'm not as fit as that gardener of yours. The chances of me winning in a fight against them seem pretty slim."

Bryant replied, shutting out the heavy heartbeat in his ears as best he could. "There's no need for you to win, Corbin. So long as we can keep them distracted long enough for Portencia to get Olivia out, that's enough." He paused for a moment, eyeing the pots and pans on racks around the room. "Of course, it wouldn't hurt to take a weapon."

Corbin's eyes lit up with a spark of mischief. "I really hope this *pans* out the way you intend." The entire table groaned at his statement even as they rose and took their cooking utensil of choice.

"I sent a telegram to the sheriff on duty in this area asking him to join us here. It'll be a bit of a risk for me to wait, but I believe it would be best to go in with a second man so that I know we'll overpower him," Wynn explained. "Save the girl as quickly as you can and make for the horses. I'll get a ride back with him when we're done here." He poured himself a cup of tea and nodded to them. "Good luck and godspeed."

"Thank you, Wynn. Best of luck to you," Corbin murmured back as he grabbed his own pan and followed Bryant as the group made their way up to the west wing of the house.

True to Eryi's report, three men sat around the door; two sleeping, one keeping watch. This wouldn't be as difficult as it seemed, providing that the two sleeping gents would remain groggy once they woke. All the same, Bryant reminded himself that there was a reason for his rapid pulse and churning stomach. There was always a surprise turn of events in these sorts of scenarios.

"I'll take on the first one," Eryi mumbled. "I'm the most equipped to handle this, after all. If anyone is able to take him on, it's me. The others will surely wake up from the sounds of the fight and that's when you two will be needed to aid me.

"We'll draw them away from the door slowly. Once they're about three yards away, Portencia, you'll run in and hurry to get Olivia out of there and into the main hall. Bring her to the stables. Don't wait for us. If we don't make it out of this, at least she'll be safe." He made eye contact with Bryant and Corbin.

Bry could feel the weight of his gaze; a look that said "do you understand what you are risking?" and he knew, as he pictured Olivia's witty smile, that he was ready to risk it all for the woman he loved.

Eryi turned the corner and darted for the man, whacking him with the pan mere seconds after being spotted. They fought, throwing punches and kicks as Eryi struggled to gain control in the ambush. He used the pan in his hand as best he could to bruise the man, aiming for his head whenever he could.

Just as expected, the noise alerted the other two guards, who lazily woke up and stood to help their friend. Bryant and Corbin lurched forward, striking them both with their pans and joining in the fight, hands swinging. Slowly but surely, they drew the men away from the door.

From his angle, he could spot Portencia as she swiftly darted into Olivia's room. He silently sighed in relief. With the slight *click* of the door closing, the plan was half complete. Now, he could only wonder how long it would be before they could make their escape.

The seconds ticked by and the fighting continued. Bryant had managed a few good blows on the man in front of him, but it wasn't without gaining a few bruises himself. Keeping his focus on fighting grew more difficult with every moment that passed without sight of Portencia. What was keeping her?

With what strength he could muster, he smacked his pan against his opponent's ear and ducked out of the way to avoid a nasty punch. Out of the corner of his eye, he saw it. The door opened a sliver at a time, revealing the two women standing behind it. Unfortunately, it creaked loudly as they left the room, immediately alerting the guards to the pair.

Bryant covered the space between his guard and Olivia, keeping the man engaged and unable to nab the lady. He heard a sharp yelp from behind him and prayed it wasn't what he suspected. A sinking feeling in his gut suggested he knew better.

One of the larger guards made his way into Bryant's peripheral. He wrestled Olivia in his arms, dragging her to the window. He threw it open before shouting to the duke. "Everything stops now or I throw her out!" All sounds of battle stopped in that single second.

"Lord Arioch wouldn't be very happy if you did that."

The man grinned with cracked teeth. "He also wouldn't be very appreciative if I let you steal his girl away from him. Considering the two options, I believe he'd far prefer this over that." He stepped closer to the window, shoving Olivia's head so that it dangled outside. She stiffened, causing Bryant's heart to leap in fear. Out of the corner of his eye, he spotted Eryi stepping forward.

"You don't want to do that," Eryi stated. "The constable is just in the other room. You kill her and he kills you. A fair trade, but not one in your favor. Let the girl go free."

The man eyed Eryi warily but didn't loosen his hold on the girl. "The constable wouldn't dare hurt me. He's not the sort to kill unless he has to. Even if I did drop her, he would do nothing more than arrest me. I've escaped from his baidch prison before. I'll do it again with ease."

"Let. Her. Go," Corbin echoed with stern force in his voice. "Let her go or there *will* be consequences. Let her go or I'll make *sure* that Wynn kills you to avenge her."

"I don't think so," he responded, lifting Olivia's feet off the ground. "And every moment that you stand there trying to free her, you're killing her. Now, go on your way and everything will be—" He cut off as an arrow pierced his skull. His arms went limp, dropping Olivia back onto the ground.

Bryant ran to her and pulled her away from the window, wrapping her in his arms as though she'd dissipate if he didn't hold her tightly enough. A few clangs behind him brought welcome relief to the fear in his veins. Olivia was safe. With the hem of his suit coat, he wiped the few drops of blood from her face. They would be alright.

"What just happened?" Corbin asked, slowly backing away from the window.

"The Most High sent us our miracle," Bryant whispered.

"In the form of Wynn's constable buddy, I suspect," Eryi added as he helped Bryant and Olivia up off the floor.

He held Olivia's hand as they walked to the kitchen, unable to let go of her for fear that she'd disappear from him again. The adrenaline of what had just happened left him shaking and he suspected it wouldn't wear off for a long while.

The housekeeper offered the group some more tea and a teacake to Olivia with a warm, apologetic smile. "There, there," she cooed as she pressed a cup of tea into the girl's hands. "You're all right now."

A knock echoed from the door as the other constable stepped inside, a crossbow in his hand. "My apologies if I startled any of you. I thought you might need a bit of assistance. How is the girl?"

Olivia straightened, her voice trembling as she spoke. "I'll be alright in time. Thank you, sir."

"Come on, Hosea," Wynn greeted, gesturing to the hallway. "We've got an earl to arrest for kidnapping. I suspect that there will be *numerous* additional charges once we get him talking."

The two of them left the room with pistols drawn as Corbin stood. "We should get going as well. Wouldn't want to leave your mum worrying longer than she ought."

"Right." Bryant stood and offered his hand to Olivia. "Come, my lady. Your steed awaits." The exhausted group stumbled out to the stables. Bryant pressed a kiss to his dear's hand as he helped her up onto a horse, unable to resist the show of affection after the chaos and uncertainty of the day. He'd almost lost her entirely. By the grace of the Most High, however, the dominoes had fallen into just the right places for her rescue. As he mounted his own horse, he sent a prayer of gratitude for their protection and for the miracle sent to them.

Indeed, we felt like we had received the sentence of death. This happened that we might not rely on ourselves, but on God, who raises from the dead. 2 Corinthians 1:9

Epilogue

March 6th
Pattermar Manor

Bryant stood before the looming doors of Pattermar, palms sweaty and heart racing. He knocked thrice, awaiting the moment that the butler allowed him entrance, just as he had done so many times in recent weeks. Today was a very special day.

The estate manager greeted him with a large grin. "She's out on her morning ride at the moment. One of the stable boys can saddle Ares if you'd like to catch up with her."

"Thank you," He shook the man's hand before dashing out to the stables, where he found that Ares had already been readied for a ride. A grin tugged at his lips. He oughtn't be surprised that his joining Olivia had been anticipated. Their engagement was all but inevitable.

That reality didn't keep his heart from thumping loudly in his chest. Nor did it keep his stomach from dropping as he thought out what he was going to say. She was the woman that he would spend the rest of his life with and he wanted to start off on the right foot. He wanted to sweep her off her feet and show her the heart that belonged to her and her alone.

Catching up didn't take very long. She'd stopped to sit beside an old building, idly picking the wildflowers that grew alongside the grass. Ivy had taken over the walls of the building, aiding the spread of the wildflowers so that bunches of them covered the old wood. He couldn't have asked for a more beautiful setting.

She met his gaze as he dismounted. Her stare alone was enough to bring heat to his cheeks. "Hello, Your Grace. Or, shall I call you Sir Detective, given your hat?" She smirked, extending a hand to pull him down beside her instead of rising to stand with him. "I'm rather glad that the rain washed away most of the snow and that the sun washed away most of the rain. Picking wildflowers is rather bothersome in the mud." She handed one of said flowers to him, twirling its stem as she gave it up. "How do you do, Your Grace?"

He took the stem, continuing its slow twirl as the petals snapped off all at once. "I'm quite well, thank you. Though, I wasn't the one to endure so much in such little time. Are you doing well, my lady?"

"Quite well, though my relationship with my household is still on the rocks. It's difficult to come to terms with everything. After the actions of my estates manager after my parents' death, I suspect it will be a long time before I can respect him again.

"Wynn comes by nearly every day to assure us that Kegg is still in prison. He's tempted to hand him off to the king's men, given the earl's status. Not to mention that it'd be rather dangerous to have someone as crafty as he is hiding away in a public jail cell. I agree that it's best to send Kegg to the Tower; but, of course, my opinion isn't the one that matters in this instance."

He would have argued if it hadn't been true. Truth be told, though, no one could make that decision except the court justice, and him only with the king's approval. "Well, I have a situation that *does* require your opinion, my lady."

She tossed a humored glance his way. "Is that so?"

"Yes. One that I'm certain you'll be glad to hear." Every word he spoke sent his stomach lurching with new fears and anticipations.

"Out with it, then. What matter requires my input?"

He took a deep breath and moved away from her so that he could get onto one knee. "My lady, I'd like nothing more than to attend plays with you and spend afternoons together on promenade around the city *without* the fear of something going wrong or someone watching who shouldn't be."

He really had meant to ask without mentioning Kegg or any of the incidents before, but it was somewhat unavoidable. The entire history of their relationship had revolved around the earl's schemes, after all. Not talking about it was like not telling stories of her to his friends. It was the natural way of things.

"I reasoned that you deserved a proper courtship, where we can get to know each other in truth without fear of what might come next." The words slurred together as they rushed out, the fear in his heart causing him to lose his composure. "However," and he noted the look of disappointment on her face, "that can hardly stop me from the question that has been on my mind for weeks now." He pulled out a ring, hand picked by his mother to ensure feminine approval. "Will you, Olivia, promise to be my lawfully wedded wife?"

A soft smile slowly replaced the grin on her face. "I'd like nothing more, Your Grace." She placed her hand in his, blushing when he slid the ring on, brought it to his lips, and pressed a kiss to each of her knuckles. "I couldn't be happier to spend the rest of my life as your wife, Bryant."

His heart melted at her words. "Nothing would bring me more joy. And, after all of that is done, I promise to grow old with you. I mean it with everything in me."

And he did.

The end.

Author's Note

I hope you have enjoyed this venture into the world of Kestia. It has been a pleasure telling Bryant's story. There are a few things you might be wondering that I will address here.

The world my novels take place in is called Kestia. While being rather similar to earth, particularly in its development, there are some key differences that I would like to highlight.

The history of this world varies significantly from our own. Though the development is similar, particularly in language and culture, the general geography and major events have changed. Shepherd cites the conquering wars of Alastair, one of the founding events of Deravail. This is not based on any specific event in our world, to my knowledge, but is a general event that aligns with how most old countries were formed. The same is true for the rest of Kestia and its history.

Brigham cites a book titled "Idris Hopewell's Guide to the Daoine Sith and Other Magical Creatures." The Daoine Sith is a term for the Scottish fae - brownies, selkies, banshees, and the like. While I keep as close to the original folklore as I am able, some details have been added or changed to provide a unique presence in my book. Not every creature is part of the Daoine Sith, such as Thanatos, but each race/creature is categorized here as the fae, as a tie between this world, that is, the material world, and the spiritual one. There is more to what we see than flesh and bone.

For my fellow nerdy friends, rest assured that I am (albeit slowly) working on a physical copy of the guide. I grew up reading

Spiderwick Chronicles, and jumped at the opportunity to develop a field guide of my own.

Where are we going now? Following this publication is Corbin's book, hopefully to be released in 2026. I have already made great progress on his story, and hope to share it soon.

You may have noticed that not everyone has a happy ending. Brigham, particularly, still faces many of his same struggles. Fear not, my darling reader, for his journey will be addressed in time. Due to the heavy subject matter his book will address, it won't be published for a few years. I want to ensure that I depict his story realistically, while collaborating the different elements needed for his happy ending. His story is far from over.

I hope this novel has inspired you, or at least enticed you to continue on the journey of my Braxden boys. Many adventures await us ahead. Go with God, my dear. Your own story is waiting for you.

Acknowledgements

I will keep this as brief as I can, but there are several people that should be highlighted here with my gratitude. First and foremost, you, my dear reader. Thank you for supporting me by reading my debut novel. Thank you for sharing this journey with me.

I'd like to thank the late Eloise Anderson, a woman I knew as a teenager. She was an encouragement to me all throughout the time I knew her. Upon every visit, she would ask how my brothers were doing, and how my book was coming along. It's here now, and I cannot wait to show her in Glory.

Next up are my parents. Thank you so much for all of your support throughout my life, my academic pursuits, and in my writing. Thank you for caring about who I would become as an adult, and for taking the time to instill in me goodness, truth, and love. I don't thank you often enough. Love you both.

A hearty thanks to my friends, who have encouraged me, read my material to disprove my imposter syndrome, and lifted my weary heart. Thank you so much for going through this by my side. My particular thanks to those I met through Gull Lake, Da Girls, church, and school.

Thank you to my kickstarter donors, many of whom are personal friends, who have financially supported this project before its publication.

For the cover art, and for your ongoing support, thank you, Miss Poppins. The cover is amazing, and I'm excited to work with you on future projects. Thank you for all you have done to help me over the time we've known each other. Your friendship means the world to me.

To my friend Cass, for everything. For putting up with my rants and rambles, for giving me advice when I was lost, for speed reading my novel to put at ease my worries of its quality. Thank you for being there through some of my darkest moments, for checking in on me when I wasn't well, and for all your prayers. Love you, Cass.

Finally, to my Lord Jesus. Without You, this book wouldn't be possible. Thank You for lifting my heart, for saving my soul, and for forgiving me, a great offender against You. Thank You for defending me and for keeping me in Your peace. May all I do be for Your glory.

www.ingramcontent.com/pod-product-compliance
Lightning Source LLC
Chambersburg PA
CBHW010731271224
19448CB00025B/124

9 798991 818506